DISGRACE

BRITTAINY CHERRY

Disgrace

By: Brittainy C. Cherry

Disgrace
Disgrace
Copyright © 2018 by Brittainy C. Cherry
All rights reserved.

Without limiting the rights under copyright reserved above, no part of this publication may be reproduced, stored in or introduced into a retrieval system, or transmitted, in any form, or by any means (electronic, mechanical, photocopying, recording, or otherwise) without the prior written permission of the author of this book.

This is a work of fiction. Names, characters, places, brands, media, and incidents are either the product of the author's imagination or are used fictitiously. Any resemblance to actual events, locales, or persons, living or dead, is coincidental.

This eBook is licensed for your personal enjoyment only. This eBook may not be resold or given away to other people. If you would like to share this book with another person, please purchase an additional copy for each person you share it with. If you're reading this book and did not purchase it, or it was not purchased for your use only, then you should return it and purchase your own copy. Thank you for respecting the author's work.

Published: Brittainy C. Cherry 2018
brittainycherry@gmail.com

Editing: Ellie at Love N Books, Editing by C. Marie and Jenny Sims at Editing 4 Indies
Proofreading: Virginia Tesi Carey
Cover Design: Quirky Bird

To those who've been left behind:
May you remember the sound of your own heartbeats.

"Someday, somewhere—anywhere, unfailingly, you'll find yourself, and that, and only that, can be the happiest or bitterest hour of your life."

-Pablo Neruda

PROLOGUE

Jackson
Ten Years Old

What a stupid dog.

I'd spent years trying to talk my parents into letting me have a pet, but they didn't think I was old enough to care for an animal. I promised them I could handle it even though I couldn't.

Nobody told me puppies never shut up or listened.

Dad said it was pretty much the same as having a kid—because I kind of never shut up or listened either. "But the love is worth it," he'd say whenever I complained about the new family member being bad. "It's always worth it."

"Always and always," Ma would agree.

The word "always" seemed a bit like a lie because the stupid dog was annoying me so much.

It was past my bedtime, but I wanted to finish the sunset painting I'd been working on. Ma taught me a new technique using watercolors, and I knew I could become really good if I stayed up late practicing.

Tucker kept whimpering as I was trying to add some orange to the picture. He nudged at my leg, and then knocked over my water cup, spilling it all over.

"*Argh!*" I groaned, going to get a towel from the bathroom to clean up the mess.

Stupid dog.

When I came back to my bedroom, there Tucker was, peeing in the corner of my room.

"Tucker, no!"

I grabbed him by the collar and pulled him to the backdoor of the house as he lowered his ears.

"Tucker, come on!" I grumbled, trying to get the dog to go outside to use the bathroom in the rain. He wouldn't budge, not a lick. Even though he was a big black lab, he was pretty much still a baby at only four months old. Plus, he was afraid of thunder and lightning.

"*Go!*" I barked at him, yawning because it was already past my bedtime. Plus, I wanted to finish the sunset painting before morning so I could show Ma. She was going to be so proud of me.

One day, I'd be able to paint as good as her—if only that dog would leave me alone!

Tucker whimpered and tried to wrap behind my legs. "Come on, Tuck! You're being a big baby."

I tried to push him into the backyard, but he wouldn't let me. The water slammed against the patio, and when a loud clap of thunder roared, Tucker booked it past me and raced straight into the living room.

"Ugh," I groaned, slapping my hand against my face as I followed him. The closer I grew, the more nervous I got as I heard Ma and Dad arguing in the living room. They'd been arguing a lot lately, but whenever I walked into the room, they pretended they were happy.

I knew they weren't, though, because Dad didn't smile as much as he used to, and Ma always had to wipe away tears whenever she saw me. Sometimes, I'd walk in on her, and she would be crying so hard that she couldn't even talk. I'd try to help her, but she had a hard time taking each breath.

Dad told me they were panic attacks, but I still didn't understand why Ma was having them. She had nothing to panic about; Dad and I would always take care of her.

I hated that more than anything—I hated when Ma was so sad that she couldn't breathe.

Over time, I'd learned to just hold her until the panic passed. Then we'd just sit and breathe together.

Sometimes, it took a while.

Other times, it took even longer than that.

I snuck into the room quietly and sat on the floor behind the couch as I listened to my parents fight. Tucker moved over to me and climbed into my lap, still trembling from the rainstorm. Or maybe he was afraid of their shouting.

Stupid dog.

I wrapped my arms around him because even though he was a stupid dog, he was mine. If Tucker was scared, I'd take care of him.

My stomach hurt as I listened to Dad beg Ma not to go.

Go? Where would she go?

"You can't leave, Hannah," Dad said, his voice sounding so tired. "You can't just walk away from your family."

Ma sighed, and it sounded like she was crying, too. *Just breathe, Ma.* "We can't keep doing this, Mike. We can't keep going in this circle. I just…"

"Say it," he whispered. "Just say it."

She sniffled. "I don't love you anymore."

I saw Dad stumble back a bit, and he pinched the bridge of his nose. I ain't ever seen Dad cry, but that night, he wiped tears from his eyes.

How couldn't Ma love him anymore?

He was my best friend.

They both were.

"I'm so sorry, Mike. I just can't do this anymore… I can't keep lying to myself and my family."

"You sure use the word family loosely nowadays."

"Stop it. Jackson is my world, and you know I care about you."

"Yeah, just not enough to stay." Ma didn't have anything to say to that as Dad began to pace. "You're really going to leave Jackson for some other man?"

She shook her head. "You make it sound like I'm abandoning my son."

"Well, what are you doing? You have your damn bags packed at the front door, Hannah. You are leaving!" he snapped, which was something he never did. Dad was always pretty levelheaded and never lost his temper. He took a deep breath and lowered his head, lacing his fingers on the back of his neck. "You know what? Fine. You do whatever you want. If you want to go, go. But I swear to God, you better stay gone because I'm tired of begging you to come back to me."

He walked out of the room, and my chest hurt so much. Ma grabbed her suitcases, making me leap up from the floor to rush over to her. "No! Ma! Don't do it!" I cried, feeling as though everything inside me was set on fire. I couldn't lose her. I couldn't watch my mom walk out and leave me and Dad behind. We were a team, a family. She couldn't leave us. She couldn't go...

"Jackson, what are you doing out of bed?" she asked, alarmed.

I threw myself at her and began to sob into her arms. "Don't go. Please, don't leave me.

Please, Ma, please don't go. Please..." I fell apart, pulling at her clothes as she wrapped her arms around my body. I shook against her and kept begging her to stay, but as she soothed me, she still pulled back a bit.

"Jackson, calm down, okay? Everything's okay," she promised, but her promise was a lie, because how could everything be okay if she was leaving?

"I'm sorry Tucker peed in the house yesterday! And I'm sorry I didn't do my chores, but I promise I'll do better, and I'll take better care of Tuck. I swear, Ma. Please, I'm sorry. Please just don't go," I cried, trying to pull her closer. "Please, Ma. Please stay. Please..."

"Jackson, honey," she said with her voice so gentle and calming, but tears fell down her cheeks, too. "You did nothing wrong. You are perfect." She moved in and kissed my nose. "You are my world. You know that, right?"

"Then why are you leaving?" I asked, my voice cracking.

She sighed and shook her head. "I'm not leaving you, baby. I promise, I'm always going to be here. Over the next few days, you and I will talk, and I'll help you understand. I just can't stay here tonight. We're…your father and I…"

"You don't love him."

"I…we…" She sighed. "You're too young to understand. But sometimes parents, even though they really want to try, just fall out of love."

"But he still loves you, so maybe you can start loving him again."

"Jackson…you're too young to get this. But do know that I'm not going anywhere. Not really. We're just going to find a new normal. It might be rocky at first, but we're gonna find our footing. I promise. Okay? You'll see that everything will be fine. We'll be even happier! And, sweetheart, I need you to understand that you did nothing wrong. I just need you to be strong for a little while and take care of your father, all right? Can you do that?"

I nodded.

"I love you, Jackson." She kissed my nose once more and pulled me into a tight hug. "Always and always."

She said those words, but then she still let me go.

She grabbed the handles of her suitcases and walked out into the thunderstorm, leaving us all behind.

As she left, I hit the floor and cried as Tucker walked over to me and licked the tears that fell from my eyes. "Go away, Tuck!" I shouted, shoving him, but he just came back, wagging his tail back and forth. He didn't even care that I pushed him away because every time I pushed him, he came back. I allowed him to crawl into my lap because I knew he wouldn't give up. He was so annoying. I wrapped my arms around him and kept crying as I held him.

After a while, I stood. Tucker followed right behind me as I walked into the kitchen where Dad was standing with his hands on the edge of the countertop. In front of him was a glass and a bottle of stuff that I wasn't allowed to drink.

"Dad? You okay?" I asked. His body tensed up at the sound of my voice, but he didn't turn around to face me. He only gripped the edge of the countertop tighter.

He sniffled a bit before downing the liquid in his glass and then pouring more. "It's past your bedtime, Jackson," he told me, his voice stern.

"But Dad..." I felt sick. I felt like I would throw up any second. "Ma left..."

"I know."

"We should go follow her. We should go get her back... We should go—"

"*Stop!*" he hollered, slamming his hand against the counter as he turned to stare my way. His eyes were red and filled with emotions. "Go to bed, Jackson."

"But Dad!" I cried.

"*Bed!*" he snapped once more, his anger throwing me off. I'd never seen Dad angry, especially with me. He took a breath and looked at me. I'd never seen that look in his eyes before. He looked so...broken. He frowned, turning back to his glass, and sighed. "Just...go to bed, son."

I headed to my room and flopped onto my bed as Tucker leaped up beside me and laid down. "Go away, stupid dog," I grumbled, tears still falling from my eyes. He nudged himself closer to me and snuggled under my arm as my chest continued to hurt. "Just go away."

But still, no matter what I did or said to him, he stayed.

Good boy, Tuck, I thought to myself, holding him closer. *Good boy.*

CHAPTER ONE

Grace
Present Day

In the dark, vacant foyer sat five pieces of mismatched, tattered, and torn luggage. They each held a part of me within them. The purple suitcase was from our first trip to Paris, our honeymoon. We stayed in a tiny hotel room where we could touch both walls if we stretched our arms out. We spent many drunken nights in that filthy little room, falling deeper in love as each second passed by.

The floral suitcase was from our getaway after my first miscarriage. He surprised me with a trip to the mountains to help me breathe. The city air was stiff, and my heart was broken. Even though my heart remained shattered at the high altitude, the air was a bit easier to take in.

The small black suitcase was the one he packed for me when I landed my first grown-up job as a teacher. He also used it for the trip after my second miscarriage; that time, we went to California.

The green one was from my cousin Tina's wedding in Nashville when I twisted my ankle and he carried me around the dance floor as we laughed all night long. Last but not least, the tiny navy one was from when he came to my college dorm to stay overnight. It was the first time we ever made love.

My heartbeats raced as I leaned against the living room wall, staring at the packed bags from a distance. Fifteen years of history in five pieces of luggage; fifteen years of happiness and heartbreak stolen away from me.

He hurried out of the bedroom with a duffle bag on his shoulder. His body brushed past mine, and he glanced down at his watch.

Gosh, he looked handsome.

Then again, Finn always looked handsome. He was much better looking than I was, and that wasn't me having low self-esteem. I thought I was beautiful, with every curve and extra pound that rested against my hips, but Finn was just more beautiful. Every couple had someone who was prettier, and Finn filled that role.

He had these crystal blue eyes that shone whenever he smiled. I loved when he wore the color olive because his eyes had a hint of jade in them. His dirty blond hair was always buzzed super short, and his smile...

That smile was what had made me fall in love.

"You need help?" I asked. "With the luggage?"

"No," he said sharply, not looking my way once. "I can handle it." His body was tense, unwelcoming. I hated how cold he was being, but I knew I'd made him that way. I had kept him at a distance for so long, and then he had let go.

He wore the yellow polo I despised. It had a rip under the arm and a nasty stain on the bottom that wouldn't come out no matter how hard I tried to scrub it out. I blinked once, trying to capture that ugly shirt in my mind.

I'd miss it even though I hated it so much.

I sighed as he dragged the suitcases. When he packed the last one in his car, he came back into the house and glanced around the foyer as if he was forgetting something.

Me.

He was forgetting me.

His hands raced across his head as he grumbled, "I think that's everything. We should get down to the bank to sign the papers. Then I have to get back on the road to Chester, and I guess you do, too."

"Okay," I said.

"Okay," he replied.

Chester, Georgia, was home to us. It was the small town where we grew up, fell in love, and promised one another forever. Finn had been down there for the past eight months since taking a resident position at the hospital. It was eight months ago when he asked me for a separation. It had been eight months since he said we should put the house on the market. It had been eight months since he walked out of my life, and I hadn't heard from him until our house sold in Atlanta.

He walked out on me and didn't look back until he was forced to do so.

But still, I loved him even though he didn't feel the same.

No one back home knew we had separated—not even my best friend, Autumn, or my sister, Judy. I told those two everything about my life except for the parts that made me cry at night. I didn't have the nerve to tell anyone my husband hadn't been mine for months now. If I told them, then that would've made me a failure, and all I ever wanted was for Finley to somehow begin to love me again.

I oftentimes wondered when he'd stopped.

Was it one singular day, or a string of moments that merged?

Did love disappear because of heartache or boredom?

Maybe a little bit due to a disconnect?

Can something disconnected ever be plugged back in?

"One more go-round?" I asked Finn as we stood in our empty living room. He'd driven back into town to sign the paperwork on the closing of our house, and he hadn't truly said much of anything to me.

My stomach had been in knots when he arrived. In my mind, I'd envisioned him showing up with flowers, some wine, and maybe telling me that he wanted me to be his again...but in reality, he showed up cranky, empty-handed, and fully ready to move on.

"No, I think we're good. Let's go to the bank, sign the paperwork, and then call it a day. I have a five-hour drive back to Chester, plus I still have to work tomorrow," he grumbled, running his hands through his hair.

I didn't have a clue why he seemed so annoyed.

He hadn't seen me in months, yet the moment he stood by my side, he was once again unhappy.

He hardly even looked my way.

What I'd give for him to look my way...

"I'm just going to look around once more," I told him, trying not to sound so heartbroken even though everything within me ached.

"We already looked twice."

"Just once more for memories." I smiled, slightly nudging him in the arm. He didn't smile back, just glanced at his watch.

"We don't have time for this. I'll meet you at the bank," he told me, walking away. He never glanced back once as if leaving me was the easiest thing he'd ever had to do.

I supposed after you walked away once, it only became easier.

I stood there, still a bit heartbroken, but when I heard him clearing his throat, I turned around and stared his way.

He looked up at me, and now I wished he hadn't. His eyes held all the hurt I felt in my chest. "Look, I didn't want it to end like this," he told me.

I sighed.

I don't want it to end at all.

I didn't reply. No matter what I said, it would still be over.

He had made a choice, and it wasn't me.

"I...it's just...after everything..." He cleared his throat once more, taking a few moments to search for words he couldn't find. "You closed yourself off, Grace. You made it impossible for me to even come near you, and...I mean, Jesus! We hadn't had sex in over a year."

"You had birthday sex."

"Yeah, sex only because I turned thirty-two—what kind of life is that? And you kept your socks and tank top on."

"I get cold."

"Grace." His voice was stern and annoyed. I wondered when I'd started to annoy him. Had it just been lately, or had it been that way for years?

"I'm sorry."

"Don't do that," he groaned, running his hands through his hair again. "Don't be sorry. I know what you went through was hard and impossible, but dammit, I was there for you, and you wouldn't let me in."

He wasn't wrong. I'd shut him out. I'd shut everyone out; it was the only way I knew how to avoid self-destruction.

"I'm sorry," I repeated.

He took one step toward me, and I prayed he'd take more. "Grace…say something, *anything* other than you're sorry. See, this is what pisses me off. You're so passive-aggressive with everything. You don't talk; you just keep all your feelings in your head."

"That's not true," I argued. At least, it didn't used to be true. There was a time when all I ever did was express my heart to Finn. Then there was a time it all became too much for him. He never said it, but his facial expressions revealed his truths. Whenever I cried, he'd roll his eyes. Whenever I voiced my pain, he'd tell me it was late, and we'd talk in the morning.

Morning conversations never came, and then my voice slowly became mute.

Maybe that was what love is, though: something that fades over time and then becomes hauntingly still.

"It's true," he asserted confidently. Everything Finn did had a layer of confidence to it, and that was a major reason I'd fallen in love with him. He walked the earth as if he knew he belonged, and that was such a powerful trait. He was two years older than me, and when we first met at my parents' annual summer gala, everyone's eyes were on Finley James Braun. He was Chester's finest. If you ended up with Finn, you ended up blessed.

He was smart, handsome, and confident.

All the girls were obsessed with him—every single one. If it weren't for Mama pushing me into his arms when I was fifteen years old, I would've never had the nerve to talk to a boy like Finn on my own.

Back then, I never thought I was good enough for him.

I still didn't.

Finn pinched the bridge of his nose, obviously irritated with me. "You don't open up. All you ever do is act passive-aggressive."

"Yes, well, all you ever do is cheat," I barked back, the words rolling off my tongue as if I'd been waiting for the perfect moment to fire them off.

Oh, that stung him and seeing him stung only hurt me.

"I'm sorry," I told him. I wasn't a mean person—not in the least. I hadn't known I had a mean bone in my body, truly. My parents raised my sister and me to be kind, considerate, and filled with compassion. If someone described me, they'd never even consider the word cruel, but then again, when one's heart is breaking, sometimes things are said out of character.

An unnatural rigidness overtook his body. He took an unsteady step backward, and his eyes glassed over. Finn hated being reminded of his betrayal, and that was all I'd been doing for the past few months. Sometimes, I'd leave him voice messages when my anxiety was too high and ask him why he chose another woman. I'd ask him if she was better than me. I'd ask if her kisses ever tasted like mine.

That bothered him so much and might have been the final straw for him in deciding to leave me: my inability to let the other woman leave my mind.

My husband wasn't a cheater except when it came to her.

Her.

I hated her even though I didn't know who she was.

I hated her in a way I hadn't known I could hate a stranger.

How dare she steal something from me that wasn't hers to take? How dare she swallow my husband whole while I was still trying to breathe him in? How dare she break my heart and not even care about the shards of brokenness piercing through my soul?

"Is that really what you want to say? Do you really want that to be the last thing you say to me?" he asked, still reeling from my words.

Gosh, I hated his face because I still loved it.

So many emotions coursed through my veins—so much confusion, so much internal struggle, so much aching. I felt lonely before he even walked away. My mind formed thoughts that made no sense.

Stay. Go. Don't leave me. Walk away. Love me. Let me go. Breathe life into me. Let me die.

Stay.

Go…

"I'm sorry," I said softly. I knew he didn't want to hear those words, but they were the only ones that came to my mind.

"Come on."

"I'm sorry I couldn't…I…"

"Grace." He stepped toward me, but I held my hand up, making him halt his movement. If he came any closer, I'd fall into his arms, and I was certain he'd drop me. He took a breath in through his mouth and whispered, "I made a mistake. She meant nothing to me."

She.

"Say her name," I demanded, knowing it was catty but not caring. I was tired of it. I was tired of Finn skirting around the subject of his infidelity. I hated how he pretended I was responsible for his mouth pressing against another woman's lips, breasts, and hips…her neck, her stomach, her thighs…

Stop.

I hated my thoughts. I'd never imagined my brain could so clearly envision my husband's mouth on another woman, but alas, the mind was a weapon of mass destruction.

"What?" he asked, playing dumb. Finn was a lot of things, but dumb wasn't one of them. He knew exactly what I was asking.

"After all this time, you've never told me her name because if you did, that would make it real. That would make this final."

His mouth hovered opened for a second as debate swirled in his mind, considering how real he needed this to be, how real he wanted it to become. Then he spoke. "I can't do that."

It was a whisper…his words, his guilt, his disgust.

"If you've ever loved me, you'll tell me."

"I…" He grimaced. "I can't. I can't do that, Grace. Besides, it's over and done with anyway."

"It's no big deal. I don't care at all, really. I just hope she was ugly," I joked, but he missed what was happening inside my chest, the fire that was burning me from the inside out.

My heart…

How could the broken pieces keep on shattering?

I sniffled.

He sighed. "We should get going."

"I'm just going to check the rooms one last time," I told him.

He parted his lips to scold me, but he didn't argue. He was tired of arguments, as was I. There came a point when words became exhausting because neither side was truly listening. "I'll just meet you at the bank, all right?"

I listened to the front door close, then slowly moved through the house, allowing my fingers to softly glide along every surface, every doorframe, every wall. Once I reached the last emptied space, I walked inside and stared at the four walls, the walls I'd had so many plans for, the walls I'd thought my future belonged within.

"Over here, we'll put the dressers and the changing table, and the crib will go here! We can get the kind that turns into a bed down the line, and over it, I want to write the baby's name in those big block letters with some kind of quote and—" I was out of breath with excitement, and Finn walked over to me, wrapping his arms around my body, pulling me close.

He kept smiling as he shook his head back and forth. "Don't you think we should wait until we're actually pregnant before we plan the nursery?"

"Yes," I agreed, biting my bottom lip, "but after ten positive pregnancy tests over the past two days, I think we're on the right path."

Finn's eyes lit up faster than I'd ever seen. I loved how his blue eyes were always so stunningly blue. Those eyes still gave me butterflies, even after so much time.

"You're…?" he started.

I nodded.

"You mean, we're...?"

I nodded.

"So we're going to have...?"

I nodded.

His eyes watered over, and he lifted me, swinging me around in the air and planting kisses all over my face. When he lowered me back to the floor, he looked at me in such a way that, even without words, I could feel his love.

"We're going to have a baby," he whispered, pressing his lips softly against mine.

"Yes." I brushed my lips against his, and when he exhaled, I took a deep breath. "We're going to have a baby."

The room darkened as I flipped the switch to shut off the light, and as I walked away from the space, the memories still lingered.

I'd thought those memories would be the ones I always cherished, but as the days and years passed by, those beautiful memories became my pain.

After turning off all the lights, I picked up the last suitcase left in the house—a black one with pink flowers. It was from the time Finn and I brought back too many souvenirs from our honeymoon.

I pulled the suitcase away from a place I'd thought would always be home, and I mourned the ideas of a future that was no longer mine.

CHAPTER TWO

Grace

It only took a few minutes to sign the paperwork at the bank and turn our keys over to the banker. I sat directly beside Finn, but still, he felt miles and miles away. When we stood to leave, he walked to his car, and I walked to mine.

"Finley," I called out, uncertain why his name had even fallen from my mouth. He looked up and arched an eyebrow, waiting for me to speak. My lips parted, yet the words I wanted to come out stayed dancing in my mind. *Let's grab lunch and maybe a movie for now… until you love me again.*

"Nothing. Never mind."

He released a heavy sigh. "What is it, Grace?"

"Nothing, really." I rubbed my hand up and down my arm.

"Here we go again," he muttered, and my chest tightened.

"What's that supposed to mean?"

"You're just doing that thing you always do."

"What thing I do?"

"That thing where you start to express your feelings and then you pull them back, saying never mind. Do you know how impossible that makes it to communicate?"

"I'm sorry," I whispered.

"Of course, you are," he replied. "Look, I have to go. When we get to Chester, we can tell our parents we're splitting. We should probably do it separately. We're gonna have to face these kinds of things on our own, so we might as well get used to it, okay?"

Stay strong. Don't cry.

"Okay."

I was on my way to spend the summer in Chester, seeing how my apartment in Atlanta wouldn't be ready for me to move into until August. On one note, moving back to Chester terrified me because it wouldn't take long for people to realize Finn and I weren't together anymore. On another note, I was secretly excited to be in the same place as Finn. On the same sidewalks where we first fell in love. Maybe having that connection would make him look at me the way he used to. I had a summer to make my husband fall in love with me again.

I climbed into my car, and when I turned the key, the engine sputtered. *Oh no.* I turned it again, and it made a scratching noise. Finn cocked an eyebrow my way, but I tried to ignore his stare. My car was ancient, a little pink Buick I'd had since the day I left for college. The only thing I'd had in my life longer than that car was Finn, and now that he was on his way out, Rosie was the oldest thing that belonged to me.

That late morning, she'd developed a cough.

"Do you need me to look at the engine?" Finn asked, but I wouldn't look at him. I couldn't, not after he snapped at me and made me feel awful just for being me.

"No. I'm fine," I told him.

"Will that thing even make it all the way to Chester? You should've gotten a rental car and trashed that piece of junk."

"It's fine," I told him, turning the key and hearing that nasty sound once more.

"Gracelyn—" he started, and my nerves were at the edge of panic.

"Just go, Finn. You made it perfectly clear that you don't want to be here, okay? So, just go." *Unless you stayed…*

He frowned and stood a bit taller. "All right, I guess I'll go."

"Yes. You should." *Unless you stay…*

I was pathetic.

His lips turned down. "Bye." He left me there along with our history, closing the door on the chapter of our story, one I was still trying to rewrite.

My chest tightened, and I called after him. "Finley," I shouted, making him turn my way.

"Yeah?"

My fingers wrapped around the steering wheel. Those fighting words in my mind wanted to escape. They wanted my lips to be their battleground, but I couldn't do it. I couldn't beg my husband to stay with me, not after all we'd been through. "How did this happen? Where did we go wrong?"

"I don't know." He grimaced. "Maybe some things just aren't meant to be forever."

But what if we were meant to be, and instead of trying to pull our boat back to shore, we were willingly letting it slip away?

Tears fell from my eyes, and I hated that he saw them, but at the same time, I needed him to witness my pain, to witness how he'd hurt me. I needed him to see me aching, and I needed to remind myself he was no longer the man who could comfort me.

He rubbed the back of his neck. "Grace?"

"Yes?"

"I love you."

I nodded slowly. "I know."

I believed him, too. Judy would call me foolish to believe in my husband's love, but I knew a few things about love that my little sister had never learned. Love was a messy emotion that didn't walk a straight line. It worked in waves and loops of ups and downs. It was a screwy emotion that could somehow still exist amidst the ultimate heartbreak and betrayal.

Finn loved me, and I loved him back in a twisted and painful way. I wished there was a way to stop it—to shut off the love faucet, and make my heart stop feeling.

But still, it felt.

Still, it burned.

In the dark trunk of his car sat five pieces of mismatched luggage, all of which were tattered and torn, all of which held a part of me within them.

I watched them all drive away.

I sat there in the parking lot with only a wish and a prayer that my car would start, but luckily, my parents taught me that that was all one needed in life. You just needed faith the size of a mustard seed that no matter what, things would work out.

I kept trying to turn the engine and then paused for a moment.

Dear God, it's me, Gracelyn Mae…

When Rosie finally started after about five more attempts, I closed my eyes and took a breath before I drove away. "Thank you," I said softly.

It was nice to know that even when I felt alone, there was something bigger than me to believe in.

"I hope this is the right choice," I muttered to myself as I began my drive to Chester. Back where we came from, everyone believed Finn and I were still in love, living our happily ever after.

He hadn't told a soul, and I hadn't either. Maybe because we knew the type of people who lived in the town where we grew up. Maybe we hadn't told anyone because we both weren't ready for their judgments, their thoughts, their opinions.

Their *advice*.

Chester was a small town in Georgia about five hours from Atlanta, and when I said small, I mean everybody knew everybody's middle name and when they had their first kiss—at least the fairy-tale romance story of it, not the actual truth.

In a place like Chester, everyone lived on semi-truths—you

know, where one only told the side of the story that made them look like a proper lady or gent.

Everyone knew I was coming back to town because they knew Finn had landed the position at the hospital, but what they didn't know was that when I came back, I wouldn't be laying my head right beside his.

I hadn't made plans for where I'd stay; a silly part of me thought Finn would come back and we'd somehow end up back in love. Even though that wasn't how it went, I wasn't too worried about finding a place to lay my head that night. My family would be there for me, always and always.

In Chester, the centerpiece of the whole town was Zion Church, which sat right in the middle of downtown. The church was the heart of the town, and my father, Samuel Harris, was the man who ran it, just as Grandpa James had before him, and Great-Grandpa Joseph had before him. Daddy never said it, but I was certain he was disappointed when he didn't have a son to take over the church someday after he stepped down.

He had asked me, and I'd respectfully declined. Finn had gotten into medical school in Tennessee, and like the good wife I was, where he led was where I followed. I followed him many different ways throughout his schooling, and I thought Atlanta was the final stop. When he told me he applied for a position in Chester, I had to admit I was surprised.

He used to say he never wanted to return to small-town life, always said it suffocated him.

Dad respected my choice of not wanting to take over the church and said he was proud of me, and Mama respected that I stood by my husband's side. There was a reason her favorite song was "Stand by Your Man" by Tammy Wynette.

The church was an integral part of my family's history, and the whole town of Chester gathered in the building more than once a week for sermons, prayer circles, Bible studies, and pretty much any bake sale that took place. Church on Sunday morning was just as common as football on Fridays and whiskey on Saturdays.

In a way, my family was royalty in small-town USA. If you knew the church, you knew our family, and if you knew our family, you knew our wealth.

Daddy claimed the money didn't matter and that his main purpose was to give back to the community and serve God, but Mama's red-bottomed shoes and flashy jewelry told a somewhat different story.

She reveled in being small-town royalty. She was Queen Loretta Harris, the pastor's wife, and boy, did she take that role seriously.

The closer I got to Chester, the tighter my stomach knotted.

It'd been years since I'd packed up my life and relocated with Finn, and the idea of returning home without him terrified me. I hated how loud my insecurities were lately, hated that I cared so much about how the town would judge me.

What would people think?

What would they say?

Worst of all, how would Mama react?

CHAPTER THREE

Jackson

"Five hundred today, five hundred next week," I dryly told the woman who kept beating her fake eyelashes toward me. She tried her best to push out her chest in my direction, but it was pointless. I'd already seen what was under that blouse, and there wasn't much for her to push out.

"But…" She started talking, but I tuned her out. Nothing she could say would interest me. Nothing about small-town USA interested me in the least.

Everything about Chester, Georgia, was a pain in my ass, and I hated that I somehow got trapped there.

It was all so damn annoying, from the small-town gossip to the small-minded folks. The people acted as if they were straight out of a cliché movie with every corny, fictional small-town stereotype, though I supposed the stereotypes had to come from some truth. Maybe Chester was the case study for those shitty films. Either way, I hated the place.

One couldn't quite call the people of Chester ignorant to the realities of the real world outside of their small quarters because they *weren't* unaware of life in the real world. They knew what was happening outside the town.

They knew the current state of the union was a disaster. They understood the poverty sweeping our nation, the drug trafficking stories. They damn well knew about the wildfires, school shootings, marches at the nation's capital, and rallies for clean drinking water. They knew about our president, both past and present. Yes, the people in Chester, Georgia, knew all about the workings of the real world, they simply much preferred to speak about why Louise Honey wasn't at Bible study on Thursday night, and why Justine Homemaker was too tired to make homemade cupcakes for the church bake sale on Friday.

They loved to gossip about shit that didn't matter, which was one of the many reasons I hated living there.

For all the hate I had for the town, it was nice to know the distaste was mutual. Chester's townspeople hated me just as much as I despised them—maybe even more.

I'd heard people's whispers about me, but I didn't give a damn. They called me Satan's spawn and it had bothered me when I was younger, but the older I got, the more I liked the ring of it. People had harbored an unnecessary fear of my father and me for fifteen or so years. They called us monsters, and after some time, we stepped into on the role.

We were the black sheep of Chester, and I didn't mind one bit. I couldn't have cared less if those people hated me or not. I wasn't losing any sleep over it.

I kept my head down and ran my dad's auto shop with the help of my uncle. The worst part of the job was dealing with people from town. Sure, they could've left Chester to find another auto shop, but alas, to them, venturing into the outside world was even more terrifying than dealing with my father and me.

That was why my current situation was so damn annoying: I had to deal with idiots.

"I'm just sayin' you owe me five hundred dollars by the end of the day. I take Visa, Mastercard, check, or cash," I told Louise Honey as she stood in front of me in her pink dress and high heels, tapping her fake nails on my desk.

"I thought we made an agreement last Thursday," she asked me, confused by my coldness. "When I stopped by to talk…"

By talk, she meant fuck, and we'd happened to do that all night long.

That was why she had missed Bible study—because her small tits were bouncing in my face.

The women of that town had no problem hating me when the sun shone while moaning my name when the shadows of night fell. I was the secret escape from their fake realities. A challenge for their well-behaved Southern souls.

"Was our agreement made before or after you sucked my dick?" I asked dryly.

"During," she replied in a whisper, her cheeks turning red. She was acting shy, which must've been part of her act to get her bill lowered because she hadn't been so bashful when she'd asked me to tie her up and slap her ass.

"Any deals made with your lips around my cock are null and void," I stated. "Just leave the payment on my desk. Half today, half next week, all right? Or I'll just give your boyfriend a call and see if he'll pay it."

"You wouldn't!" she cried. I stayed quiet, and she stood tall and quickly pulled out her checkbook. "You're a monster, Jackson Emery!"

If I had a dollar for every time I'd heard that…

"Thank you for your time. We at Mike's Auto Shop appreciate your loyalty to our company. Have a blessed day, sweetheart. Now, if you could please let yourself the fuck out of my shop, Louise—"

"My name's Justine, you jerk!"

Oh. Justine…

Names weren't something I cared about. They made things personal, and I didn't do personal.

"As long as your name is right on the check, we're good," I replied.

"You're an awful, awful man, and you're going to die alone!" she barked, storming out of the shop.

"Joke's on you," I mumbled to myself. "Most people die alone."

After she left, I returned to the car I had been working on as Tucker napped in his dog bed in the far-right corner of the shop. If my black lab was good at anything, it was napping in his dog bed.

He was an old man, fifteen years old, but out of the two of us, it was clear that I was the grump. Tucker just went with the flow in the same way he always had. When I was down in the darkness, he was always the happy spark of light.

My faithful companion.

As I worked on the car, my father walked into the shop, and by walked, I meant he could hardly remain standing. I hadn't seen him since the day before when I dropped off groceries. His house had been a mess, but that didn't shock me. His place was always a mess because he didn't care enough to clean it up.

He looked identical to me in almost every way, except for his constantly bloodshot eyes and skinny body. He scratched his salt-and-pepper beard and grunted. "Where are my keys?"

I had taken his car keys away from him four nights earlier—crazy how he was just noticing they were missing.

"You can walk anywhere in town, Dad. You don't need your car."

"Don't tell me what I need," he mumbled, stretching his arms out. He wore a dirty T-shirt and a pair of torn and ratty sweatpants. It was his normal wardrobe even though I bought him new things every now and then.

"What do you need? I can get it for you," I told him, knowing he had no business getting behind a steering wheel. Even though his license had been revoked long ago, he still tried to drive around.

Ever since he pissed on the damn float at the Founder's Day parade, the townsfolk were just looking for a reason to get him locked up again, and I didn't want to deal with that.

"Gotta get some food."

"I just restocked your fridge. You should be good."

"I don't want that shit. I want a pizza."

I glanced at my watch and cleared my throat. "I was gonna go grab a pizza, too. I'll get you one."

He grumbled some more before turning to walk back to his house. "And some beer."

I always casually forg0t the beer.

"Tuck, you wanna go for a walk?" I asked my dog. He lifted his head to look at me, wagged his tail, but then plopped right back down and went back to sleep.

That was a clear no.

Going downtown was always a bit stressful. My father and I didn't belong in a place like Chester, but still, there we were. Over the years, my dad had done a good job of getting everyone to despise us. He was the town drunk, the filth, and the OM—original monster. I was twenty-four years old, and I harbored more hate inside me than the average man. Everything I'd learned about hating people, I had learned from my father.

Nobody took the time to get to know me because they knew my father's reputation well enough. Therefore, I never introduced myself to them and their judgments.

Plus, I was a monster all on my own, and it didn't take anyone long to realize it.

I took right after my pops.

As I approached the pizza shop, I heard the whisperings of the people around me. I always noticed how they moved away whenever I approached. They called me a junkie because I used to use drugs. They called me a drunk because my father was one. They called me white trash because it was the only clever title they could come up with.

None of that bothered me because I didn't give a damn what they thought.

Small-town people with small-town minds.

When I was younger, I'd get into a lot of fights with people who would talk shit about my father and me, but eventually, I learned they weren't worth my time or my fists.

Every time I got into a fight, they savored it. Every time my fist met a jerk's face, they used it as justification for their fabricated lies. *"See? He's wild. He ain't nothing but a lowlife."*

I didn't want them to have that power over me; therefore, I became silent, which seemed to scare them even more.

When they whispered, I kept quiet.

When they spat at me, I walked on, though if I was feeling wild, sometimes I'd growl at them. It scared them shitless. I was certain some of them actually thought I was a werewolf or something.

Idiots.

"He's just like his father—a no-good piece of trash," someone muttered.

"I wouldn't be shocked if Mad Mike died in his own vomit," a fellow customer remarked, his voice low but not low enough for me to miss his comment.

I paused my footsteps and took a deep breath.

Those words hit me the hardest because I wouldn't have been shocked either.

I listened to them talk about my father dying, and flashes of my past shot through my mind. I closed my eyes and took a deep breath. I wanted to use. I needed something to fix my current fucked-up mind. Just a little, nothing too major…just one small hit…

My heart pounded against my chest, beating me up inside, crying for numbness, crying for me to bring it back to a level of comfort it missed.

I looked down at my wrist and saw one of those stupid ass plastic bracelets that read *Powerful moments*. Dr. Thompson had given it to me a few years back when I entered rehab. I could almost see his aged head of hair and kind eyes staring into mine, reminding me that I was stronger than my worst moments.

"Those times you feel lost and afraid and weak—those are your moments for a breakthrough. Hidden beneath those dark moments is your power. Take those weak moments and make them powerful. Make them matter, Jackson. Make them count."

Dr. Thompson had me snap the bracelet against my wrist whenever I felt weak had or got the urge to use.

My wrist was currently red as hell.

Even so, I kept snapping it. It was a reminder that my next move would be real, just like the pain. The next choice I made would control my other choices down the line.

My choice couldn't be drugs.

I didn't use those to curb my emotions anymore.

I didn't use those to make me feel empty inside.

I'd been clean for years, and I didn't want that to change. Especially due to the people of Chester.

Doing my best to ignore the ignorant people around me, I glanced outside then paused when I saw a car flying through the one and only stoplight in town. By stoplight, I meant the flashing yellow light. The car moved recklessly, and a knot formed in my gut as I realized it had no plans of slowing down.

I groaned. "You're going to crash," I muttered to myself before releasing a heavy sigh and breaking out into a run toward the unstable vehicle. "You're gonna fucking *crash*!"

CHAPTER FOUR

Grace

I'm going to freaking crash!

"No, no, no!" I muttered to myself as I tried to control my uncontrollable car. Seconds before I'd pulled into Chester, my car had begun to hiccup, but I'd figured it would make it safely to my sister's house before it gave out on me completely. That wasn't the case.

I tried to hit the brakes, but the pedal went to the floor of the car and nothing happened.

"No, no, no," I begged, feeling the vehicle start to shake.

I flew through the flashing yellow light at the intersection of Grate Street and Michigan, and I shouted as people scurried out of the way so I wouldn't hit them. I hit the curb a few times, trying to maneuver the car a bit, but nothing was working. Taking a deep breath, I said a small prayer, but it seemed my link to God was a bit delayed at the moment.

Panic filled my heartbeats as I headed straight toward the auto shop at the end of downtown.

How ironic would that be? Crashing into an auto shop.

I reached for my phone that sat on the charger, only to realize the car hadn't been charging at all and was completely dead. Just my luck.

"Take your foot off the brake. It's already flooded," a deep voice said, making me turn around to look out the driver's window.

"It won't stop!" I said, my voice shaky.

He was running right beside me, keeping up with the wild runaway vehicle. "No shit, Sherlock. Unlock your door and slide over to the passenger seat," he ordered.

"But I can't take my foot off the brake, I—"

"Move!" he ordered, sending chills down my spine.

I did as he said. The man quickly hopped into the moving vehicle, did some magic trick moves with the keys, and brought the car to a halt.

"Oh my gosh," I said, my breaths heavy. "What did you do?"

"Put the damn car in park and turned off the ignition. It's not brain surgery," he said with such distaste on his tongue. He opened the driver's side door and stepped out. "I'll push you to the curb."

"But..." I started, uncertain of what to do. "Do you need help?"

"If I did, I would've mentioned it," he grumbled, obviously annoyed.

Well *then*.

The car began to move, and I kept glancing back, watching him push the four-thousand-pound vehicle. He looked as dark and broody as one could with his black crew neck T-shirt, dark black jeans, and black Chucks. A baseball cap hid his hair, but the ends curled under the edges. His brows were knit tightly, and his face was so stone cold I was certain he didn't have a clue what it meant to smile. His biceps sat on biceps as he pushed with all his might, taking me to the side of the road. The moment I made it there, I hopped out.

I knew who he was—the whole town did—though, we'd never really interacted. He was Jackson Emery, the bad seed of Chester.

Rumor had it he'd started the fires in the park during summer of 2013, and he had been the cause of more than a handful of divorces. He was known to sleep with his fair share of Chester women; there was no secret about that.

Jackson Emery wore his trouble on his sleeve like it was his full-time job.

"Thank you for that. You didn't have to help me," I told him, giving him a smile.

He didn't make eye contact at all, just grumbled. "Didn't look like you were gonna help yourself. Maybe you shouldn't drive a shit car. It's obviously a death trap," he replied dryly.

No smile.

No smirk.

No sarcastic, funny undertones.

"I beg your pardon?" I asked, somewhat shocked by his words.

His facial expression remained unwelcoming, and his top lip twitched. Removing his hat from his head, he held it against his black shirt while one hand raked through his hair. With a lingering sound of detestation in his voice, he said, "You could've killed someone, driving like an idiot like that."

"I didn't know it would break down," I told him, feeling knots in my stomach.

When his cold stare finally met mine, chills ran down my spine. His eyes were so intense, so dark they almost seemed hollow. At first, his gaze appeared confused by my entire existence, and then he looked intrigued, as if he recognized me from a dream within a dream. I knew it wasn't the time to be deciphering the facial expressions of Jackson Emery, but in all honesty, I couldn't help it. I'd encountered with many individuals throughout my lifetime, but I'd never seen one so hauntingly dark. His confusing look bewildered me. His intriguing look gave me anxiety.

"You're one of those Harris people?" he asked. It was weird being called a Harris after so many years of being a Braun.

By the way he said my last name as if I were covered in Ebola, he obviously wasn't my family's biggest fan, so I wasn't certain how to reply.

"Yes."

He grimaced. "Didn't know I was dealing with one of Chester's royalty. I guess I shouldn't be shocked by your stupidity then."

"That's not very nice," I said softly.

"Yeah, well, I'm not a very nice guy."

"I know you, too," I said, nodding his way. "You're Mike Emery's kid, Jackson."

He had to be at least five years younger than I was, but with the wrinkles around his frown and his five-o'clock shadow, he appeared older.

"Trust me, sweetheart, just because you know my name doesn't mean you know me." He swiped his hand beneath his nose. "You don't know anything about me."

I'd never been called sweetheart in such a demeaning tone.

"You don't know anything about me either, but it seems you have your own judgments on my family."

"With good reason."

"And what reason is that?"

He blinked, and once again, the cold, isolated stare returned. He placed his cap back on his head before he parted his lips again. "Your car's a piece of shit. You could've really hurt someone today."

"I didn't know."

"There's no way a car in this bad of shape didn't give you any signs."

Well…he wasn't wrong about that.

As he spoke, intense annoyance painted his words. "You knew it was pretty bad off. You made a choice, and it was stupid," he replied. "Don't worry, though, I'm sure your daddy will buy you a new one soon enough."

The *nerve* of this guy. He sure did live up to the fables I'd heard about him.

"I bought this car on my own," I said, somewhat annoyed. It had been the first grown-up purchase I'd ever made in my life, and she'd been through the good and bad days with me. My pink Rosie. It was one of the only things I could claim I'd done on my own, other than my teaching degree, though, even with that, my parents had helped pay. Jackson didn't have a clue how much that car meant to me, how much doing something for myself meant, so screw him for judging me. "Just because my family has money doesn't mean I do."

"That's the type of shit rich kids say to make themselves feel somewhat human."

"Are you always such an asshole?" I asked, placing my hands on my hips.

"Oh, the Bible girl cusses. You better repent," he barked, popping open the hood of the car.

"What are you doing?" I asked, but he ignored me as he began fumbling around.

"What does it look like I'm doing? Trying to fix the shit you let break." Smoke seeped from the engine, and he pulled and pushed things around as I studied his every movement.

"Just be careful. I don't want it worse off than—"

He tilted his head and cocked an eyebrow. "Trust me, you can't get worse off than this. I found the problem."

"What is it?"

"Your car's a piece of shit."

I blew out a hot breath. "Is that the technical term?"

"Something like that." He stood straight and wiped his grease-covered fingers on his jeans. "If you want my opinion?"

"Is it a jerky opinion?"

"Yup, it is."

"Go for it."

"Never step foot in that car again. There's a ninety-five percent chance it will blow up. I'll have my tow guy pull it into the shop." He took out his phone and began sending off a text message. When he looked up at me, his eyes grew even gloomier. "Jesus, I didn't mean to…" He paused and brushed his fingers over his temple, leaving black oil marks. "Come on. For fuck's sake, don't do that," he groaned, gesturing toward me.

"Do what?"

"Cry."

"I'm not."

He cocked an eyebrow and stared at me as if I were insane.

I lightly touched my cheeks and felt the wetness.

Crap.

I am crying.

I choked on my next breath and began sobbing, covering my mouth with my hand.

"Can you just…not do that right now? Can you not fall apart?" He asked it in a way that sounded more like a demand.

"I-I'm t-t-trying not to," I mumbled, unable to control myself. I hated this. I hated not having control over my emotions, over my feelings. Lately, the smallest thing could send me into a whirlwind of sadness, and I hated it. Losing my car—losing the one thing that was mine and mine alone—was breaking my heart.

He sighed again. "You should really pull yourself together."

"Don't tell me what to do," I sobbed, annoyed by him being there and annoyed that I couldn't stop crying.

"You look like a hot mess."

"I'm not a hot mess!" I snapped. I just had hot-mess tendencies…

He grimaced, something I assumed he did often. "Well you sure look the part."

"Can you just go away? Please?"

"Not till Alex gets here to tow the car. It's on the house."

"What?"

"That means you don't have to pay for it."

"I know what 'on the house' means."

"Then you shouldn't have asked."

I was offended by him, and by his offer to help with my car. How could he be so rude to me and then try to be helpful? That wasn't how things worked in the real world. Life wasn't a Sour Patch Kids commercial—you couldn't first be sour then shockingly sweet. "I don't want your help."

"You sure needed it a minute ago."

"I didn't ask you to help me."

"You didn't refuse it, either."

I took a deep breath. *What is wrong with this guy?* It was as if he found pleasure in arguing with me. "Well, now I'm refusing it."

"Too late. He's already on his way," he said, nodding toward the tow truck that was headed in our direction.

"I don't want it!"

"Fine. When he pulls up, you tell him that and make him realize you're wasting his time." He rolled his eyes and shrugged. "Your call, raccoon eyes."

"I don't even know what that means!" I huffed back at him.

He pointed at my eyes.

Crap, again.

My mascara was running.

"Some guy hurt you?" he asked, a hard look on his face.

"Yes."

His bottom lip twitched, and he stepped back. Right as I thought he would open up, just when I thought he would offer me some words of wisdom to make me feel better, he blurted out, "Don't be so fucking dramatic. No dick is worth falling apart over."

Oh...well then. "That's exactly what I didn't need to hear."

"It's true, though. You're crying over someone who probably isn't worth it."

"What makes you think he's not worth it?"

"Because. You're. Fucking. Crying. People don't sit there sobbing over someone who makes them happy."

A chill raced down my spine as he snapped at me.

"Why do you have to be so dang straightforward?" I snapped back, my emotions jumbled up from his unnecessary harshness. "Why couldn't you just say something nice and leave it at that? Or, you know, not say anything at all?"

"People don't need nice; they need the truth. I find it ridiculous that a guy has this kind of hold on you. Have some self-respect. It's insane to give full control of your emotions to someone who doesn't give a damn about you."

"He does care," I argued, though I knew it was a lie, feeling as if I had to stand up for my hurts. If Jackson knew Finn hadn't cared about me at all, it felt as if he'd won somehow. "You don't understand. We have history. It's not just some silly fling like what you have with all those random women."

He stood taller, his face tensing. "Oh yeah, that's right, you know all about me, don't you, princess?"

The discomfort caused by my comment was apparent, and I instantly felt bad. "I didn't mean to offend you…"

"You can't offend me because I don't give a damn what you think, just like the dude who hurt you."

"You don't have to be rude. I'm just saying, what Finn and I have…" I paused and took a deep breath. "What we had was real."

"Had. Past tense."

"That doesn't change the fact that he's the love of my life."

Jackson rolled his eyes so hard, I thought they'd get stuck in the back of his head. "That is the stupidest thing I've ever heard in my life. Yes, the love of your life would be the guy who made you cry without giving a fuck about your feelings."

"How do you know he doesn't care about my feelings?"

"Trust me, he doesn't."

"What do you know? You probably don't even know what love is."

He grumbled and stuffed his hands into his pockets. "You don't got to know what love is to know what it isn't. Go ahead, though, keep crying over a dick who's not even thinking of you. Trust me, princess, no number of tears from you is ever going to make him love you, but, by all means, keep crying. Hell if I care."

He didn't say another word. As the tow truck pulled up, I was one hundred percent ready to tell the driver I didn't need his help, but when he stepped out of the vehicle, he gave me the kindest smile. He was a bigger guy, not chubby but built, and his body was covered in tattoos. He was older too, with his fair share of gray hairs. The way he smiled had a way of canceling out all the rudeness Jackson had shot my way.

"What do we got here, Jack-Jack?" the guy asked, patting the top of my car. I glanced at the name sewn onto his work shirt: *Alex*.

"A piece of crap. I was gonna have you tow it into the shop to take to the scrapyard later, but she said she doesn't want your help.

She just wanted to waste your time," Jackson replied dryly, making Alex frown.

"Oh…"

"I didn't say that!" I protested quickly, giving Jackson a narrow stare before turning toward Alex. "I'd love for you to help me out."

He grinned brightly as if all he knew how to do was smile. "It's no problem. I'd love to help you out. Let me just hook it up. Do you want me to drop you off anywhere?"

"No, really, it's fine. I can walk. I just have to grab my luggage." I walked to the back of the car and opened the trunk. Before I could grab the suitcases, Jackson was there with his mean look, lifting them up for me.

"Stop that," I barked, grabbing it from him.

"Stop what?"

"Being nice to me when you're still an asshole."

"Man." He whistled low. "You'll have to ask your god for a lot of forgiveness with that potty mouth, princess."

"Don't call me princess," I snapped.

"Okay, princess."

Oh my gosh, I hate him. Instant love isn't actually a thing, but instant hate? So, so real.

"You all good here, Alex? I'm gonna head to get food," Jackson said.

"Yup, all good, Jack-Jack," Alex replied with that same Southern charm.

"Alex?" Jackson's brow knitted. "Stop calling me Jack-Jack."

"Okay, Jack-Jack," he replied, giving me a wink.

"Not so fun when it's happening to you, now is it?" I remarked.

Jackson just grumbled and walked away.

As I watched him leave, another chill shot down my spine. "Is he always that nasty?" I asked Alex as he began hooking up my car.

"Just maintaining his Chester persona, but don't take it personally. Jackson's all bark and no bite. He's harmless."

"That's not what I've heard."

"Yeah, well, people are always spreading some kind of gossip. I'm sure there have been rumors about your family, too, but I like to be my own judge of character." He grinned and nodded toward my car. "We're all hooked up here, so you're free to go. I know Jackson said the car is fried, but if it's okay with you, I'd love to get under the hood and play around."

"Oh, no, you really don't have to. I know it's an old car, it's just…" I took a breath.

I was so tired of losing things lately.

"This thing means a lot to you, doesn't it?" he asked.

"Yes, it does."

"Then let me try."

I smiled. "I'd really appreciate that. Thank you."

"No problem. Cars are like puzzles for me—I love trying to figure out how to make the broken pieces fit together. Here, if you can just fill out this form, then I'll be out of your hair. I'll give you a call sometime next week to stop in for an update."

"Sounds good. Thank you so much. You have no clue how much this means to me." I filled out the paperwork then thanked Alex one more time, before grabbing the handles of my bags and starting off down the road.

I wasn't certain if Alex knew it, but I was in desperate need of his kindness, especially after crashing into Jackson Emery and the rain cloud hanging over his head.

CHAPTER FIVE

Grace

"Grace, what's going on? What are you doing here?" Autumn asked as I stood on her front porch with my suitcase. When life fell apart, I was always thankful that best friends existed.

"Sorry I just stopped by without calling, but my phone died, my car died, and…" I paused briefly as my eyes watered over. "I think my marriage died, too!" I sobbed, covering my face with my hands. I shook my head back and forth and took a breath, trying to pull myself together as best I could. Autumn's eyes watered over, and she placed her hands against her chest. We were those kinds of friends —whenever one cried, the other's tears weren't that far behind.

"Oh my gosh, Grace…" she whispered, her voice cracking.

"I was just hoping I could stay here for a while," I told her, walking into her place with my suitcase. "I would've asked you earlier, but for some reason, I thought Finn would come around and still want me."

I sat down on the couch and took in a few deep breaths as my head stayed lowered.

My heart, my brain, and my body were all exhausted.

It had been a long day.

"I just...I wish you would've called," Autumn said flatly.

"Yeah, but I know how busy you've been," I said, looking up toward her. Tears were still falling from her eyes, and the heaviness in her stare seemed almost as sad as I felt.

"It's okay, Autumn. I know I'm a bit of a mess, but I'm better now that I'm..." I glanced at her table, where one glass of water and one opened beer sat. Autumn didn't drink beer. She always thought it tasted like garbage. "I'm sorry, do you have company?" My chest tightened. Then, I noted a small red thong under her chair. "Oh my gosh, are you on a date? I'm so sorry! I should've called."

"Grace..." she whispered.

Her lips parted once more, but she couldn't speak. Her body trembled, and no words were coming out of her mouth. I looked around her place and noticed a pair of tennis shoes...shoes I'd seen before. Then there was a shirt sitting on her chair.

My eyes zoomed in on the yellow polo.

I slowly stood and walked over to it.

"Gracelyn," Autumn whimpered, but now I knew the tears weren't falling for me, but rather for her own emotions.

I picked up the yellow polo, studying it. It had a rip under the arm and a nasty stain on the bottom that wouldn't come out no matter how hard I tried.

I looked up at my friend.

My best friend.

My person.

My life.

Fire burned in my stomach, and tears flowed from her eyes. She became overwhelmed with emotion and began sobbing uncontrollably.

"It was you...?" I whispered.

"Oh my gosh, Grace!" she cried. Her hand landed over her

mouth to control her sobbing mess, but still, I watched her fall apart in front of me.

It was her.

Not a random woman, but her.

Her.

Autumn.

The woman who'd been through wars with me.

I hadn't been able to really get in touch with her lately, and when I had, she'd ended our calls fast, always telling me she'd call me back, yet she never had.

I understood now.

What I didn't understand was how she could have done this to me.

She'd been in my home. We'd laughed together. She'd told me how amazing Finn and I were as a couple. She'd said she envied us. I'd cooked dinner for her and her ex-boyfriend Erik. When Erik had cheated on her, I'd comforted her, telling her she was better off without him and she'd find someone worthy of her love.

I hadn't meant my husband.

"Oh my God, oh my God," she said, still crying.

I felt her tears against my cheeks.

Wait, no…

Those were my own tears. The disbelief of it all shook me to my core. How was this a thing? This couldn't be a thing. I felt as if I were in a nightmare, unable to open my eyes and wake up safely in my warm bed. Was it all a mirage? Autumn would never do that to me. Finn would never hurt me in that way—at least that was what I'd thought. As it turned out, though, my thoughts were wrong, and their hearts were jaded.

I blinked my eyes, but still, I saw her.

My stare scanned up and down her body, taking in every inch of her. I studied her curves. I studied her tears. She was a beautiful crier. I hated that even when she cried, she looked like a goddess. She looked like everything I hadn't been in so, so long.

Oh.

That hurts.

"Is he here?" I choked out, standing tall yet feeling as if I were crashing down. She just kept crying. He was there. Those were his tennis shoes. I puffed out my chest. "Finley!" I shouted as I darted through her house.

I knew every inch of Autumn's home. I knew every corner. When she'd moved in, I'd taken a weekend trip back to Chester just to help her organize it. I checked the closets, the bathroom, the corners, under the beds.

When I opened the pantry door, my heart clenched, and those blue eyes stared straight into mine. My husband was hiding beside the garlic powder and sea salt in an attempt to avoid coming face to face with me.

Shirtless.

"Grace—" he started, but he shut up quickly when I slapped my hand against his face. "*Shit!*" he hollered.

"Oh my God!" I cried, feeling overwhelmed by betrayal, pain, and sadness. My hands flew over my mouth. "Oh my God, oh my God!"

I was an ugly crier. I could only imagine how hideous I looked in that moment.

I looked nothing like her.

There were so many nights of my life I'd wished I looked like her.

"I'm so sorry." Autumn sobbed, holding her hands over her heart as she continued to fall apart. "I'm so, so sorry, Grace," she repeated, and every time she spoke, I thought about dying right then and there.

I pushed past her, rushing out the front door. My vision blurred, my mind jumbling. I couldn't think straight.

"Grace." I heard him behind me, and I flinched at the sound of his voice. That voice had once filled me with so much happiness. It was what I had fallen in love with—so smooth, so deep—was now so unbelievably hurtful.

"No," I said adamantly, watching Finn emerge from inside my personal hell and walk toward me. He wasn't irritated with me like

DISGRACE

he had been in Atlanta, but the guilt swam in his eyes. "Don't talk to me."

"I just…" He pinched the bridge of his nose. "I didn't know how to tell you. We didn't know how to—"

"*Autumn*, really?!" I cried, shoving my hands against his chest. "My Autumn! You-you-you monster!"

He let me hit him, and that made me angry. I wanted him to fight back. I wanted him to lay his hands on my body instead of delivering blows to my heart. I wanted it to hurt. "You said she meant nothing to you. You said she meant nothing! You slept with my best friend!"

"I know. I mean, we…it's…"

"I swear to God, Finley, if you say it's complicated, I will rip your head off your body." I never swore to God unless I truly meant it.

"I still care about you, Grace. I didn't tell you because I didn't want to hurt you," he said.

Slap.

I slapped him again, and again, and again. How could he use those words? How could he say that to me? How could a small corner of my heart somehow stupidly believe him?

"How long?" I asked him.

"Grace…"

"How. Long?"

He lowered his head. "Since I moved back here."

"Wait…so she wasn't…" I took a breath. "You cheated on me with someone else before her?"

"Gracelyn—"

"Were there more? More than the two of them?"

He went mute.

Ohmygosh.

"I hate you," I pushed out. "I hate you. I hate you!" I kept hitting him. My hands slammed into his body repeatedly, and he didn't even try to stop me because he knew he deserved it.

"I was going to tell you. I just…" He swallowed hard. "After everything we went through—"

"No," I cried. "You didn't go through it. You didn't go through it—*I did*. I went through it," I shouted, my hands wrapped around my body. I had no one to hold me, so I was in charge of holding myself. "I went through it all, and y-y-you…" Tears blinded me as I stared at a man I'd once thought was mine. The ache in my chest burned throughout me, and I choked out my final words. "You broke me, Finley. You broke me."

My chest was on fire, each breath more difficult than the last. He reached toward me, and I ripped my arm away from him. He couldn't touch me. I was no longer his to hold.

I headed toward town to try to get some air, to try to come to grips with what had just happened, but it didn't take long for me to realize I'd made a major mistake by walking through downtown Chester. Everywhere I turned, I ran into the familiar face of someone who wanted to talk to me, wanted to ask me questions, wanted to know why my eyes were flooded with tears.

Each person made my heart crack. Each question singed my skin. I wasn't in the right mindset to deal with anyone or anything.

I can't breathe…

I began rushing, trying my best to avoid people on the whole. Everyone in town seemed so happy, and that was hard for me. It hurt more than I thought possible to push my way through a space filled with happiness. Everyone was alive, everyone was filled with life, and my insides felt hollow.

Whenever I blinked, I was certain I was seconds away from falling apart.

How was it possible?

How could one be in the middle of a town, surrounded by people who knew you, yet feel so unbelievably alone?

I took a moment to slow down in front of the pizzeria, leaning against the brick wall and trying to inhale, but the air was still hard to take in.

My body was sweaty, and my vision blurry. Whenever I blinked, I saw him with her. Whenever I breathed, the shards of my heart stabbed my soul.

I was seconds away from a mental breakdown, moments away

from losing myself when a hand landed on my shoulder and I flipped around, panicking as I made eye contact with Jackson. The palms of my hands were sweaty, and my heart pounded rapidly against my ribcage.

"Hey," he said, holding his hands up in surrender. The concern on his face was heavy, and I was surprised to find that a man like him could be concerned.

I must've looked that bad off.

"I-I-I..." I tried to say I was okay, nodding so he wouldn't worry. "I'm o-okay. I think I'm j-ju-just..." I couldn't push the words out, so I started waving my hands toward me, trying to collect my next breaths, and Jackson shook his head.

"You're having a panic attack," he told me.

I nodded once more. "Yes. That." My hands fell to my chest, and I swore any second I'd be okay. I had to be okay. There had to be a point when the breaking pieces stopped breaking, right?

"Come here," Jackson said, holding his hand out toward me.

"I'm...I'm f-fine," I stuttered, but he just shook his head as people walked past us on the street, whispering and staring.

"Princess," he said, his voice low. He moved his hand closer and gave me the gentlest stare. "Trust me."

I didn't. I didn't know what trust was anymore. The two people who were supposed to always stand by my side had ruined my idea of trust, but...

I needed to breathe.

Just for a moment.

I took Jackson's hand, and he walked me around the corner to the alleyway. Stepping back against a mural, we leaned against the brick wall. As I began to fall apart, I tried to apologize to him, but my words came out jumbled and incoherent.

"You're fine," he said sternly.

I kept huffing and puffing, but nothing was working. As my body was about to hit the concrete, as I was about to surrender to my pain, I was surprised when I melted into Jackson Emery's arms.

He caught me.

He held me.

He wouldn't let me fall.

I yanked on his shirt, pulling him closer as I fell apart against him. I wanted to be brave, wanted to end my meltdown, but for a split second, as Jackson held me, it felt okay to have my moment and fall apart. When my sobbing became too intense, when it felt like anxiety and panic would swallow me whole, he held me closer.

"You're okay," he soothed, his voice deep and steady. He let me go as I kept trying to regroup. "Hey, come here," he said, lowering himself to the ground. "Just sit down for a second. Breathe."

Easier said than done.

I sat down beside him, leaning my back against the mural of our town.

"Good," he told me. "Now lower your head between your legs and take deep breaths."

"I-I ca-can't..."

"Yes, princess, you can. Just slow down. Lower your head and lace your fingers together on the back of your neck. You can do this."

I did as he said, and every time I tried to apologize, he told me to stop and just breathe.

Slowly but surely, my heartbeats began to return to a normal pace. Slowly but surely, embarrassment filled me as I raised my head and found Jackson's intense stare on me.

I wiped my eyes and inhaled. "I'm so sorry."

"Stop saying that."

"Sorry," I murmured, making him roll his eyes.

"I said stop saying that."

"Sor—" I started but then caught myself. "Okay."

He sighed, his face still hard. "Okay."

I combed my hands through my hair and shook my head back and forth. "You can go, I swear. I'm just a bit of a hot mess, remember? I should probably get going, too," I said, moving to stand, but he placed his hand on my forearm.

"Just give it a minute. Let your body calm down. Panic attacks take a second to disappear completely."

"You've had panic attacks before?"

He fiddled with his hands and looked down at the ground. "My mother used to suffer from them." He kept staring down at his hands before saying, "You'll be fine. Just give it a minute, all right? Take small breaths."

Take small breaths.

I can do that.

We sat in silence, both staring forward and letting the warm night air touch our skin.

"What's your story?" I asked, tilting my head toward him, somewhat confused by his entire existence. He was so mean, so dark, but at the same time, he managed to somehow be gentle…

A gentle monster.

"You know my story, remember? You said you know me. Everyone in this place seems to know me," he replied, almost growling. "I'm the town asshole, and that's all there is to it." He stood and then cleared his throat. "Just give it about five more minutes, all right?"

"Okay. Thanks."

He brushed his hands on the back of his neck and shook his head. "Stop talking. Just breathe."

His hazel eyes locked with mine, and we spent a moment taking one another in. It was as if we truly saw each other for the first time. As I looked into his eyes, I recognized something I saw in my own soul: loneliness.

The way he stared made me think he recognized it, too.

He glanced my way one last time. He didn't smile, but he didn't frown, and somehow, that felt like a small victory.

As he left, I silently thanked him again. After an evening of drowning, the town's bad seed was the one who'd helped me come up for a small breath of air.

CHAPTER SIX

Jackson

"I see we're out and about, making new friends," Alex remarked as I walked back into the shop with a pizza a while later. I tossed it in the break room then came back out, arching an eyebrow in his direction.

"What the hell are you doing?" I asked as he stood under the hood of that disgustingly pink automobile.

"What does it look like I'm doing? I'm working on Grace's car."

"I said take it to the scrapyard, not here."

"Oh? Did you? I must've missed that," he lied. Alex was a great listener; he never missed a word anyone said. "Well, since it's here…" He smirked at me, and I rolled my eyes, making him laugh. "Come on, man. It could be our newest passion project. We've been looking for the perfect new toy to play with."

I walked around the car, kicking one of the tires. "There's nothing about this thing that makes me passionate. It's a piece of shit. It's seriously a piece of actual shit. If it were an animal's shit, it would be a monkey's. If it were a person's shit, it would be yours. It's the worst piece of shit that ever existed."

"Hmm…" Alex whistled low. "I'm glad to see you've been working on watching your language, and really? You think monkey shit is worse than hippo shit?"

"Well, I guess it depends on the size of the monkey."

"No, Jackson"—he shook his head—"it doesn't."

"I'm serious, man. Get this out of the shop."

"Listen, kiddo, you know I love you like you're my own son, but I think it's childish that you are refusing a perfectly good learning experience on this pink hot mama because of the hate you have for the family it belongs to."

"That family is nothing but shit," I barked. "You should hate them, too."

"Yes, sure, of course. But this"—Alex hugged the car—"this is a precious baby. It didn't choose its family. It had no say in who owned it. It's just sitting in our shop, looking for a little love. Can't we give it a little love, Jack-Jack?"

He gave me his best puppy-dog eyes, and he knew how much I hated when he did that.

Alex was my uncle, my mother's older brother, and he'd moved to Chester a few years back when Dad wasn't in any shape to take care of the shop or me. He was pretty much the only person in the whole town I gave a damn about.

We were close, at least as close as I allowed people to get, which wasn't saying too much.

His body was coated in tattoos, and if you found a spot that wasn't, he'd be quick to fix that issue. He spent all his free time working at a tattoo parlor right outside of town. He had dark black and gray hair that he always combed back and piercings all over. If you passed him on the street, you might jump out of your skin in fear until he started talking to you about the latest avocado mask he'd discovered.

He was one of the most positive people in the world, and I was the complete opposite. But, at the same time, our connection made sense—we balanced each other out.

"My dad's going to throw a fit if he finds out a Harris's car is in his shop," I warned. If anyone hated the church more than I did, it was my father.

"He won't even know," Alex said, shaking his head back and forth. "I promise I'll keep our dirty little secret."

"*Your* dirty secret. I'm not working on that car. I want nothing to do with it or that family." The only reason I agreed to let the car stay was because I knew he wouldn't give it up until he got his way. "But just to be clear, I'm not happy about this."

"Just to be clear, you're never happy, so I'll take that as a good thing. Anyway, I know you and your pops got your issues with that family, but I liked her."

"You like everyone," I remarked.

"Yeah, but you gotta admit, she was beautiful in a way—even with the puffy eyes."

He wasn't wrong; Grace Harris was beautiful. She had long blond hair and wide blue doe eyes that were filled with fear and wonderment all at once. I'd have been lying if I'd said I hadn't noticed that her curves fell in all the right places, but that wasn't shocking. All the Harris females were easy on the eyes. They walked and talked as properly as a Southern belle could—except for Grace when she was falling apart. For the most part, they stood for beauty, charm, and elegance—on the outside, at least. On the inside, they had the ugliest souls, and I wanted nothing to do with them or their piece-of-shit cars.

I still wasn't sure why I'd stopped to help her in front of the pizza place.

It made no sense whatsoever except for the fact that her breakdown reminded me of my mother.

"Hey, Jack-Jack?" Alex called out, and this time when I looked over at him, I saw the worry in his eyes. It was the same worried look he always gave me when he thought I would fall overboard. "How are you doing? Are you doing okay?"

"I'm fine," I said. That was what I always said when Alex asked me that question.

Even after I overdosed and almost lost my life over a year ago, I replied in the same fashion. *I'm fine.*

I was always fine, even when I wasn't.

"All right. Well, hey, if you don't want this car to be your new project, you should still find yourself a hobby or something to keep your head on straight. You still doing art and stuff? Maybe you should pick that up again. Are you dating? Maybe go out on some dates, or hell, knit a sweater—anything, really."

"Yeah. Okay."

"I'm really proud of you."

"I haven't done anything," I replied dryly.

"Exactly." He nodded. "You haven't gone off track and fallen back into your old habits. I'm just proud of you, and if you ever need someone to talk to, I'm here."

I shrugged. "Thanks."

"Anytime, Jack-Jack."

"Oh, and Alex?"

"Yeah?"

"Stop calling me Jack-Jack."

I went back to the break room and grabbed a few slices of pizza to take over to my dad's house. When I walked into his living room, I found him passed out drunk on the couch. Sometimes, I pretended he'd passed out from exhaustion, but the truth of the matter was the whiskey lullabies were what put him to sleep most of the time.

I tossed the pizza into the fridge and grumbled as I cleaned up a bit. Dad stayed knocked out on the couch, and every now and then, I'd wander past to check that he was still breathing.

There had been a time in my life when I believed my old man would live forever. There had been a time when he was my hero, and I had thought he could defeat any villain in the whole wide world.

Funny how time had changed my hero into my worst villain.

Funny how life had destroyed my father's soul.

After I finished at my father's house, I walked to my cabin and went inside. Every piece of that place held a part of my father before the alcohol had overtaken his soul—the paint on the walls, the hardwood floors, the tiles in the bathroom. Everything about the cabin told the story of the man he once was before his life began to crumble.

I'd helped him fix up the place when I was a kid—before Ma left and before Dad found himself addicted to the bottle.

Each night, I sat there in the dark, looking around the space. In the corner of the living room sat an easel and art supplies, and in the spare bedroom, bookshelves filled to the brim with novels lined the walls. Throughout the whole cabin was framed artwork; no room went without one of Ma's masterpieces. That was the last part of her I still held onto. The cabin was both a gift and a curse to me, reminding me of the past, contrasting sharply with and the present day. It was now a place filled with hollowness.

I welcomed the emptiness and I allowed loneliness to be almost all I knew, and then when it was all too much, I took on my hobby.

Alex didn't know I already had something to keep me away from the drugs.

Over the past few years, I'd entertained different women in my bed almost every night. It wasn't anything I was proud of, but it distracted me from my reality. Some I'd hooked up with before, but I usually didn't remember that until they informed me. Others acted as if it was an achievement to get in my bed and just giggled like damn teenagers.

Sarah, Michelle, Jamie, Kay, Lisa, Rebecca, Susie…
Sky blue eyes, chocolate eyes, hazel, light brown, green, sable…
Each one helped me forget for a while.
Each one shut off my brain.
Each one became my new kind of drug, and slowly but surely, I became addicted.

No one ever stayed the night. I didn't want them to stay; I just wanted them for a few hours to help me forget. It was the same thing every time: sex, no talking, leave. Sex, no talking, leave. The night Hazel Eyes was leaving, she told me we'd had sex before, and she liked me better when I was doped up.

"Yeah? Well, I liked you better when your mouth wasn't running and was wrapped around my cock."

"You're such an asshole," she exclaimed, acting as if she hadn't been just as rude a moment before. "You're disgusting."

"Both sets of your lips didn't seem to mind fifteen minutes ago," I replied dryly.

It was her turn to flip me off, and I probably deserved it. I could be a real asshole sometimes. The thing was, it seemed people seemed to like the assholes more than the nice pathetic guys.

Hazel Eyes would probably call me up to fuck again soon enough. It was as if women had a magnetic pull to guys who treated them like trash.

Then when they left, I was alone again.

Well, not completely alone.

Tucker was older than before yet still so loyal. Each night, he'd slowly move in my direction, wagging that tail of his, and then he'd crawl into my lap on the couch. Sometimes, I had to help him into my lap, but he always came close to me.

Even on the nights when I felt as if I deserved to be alone.

But still, no matter what I did or said to him, he stayed. He was my friend. The only one I had, and the only one I needed.

Good boy, Tuck, I thought to myself, holding him closer. *Good boy.*

Jackson
Six Years Old

"Ma? Can I have a new name?" I asked one day, walking onto the front porch where she sat painting the sky again. She always painted the sky, and she was really good at it, too.

She tucked her paintbrush behind her ear and raised an eyebrow at me. "What do you mean can you have a new name?"

"Today at school someone told me my name was stupid, and that's why they didn't want to play with me."

Ma's mouth dropped open, and her eyes watered over. "Someone said that to you?"

"Yeah. Can I change my name, so I can make friends?"

That's all I wanted.

I wanted the kids at school to like me. We'd only lived in Chester for a few months now, and I hadn't made any new friends. Dad told me to give it time, but the more time I gave it, the more people told me why I couldn't hang out with them. Tim Reeves was having a birthday party and invited everyone in our class except me because I was the weird new kid.

I just wanted to go to a party.

"Jackson, honey, your name is perfect. Anyone who tells you they don't want to be your friend because of your name isn't the type of people you want to be friends with, okay?"

"I'll be friends with anyone," I promised her. "Maybe if my name was Eric or something."

Ma frowned. "Come on, love. We're going to go have an art lesson."

I groaned. I didn't want to do art. Whenever there was a problem, Ma always used art to try to fix it—to teach me. I didn't want to learn, though.

I just wanted friends.

"But Ma—" I started, yet she gave me a stern look.

"Jackson Paul," she scolded, using my middle name. I stopped talking because whenever Ma used my middle name, I knew she wasn't going to let me slide.

She gathered some things from the house.

Paints, paintbrushes, a white bedsheet, two long sticks, wire, and clothespins.

"What are you doing?" I asked.

"You'll see. Come on. Let's go out to the field."

We walked through the trees in the back of our house toward an open lot of land. That was where Ma had me paint the sunsets with her at least twice a week.

I waited not-so-patiently as she set up her "canvas."

She staked the two sticks into the ground with a bit of distance between them

Then, she tied the wire to the top of each stick, connecting them. Next, she took the sheet and attached it to the wire with the clothespins.

She turned my way, smiling. "You know where your name came from?"

I shook my head.

She picked up a paintbrush and covered it with blue paint. Next, she splattered the paint against the sheet. She added a new color to her brush and did the same thing. It looked like a mess, but a nice mess somehow.

I didn't know messes could look nice.

"His name was Jackson Pollock, and he was unique. He was known for his drip painting technique like this. Here, try it." She handed me the paintbrush, and I started making a nice mess, too.

"He was an individual, Jackson, and he went against the norm. He didn't try to make people like him by being something he wasn't. He didn't care what others thought of him. He was just himself, and he was extraordinary." She walked over to me and tapped me on the nose. "Just like you. Do you know what his original first name was?"

"What?"

"Paul."

I grinned ear to ear. "Like my middle name? Jackson Paul?"

"Exactly. Your father and I named you that because you are extraordinary, too, honey. One day, the right people will show up, and they will realize how special you are. They will see you for everything you are and love every piece of it just like your father and I love you. They will be your friends. Okay?"

I nodded. "I guess until those friends come, I got you and Dad to hang out with me."

"Yes, Jackson." She pulled me into a hug and kissed my forehead. "You'll always have us."

We went back to painting, and it was a lot of fun.

After we finished, I looked at our artwork. "Hey, Ma?"

"Yes?"

"You think I can be as good as you at art one day?"

"No, Jackson," she told me, shaking her head, "you'll be better."

CHAPTER SEVEN

Grace

Growing up, my sister and I never really went without. We grew up on acres of southern land in a house that was bigger than it needed to be. Daddy never really cared about having a home that size, but Mama felt they deserved it. As if God put the money in their hands, and they did enough for the community, therefore they were allowed to swim in God's blessings.

Mama was right about one thing—Daddy did deserve it. He worked hard to get to the position he was at, and he never took that for granted. He believed in the church more than anyone I ever knew, and for every acre of land he owned, he gave back to the community.

My sister and I had a certain role to play as pastor's children. Mama always taught Judy and me that we had to act a certain way throughout all our lives. The Harris girls were always supposed to be proper, prose, and beautiful. Not just an outer beauty, but we were to hold beautiful spirits, too.

For the most part, we took those roles very seriously. People looked up to our family, which meant we had to create a world worth looking up to. We were blessed, which meant that we had to be other's blessings.

That meant we always had to be perfect in public. There was no place for flaws. So, whenever we faltered...whenever the world hit us, and we'd stumble, my sister and I fell against one another.

I knocked on Judy's front door, and the second she opened it, her eyes filled with tears.

"Oh my gosh, Grace! What's wrong?! What's going on?" she asked, but she didn't wait for a reply before wrapping me into her arms.

I began sobbing uncontrollably onto my baby sister's shoulder as she gently rubbed my back.

"Can I stay with you and Hank?" I choked out, unable to say anything else at all, but that seemed like more than enough for Judy.

"Always, Grace," she whispered, pulling me closer to her body. "Always and always."

I told her and Hank everything. The words poured out of me, and truthfully, so many of them were hard for me to believe. It all felt like a nightmare that I simply couldn't wake from.

As we sat on the living room couch, Hank kept refilling Judy's and my wineglasses. Hank was such a gentle man. I'd never once heard him raise his voice, and he never saw the bad in anyone.

Even when Judy and I slipped into our gossipy nature, Hank never spoke a word about a soul. His main goals in life were living it to the fullest and taking care of his love. And boy, did he love my sister. There were so many times I'd catch him staring at her when she wasn't looking, and it would give me butterflies.

"I'm so sorry, Grace," Hank told me, giving me a slight frown. "I can't believe he'd do that to you. I can't believe they'd both do that. I just...I can't believe it." He appeared stunned. Finn was one of his closest friends, and he just kept saying he couldn't believe it could happen.

Me either.

We stayed talking for a while, and when the doorbell rang, Judy hopped up to answer it.

I turned to face Hank and crossed my arms. "Hank, can I ask you something?"

"I didn't know, Grace," he said as if he could read my mind. "I had no clue about Finn and the cheating, and if I'd known, I would've told you. I understand why you think I wouldn't, seeing how he's my friend, but you're family, Grace. I swear on my grandfather's grave, I would've told you. And truthfully, it's hard for me to even realize who Finn is anymore, or how he could do this to you."

I lowered my head and stared at their carpeted floor. "Thank you, Hank."

"Always and always," he replied, stating my family's favorite phrase. Those were the words my family had always exchanged with one another since the beginning of time. *Always and always.* It was a promise that no matter what, we'd stand by one another—through the good days and the bad.

Every time I heard the words, I felt less alone.

"You have some nerve showing up here!" Judy barked, making both Hank and me jump up from the couch. Judy never raised her voice—ever.

"I'm sorry, Judy. It's just…"

My skin began to crawl as I heard Finn's voice. "Is Grace here?"

"That's none of your business," Judy snapped again. "You should go."

Oh, sister, I love you.

"Yeah, of course, it's just…" He paused, and I heard something moving. "She left her suitcases at Autumn's place."

It was painful when hearts stopped beating.

I listened to Judy pulling the suitcases into the house. "Fine. Now leave."

He didn't say another word, and I was certain he was walking back to go find Autumn.

"And Finley James?" Judy said, using his middle name. That was how you knew my sister was serious—when she used a person's middle name.

"Yes?"

"You should be ashamed of yourself. Both of you."

"Is she okay?" he asked, and it almost sounded as if he cared.

"She will be," she swore. "Because she's strong. She's stronger than any betrayal you could've ever brought to her doorstep."

Then the front door slammed.

It *slammed*.

Judith Rae never slammed doors.

As she rounded the corner, her eyes locked with mine. We could've easily been twins, she and I. She always said I had Dad's crystal blue eyes, and I always said she had those bluest of blues. We smiled the same too, a bit of a lopsided grin to the left side. Our hair was long and naturally blond. Mama would've killed us if we ever dyed it—because one didn't mess with God's creation. Also, our hearts kind of beat in the same rhythmic pattern.

If sisters were soul mates, Judy would be mine.

"So," she breathed out, giving me a gentle smile. "How about some more wine?"

I hadn't slept a wink the prior evening. The next morning, the sun came up, and I watched it rise with a cup of coffee in my hands. I stood on the back porch, feeling the warmth against my skin. It amazed me how hollow I could feel, watching the morning light fill the sky. Dad used to always tell my sister and me that the morning sun was Jesus' kisses against our skin.

As a kid, I never mentioned the scientific truths I learned at school about the sun rising and setting because it wasn't really my place. Sometimes, people needed to believe what they needed to believe to get through each day.

That morning, I needed to believe in the kisses.

"You're up too early." Judy yawned, walking out of the house still in her pajamas.

"Just wanted to feel Jesus' kisses," I joked, taking a deep breath of the crisp morning air.

She walked over to me, took my cup of coffee, and sipped it. "How did you sleep?"

"I didn't."

"Makes sense. I didn't sleep at all either. It took everything for me not to go into your room and check on you. I've been so worried."

"I'll be fine," I said even though I wasn't certain I'd be okay, but I had faith. At least enough to get me to every next breath. "Everything always works out, right? Don't worry about me."

"You're my sister, my heart, Grace. I'm always going to worry about you."

I believed her. The same way she worried about me was the same way I worried for her.

"I just wish I could do something for you. I wish I could take away all your hurting. I'm just really sorry," she told me, so truly sincere, "for what they did to you."

We stood there staring out into the morning light, and as my hand rested on the porch railing, my sister placed her hand on top of mine. I didn't know why, but her gentle touch made tears fall from my eyes as we stared out at the waking sun. For a moment in time, I felt less alone. Maybe that was the whole point of family—to make you feel less alone in a lonesome world. Sometimes, family got it wrong; sometimes, they said and did the wrong things because they were, after all, only human. Yet then there were those moments when they were right on time with their sparks of love.

Home is healing.

"Did you bring clothes for church service?" Judy asked, yawning again. "Or do you want to borrow some of mine?"

"I don't think I'm gonna go. I'm not really in the small-town church mood today."

Judy laughed, tossing her head back, and then when she stopped giggling, she looked at me and her jaw dropped. "Wait, you're serious?"

"Yeah, I am."

"Grace. You're the daughter of the pastor, and you're back in Chester. Everybody already knows you're back. Do you know what it would do to Mama if you didn't show up? She'd have a heart attack."

"Mama will be okay," I lied. I knew she wouldn't.

Judy cocked an eyebrow. "I can already hear Mrs. Grove badgering Mama with questions of why you weren't at service, which would lead to Mama badgering you. Do you really want to deal with that?"

I sighed. I didn't, but I wasn't certain I was ready to talk to anyone, really. I hadn't even been able to look in the mirror without tearing up. Plus, I'd already been receiving text messages from the townsfolk who saw me at my lowest of lows with Jackson yesterday. They kept asking if I was okay, and it was all so much. The idea of facing the whole church seemed so unbelievably overwhelming.

Judy must've noticed my hesitation because she squeezed my hand. "Don't worry about it. Mama can be a bit peeved for a minute, but that's nothing new. The most important thing right now is taking care of you and that heart of yours, okay? I'll cover for you and tell everyone you weren't feeling well."

I laughed. "You'd lie in the church for me?"

"I'd do anything for you, Grace. Anything."

"Even help me hide a dead body?" I joked.

"Only if it's Finley James'," she replied.

That made me smile, but then I felt guilty for thinking about Finn being dead.

It was sometimes hard to be God's follower when the Devil's whisperings sounded more satisfying.

We went back to staring at the horizon, and every now and then, I took a few small breaths.

CHAPTER EIGHT

Grace

Only a handful of people in town didn't make it to church service on Sunday mornings, and Josie Parker was one of those individuals. Her mama, Betty, opened the doors of The Silent Bookshop a few years back after her husband, Frank, lost his hearing in a freak car accident. For a long time, Frank struggled with depression, but the only thing that kept his head above water were the words in the novels.

Each night for months, Betty sat beside her husband, holding a book in her hand, and they'd silently read the words together, flipping the pages as their fingers brushed against one another.

Whenever you saw them in town, they were either holding hands or holding a book. Their haven lived between their love and their novels, and when the idea of opening a bookstore where the one and only rule was complete and utter silence, Betty dived right in.

I spent many of my teenage years inside that store, sitting in the back corner and falling in love with men and women from faraway places. It was because of that shop that I knew I wanted to become an English teacher. I wanted to teach children the importance of words.

Words had the power to transport a small-town girl to worlds she'd never imagined. When I turned sixteen, it was that same bookshop where I received my first job, too. Sometimes, that place felt more like home than my actual home.

As I walked into the shop, I could smell them all—the adventures hidden behind the covers. The heartbreaking stories. The heart healing ones. The stories of love lost and found. The stories of self-discovery. The stories that made you feel less alone in a lonely world.

There was no better feeling than falling in love with people you'd never truly meet, yet still, they felt like family.

The bookshop was set up in such a unique way. When you entered, you walked into the front lobby where you could speak. A coffee area was set up with countertops and bar stools. On the countertops were crossword puzzles that changed each day, and as you drank your beverage, you'd fill in the puzzles and chat with the barista about the latest gossip in Chester.

To the left, you'd find a set of doors carved out of wood—made by Frank—that had handwritten famous first lines from classic novels. Over the doors, a sign read, B*ehind these doors, the story begins.* Once you stepped foot inside that space, dozens and dozens of novels surrounded you. The bookcases touched the high ceilings, and ladders scattered throughout the area allowed you to climb high to find that one certain read you hadn't even known you'd been searching for.

Tables were set up throughout the space where people could sit and read. The only rule was complete silence, like a still bear sleeping through the depths of winter. The only sound ever heard was people tiptoeing through the space as they searched for their next book.

I loved the solitude that The Silent Bookshop offered. It was a safe place where the only drama allowed was found within the stories.

"Well grand day, if it isn't Gracelyn Mae returning home," Josie remarked, using sign language to speak as I walked into the shop. She always signed her words as she spoke. It seemed like a first language to her, and every sign I knew was because she taught it to me. Her blond hair sat in a bun on top of her head, and she still had that deep dimple in her right cheek that always appeared whenever she smiled—and Josie Parker was always smiling.

We'd graduated high school together, and she was hands down the class clown. Yet outside of that, she was also a good person. Her comedy never came at the cost of others. She'd make fun of herself before another person, and I always adored her positive outlook on the world. Plus, in town, she was one of the only souls I trusted to keep my secrets. She was the girl who allowed me to step out of my perfect persona to be free for a bit of time. When we were kids, Josie would bring me Diet Coke with a few splashes of whiskey, and we'd sit in the park people watching while tipsy.

Mama would've killed me if she knew I was drinking whiskey in high school, but I never had to worry about that with Josie by my side.

With her, my secrets were always safe.

Maybe that was why I wandered her way. Maybe I was hoping she'd be able to shine some light on some of my dark days.

"It's been too long," she said before pulling me into a hug.

"I know. I've missed this place. Everything about it, I've missed."

"Well, it misses you too, but we understand you getting out of this small town. Following Finn for his dream was a noble thing, but I'm glad to hear he's working at the hospital now, which means you're here, too, yeah?"

"Yeah, but only for the summer, though. I still have my teaching job back in Atlanta."

"Oh? So you are doing the long-distance thing?"

"Well…"

My bottom lip quivered, and she noted it. "You know what? No need to answer my questions. I'll shut up real quick." Something about Josie just warmed up hearts. She was such a positive energy and such a genuine heart. "Now come on. Sit down. You still drinking coffee over tea?" she asked me.

"Yes, sure am."

She shook her head in disappointment. "One day, I'm gonna make you a cup of tea, and you'll be forever changed. But for now, I'll make you a nice cup of joe."

I snickered. "You studied abroad for a few months in England and came back a changed woman."

"I also married a British boy from those studies and dragged him back to Chester. So, the least I can do is drink tea." She grabbed the largest mug in the shop and poured the coffee to the brim, then she sat it in front of me. "So how does it feel to be back in Chester?"

My eyes watered over, and my stomach knotted, but I did my best not to cry.

She frowned. "Are you okay?"

"Truth or lie?"

"Always truth." She walked back around the counter and sat on the barstool beside me with her hands wrapped around her mug of tea. "So what's the story?"

I huffed out a laugh. "Honestly, I don't even know where to start."

"Well, I never liked a book that started in the middle," she joked. "So let's start from the beginning."

And so, I did.

I told her everything that unfolded with Finn, and when the tears fell from my eyes, she was quick to wipe them away. She didn't offer any advice, and she didn't push me with options of what I should and shouldn't do. No, she simply listened.

Sometimes, all a person needed was another to listen to their uneven heartbeats.

When I finished talking, she gave my knee a squeeze. "So you're not okay."

"I'll get there."

"Yes." She nodded. "You will. But until then, if you need a safe place to escape, you can always come here. Also, we always have a spot for you on the staff."

"You don't have to do that for me."

"Yeah, but I want to, and you know my mom wouldn't have it any other way. Even though I love this town, I know how overwhelming it can get sometimes. Plus, I get the feeling that your heart needs a break. So, if you want that break, you can take it here."

"I might take you up on that offer."

"It's yours for the taking." She paused and scrunched up her nose. "I always hated Autumn," she told me.

"I wish I could say the same."

Right as I was about to change the subject, the front door of the shop opened and in walked Jackson. He didn't look the least bit intrigued that Josie and I were in the shop. In fact, he moved as if he couldn't even see us. The way he traveled made it seem as if he was bored with everything in the whole wide world. He was simply moving to get from point A to point B with no real drive to even explore the idea of a point C.

A chill ran over my body as he walked straight through the set of wooden doors without looking toward either of us.

"Well, he sure is an intriguing personality," I muttered.

Josie laughed. "That's just the normal Jackson Emery for ya. He doesn't really interact with people much when he comes in here—and he's here every day."

"Seriously?"

"Yup. One of our best customers, too. He sits in the back room for two to three hours reading, and he always leaves with new book purchases. I swear, most of the shop's income probably comes from that man."

"What kind of books does he read?" I questioned, curiosity striking me. You could tell a lot about a man based on the type of books on his nightstand.

"Only one genre—young adult."

"Young adult? Really?"

"Truly. Weird, huh? He doesn't very much seem like the young adult type, now does he?"

"Not at all." *Interesting...* "Everyone calls him the devil in town, and when I crossed paths with him, at first, I had to agree. He was awful. A really mean person. But then...then there were moments when he was just so gentle. Like a whisper."

Josie nodded. "Yes. He's rough around the edges, but he's not the devil—not by a long shot. But best believe he ain't no saint, either. I don't know much of his story, but it can't be that easy of a read. His father is a handful, and Jackson is the only person around who takes care of him. His uncle helps out a bit, but he has his own tattoo business outside of Chester, so he keeps busy, leaving Jackson to care for his dad. I swear Mike Emery finds himself locked up more often than not from his drunkenness, and Jackson is the only one there to ever bail him out. That can't be easy—having to be a parent to your parent."

Josie was so unique to the town of Chester. She saw things and people in ways that no one else quite could. The same could be said about her parents. They saw the beauty in the ugliest shadows, and I adored that quality about their family. It took a special soul to see past others' scars.

"How do you do that, Josie? See the good in everyone and find understanding for why people are the way they are?"

She shrugged her shoulders. "My parents taught me to zoom in, ya know? It's easy to judge others from afar. It's easy to look at someone from outside your world and make blanket statements and judgments on who those people are. Because when you see others' flaws, you somewhat justify that your flaws are better than theirs. But when you zoom in, when you truly look at the person beside you, you'll see many of the same things. Hope. Love. Fear. Anger. Once you zoom in, you realize we are all similar in so many ways. We all bleed red, and even monster's hearts can break. Just gotta remember to always zoom in."

To always zoom in...

I liked that more than I could express. I wasn't the perfect person. I judged others without being aware of it at times, and that was one flaw I knew I had to work on. Just like Jackson, I, too was far from a saint. I needed to zoom in more often.

"After my dad's accident, he turned to the bottle for a while, too. Did you know that?" Josie asked.

"No, I had no clue."

"Yeah, we were young when the accident happened, so it's not shocking. For a good while, he suffered from depression. People judged him hard, and if he didn't have my mom to help him through the dark days, he could've easily turned into Mike Emery. And I could've easily become Jackson. I feel like the whole world could be Jackson or Mike, based on one left turn."

"That's true…" I swallowed hard. "I guess I never thought of it like that."

"But then again, who knows? I could be wrong, and Jackson could seriously just be a total asshole who just sleeps around," she joked. "But watching him with that dog of his is the biggest turn-on in the world to me."

"His dog?"

"It's an old black lab. You'll see him in town with him. Just watch how he treats that dog, and you'll realize more than just darkness lives in that boy."

We spoke for a few more minutes before I found myself walking into the silent book area. As the door closed behind me, I inhaled deeply, looking around at all the beauties against the wall.

Hello, friends.

There were so many words throughout the space that I wasn't quite certain where to even start. I loved the idea of falling into the pages more than ever now since my own story was quite a mess. I'd rather read another's happily ever after than waste time debating my own.

As I walked through the aisles of books, my fingertips danced across the spines. I smiled at those who looked up toward me, and ninety-nine percent of the individuals smiled back, with warm, welcoming looks. But that one percent…

Jackson sat in the far-left corner of the shop. It was the darkest corner with only a small flood of light from a small window. My eyes fell to the book in his grip.

Children of Blood and Bone by Tomi Adeyemi.

Gosh, he was so complex. A big, muscular, mean man reading young adult novels.

Fascinating.

Right as I studied the cover of the novel, I felt his eyes on me. I lifted my head a bit, and his eyes burned into me with a look of complete disgust. The corners of his lips stayed turned down, and he slightly grumbled before looking back down at his book and flipping the page.

Knots formed in my stomach and my nerves twisted up with confusion of the boy who seemed to despise me more than anything. I tried to understand why he was the way he was toward me. I tried my best to zoom in on him and see his true colors.

"Hey, Jackson," I said, nodding his way.

He looked up, then back down at his book. "No talking in here," he muttered, flipping his page.

"I know, but I just wanted to say thank you for yesterday, for when you—"

"You can't talk in here," he hissed once more.

A chill raced down my spine. "I know but—"

"Listen, princess, I get that you might think you're beyond privileged, and that rules don't apply to you, but please, just take your comments elsewhere, cuz I don't want to hear them."

Wow.

Mean Jackson was back in full force.

"Just go away," he told me, his voice hard and mean.

And without a single sound, I did exactly that.

CHAPTER NINE

Grace

As I walked up to Judy and Hank's place after spending most of the day in The Silent Bookshop, I saw the panic in my sister before she even spoke a word my way.

She rushed out the front door, whisper-shouting, "Grace, listen, I'm so sorry, I didn't know this would happen, and you're going to kill me because I let it slip, but I didn't mean to let it slip, and I'm so sorry!"

I cocked an eyebrow. "What are you talking about?"

"It's Mama."

"What about her?"

"She's here, and she knows about Finn."

"What? How?"

"Well, she doesn't exactly know, but people were gossiping at the service about how they saw you and him fighting in town last night. They asked her about it, asking if you two were okay."

Oh, great, people were already running their mouths about Finn and me. That didn't take long.

"Mama was so thrown off, but she smiled through it all. Then she gave me a good talkin'-to...and she invited herself over for dinner. Which is happening now." The guilt of it all swam in Judy's eyes, but it wasn't her fault.

I gave her a tight smile and told her it was okay. Mom would've found out anyway. I just wished she hadn't learned it from random people in the church. Even though she smiled through it, I knew that being blindsided would've upset her.

"We better get inside before she loses her mind even more," Judy warned.

"Where's Hank?"

"Are you kidding me? The moment he found out Mama was coming over, he got out of dodge."

Smart man. "What about Dad? Is he coming?" He worked pretty well as a buffer between Mama and me when we ended up butting heads, which was inevitable. If anything, I was a daddy's girl through and through, so I always did better when family dinners involved him.

"Mama said he's working at the church tonight, so it's just the three of us."

"Oh." I groaned. "Wonderful."

The moment we stepped into the foyer of the house, Mama was there wearing the biggest frown of her life, and her arms stretched out to embrace me.

"Oh, Gracelyn Mae." She sighed, shaking her head back and forth. "You look awful."

Home sweet home.

"I was blindsided at the church today," Mama told me as we sat down at the dining room table. "You could've given me more warning, Gracelyn Mae."

"I know, and I'm sorry, Mama. I didn't know anyone saw Finn and me last night."

"This is Chester. Someone is always watching."

She wasn't wrong about that.

"I just cannot believe this is happening." Mama gasped, seeming completely stunned after learning about what happened between Finn and me. I'd never seen Mama so distraught. She kept shaking her head back and forth in disbelief.

"It's really okay, Mama. You don't have to be so heartbroken," I told her, pushing my food around on my plate.

"You can't just give up, though, Grace. You can't walk away from your marriage. Your vows!" she cried. "Didn't your vows mean anything to you?" I doubt she meant for her words to hurt me so much, but lately, hurting was all that my heart did.

"Mom, come on," Judy cut in, trying to protect me.

"Of course, they meant something to me," I whispered, my stomach in knots from her words. Those vows meant *everything* to me.

"Through sickness and health, Grace. Obviously, Finn is dealing with a demon of the mind. He's not himself. He wouldn't ever willingly hurt you, and our family has never had a divorce—ever." Her overly dramatic reaction was exactly what I expected because everything about my mother was over the top. "What will people say?"

What will people say?

That was her concern?

I couldn't even reply.

I was currently dealing with my breaking heart pains.

"Grace, it's like you're not even fighting for him," Mom said.

"I'm not," I told her.

"Don't you love him?"

I wouldn't answer her.

"Don't you care?"

Still, I couldn't voice my feelings.

"How can you be so selfish?" she asked me, and I giggled. I

giggled because she was so serious. I giggled because sometimes laughter was the only thing that kept me from falling apart.

"Selfish? How am I being selfish?" I asked, passing the bread bowl to Judy. She gave me the sincerest frown, and I was so thankful she was my person. Without her there, I would've shattered.

"Our family has generations of marriages, long-lasting marriages, and not a single divorce, not ever. Now you want to be the one to soil that? To ruin your family name?"

I rolled my eyes. "Mom, you and Dad don't even share a bedroom."

"He snores."

"And probably can't put up with you," I muttered under my breath.

"Please speak up, Grace. I hate when you mumble," she scolded. "You always do that, get so mumbly. Pronunciation is important when you speak. As a teacher, I'd think you'd know this."

"Sorry. But, look, Finley and I both agree that a divorce is the best idea for us." That was a lie. A part of me still wanted my husband to love me, but he hadn't chosen me. He'd chosen her, and I was certain he didn't have any plans to change his mind.

"He's agreeing to please you, Grace. He doesn't want a divorce. He just thinks that will make you happy. All he ever did was try to make you happy."

"Make me happy?" I questioned, shoveling bread into my mouth. I ate carbs at an unattractive rate when I was nervous, or irritated, or happy—heck, I ate carbohydrates for a living. My hips were living proof of that. "He slept with my best friend, Mom, okay? So, please, tell me how he only wanted to make me happy."

"He slept with Autumn?" she asked, stunned.

"Yes."

"Oh my gosh," Mom said, bearing the same grimace my sister did when she found out about Autumn, but her next words were nothing like Judy's. "How could you let this happen?"

My jaw hit the floor. "What?"

"That came out wrong, but don't you see?" Mom exclaimed. "You pushed him into the arms of another woman, Grace."

"Please tell me that came out wrong, too," I begged.

"You see it, though, right? Don't you see that? After the last incident—"

"Miscarriage," I corrected her. She flinched. She always called it an incident because the actual word brought her discomfort. Too bad. I'd lived a lot more discomfort with the word than she had.

"Yes, after that. After the last one, you shut down. I even gave you all those articles on adoption and surrogacy, and still, you wouldn't even try for Finley. The church offered you a prayer circle, and you wouldn't even show up."

"Maybe praying doesn't fix what's broken," I barked her way, feeling my blood pressure rising. I could hardly believe what she was saying, but then again, I could. I knew my mother and how she believed so strongly in my flaws.

Her eyes watered, but she didn't cry. "You don't mean that. You're just hurting right now. Prayer changes everything."

"Everything but this," I told her. I prayed for a child. Every single day, I prayed, and the prayers went unanswered. Then I prayed for my husband, and those, too, were received with silence.

"You didn't even try, Grace," she said, her disappointment loud and clear.

She spoke her words as if she didn't know how cruel she sounded. I hadn't even tried? If only she knew how much my body knew of my failed attempts. If only she knew how looking in the mirror each morning, knowing you couldn't give your husband what he'd always wanted made one feel. If only she recognized how, for years, the only word I knew was "try," second only to "fail."

"And I think that's my breaking point," I blurted out, tired of talking about my marriage, my faults, my disappointments. I had no words left for her. I pushed my chair away from the table, stood, then walked to the spare bedroom and closed the door behind me.

I lay on the queen-size bed as I listened to Judy try to tell our mother why she was wrong in every fashion. Mom wasn't hearing it, though. She had her way of life and never understood that others' lives didn't need to mirror it.

"Judith, you cannot always protect your sister and her actions, and she is your older sister, after all—it's not your job to make excuses for her," Mom barked.

"I'm not making excuses," Judy replied. "I'm trying to show you a different side. She's your daughter, and she was betrayed in the worst way possible. By the two people who she thought truly cared about her. I mean no disrespect, but maybe now's not the time to come down so hard on her, Mama."

"Yes, well, I'm going to go speak to her one last time before I leave."

I sat up on my bed and cussed under my breath.

Her footsteps were growing closer, which made my stomach knot up more and more.

"Grace?" she asked, not waiting for a reply before opening the door. She looked my way as I sat with a pillow in my lap, staring at her. "I'm sorry you got upset."

That was how she always apologized—a non-apology. Not, *I'm sorry I upset you*, but *I'm sorry you got upset*.

There was a big difference. She never took the blame for her actions, only apologized for others taking offense.

"It's fine. No big deal."

"But"—she shook her head—"it is a big deal. This is your life, Grace. Do you really want to ruin it at this point? You're almost forty. Do you really want to start all over?"

I was thirty—how was that almost forty?

Even if I was forty—what was so terrifying about starting over?

I'd rather start over at forty than stay somewhere miserable for the next forty years.

"Mom, no offense, but can we not do this tonight? I'm tired and mentally checked out."

She nodded. "Okay, but we should talk about this later. Maybe we can look into therapy." That was Mama's fix to everything—first prayer, then therapy. She walked over to me and kissed my forehead. "I'm only this way because I love you, Grace. I hope you know that."

"I love you, too, Mom." That wasn't a lie.

I loved my mother, but oftentimes, I wondered if I liked her. I wondered if she wasn't my mom if I'd like her as a fellow human. Most signs pointed to no, but still, I loved her as the woman who gave me life even when she told me I needed Jesus's help to fix my womb.

I listened to Judy say goodbye to Mom, and when the front door closed, I let out a sigh of relief.

It only took a few seconds for my sister to pop into my room, the palms of her hands rubbing against her eyes as she groaned. "That was fifty million times worse than I thought it would be, and I thought it would be awful." I scooted over on the bed and patted a spot beside me. She gladly took it and leaned her head on my shoulder. "I'm so sorry, Grace. If I'd known she would be that bad—"

"You'd what? Tell her not to come over? Let's face it, this night would happen regardless. It's fine."

"Ugh, yeah, but she's just so…so…ugh! She's so mean to you. I couldn't imagine ever saying the things she said to another person, let alone to my own daughter. It just pisses me off."

Her face was bright red, and I felt her body shaking as she grew more and more upset about the things Mama had said to me. I almost laughed out loud because seeing Judy so angry was such the opposite of who she was ninety-nine percent of the time. Her version of cursing was saying "pisses me off," and it took a lot for her to get to that point. Mainly, she only grew angry if someone attacked the people she loved the most.

"You're my favorite person," I told her.

"You're my favorite person," she replied. "I'm just shocked neither of us picked up smoking to deal with her stressful ways over the years."

I laughed. "Or cocaine."

Judy smiled my way and shrugged. "I have no idea how Dad has spent so many years with her dramatics."

"A separate bedroom helps."

Judy looked up at me and clasped her hands together. "This is going to be good for you, Grace—a reset to your life, a rebirth. Please do me a favor and don't let Mom get too much into your head. I know you overthink things, but this is good. You made the right choice. Finn is a piece of crap, and don't even get me started on Autumn. I knew something was off with her from the first day I met her. I hate her. I hate him. I hate them."

"I appreciate the hate."

"I'll always hate for you. I love you, sister."

"I love you, too."

"What can I do? How can I make you feel better?"

I shrugged. "I think I need some time alone."

She frowned. "Not to overthink, though, right?"

"I think overthinking is the only thing my mind can do right now."

"Grace…"

"I'm okay, Judy, I swear. I just need some time."

Judy agreed even though she didn't want to do such a thing. She left the room, and I lay there in the bed with only my thoughts.

That was the worst companion I could've had that night.

After a while, my phone began to ring, and Finn's name flashed across the screen. I didn't answer because I knew if I did, he might've lied to me, and I stupidly might have believed him. He called me three times after that and left a voice message every single time.

Like a fool, I listened to them.

He asked me if we could talk. He begged me to hear him out.

Yet I didn't have any desire to see him anytime soon, so in the darker room, I sat as my anxiety began to build. Anxiety was a wild beast. It attacked me most in the quiet moments when the world was calm and I, too, should've been calm. Yet that was when my mind began to spin. I stayed in bed, overthinking every aspect of my life. My heart and my mind were at war.

There was no way I'd be able to sleep. My body was exhausted, yet whenever I closed my eyes, Finn popped in my head. Right after his image, I'd see Autumn and her beautiful tears and her perfectly perfect body.

Walking over to the full-length mirror in the corner, I inhaled deeply and exhaled it slowly. There were purplish bags beneath my eyes, my T-shirt was tucked into only one side of my jeans, and my hair looked awful.

I couldn't blame Finn, really. I hadn't put a lot into myself over the past few years. Even though it hurt me, I understood why his eyes wandered. Maybe Mama was right. Maybe part of the flawed marriage had to do with me.

Unable to shake off my hurts and Mama's insults, I did the only thing I could think of that would make me feel better.

I went to visit Dad at the church. If anyone in the world knew how to soothe sad hearts, it was the first man who ever loved me.

Walking into the church, I felt the emptiness of the space that was recently packed with individuals full of belief or searching for hope. I couldn't help but smile as I saw Dad standing at the podium, wearing his thick-framed glasses and staring down at his upcoming sermon. He was such a handsome man. He had a head full of hair peppered with gray, crystal blue eyes like the sea, and a smile that could make the saddest soul feel whole.

Judy always said I had his eyes, and I always noted that she had his smile.

As he spoke into the microphone, his voice would echo throughout the space, bouncing off the walls. Then he'd grimace, shake his head back and forth, and mark up his sheets of paper.

"No, no, no, that's not it," he murmured into the microphone, displeased with his delivery.

"It doesn't sound that bad to me," I shouted, making him look up from his papers. I started walking down the aisle toward the front of the church, and as I drew closer, his smile grew brighter.

"Tell me I'm not seeing a ghost and my daughter really is back in town," he said, removing his glasses and placing them on top of his head.

"Not a ghost yet," I replied, walking up to him. It only took seconds for him to wrap me in an embrace.

"It's been too long, ya know," he told me, holding me tighter. "We missed you at service this morning."

"I know. Sorry about that. I wish I could've made it."

As he let me go, he took a step back and smiled my way. "You look beautiful."

I laughed. "Makeup works wonders."

He shook his head. "No, it's not makeup." He linked his arm through mine and walked us down to the front pew. We sat, and he kept smiling his bright smile my way. "Not that I'm not happy for the sweet reunion, but what brings you back to Chester, baby girl?"

I raised an eyebrow, bewildered. "Mama didn't tell you? I was certain she would have after our falling-out tonight."

"Falling-out?" he asked, baffled. His thick eyebrows knitted, and he rubbed the nape of his neck. "I haven't heard a word from her. So what's going on?"

My chest tightened. A big part of me hoped Mama had already gotten to Dad so I wouldn't have to watch the disappointment hit him as he learned about the failure of my marriage. As I swallowed my pride, I proceeded to tell him everything that had happened with Finn. I couldn't look him in the eyes as I told him, though. The guilt and embarrassment were too difficult for me, so my stare stayed focused on my shaking hands.

As I finished, I closed my eyes, waiting to hear his thoughts.

"Hmm..." He let out a deep sigh and placed a hand on my knee. "Marriage is hard."

"Harder than I ever thought," I agreed.

"Is it completely over?"

I snickered. "He's with my best friend, Dad. I think it's as over as it could ever be."

"No, I get that, but your heart...is your heart completely over it? Is there any part that wants him back?"

I grew quiet because the answer was yes, and that embarrassed me.

I was ashamed that parts of me still longed for him.

"There's nothing to be ashamed of, Grace," he said as if he could read my mind. "It's okay to love someone even though they wronged you. You can't pretend your feelings don't exist because you're afraid of what those feelings might mean. Sometimes, the hardest thing in the world is to love someone who broke your heart."

"I do love him," I whispered, my throat painfully raw. "I hate him, too, though. How is that possible?"

"We were created to feel, Grace. It just so happens that sometimes our feelings come out of order. It's amazing how one second, your heart can beat for love, and in the next, hate can sneak in. You're not in the wrong for anything you're feeling."

"Mama disagrees. She thinks I'm making a mistake by not fighting for our marriage."

"What do you think?"

I shrugged. "I'm really not sure. Everything spiraled so fast. I feel so lost."

"You're not lost; you're just figuring things out. And now you're home for a while, which is good. You need to be surrounded by familiar things and people. You just need to find your footing is all. Home is healing."

"Thanks, Dad," I said sincerely, resting my head on his shoulder.

"Always and always," he replied.

"Your advice was a lot better than Mama's."

"And what was her advice?"

"Therapy."

He laughed and nodded slowly. "Sounds about right."

CHAPTER TEN

Grace

"Hey, Grace, it's Alex from the auto shop. I wanted to call and let you know you can stop by any time today to check on your car. Thanks, and hopefully we'll see you soon!"

A few days had passed since I'd arrived in Chester. I hadn't really left Judy's house much since I'd come into town, and when I did, I ended up in The Silent Bookshop. Staying in one of those two places was the easiest way to avoid running into people.

I was making it my mission to avoid Autumn and Finn like the plague.

Yet now that Alex called, I had to force myself to leave my two havens and head over to the auto shop. After I slipped on my shoes, I headed outside and felt the summer breeze brushing against my face. There was nothing like the hot summers of Georgia and the way the trees exploded with the brightest shades of green.

Chester was the perfect sized town because everything was within walking distance. Though Mike's Auto Shop seemed a bit off the pathway because it was right on the edge of town. The Emery men owned a lot of acreage—nowhere near as much as my family, but they had a lot more land than most people in town did. On the far-right side of their property sat a beautiful two-level home, and in the middle was the auto shop. In front of the shop, a few broken-down and rusted vehicles placed on top of spare tires were used as decoration. It was…cute.

A wooden sign, which read Mike's Auto Shop, sat tilted against the front of the building.

Right beside the auto shop was a small cabin with a few bushes around the front. It was nothing special, but it did have that cute, homey feel to it.

When I used to dream of having a family, I always thought we'd vacation in a cute cabin like that each year.

As I pulled open the front door of the auto shop, it squeaked and dinged a bell above the door. I glanced around the shop, but no one was around. I walked to the front desk and hit the bell, hoping someone would notice my arrival. When no one did, I began walking around the shop.

Out of nowhere, a big black lab started walking in my direction. He moved so slow, though, wagging his tail. When he reached me, he sat down and kept wagging his tail.

"You must be the guy Josie told me about," I remarked, bending down to pet him. He kept wagging his tail as his breaths sawed in and out as if the short walk exhausted him. I glanced at his dog collar. *Tucker.* "You're adorable, Tucker," I told him before he stood back up and slowly walked back to his dog bed.

What a sweetheart.

"Hello?" I called out, but no one answered. "Hmph."

I waited a bit longer in the front lobby before I heard a loud banging. Walking toward the back of the shop, I saw an open door that led to the backyard. The banging grew louder and louder as I walked through the door, and there buried behind a few trees was an automobile that looked as if it had been tossed through a hurricane a few times. Standing over it with a sledgehammer, Jackson was slamming into the vehicle.

He stood shirtless and sweat dripped from every inch of his body as he kept pounding the car over and over again. Every muscle in his body was on full display, and I couldn't help but notice. How could I not? Jackson might've been the town asshole, but his body was something worth worshipping. You didn't come across men as handsome as he was very often—too bad his personality didn't match his looks.

"Hey!" I called out to him, but he didn't look up. He kept hammering away, aggression in every hit. He had earbuds in his ears, which didn't help his case when it came to ignoring me. So, I moved in closer. "Hey!" I shouted, pounding my hand against the car. He jumped out of his skin when he saw me, dropped his sledgehammer, and within seconds, he was cussing up a storm.

"Holy shit!" he shouted, grabbing his left foot in his hand, the unfortunate place that the sledgehammer happened to fall. "Fuck, that hurts."

"Oh my gosh, I'm so sorry!" I claimed, covering my mouth with my hands. "Are you okay?"

"I just dropped a fucking sledgehammer on my foot. What the hell do you think?!" he barked.

I would've called him out on his sass level, but well, he did drop a sledgehammer on his foot, so his anger seemed warranted.

He grumbled, something he was a professional at doing, and gave me a harsh look. "What do you want?"

"I got a call from Alex saying I should stop in to check on the car, and no one was in the shop. Then I heard you doing"—I gestured toward the destroyed car—"whatever it is that you're doing."

He grumbled some more, finally dropping his foot back to the ground, and he started toward the shop. I stood there for a moment, uncertain of what I was supposed to do as he limped away.

He glanced over his shoulder at me and huffed. "Are you coming or what?"

"Oh, okay," I replied, hurrying in his direction.

Once we got inside, he walked over to my car, and said, "Alex had to run out to tow someone." His face was sporting a bit of a five-o'clock shadow, and he brushed his hand against it. "He told me to update you on the car if he wasn't back."

I placed my hands on my hips and stared at the car. "So how is she doing?"

"She?" he asked, cocking an eyebrow. "Cars don't have genders."

"Cars definitely have genders. Just because you can't pick up on it doesn't mean that they don't. Rosie, here, is definitely female."

"You would be the type to name a damn car."

"And you would be the type to complain about someone naming a car," I remarked.

He grumbled again, and I smiled. I felt as if my smiling irritated him, and I somewhat enjoyed annoying him because he somewhat liked to be mean to me.

"The car's a piece of shit. Alex should've tossed it into the scrapyard," Jackson stated. "You wasted your time coming down here. It's junk." I took a deep breath, and he held his hand up to me. "I swear to God, princess, if you start crying, I'm going to lose my goddamn mind. I'm the one with a broken foot probably, and you don't see me getting emotional."

I sniffled and tried my best to hold my emotions together. "Sorry, it's just that Rosie and I have been through a lot."

"Stop calling your car a human name."

"Stop calling me princess."

"No."

"Then Rosie stays, too, and I'm going to call you Oscar."

"What the hell does that even mean?"

"Because you're grumpy—just like Oscar the Grouch."

He gave me the blankest stare. "Oh, how creative, princess."

"Thank you, Oscar. Because ya know, calling a woman princess is really outside of the box," I mocked.

"You're annoying."

"And you're a grump. But..." A knot formed in my gut, and I rubbed my hands against the back of my neck. "I am really sorry, ya know. About your foot. If you want, I can have—"

"Nope," he cut in.

"What?"

"I said no. We aren't doing this. Let's make something clear, this isn't something—our back and forth interactions. This isn't a thing."

His response perplexed me. "I never said it was a thing. All I was saying was—"

"Don't. Don't say anything."

"Stop cutting me off!"

"Then stop talking. You think I don't see how you look at me every time you're in that bookshop? Like there's something about me that you can't figure out? Well, there's not. So if you could just please leave me the hell alone, that would be great." And, like normal, he grumbled once more. "You're doing it again."

"Doing what?"

"Crying."

What? Dangit!

"Hot. Mess," he breathed out. "Just wait for Alex to get back," Jackson muttered. "I don't want to deal with you anymore."

Wow.

I think I hate you.

I went to the waiting area and sat down, leaving my purse on the table as I waited for Alex to come back. When he walked through the front door, he gave me that same bright smile. "Hey, Grace! Thanks for coming in! Have you been helped yet?"

"Not really. I mean, Jackson spoke to me, but he wasn't really helpful, per se. He told me the car was a piece of crap and not worth saving."

Alex crossed his arms. "Where is he?"

"He's outside banging a sledgehammer against some car like an insane man."

"Oh." Alex frowned and shook as if a chill had run over him. "Don't take it personally. He's having a bad day."

I sarcastically laughed. "How can you tell? It seems as if he's always in a mood."

"Yeah, but…" Alex frowned. "When he's out there, hitting those cars, it means he's in a bad mood. Like, really bad mood. There's no getting through to him when he's like that."

"He's not the easiest person to deal with."

"That's true, too." He snickered and nodded, walking toward my car with me. "He's not as bad as everyone says."

"No," I agreed. "He's worse."

"That's just because you don't know him. The Jackson I know is one of the nicest guys, but he doesn't show it the same ways as others do. If you watch closely, you'd see it every now and then."

"So what you're trying to tell me is that somewhere inside that person's body over there is an actual heart?"

"Yes." Alex smirked and leaned in toward me, whispering. "And sometimes it even beats."

Wow.

What an odd concept.

"Listen, I know the shit people say about him, and I know the rumors that get tossed around, but those lies aren't Jackson. The truth is, he's one of the best humans on this here Earth. It's a shame the world is missing out on knowing him because they are so stuck in their false realities of the man that he is. He might be my only nephew, but if I had more, he'd still be my favorite."

"He's your nephew?" I asked. "Mike is your brother?"

"No." He shook his head. "His mother was my sister."

Was. That word hit me so hard, and my next breath was stolen from me. "I'm sorry for your loss."

"Thank you. It's been over fourteen years. Hannah was…" His words faltered, and he cleared his throat. For the first time, I witnessed Alex frown, and it was the saddest moment. His always happy eyes became a bit dimmer. "My sister was a good person. Not a day passes that I don't think about her. Not a day passes when Jackson doesn't, too."

"I'm truly sorry. I couldn't imagine what going through something like that is like."

"It's worse than anyone could ever believe. What Mike and Jackson both went through…" He took a deep breath. "No one can understand that kind of suffering. Not even me."

It made it seem as if there was a lot more to the story, but I didn't ask any questions. It wasn't my place.

He shook his head back and forth and washed away his somber stare. "But listening to my family's woes is not why you're here. Let's talk about your car."

"Oh yeah, the car," I muttered, still somewhat thinking of the monster that had greeted me.

"Do something for me." Alex scrunched up his nose, rubbed the back of his neck, and then tossed me the set of keys. "Give the engine a turn."

I did as he said, and a high-pitch sound came through before it began to smoke.

"That can't be good." I laughed.

He agreed. "Yeah, but it's a better sound than before. I'm not giving up on it just yet."

"Yes, you are because it's a piece of shit!" a person snapped, stumbling into the space. "I don't know why you brought that into my damn shop."

I looked up to see a grown man wavering back and forth with a whiskey bottle in his hand. He was almost Jackson's exact twin, except aged with wrinkle lines, gray hair, and an even more pronounced permanent scowl.

I didn't know someone could scowl more than Jackson.

Alex's persona shifted at the sight of the man. "Mike, I thought you weren't coming in today."

"It's my shop. I'm allowed to come and go as I please. Don't forget it," he hissed, walking over to the car. He tossed the hood down and tapped it twice. "Take this to the scrapyard." He took a swig of the whiskey and then finally glanced my way. The moment he met my stare, I swore I saw hatred swim in his eyes. "I know you," he hissed.

"I don't think so," I replied, nerves building in my gut. Out of the corner of my eye, I could see Jackson in the back corner of the shop, looking our way.

His frown was identical to his father's.

"I've seen the likes of you. You related to those people at the church?"

"My father runs the church."

"Hmph. You're a PK," he groaned, taking another drink.

"A PK?" Alex asked, but I knew the term. It'd been tossed my way all my life.

"A pastor's kid," I answered.

"I don't want nothing to do with you people," he scolded me. "So take this piece of shit car and get out of my shop."

"But Mike, I think I can fix it," Alex started. It was clear Jackson's father made him nervous. The same kind of nervous he was making me feel. It was scary being around unstable individuals because you never truly knew would come next.

"We ain't fixing shit for this bitch."

Chills down my spine.

Knots in my stomach.

"Dad, knock it off. Don't be a fucking asshole," Jackson barked from afar, growing a bit red in the face. I didn't know someone could make Jackson seem so soft, but his father sure did. "You're drunk."

"I might be drunk, but I ain't stupid." His eyes stayed glued to me. "I know what kind of people that church brings up, and I don't want nothing to do with any of them. The way they act like they give a damn about people, but really, they just take their money and live in their mansions. You think I don't see how y'all look at me when I go into town? The way you look at my boy? Like we're some lowlifes?"

"I don't know you," I whispered, my voice shaky. I only knew the stories people told, and those stories were terrifying. Though, all the stories seemed a bit based on facts that afternoon.

"Yeah, but I know you and your type. I don't want you anywhere near this place again, you hear me? Take yourself and that dirty money of yours elsewhere. We don't want any of the Harris's filth near us. Especially the daughters. Everyone knows the biggest whores are the daughters of a pastor. Now piss off and tell your God to do the same thing."

Did those words really just leave his drunken mouth?

My lips parted to speak, but nothing came out. I was stunned into silence.

I turned slightly and found Jackson's eyes on me. He frowned as if he felt bad for me, which made me feel even worse.

I didn't want to cry in front of Mr. Emery because that seemed like it would've been a victory for him. He was intent on making me feel as though I was nothing but darkness, and the way his eyes pierced into mine made me want to vomit. I wasn't certain what to do, so I turned around on the heels of my feet and stormed out of the shop.

"Hey!" Jackson shouted after me. "Hold up!"

I whipped around flustered. "I get it, all right? You guys hate us. I won't come back."

"No, it's…" He sighed, rubbing his hands over his face. He didn't say anything, and he went back to his dark, sulky look.

"What is it, Jackson?!" I snapped, annoyed by the likes of him and his father.

He spoke low. "You forgot your purse," he said, holding it out to me.

I snatched it from his hands and muttered a thank you even though he didn't deserve it.

"Listen…" He cleared his throat. "What he said to you…that was too much."

"Everything he said was too much."

"Yes," he agreed. "My dad's a lot sometimes."

"Ha. That's putting it nicely."

"He has these issues with your family. He's been through some stuff with the church after the incident a few years back."

"You mean when he drove his car into the church while drunk? Then he proceeded to walk into the service and cuss everyone out? There's a reason people call him Mad Mike."

Jackson twitched. "Don't call him that."

"That's what everyone calls him."

"I fucking know that's what everyone calls him," he growled, making me take a step backward. He locked eyes with me, and unlike his father's stare, I swore I saw a pained expression. As if he was fighting against his true urges. I took in a sharp breath. *Always zoom in...* "Just because everyone calls him that doesn't mean you have to, too."

"Sorry." I saw how the nickname affected him, how it hurt him, and right away, I regretted saying it to him. I wondered how often he heard that name as he walked through town, and I wondered how often his heart skipped because of it.

"I know he's an asshole, but everyone always brings up that one incident about him, and it's labeled him forever. He was having a rough morning that day."

"From what I hear, it was more than rough. He took a sledgehammer to the pews." The same way Jackson took a sledgehammer to the car outside.

"It was a *really* rough morning," Jackson replied.

"Jackson, come on," I argued, annoyed by how he was defending that grown monster for his actions.

He tossed his hands up in defeat. "Yeah, okay, I get it. My dad's a fucking asshole. If anyone knows that best, it's me. Back then, he made a mistake—a big one—but the way the town turned on him was uncalled for. Hell, they tried to shut down his shop! They tried to burn it down. They tried to run us out of town. They protested on our lawn and called us things that you wouldn't think would come out of the mouths of 'saved' people."

"But what he did—"

"Was wrong, yeah, I get it. But he's broken, and instead of showing up with that compassion bullshit this town is always pretending to have, they showed up with malice. They broke him even more and made him harder, colder. They painted us as these awful beasts and then got mad because we became the damn nightmares they created. I was just a kid. I watched these people, this town, attack my father and me because of a mistake."

"I'm so sorry that happened, Jackson, I really am, but I don't see why you and your father are so against my family. We weren't the ones storming your place." We hadn't done a thing to the two. We took no part in the malice they received.

"Come on, you can't be that stupid," he said, seeming somewhat disappointed in my lack of understanding. "We all know who runs this town. Your family are the royals of Chester."

"So…? They still weren't the ones attacking you."

He clasped his hands behind his neck and cocked an eyebrow. "Listen, princess, if your father or mother would've stood up in the church and said, 'Stop,' it would've all come to an end. They could've shown compassion for my father, who obviously wasn't doing well, but they stayed quiet. They never spoke up for him. Or me."

My stomach ached. "Why don't you guys just leave? Why stay in a town that makes you feel so unwelcomed?"

He glanced back toward the shop where his father was still wandering around wasted, arguing with Alex and stuffed his hands into his pockets. "We got our reasons, and we ain't gotta explain shit to no one," he muttered. "Especially to a Harris."

"Are you always this hard?"

He shut his eyes, and his bottom lip twitched a bit. "Yes."

"If I hated this town as much as you two did, I'd move on."

"To what? This is the only damn home we got." He shifted his feet around. I saw the debate in him as he battled with himself about whether to open up to me or stay shut down. "I went to her, ya know—your mother," he told me, his voice cold as stone.

"What?"

"I was sixteen when I went to your house. I remember it like it was yesterday. I knocked on the door and spoke to your mother, asking her for help. It was right after some assholes jumped me and beat the shit out of me as I was going to get groceries."

"What did my mom say?"

"My dad made his choices; therefore, the townspeople are allowed to make theirs, too. She said she didn't owe us a thing."

No…that's impossible.

"You're lying. I know my mother can be hard sometimes, but she's not evil. She wouldn't say that. She'd never turn her back on someone like that," I swore to him. "Especially not on a kid."

"Whatever you say, princess. You keep believing in that precious queen of yours," he barked. "I shouldn't have expected you to understand shit, based on the people who raised you."

"What made you such a jerk?" I snapped his way. His jawline was chiseled, and the intensity in his stare made my body slightly tremble. But then, there was a moment. It was tiny, so tiny that anyone who wasn't zooming in would've missed it, but I noticed. He blinked, and his eyes softened. He stepped back as if my question had stunned him. The corner of his mouth twitched, and I swore I'd never seen a man look so broken.

He knew the answer to my question. He knew exactly what made him the man he was, and that fact truly hurt him to his core.

"Jackson," I whispered, feeling as if I'd crossed an invisible line.

"Can you do me a favor?" he growled low as his stare once again grew dark. "Can you just leave? Go run off to your mommy. I'm sure she has more lies to feed you," he breathed out before he turned around and left, leaving chills racing down my spine. He seemed to leave that impression on me every time we went our separate ways.

I walked back through town, and when I heard the high-pitched voice of Charlotte Lawrence calling my name, I began walking faster, pretending not to hear her. Though, she stayed right on my path.

"Grace! Grace! It's me, Charlotte!" she shouted as I listened to her heels click-clacking against the sidewalk.

With a deep breath, I paused my steps, knowing she would've chased me throughout the whole town for as long as it took to get my attention.

I turned around and saw Charlotte in all her glory. She graduated in the same class as Finn and had been in love with my husband for as long as I'd been. Though, she'd deny it forever and always.

She wore a yellow sundress and bright pink five-inch heels, which were her staple. I'd never seen Charlotte in any other type of shoe.

"Oh, hi, Charlotte," I said, giving her the fakest smile.

She bent over for a minute, catching her breath. "Oh Mylanta, Grace, I didn't think I'd catch you."

"Well, you did."

"I tried talking to you yesterday when I saw you going to the bookshop, but I don't think you heard me calling your name."

No, I did.

"Oh? I'm sorry I missed you. I actually better get going, though. I have a lot—"

Charlotte placed her hand on my shoulder, ignoring my words. "You doing okay? You know, I've heard some rumors floating around about Finn and you, and—"

"We're fine," I lied with a big, bright smile. "Finn and I are fine." I felt somewhat bad for lying, but the last person I wanted to deal with was Charlotte Lawrence. Charlotte was the editor in chief of Chester's newspaper and the nosiest woman in town. The newspaper read more so like a gossip column than an actual paper. She lived her life by the theme, "If it bleeds, it leads." Plus, due to her love for my husband, she was probably doing a praise dance when the rumors started to spread.

"It's complicated, though, right?" she asked. "People said they saw you two arguing outside Autumn's house? Is that true?" she queried. "And did you slap him? I heard that, too."

"Charlotte." I sighed, my voice low.

She smiled big. "Sorry. You're right. That's none of my business. Lord knows marriages are hard work."

I cocked an eyebrow. "Charlotte, you've never been married."

"Yes, but I can only imagine how hard it must be going through a divorce," she echoed.

"No one said we were going through a divorce."

"Oh? So…you're staying together…?" she asked, crossing her arms and zooming in to see my reaction.

"You know, Charlotte, I don't really feel comfortable talking about this with you right now."

"Of course, I won't pressure you to talk. But if you ever need listening ears, I'm always here for you. You know, I always envied

Finn's and your relationship. I always said if I married a man, I'd want him to be just like Finn. He treated you like a queen."

"Yeah," I huffed. "Something like that. Okay well, I better get—"

"Oh, Grace! I almost forgot," she cut in, placing her hand on my shoulder. "Me and a few ladies from town get together at my parents' house every Friday night for chitchat and empowerment. I wanted to invite you. It's so important as a woman to feel as if you have a tribe of females behind you to help lift you up. We drink wine, discuss current events, and push one another to be our best. Why, just last week we helped coach Lacey Weeds to apply for a different spot at the newspaper. She wanted more of a role, and us girls helped her realize her worth and gave her that extra push to go after it. Of course, I had to turn down her request when she came to me at work, but at least she tried for it, which was the important part."

"You told her to go for a job position, and then told her she couldn't have it when she came to you?"

Charlotte pursed her lips together. "Yes, bless her heart, she just wasn't a right fit. But now she can try again next year." Wow. What a gem Charlotte was. "Anyway, I'm sure we could help you, and we'd love your help inspiring each other."

"I'm actually busy that day, and—"

"Really? Because your mom said you were free and you'd definitely be there. It's at seven p.m., and I put you down for a dessert. I hope that's fine. Okay, Grace, I gotta run! See you Friday!" She blew kisses my way and hurried away before I could even disagree.

I guessed I needed to find a brownie recipe sooner than later.

CHAPTER ELEVEN

Jackson

Grace gave her time and energy to any and everyone in town without any thought to it. I'd seen different nosy individuals who thought it was their job to butt into her personal life stopping her all the time. Yet instead of telling them to fuck off as she should've, she smiled, stood tall, and responded to their questions with such elegance.

It was sickening to watch.

They were emotionally draining her, and she was giving herself to them as if she hadn't even cared a bit for their bluntness and disrespect.

"Well, bless your heart, Gracelyn Mae. I don't even know what I'd do if my marriage was on the rocks. But you're strong. I'm sure you'll make it through. Plus, you're not that old, so maybe you'll find someone else. Or maybe Finn will take you back. Otherwise, there are always cats. I'm praying for you, sweetheart," an old woman told Grace in the marketplace while Grace was simply trying to buy flowers. She'd been standing there for over ten minutes, trying to check out, but people kept butting into her time and space as though they didn't give a damn about her feelings at all.

Once the old hag walked away, I grumbled as I brushed past Grace. "You just allow anyone to treat you like crap, huh?" I asked her.

She turned my way, and goddamn, her eyes were still beautiful. I wondered when that would go away.

She blinked once. "What are you talking about?"

"For the past forever minutes, people have been so belittling to you."

"What? No, they haven't. They are just giving me their prayers."

"With prayers like that, who needs curses?"

Her eyes narrowed. "What are you talking about, Jackson?"

"Everyone in town has been eating you alive over the past few days, and you're just allowing it to happen."

"Have you been watching me?"

"No."

Yes.

Maybe.

She cleared her throat. "Well, all I'm saying is, you don't know these people like I do. They are just being caring, that's all."

"They are abusing you, and you're freely allowing it!" I barked, annoyed by how ignorant she was being. They were pretty much spitting in her face, and she was pretending it wasn't happening.

"Why do you even care, Jackson?" she wondered out loud, raising an eyebrow.

"I don't," I snapped.

"Then why are you standing here talking about it?"

I released a low growl. "You're right. Go ahead, let them mock you to your face. Let them treat you like shit, look down on you, and suck you dry of all your energy. But when the day comes that you're burnt the complete fuck out, remember I told you so."

"How can you be so sure about that, huh? How can you be so positive that people are using me?"

"Because I know how people work. They think so little of you, and you know why?"

"Why?" she asked, her voice unsteady.

"Because you think so little of yourself. People only treat you the way you treat yourself. And I know exactly what they are going to do to you if you keep this up." I leaned in closer to her, and our eyes stayed locked. We were so close that I felt her uneven breaths against my skin, and I was certain she felt mine. "They're gonna bleed you out till you're nothing, and then they're gonna ask how you died."

She swallowed hard, and her eyes watered over, but she stood as tall as she could and tried her best to hide the trembling in her hands as she held her flowers.

"Let me guess," I said. "This is the part where you cry."

"Yes." She nodded slow, taking a deep breath. "And this is the part where you leave."

The corner of my mouth twitched, and I turned to walk away when she called me once more. "Why do you treat yourself like that?"

"Like what?" I asked.

"You said people treat you the way you treat yourself. Then why do you choose to treat yourself like a monster?"

Her words pushed me, and I almost wavered. "Because that's exactly what I am."

Jackson
Eight Years Old

"This is stupid!" I snapped, knocking my canvas over in the open field as Ma tried to teach me a new technique for the sunset. She'd been showing me for over an hour, and I couldn't do it. It was stupid, and art was stupid, and I was done with it all.

"Whoa, whoa, whoa," Ma remarked, arching her eyebrow. "What was that? Since when do we act out like that?"

"I can't do it! I don't want to do this," I said, swallowing hard. I was angry, and I didn't want to paint anymore. I just wanted to go home.

Not to our new home, but our old one.

The one where I had a few friends.

"What's wrong?" Ma asked.

"Nothing."

"Jackson, what is it? I know you're not mad at the painting, because you were doing great. So tell me the truth. What's wrong?"

I took a deep breath. "I don't understand why we have to live in this stupid town! Nobody likes me, and they just pick on me about everything. I hate it here, and I want to move!"

"Are people bullying you again?" she asked me.

Tears fell from my eyes. She said "again" like everyone had stopped bullying me at some point. I was tired of people judging me for how I looked. I was tired of people laughing at me because sometimes I couldn't score a goal in gym class. I was tired of not fitting in.

I was tired.

"Come here," she told me.

"No."

"Jackson Paul."

I sighed.

I walked over to her and she took my hands into hers. "What are you?" she asked me.

I mumbled a word.

"Louder," Ma said.

"I said I'm extraordinary."

"That's right, and even on the bad days, you are extraordinary. These mean people, they don't get to run you away. They don't get to hurt you, and come Monday, I'll be marching down to the school to talk to the principal about doing something about this. But we are staying in this town."

"Why?"

"Because we don't run. We don't let people run us away. We have a right to be here, to be happy, and that's exactly what we are going to do, okay? We are going to be happy."

I sniffled. "Okay."

"And you are going to get this technique down tonight. Do you know why?"

I sniffled. "Because I'm extraordinary?"

"Yes, my love. You. Are. Extraordinary."

CHAPTER TWELVE

Grace

Finn had been calling me each day, but I never answered. Every time he left a voice message, I deleted it. I knew if I listened to his voice, I would miss him, and he didn't deserve to be missed. My brain understood that fact, yet my heart had its own thoughts on the subject. Avoiding him was the best option for me.

I did my best to keep to myself. When I went to The Silent Bookshop, Jackson was normally there, yet we didn't interact. He sat in the far-left corner of the shop while I sat at the table in the far-right.

Sometimes, we'd cross paths while searching for books, but he made it his mission not to look my way, so I did my best to stay out of his way, too.

Something about him made me so uneasy. The way he approached me in the marketplace was so odd. He came off so aggressive but also protective all at once, and it gave my head the biggest migraine.

I did catch him one afternoon with Tucker, and Josie wasn't lying—it made my heart swell. I was walking through Kap Park when he and Tucker arrived. Tucker seemed to have trouble walking on his own, so Jackson carried him in his arms. Jackson wore a backpack, and once they found a spot in the sun, he pulled out a blanket and chew toys for Tucker. He laid his old faithful down on the blanket and just sat with his dog. Every now and then, he'd pet Tucker's back, and say, "Good boy." It almost looked as if Tucker was smiling as he slowly wagged his tail and rested.

Jackson cared for his dog with nothing but love. I didn't know a man like him could care for something in that way. His love was so quiet, yet somehow so loud. The way he loved Tucker was the way every person should've been loved: unconditionally.

When he looked up and saw me watching them, I started walking away fast.

He didn't look at me the same way he looked at Tucker.

When Jackson's eyes locked with mine, I only saw hate.

On Friday evening, Judy joined me at the bookshop, something she never did. Yet she'd been very close since I'd been back to town, making sure I was okay. She wasn't as big on reading as I was, so she casually flipped through some pages as we sat in my corner.

"We can go," I whispered, watching my sister twiddle her thumbs from boredom as she leaned back in her chair.

"Shh..." she scolded me. "Silence is golden."

I laughed. "You're bored out of your mind."

"What are you talking about? This is the best. Books and words, words and books. It's amazing."

A person shushed us from afar, and we couldn't help but snicker some more. "Want to go get ice cream?"

Her eyes widened with glee. "Now you're speaking my language."

As we began to walk away, I glanced in the direction of

Jackson's corner and noticed he was gone. I wondered what books he'd taken with him that night.

Then I wondered why I wondered.

We walked the streets of Chester, Judy talking about how the planning for the Peach Festival was coming along, and I was listening closely until my eye caught a crowd of teenagers, laughing and throwing items at something. A few had a garbage bin in their hands and dumped it upside down on the thing. The closer I drew, the more nervous I became.

They weren't throwing trash at something—they were hitting someone.

"Hey!" I shouted, hurrying over. "Stop that!" I ordered. The second the kids turned around and saw me, they took off running in different directions. As I neared the individual covered in trash, I became concerned.

"Mr. Emery, are you okay...?" I asked, bending down to help him up.

He was completely plastered, and the smell of whiskey and urine was strong. He'd wet his pants. *Oh no...*

"Is he okay?" Judy asked, her voice shaky.

"Mr. Emery, let me help you up," I said as he batted his hand at me.

"Leave me alone!" he barked.

"But, here. I can help you get home, and—"

"I said piss off, b-b-bitch!" he hollered, slurring his words. I didn't take offense to them, though. I doubted he even knew who I was at the moment. His eyes were hardly opened. He was so far gone.

"Grace, maybe we should just let him be..." Judy whispered, her voice shaky with nerves.

"I'm not going to leave him here," I told her.

"I can go get Sheriff Camps," she offered, making me hastily turn to face her.

"Judy, no. No cops. I can handle this." The last thing Jackson needed was the stress of bailing his father out of jail.

"But Grace…" my sister started.

"Really, Judy. It's fine. You can go home." She looked at me with concerned eyes, but I gave her a comforting smile. "Seriously, I got this."

"No. I'm helping you," she said, not allowing me to take on Mike Emery alone.

I went back to looking at Jackson's father, covered in trash. He kept telling us to leave, but I ignored him. There was no way I was leaving his side, and there was no way Judy would leave mine. I didn't need more kids to gather around and abuse him, or even worse, the cops to pick him up and take him in.

I did the only thing I could think to do: I helped Mr. Emery up from the trash, and Judy helped too. We started to walk him home even though he pushed against us. "Go away, you fucking ugly bitches," he growled, and for a moment, I considered it, but then Dad's words crossed my mind.

If you turn your back on one, then you turn your back on all…

Halfway though, he simply gave up and let us drag him home.

"I don't n-need you," he muttered, drool rolling out of the side of his mouth as he slurred his words. I reached into his pocket and pulled out his set of keys to unlock his door, and we brought him inside.

The house was a mess. There were empty beer cans scattered throughout the space, and old food sat on dirty dishes stacked high in the sink. I kept pulling Mr. Emery through the house until we reached the bathroom.

"We need to put him in the shower," I told Judy, and she was quick to help me without any questions.

"You'll hate me for this," I muttered. "But then again, you already hate me, so it can't get any worse." He sat down and scrunched over, mumbling to himself. I reached into his front pocket and grabbed his phone before I turned on the cold water. He reacted instantly to the feeling.

"What the fuck?!" he shouted but was still unable to stand.

I couldn't let him sit in his own urine and the filth from the garbage bins. "You're okay," I told him.

"I don't need y-your help. Fuck you, whore," he kept repeating, but his shoulders slumped over as he shut his eyes and allowed the water to run over him. I turned the water to a warmer temperature before grabbing his cell phone and dialing Jackson's number.

The moment it began to ring, Jackson was quick to answer.

"Yeah, Dad?"

"Hey, Jackson? It's actually Grace…"

His voice grew alert. "What's going on? Is my dad okay?"

"He's, um, he's okay. He's just a bit wasted. I found him in town almost passed out, and a few kids were messing with him. I brought him back to his house. I just thought you should know."

"Shit," he whispered under his breath. "I'm so sorry. I'll be over there soon. You don't gotta stay with him."

"No, it's fine. I'll wait with him. I'll probably need your help getting him into clean clothes."

"I'm so—"

"Jackson."

"Yes?"

"Don't say you're sorry. I'll see you soon." I hung up the phone and turned to Judy, who still had a look of worry in her eyes, but I knew it was for Mr. Emery's life. She cared about everyone equally because that was the only way her heart knew how to beat. "You can head home, Judy. I'll be there soon."

"Are you sure? I can stay and help…" she told me.

"No, really, it's fine. Jackson will be here soon, and then I'll head home." She gave me an uncertain frown, and I reached out and lightly squeezed her arm. "Really, Judy. We're good here."

"Okay, but call me if anything changes."

"I will do. And Judy?"

"Yes?"

"Can you not tell Mama about this?"

"Of course, I won't."

I thanked her for that, and then she left.

I shut off the water and began to dry Mr. Emery's hair, but he kept pushing my hands away and calling me names. That didn't stop me from trying to help.

After I dried him the best I could, I went searching for dry clothes for him to change into once Jackson made it home. I walked into his bedroom and I paused at his dresser. A dusty framed picture sat on it of Jackson, Mike and his late wife. They were all laughing in the photograph. A beautiful memory snapped into a forever keepsake. I moved my fingers across it lightly and studied the family.

They once looked so happy and full of life.

It was amazing how tragedy could change a person forever.

I shook off the feeling of sadness and gathered Mike's clothing.

Then I went back to the bathroom and waited on the floor, making sure Mike didn't get sick and choke on his own vomit. He leaned against the tiled wall with his eyes closed, and his mouth parted. Every now and then, I waved my hand in front of his mouth to make sure I could feel his breaths.

The moment the front door opened, a wave of relief hit me. Jackson rushed through the house, calling for his dad.

"Over here, in the bathroom," I replied.

He stepped into the room, and his eyes fell to his father. "Jesus, Dad..." he softly spoke, disappointment dancing through his sounds. He raced his hands through his hair.

"He pissed himself?" he asked.

"Yes."

He cringed. "I got it from here. You can go."

"Are you sure...?"

"Yes," he said, uninterested in any more words. "Go."

I stood and gave him a broken smile. "If you need anything..."

"We won't."

"Okay."

I walked past him and then felt a small touch to my forearm. My eyes fell to Jackson's hand against my skin, and my stomach flipped.

Oh...

I forgot what that felt like—to be touched ever so gently.

I looked up and found his hazel eyes staring into mine. As his lips parted, his words somersaulted off his tongue. "Thank you for bringing him back here. You didn't have to do that."

"Yes, I did."

As I walked away to allow Jackson to help his father change into clean, dry clothing, I had a feeling I shouldn't leave him alone to deal with everything on his own. As he took care of his father, I helped clean up around the house, tossing the dishes into the dishwasher and throwing the empty beers into the trash can.

After Jackson helped his father to bed, he came out with such a look of distress on his face.

"He's knocked out. I placed a garbage can next to him. Hopefully, he won't need to use it."

"I hope he's okay."

"Why are you still here?" he asked, and I wasn't very certain. He glanced around the space. "Did you clean up?"

"Only a little. I just wanted to make sure you're okay. Are you okay?" I asked, nodding in his direction. After the words left my mouth, I realized how stupid the question was. Of course, he wasn't okay.

"I'll be fine," he replied with knitted brows. He was repeatedly snapping a band on his wrist. So much so that his skin was turning red.

I hugged my body with my arms. "It has to be hard living in a place where you feel like you don't belong. I'm sure your reasons for staying are valid, but that doesn't make it any less hard. Plus, with the shape your father is in, that can't be easy." He didn't reply, so I kept talking. "I know you don't know me, but if you ever need a person to talk to—"

"I don't," he snapped, and when the words harshly fell from his tongue, his mouth twitched.

"Okay."

His bottom lip twitched. "It's not you. I don't talk to strangers, and it just turns out that everyone's a stranger."

"Except Alex."

"Yes. Except Alex, and even then…"

I nodded in understanding, then swayed back and forth a tad bit. "I, uh, I'm Grace. I love puzzles, but I never finish them. I'm the worst person to take out to eat because I can never decide what to order. I think bananas are weird, but I love banana cream pie. I can't do a cartwheel, but I can eat a whole pizza in one sitting, which some might find gross, but I find impressive. I still have my wisdom teeth even though they bother me during full moons, and—"

He narrowed his eyes. "What are you doing?"

"Telling you about myself so I'm no longer a stranger to you. Therefore, you won't feel weird talking about things to me."

He almost smiled, or at least, I pretended he did. Every now and then, I imagined what it would look like if his lips curved up into a grin. I bet a smile would look so good on him.

"Why are you so set on trying to get me to open up?" he asked.

"Because, even though you don't see it, I think we have things in common. Plus, you're the only person in this town who makes me feel like I don't have to pretend to be something I'm not."

"What are you pretending to be?"

I swallowed hard and shrugged my left shoulder. "Perfect."

"I know what that's like." He spoke low, unease in his tone. "To have to pretend to be something you aren't."

He was opening up, slowly, quietly, softly…

Please stay open.

"What are you pretending to be?" I asked.

"Angry."

"But what are you really?"

"Lost," he truthfully confessed, and I felt his words deep in my soul.

"Me too," I told him. "So much, me too."

His shoulders rounded forward, and his stare dropped to the floor, but no words escaped him.

I stepped toward him. "If you need anything—"

"I don't. We don't."

"But if there ever is a time you do need anything, I'm here. Even if it's just loading the dishwasher."

He appeared so perplexed by my offer—almost angry that I'd

say those words—but he didn't say anything in response to my offer, which made me grow a bit uncomfortable.

"I should get out of your hair, though. I don't want to take up your night."

He nodded in agreement and walked me out to the front porch.

"I'll walk you home," he offered, his voice intense, but I didn't take offense to it. It seemed that intensity was all that Jackson really knew how to be.

I shook my head. "I'll be fine."

He grumbled, and the corner of his mouth twitched. "It's late."

"We're in Chester," I joked. "It's pretty safe."

"You never know what kind of weirdos there are in small towns."

"I think I can handle it."

"But—"

"Really," I cut in. "It's fine."

"Are you always this stubborn?"

"That's funny." I grinned. "I could ask you the same thing."

He almost smiled, and I almost loved it.

"Well, if you're sure," he told me, his deep voice still uncertain.

"I am but thank you for the offer."

As I turned to leave, his sharp voice sounded once more. "Why didn't you call the cops?"

"What?"

"On my father. Why didn't you call the cops on him like everyone else in town does?"

My eyes locked with his, and even though his words were hardened, his stare wasn't. His eyes simply looked sad. *Oh, Jackson.* He was way too young to be that sad, that angry, that broken.

"That's simple," I replied. "Because I'm not like everyone else in town."

"Grace?"

"Yes?"

He stuffed his hands into his pockets and released a small breath. "You're nothing like your mother."

That both broke my heart and healed it all at once.

We didn't say another word. He turned and went back into his father's house, and I walked down the steps of the front porch. As I made my way back to my sister's, Jackson Emery and his father both stayed on my mind.

I said a small prayer for their hearts and hoped somehow their souls could find some kind of healing.

CHAPTER THIRTEEN

Jackson

She helped him when she didn't have to.

I didn't understand. I couldn't process what had happened the night before. Grace Harris, from the family I despised, helped my father last night. Why would she do that? Why would she reach out a hand to him and take him home? Shower him? Clean up his home?

She could've easily just called the cops on him. I should've been bailing him out of jail last night, but I didn't have to do that.

Everything I knew about her family proved the opposite of her actions, yet still…

"Where's the damn coffee?" Dad muttered, walking into the auto shop, scratching his beard. He looked like shit, but that wasn't surprising. I was actually shocked he was up before five in the afternoon.

"In the break room where it always is," I stated dryly.

He walked into the break room and went to pour himself a cup.

I tried my best to ignore the small bottle of whiskey he dumped inside before he began to sip.

"How was your night?" I asked.

He shrugged. "Fine. I just passed out."

Blacked out, you mean.

"Did you hang out with anyone?" I questioned him, wanting to know how much he remembered.

He cocked an eyebrow and sipped his "coffee." "Who the hell would I hang out with?"

"No one. Forget about it."

"Already forgotten. Also, clean up this room. It looks like shit in here. Are we running a business or a fucking dump?" he grumbled.

We weren't running anything. My father hadn't worked on a car in years. He used to be the best at it, though. I used to really look up to him before the liquor made him too far gone.

Now, he was merely a ghost of the man I used to look up to.

He hadn't a clue of the events from the night before. I wasn't sure if that was a good or a bad thing. Though, if he found out a Harris was who saved him from himself, he'd probably take another sledgehammer to the pews.

Our family didn't take handouts.

Especially from the likes of them.

Except maybe she saved him last night. If she hadn't been there to walk him home, to watch over him, who knew what would've happened.

My mind was conflicted, blurred, and I wasn't sure how to make it clear.

I not only had so much hate for Grace Harris and everything she stood for, but an overwhelming amount of gratitude also.

How could that be? How could I hate and be thankful all at once?

I didn't know how to feel, so I chose to feel nothing at all and headed back to work. My job was the only thing I had control over, and at that moment, I felt as if I needed some form of control.

Yet even as I worked, the sight of her eyes crossed my mind

every other minute. Those stupid, wide-eyed doe eyes that looked so full of kindness.

I wished she didn't look so kind.

My mind was split in two as I thought about Grace. Part of me was so thankful for her help. I wanted to believe in the kindness that she showed me and trust that she did it from the goodness of her heart. Yet another part of me wished she hadn't helped my father because that felt like some kind of leverage to me. That she had something over us somehow. That we were some kind of charity case to her. I didn't want that at all, so I'd make it my mission to pay her back somehow.

No matter what it took.

"Hey, Jackson, I got a call that I was supposed to come into the shop?" Grace said, walking in later that afternoon. "Is everything okay with the car?" As she walked up, Tucker rose from his dog bed and wandered over. He was slow and grumbled as he did it, but his tail wagged the whole time. He was committed to greeting every guest who came into the shop even though he was half blind and arthritis ravaged his body. He was in pain whenever he moved, but the idea of not giving someone a "hello" and a lick against the face seemed more painful to him than anything.

Grace welcomed his greeting, rubbing directly behind his ear as Tucker licked her face once, then sluggishly retreated to his bed. The vet had recently put him on new meds, and I worried they were making him too drowsy, but at least they were supposed to help his pain.

I cleared my throat and stood up from working under the hood of a truck. "Your car's still a piece of shit. I still think Alex should junk it, but that's not why I called you in."

"Oh? What's up?" She stood a bit taller. "Is your father all right?"

"Yes, well, no, not really, but as far as last night goes, he doesn't remember it. But that is what this is about. About last night."

"Yeah? What about it?"

I walked over to her and crossed my arms. "I don't want to owe you."

"What? What does that mean?" she asked, and I hated how her eyes were so wide. And beautiful. And kind.

Stop being so soft-spoken and kind.

"I don't want to owe you anything for helping my father," I told her matter-of-factly.

"Oh." She somewhat laughed, and I hated the sound because it sounded gorgeous, and I needed her not to sound that way. "You don't owe me anything. I just wanted to help."

"We don't want your handout," I told her.

She raised a brow and narrowed those eyes. "It wasn't a handout. I was just helping him."

"No, you must want something in return, and I don't want you or your family to hold that over us."

"Listen, I don't know what you're thinking, but please know that you're wrong. It wasn't some kind of game—me helping your father. I didn't want anything at all. I still don't."

I heard her words, but they were so hard to believe. I slid my hands into my jeans pockets, and my shoulders curved forward. "I don't get it then."

"Get what?"

"We've been awful to you…my father and I, and you still treated us with kindness. Why?"

"Jackson." She sighed, her voice almost a whisper. Her eyes softened in a way I wished they hadn't. She looked so genuinely concerned by my question, worried about my lack of understanding. "My father always taught me that you don't only treat certain people well. You treat all people equally. With love, with respect, and understanding."

"Your father," I muttered, my brows lowering. "You're close to him?"

"Yes. He's the best man I've ever known."

I hadn't a word to say to her comment. "Let me pay you back," I said, almost aggressively.

"You guys are already working on my car. That's payback enough."

"No. Alex is fixing your car, not me."

"Really, Jackson, I—"

"*Please*," I begged—yes, I pleaded. I begged her to allow me to do something, anything, so I wouldn't feel in debt to that woman and her family. I took a deep breath and shut my eyes. "Please let me do something for you."

"It's hard for you, isn't it?" she asked me. "Believing that people are good."

I didn't reply, though I doubted she expected an answer. I'd seen enough bad to believe that the world wasn't filled with goodness.

"Well," she started. "What do you want to do for me?"

I grimaced.

I didn't know.

I just knew that a handout from her couldn't be floating over my head.

"Or," she started, apparently aware that I didn't know how to pay her back. "We'll figure that out when the time comes. How about that? Deal?" she asked, holding her hand out toward me. I took her hand into mine and shook.

"Deal."

Jackson
Nine Years Old

"What happened to you?" Dad asked me as I walked into the auto shop, grumbling with my head down. I didn't look up. His voice grew sterner. "Jackson Paul, look at me."

My head rose, and he cringed when he saw me, dropping the tool in his hand. "Jesus," he muttered, walking over to me.

"It's fine," I huffed.

"You have a black eye!" he barked, anger building inside him. Dad hardly ever got angry, but whenever I was bullied, his temper grew. "Who did this to you?" he asked, lightly touching my face.

"Just those stupid kids at school. They pushed me into a locker, and my face hit the metal."

He grimaced and took my hand into his. "Come on."

We marched out to the open field where Ma was painting.

Dad huffed and puffed. "Hannah, look." He gestured toward my face. "Look what they did to his face."

Ma gasped, standing from her chair.

I looked down at the ground.

She placed her fingers against my cheeks. "Jackson, honey, who did this?"

"Just some kids at school," I explained. "It's fine."

"It's not," Dad barked. He turned toward Ma. "Talking to the school board isn't doing anything. It's time to teach him to defend himself."

Ma shook her head. "So he can be just like them? No. Fighting isn't the answer."

"Oh, and ignoring the kids is? Those monsters had the nerve to put their hands on my kid as the teachers stood around and did nothing. He's taking self-defense classes."

"Mike—" Ma started, and he spoke over her. Then she spoke over him. Then they both just yelled at one another in the open field.

My stomach hurt.

"Are you guys fighting?" I asked, my voice shaky. I hated how it made me feel, seeing them argue over one another. I'd never seen them angry with each other, and now they were angry because of me. I didn't want to make them sad. They were the only friends I had, and watching them fight made me sad.

They both stopped talking, and they looked over at me.

Dad took a deep inhale. "No, son. I'm sorry. I just…" He ran his hands through his hair. "It just upsets me when people hurt you." He held his hand out to Ma, and she took it. He pulled her close. "It upsets us both."

"But why are you yelling at one another?"

"We were just speaking loudly," Ma smiled. "We want to figure out the best way to help you, and sometimes those conversations get heated. I'm sorry, love."

"We both are," Dad agreed.

I took a breath, still feeling uneasy.

Lately, it seemed every time someone bullied me, Ma and Dad took it out on one another.

"Listen, I'm going to clean up this mess out here, and then I'll head inside to cook us some dinner, okay?" Ma said. "How about you two go read another chapter from Harry Potter and relax a bit?"

When I wasn't painting with Ma, I was reading young adult books with Dad. Ma taught me how to love art, and Dad taught me how to love words.

There wasn't a night that passed when he didn't sit in my bedroom at night, reading books to me.

Those were some of my favorite times.

He was my best friend.

He and I headed into the house, and we sat on the couch to read. As he began, I listened closely, and every now and then, he'd look up at my eye, frown, and then he'd pulled me in for a side hug.

"Do you and Ma hate each other?" I asked, worry still filling me.

He arched an eyebrow. "What?"

"You were fighting and yelling."

"Sometimes people argue. It doesn't mean they hate one another."

"But—"

"Your mother is my best friend, Jackson." His eyes glassed over, and he sniffled a bit. "She's my whole world, just like you. You both mean more to me than you could ever know."

"You love her?"

"Yes, son." A tear rolled down his cheek, and he nodded, wiping it away. "With all that I am."

"Okay." My stomach stopped hurting as much. I leaned back against Dad and nodded slowly. "You can keep reading now."

He cleared his throat and sighed, looking back at his book. "Chapter fourteen…"

CHAPTER FOURTEEN

Grace

Sunday morning church was the highlight of the week in Chester. It was a staple in our lives, and my father was the man who ran it. And boy, was he good at what he did. I just wished my attention could've been on him more that morning.

"Sit up straight, Gracelyn Mae," Mama whisper-shouted at me in the pew on Sunday morning. "A proper lady doesn't slouch."

I sat up straighter and rolled my shoulders back as I listened to Dad preach his sermon. A few people sitting behind us began to whisper, and my ears perked up as Finn's name fell from their lips.

"Yeah, he came straight from Autumn's home last night. I wonder if she even knows," they said, making my stomach twist into knots.

"It's sad to see their marriage crumble. I thought they were going to make it."

"Yes well, that's today's generation. They don't even fight for their partner anymore. I heard he wasn't the first one to step out on their relationship."

"It's always the good girls, isn't it?"

I moved to twist around and snap at the gossiping women, but Mama placed a firm hand on my knee and shook her head back and forth slightly.

"Straighter, Gracelyn Mae," she told me.

I sat up even more.

"Rumor has it Finley wanted a family, but Grace didn't want to get pregnant. Didn't want to ruin her figure. Even though it looks a bit…different."

"I noticed her weight gain, too. It's a shame."

My mind began to spin as I was forced to sit there and be ridiculed by townsfolk. I wasn't even allowed to stand up for myself because I was Gracelyn Mae Harris, the well-behaved angel of Chester, Georgia.

What hurt the most was the fact that those people who were whispering were the same ones hugging me in the marketplace. They smiled to my face while literally talking behind my back.

They're gonna bleed you out till you're nothing, and then they're gonna ask how you died.

I did my best to blink away my tears, too, because the perfect princess never cried.

"Can you just not?!" a voice snapped, making the whole church go silent. Dad stopped preaching, thrown off by the sudden shout. I turned to my left to see Judy facing the rude individuals, who had looks of shock painted across their face.

"How about you listen to the sermon instead of gossiping about things that you know nothing about?" She then turned back to the front, and the room remained quiet. She nodded once toward our father and cleared her throat, sitting up straighter like the proper princess. "Sorry, Dad. You can continue."

He did exactly that, completely unmoved by the disruption.

After the sermon, I caught Mama giving Judy a stern talking-to in the corner of the church. I moved in close enough to hear Mama preaching her own words. "How dare you embarrass us like that, Judith Rae!"

"I'm sorry, I just couldn't listen to them talk about Grace like that, and I'm shocked that you could. They have no clue what's going on in her life!"

"That's on them, but it's not your job to educate them on it. Their gossipy ways are between them and Jesus."

"Yes, well, maybe Jesus wasn't listening that closely today, so I decided to join the conversation," Judy snapped.

She *snapped* back to *Mama*.

Who was this new sister of mine, and how could I tell her I loved her with more than words?

"You're acting like a child, Judith. Stop it."

"You're acting like those people are your family. You're so concerned with how the church views you that you don't even care how your daughters do. What ever happened to always and always, Mama? When did you stop believing in it?" she asked before walking off in a huff.

I was stunned. Simply stunned. Never in my life have Judy or I stormed away from Mama. We always waited for her to leave the room in a huff and puff because that was how it was meant to be. We never sassed our mother, and she always had the last word. Until that afternoon.

I felt as if I was in a weird twilight zone, and I hadn't a clue which way was up.

Mama glanced my way and hurried over to me. "Are you happy, Grace? Are you pleased that your sister is acting out like you now?"

"No," I whispered, shaking my head. "Of course not. Mama, I didn't plan for any of this to happen."

She frowned and shook her head. "But you're not doing anything to fix it."

"What do you mean fix it? My husband left me for my best friend."

"He didn't leave you. Has he spoken of divorce papers?"

I swallowed. "No."

"So he's still your husband."

"Yes, technically, but—"

"I called him last night."

"What do you mean you called him?"

"I called him," she said matter-of-factly.

"Why would you do that?"

"I wanted to hear things from his point of view. I wanted to make sure he was okay."

My heart began to drown once more.

"He cheated on me, Mama. He left *me*, and you're asking if he's okay?"

She didn't once ask me that question. She never asked if I was okay.

She stood tall, looking as beautiful as ever, and pursed her lips together. "He's still my son-in-law, Grace. He's our family."

"I'm your daughter," I argued.

"Please listen, Grace," she whispered. "He said he still loves you."

"He's a liar."

"Bite your tongue," she scolded me. "We have known the Braun family all our lives, and Finley Braun wouldn't lie about loving you."

"You'd be surprised at what he could lie about, Mama. Plus, maybe it takes more than love to make a marriage last."

"Yes, it does. It takes forgiveness and prayer," she scolded me.

"She was my best friend. He's dating my best friend. They are still together."

"I know it's messy…" Mama started.

I huffed. "Messy?!" My voice was louder than she liked. "Come on, Mama. You're being ridiculous."

"I am not. People make mistakes, Gracelyn Mae, and if you don't show him that you still want him, you'll lose him completely. As his wife, it is your duty to stand by your husband even when he's lost. You have to lead him back home."

"But Autumn—"

"Autumn didn't stand before you and say vows. What she did was horrible, but it is no concern to you, not really. She means nothing to your life. Finley means everything. Who are you without

Finn, Grace? He's been by your side more than half of your lifetime. You both are a part of each other. Just because the days are dark doesn't mean we stop trying. Youth today are so quick to throw away relationships before even giving them a chance to heal. There's healing in time."

My stomach was in knots, and I hadn't a clue how to respond because I've somewhat been wondering the same thing. Without Finn, who was I? He'd been such a big part of my existence that I wasn't certain how to go about living without him.

Our lives had been so tangled that I was almost certain he took parts of me when he untied our love.

Who was I supposed to be now?

Was I even still a person of my own accord?

Without Finley, did I even exist?

Yet none of that mattered. Not really.

Because even if I fought for his love, even if I prayed for him to come back to me, he'd still have had an affair with my best friend. If it were a stranger, perhaps I could've moved on. Perhaps I could've found a drop of forgiveness in my soul, but with Autumn?

No.

I'd never be able to trust him again, and every second he was gone from my touch, I'd imagine him embraced in hers.

What kind of life was that to live?

What kind of woman would I be if I melted back into the arms of the man who repeatedly betrayed me?

"You aren't even going to try, are you?" Mama frowned. "You're not going to give him a chance? He'd said he's been calling you."

"I have nothing to say to him."

"Your stubbornness is going to ruin your life."

"Mama…" I whispered, blinking a few times and rubbing the side of my neck. "Can't you just choose me today? If only for one day?"

Not even a glimpse of compassion crossed her face as she glanced around the church. "Gracelyn, I need you to start acting your age instead of acting out like a child. If you are going to stay in Chester for a while, you need to act appropriately."

"Act appropriately? What are you talking about?"

"You are the daughter of the pastor, which, in turn, makes you the daughter of this town. You have a responsibility to your family, to this town, to show up with a smile and class."

"Mama—"

"I'm serious, Grace. I don't want to argue, and I'm tired of getting calls from people about how odd you're acting."

"What? What does that even mean?"

"People have been talking about seeing you wandering through town crying and how your whole personality seems"—she cleared her throat—"off. Plus, what were you doing down at that auto shop talking to that—*thing*?"

"Excuse me? Mama, do you have people spying on me?" I asked, stunned.

"Of course not, Gracelyn. Don't be ridiculous. But this is a small town, and people do have eyes of their own. You need to stay away from those Emery men. They are reckless."

"Do you even really know them, Mama? Like really?"

"I know enough."

"From Mike's one mistake years ago."

She huffed. "One mistake? You must be out of your mind to think Mad Mike has only made one mistake."

"You shouldn't call him that," I softly spoke.

"Why? That's what he is—he's insane. Since you've been gone, he's been in and out of the jail cell and piss drunk all over town. He's a pain to this town, and we'd be better off without him and his sinful son."

"Sinful son? Come on, that's a bit much." I didn't know why, but I felt the way she was judging Jackson was a bit unfair. Yes, he was mean, but could you really blame him for being that way after the town pushed him into that corner?

"Is it? He's a drug addict."

"He got clean."

"Maybe for a minute, but no lowlife like him could ever stay that way. Do you know where women go when they have the devil whispering in their ears about infidelity? Straight into the arms of that disgrace. He has ruined the relationships of many people in this town because of his disgusting habits. He's pretty much a walking STD, and that's why it looks awful when you're seen with him. You are starting rumors that don't even exist just by being seen with him. It looks appalling to have you talk to that monster. You must stay away from Jackson Emery at all costs."

"Did he come to you for help years ago? About the townspeople attacking him and his father?" I asked.

She shifted around in her heels. "A lot of people come to me for help. I am, after all, the pastor's wife."

"Yes, but did Jackson come to you, asking you to talk to the church about leaving him and his father alone?"

She stuck her nose up in the air. "I don't recall that."

"Well, he does."

"He's a liar, like his father."

"Mama," I whispered, shaking my head. "When did you become so cold? How could you turn your back on him?"

"Those two people didn't deserve my ear after what Mad Mike did to our place of worship. Thousands of dollars in repairs. Someone could've been killed."

"But what does Mike's actions have to do with Jackson? He was just a kid, Mama, and he came to you in his time of need."

"Don't preach to me about being a good person, Gracelyn Mae. You have no clue the things I've been through."

"You turned your back on a child."

"They didn't deserve my help. Not after the mess Mike made. Not after the storm he started."

"If you turn your back on one, then you turn your back on all," I said, quoting one of my favorite sermons Dad ever preached.

She knew the words, too.

For a split second, her eyes glassed over as she stared my way, but as soon as she blinked, away went the emotions. "I don't have to explain myself to you. As long as you're staying here, you need to listen to me. You must stay obedient, and you must remain graceful, or else more rumors will start about you. I know that's the last thing you want. Keep your head low and do as you're told. Do you understand me?"

"I'm not a child, Mama."

"Then please," she scolded, "stop acting like one." A few people walked by, and Mama's nerves continued to build. She stood tall and smoothed out her outfit. "You're ruining our name. You're ruining everything we work to protect."

Before I could reply, Dad walked up to us. "Everything okay?"

Mama gave him a hard look. "Are you kidding, Samuel? Didn't you see that scene your daughter made in the church today? Everything is far from okay!"

Dad smiled and shrugged. "I'm sure there will be another scene before the day is over, and people will have already forgotten about that."

"People don't forget in this town, Samuel. You should know that better than anyone," Mama remarked as she smoothed out her dress. "Now if you'll excuse me, I'm going to do damage control because it appears I'm the last sane one in this family." She hurried away, and Dad moved closer to me.

He placed his glasses on top of his head, as always, and stuffed his hands into his pockets. "You okay, Buttercup?"

I gave him a tight smile. "I'm sorry about all that, Dad. I know me coming home hasn't been the easiest for anyone."

"You coming home has been the greatest thing in this world. Don't ever apologize to me, Grace. You and your sister are my greatest blessings." He kissed my forehead and pulled me into a hug. "Always and always."

"Dad?"

"Yes?"

"Don't let go yet, okay?"

He tightened the hug and placed his chin on top of my head. "Okay."

CHAPTER FIFTEEN

Grace

In the town of Chester, you saw the same faces every single day. Even when you didn't want to. I was quick to learn that Jackson not only took Tucker to the park every now and then, but he also carried that big boy into town each day and would sit in the sun with his companion for hours. It seemed to be Tucker's happy place, and Jackson had no trouble giving his dog that joy.

Even though he hated when I looked his way, I couldn't help myself.

It was intriguing to zoom in on someone I believed was so different from me and see parts of him that matched corners of my soul.

Maybe we weren't so opposite, after all—both of us being lost and stuff.

He wasn't the only one I saw in town, though, which was unfortunate.

I saw Autumn all the time, but I did a good job of avoiding her.

I saw her first at the diner. Then again at the ice cream shop, and I dipped out before she could say a word my way.

Then we crossed paths in the grocery store.

She was wearing high heels and had her blond hair pulled back into a tight ponytail. As she pushed her cart down the fresh produce section, I paused. She looked at the bananas as if they were foreign creatures, studying every single one as if she'd never seen the fruit before.

They are just bananas, idiot. Just pick one.

The moment the thought rolled through my mind, I felt guilt.

Sorry for calling you an idiot.

Wait.

No.

She stole my husband. I was allowed to mentally call her names without feeling guilty about it.

As she picked up the bananas, she raised her head, and her eyes fell on me. "Grace," she said, my name rolling off her tongue like a disease.

She stepped backward, and I stood still.

Her eyes watered over, and I hated that it happened. She began to cry in the middle of the grocery store, tears hitting her soon-to-be-purchased fruits. Gosh, I hated her tears because they reminded me of my own pain.

The pain she caused me.

She stepped toward me, and my body tensed up. I pushed my cart away from me.

"Grace, wait. Can we talk?" she asked.

Her words stung me as they left her mouth.

She stepped closer.

I turned around and ran.

I ran.

Just to be clear, I wasn't a runner. I was certain that I didn't even know how to properly run. After about twenty seconds, I was winded, and sweating in places I didn't know sweat could come from. But, still, I kept running because I could hear her behind me, click-clacking in her heels.

Autumn was a runner.

She'd been running since she was in diapers and was one of the fastest people I knew.

As I raced down the streets of Chester, out of breath and seconds from passing out, I listened to her calm as day voice still calling after me. She wasn't a lick out of breath while I was debating if I should call an ambulance for CPR. My arms flung all over the place like an octopus as she ran like the next USA Olympian champion.

The second I could, I threw the door to The Silent Bookshop open, and Josie saw my panicked expression, though I didn't have time to say anything to her. I hastily opened the set of double doors and rushed into the silent area, where I proceeded to hide behind bookshelves.

My whole body ached as I placed my hands over my chest. My heartbeats were erratic, though that was nothing new. As I listened to the door open, I whimpered to myself. I wished I were invisible. I wish I had Harry Potter's cloak of protection so I could avoid ever actually having to face Autumn.

"Gracelyn? I know you're in here," she said, as I heard her tiptoeing in my direction. "You can't keep avoiding me."

A few people shushed her, but she didn't listen.

Who would've thought that a woman who took her best friend's husband wouldn't obey to the quiet rules of The Silent Bookshop?

She turned the corner, and I stood still, pressed up between Narnia and Hogwarts.

I was cornered. Books surrounded me on the left and right side, and Autumn stood tall in front of me.

Had she really run that whole way in heels and didn't have a drop of sweat to show for it?

I hated her.

Oh, how I hated her glowing skin.

"We should talk," she told me, wiping at her eyes.

What kind of mascara did she wear that it didn't run at all when she cried?

"You can't talk in here," I scolded her. "And even if we weren't here, I wouldn't want to speak to you."

"Please. If we are both going to be in town, we can't keep this up."

"You'd be surprised at how long I can keep this up."

"Grace."

"Go away."

"No. Not until we talk," she told me, crossing her arms. "I need you to understand."

"To understand what? How you betrayed me? How you stabbed me in the back? I'd rather not."

"It was only supposed to happen once, Grace."

It was only supposed to happen once.

That didn't make it better in any way, shape, or form.

"And it happened when Finn came to work at the hospital. We saw each other every day since I'm the receptionist there. One night, we went out for drinks, and he fell apart over you. He told me how you left him."

I huffed. "How *I* left *him*?"

"Yes. That night we had one too many drinks, and…" Her words faded.

"You betrayed me. You never called to ask me if what Finn was saying was true."

"I'd never known him to lie," she told me.

"But you were my person, not his. You were my best friend."

"Grace…"

"Please just leave me alone," I begged. That was all I wanted, really. To be left alone.

Josie walked into the space, and she glanced my way. I gave her a stare, begging her to save me.

She looked at Autumn with such distaste. "I'm sorry, Autumn. This is a quiet section. If you are going to speak, you must go in the lobby."

"But she won't follow me there," she whined. "And we have to talk."

"We aren't going to talk," I barked her way. "There is nothing you can say to me that will make me want to—"

"I'm pregnant," she blurted out, her words somersaulting from her tongue and slapping against my skin.

For a moment, I blacked out. I felt acid rising from my stomach and burning against my tongue as I stayed frozen in an unbelievable state of shock.

She shifted around in her heels. "When Finn saw you when you closed on your house, he was supposed to tell you, but he told me he couldn't. Not after all the miscarriages that you two have dealt with," she told me.

Unlike Mama and Finn, Autumn had no struggles saying the word miscarriage.

I wished she had, though, because hearing it from her made me want to be sick.

"You're pregnant?" I choked out, my body shaking uncontrollably.

She nodded slowly. "I...this..." She took a deep inhale and sniffled as tears kept falling from her eyes. "It wasn't supposed to happen like this, Grace. I swear, none of this was ever supposed to happen. I didn't expect to fall for him, and this..."

I zoned out on her. I zoned out on all the sounds surrounding me. I watched as Autumn kept speaking, but Josie took her by the arm and pulled her out of the room.

My eyes began to blur as I became dizzier by the second.

I would vomit.

No, I would pass out.

No...

I was going to die.

She did it.

She did the one thing I was never able to do. She would give my husband a child, and I was certain that child would have his eyes.

Those crystal blue eyes...

For a long time, I thought perhaps it was both of us who were the issue—both Finley and me. Yet it turned out, he wasn't at fault at all. He was able to bear children.

It was me, and only me, who was tragically flawed.

"Grace."

I heard my name but didn't flinch. I was frozen. Unable to move, unable to breathe. Unable to do anything but stand still.

"Hey! Snap out of it!" Jackson shouted my way. He placed his hands on my shoulders and shook my body back and forth, making my blurred vision clear somewhat. I looked into his eyes and blinked a few times.

Then came the tears, each one taking its precious time to roll down my cheek.

"She's pregnant," I softly spoke, staring into his eyes that weren't as hard and cold as they usually appeared. "My best friend's pregnant with my husband's child."

"Yeah." He frowned but not his normal frown. This was built around his pity for me. "I heard."

"I-I-I..." My eyes faded over, and I only saw black. I couldn't speak. I couldn't move. I didn't know what to do or how to react. All I knew was that this was not a panic attack.

I knew panic attacks.

I knew anxiety, and how it had swallowed me in the past, but this was a new feeling.

This felt like the first moments before the final descent into nothingness.

I'd never forget the moment as I stood there in The Silent Bookshop. It was one of the big moments. One of the ones that truly defined who I'd be from that point on. It was the moment that changed me from the person I'd always been.

It was the exact moment when I lost my last mustard seed of faith. It was the exact moment when I no longer believed in God.

"Come with me," Jackson whispered.

"But..." I started.

"Princess," he said, his voice smoky as it always had been. He took my hands into his and lightly squeezed them both. "Come with me."

And with his guidance, I followed him.

We walked the streets of Chester with my hand in his, and it still felt as if time was frozen. We reached his property, and he took me to the area in the back of the shop where the broken-down car sat.

He stood me in front of the car and then grabbed a pair of safety goggles and placed them over my eyes. Then he grabbed the sledgehammer and handed it my way.

"Okay, he said, nodding toward the vehicle. "Go wild."

I took a deep breath, pulled the sledgehammer over my head, and slammed it into the car. I kept swinging, unaware of how long I beat the car. I couldn't stop pounding the metal piece of junk in front of me. I slung the hammer into the back window, shattering the glass as my eyes released a floodgate. I couldn't see through the goggles, but I kept swinging over and over again, taking all the strength left in my body and releasing it onto the vehicle. I might not have had much left inside me, but I had enough power to release the anger inside me.

"All right," Jackson stated. "That's enough."

But I didn't stop. I kept pounding away at the balled-up sheet metal.

"Princess, that's enough," he said, this time sterner, yet still, I didn't listen.

Everything inside me ached in a way that I didn't know could hurt. It was as if my soul was set on fire, and it would be an eternal burn.

I swung the sledgehammer over my head, and when I was unable to swing it down, I turned to see Jackson's hands gripped around the head.

"Let go," I ordered.

"No," he replied.

"Jackson, let go," I begged, taking off the goggles.

"No."

"Let go!" I barked, this time with tears falling down my face, my heart racing faster and faster.

"Grace, please..." he whispered, his voice quiet, almost a whisper as he stared straight into my eyes. He moved closer to me, and his fingers landed against mine as he started to loosen my grip. "Let go."

I released the sledgehammer and took a few steps backward.

Jackson placed the hammer down, and he gave me the most pathetic look.

"I'm okay," I lied, sniffling. "I'm okay."

"You're not."

"No. I am. Everything's fine. Everything's always fine. Everything's—"

He moved in closer and narrowed his eyes as he stared my way. The closer he got, the more my nerves began to build. "Seriously, I'm okay. I lost it there for a minute, but I'm okay. I'm—"

"You're bleeding," he told me.

I am?

He wiped his thumb against my cheek, and when he pulled it back, I noticed the blood resting against his fingertip. Then I felt the sting.

"It's a deep cut. I think some of the glass from the car must've struck you," he said. "Come to my place. I'll get you cleaned up."

I wiped my hand against my cheek and shook my head back and forth a little. "It's fine. I'm okay. I'm fine." I kept saying those words over and over again, hoping that I'd somehow start to believe them.

"Come on," he said, holding his hand out to me. I took his grip, and a chill raced over me as he walked me to his cabin. I didn't say a word on the whole walk over, mainly because my mind was numb. We walked into the house, and I stood in his living room, where an easel was set up and a piano sat in the far corner of the place. The cabin looked bigger on the inside than it appeared from the outside, and it was a very clean place. The artwork on all the walls, many different paintings of sunrises and sunsets, was all breathtakingly stunning.

"Sit here," Jackson ordered, leading me to the couch. I did as he said, and he hurried away to get a towel and some Band-Aids. Tucker was quick to come greet me, and when he tried and failed to jump on the couch, I helped him up, and he snuggled right into my lap, wagging his tail.

"Good boy," I whispered, somehow finding instant comfort.

When Jackson came back, he kneeled in front of me with a

warm cloth and placed it against my cheek. I flinched a little, and he frowned. "Sorry," he muttered.

"It's fine," I replied.

We sat in silence as he attended to my wound, and Tucker fell fast asleep in my lap.

"Jackson—"

"Look—"

We spoke at the same time, and I nervously laughed as his fingers brushed against my face. "You first," I told him.

He swallowed hard. "I didn't mean for you to get hurt. I'm sorry. I just thought some of the energy you had needed to find an outlet."

"Is that why you hit the cars? As an energy outlet?"

He didn't reply.

I lowered my head.

"You might need stitches," he told me. He cleared his throat, and when he looked up at my eyes, the guilt in that hazel stare made my heart feel as if it were being squeezed. "I'm sorry."

"No worries," I said. "I did, after all, make you drop a sledgehammer on your foot, so I assume we're even," I joked.

"No, that's not what I mean."

He stared at me with a hard look, and his lips stayed turned down into a frown. "I'm sorry for the way I've been. For the way I've treated you."

"If I knew all it would take for you to be nice to me was my husband getting my best friend pregnant, I would've done that ages ago." I laughed, but he kept frowning.

"You don't have to do that."

"Do what?"

"Laugh when nothing's funny."

"Yes, I do, because otherwise…" As he stared at me that way, I had to turn away because I felt my emotions finally catching up with me as my heartbeats slowed down. A small, uncomfortable laugh fell from my lips. "Because otherwise you're going to be annoyed by me," I warned him.

"Why?"

My bottom lip trembled, and I felt my body start to shake as my hands covered my face. "Because this is the part where I cry."

"Yeah," he agreed. His hands brushed against mine, and he took them into his hold, lowering them from my face. "And this is the part where I let you." He moved Tucker from my lap onto another couch cushion. Next, Jackson placed his hands into mine and lifted me up from the couch and wrapped his arms around me. He held me close to him, and he became the one who held me up as I began to fall. I sobbed against his T-shirt, thinking of all the years of struggles, all the years of pain as I tried to create the life that Autumn had stolen straight from under my feet.

Every now and then, Jackson's hand gently rubbed my back, bringing about an odd sense of comfort.

As I pulled back a little, I thanked him for holding me, for allowing me to fall apart. He brushed his thumb against my cheeks, wiping away my tears that kept falling.

I laughed nervously. "Hot mess," I said, stating what he'd been calling me for the longest time.

He kept wiping my tears. "I'm sorry," he said, his voice deep and smooth. "For calling you a hot mess when I met you."

"Don't be. It's true, after all. I am a hot mess."

"Everyone's a hot mess," he insisted. "Some people are just better at hiding it."

I didn't know why, but that statement eased my mind a bit.

Jackson rubbed the side of his neck and cleared his throat. "You want water?"

"Yes. Please."

He hurried into the back of the cabin, toward the kitchen, and I took deep breaths. My fingers lightly touched the Band-Aids against my face, and I walked toward the walls to study the sunsets more closely. They were stunning. So stunning and realistic that they almost looked like photographs. Each one had the initials H.E. in the bottom corner.

"These are beautiful," I told him as he reentered the room with the glass of water. He handed the glass my way. "Who's H.E.?" I asked.

"Hannah Emery," he quietly replied as he stuffed his hands into his pockets. "My mother."

"She was an amazing artist," I told him.

He nodded once. "She was more than that." Before I could ask him anything about his mother, he shifted the conversation back to me. "Are you all right?"

I snickered. "Truth or lie?"

"Truth," he replied. "Always truth."

I took a deep breath, and tears fell as I exhaled. I couldn't even reply.

"I'm sorry you're hurting," he told me.

"It's fine."

"It's not."

He was right, it wasn't all right, and I wasn't certain that it would ever be all right.

"You were right about everyone in town. They were just comforting me so they could get more gossip. They didn't care about my heart or how it beat. They just wanted something to talk about."

"I'm sorry I was right."

"It's okay. I just…I feel like I have no one, you know? I mean, I can talk to my sister and my father, but that's pretty much it, and I don't want to burden them. Everyone else in this town just feels like a stranger to me."

"Even your mom?"

I huffed. "Especially my mom."

He cleared his throat and rounded his shoulders forward. "I'm Jackson Paul Emery," he calmly stated, locking his stare with mine. "I can't whistle, but I can do three backflips in a row. I got my car skills from my dad and my art skills from my mother. Last summer, I ate twenty-five hot dogs in a row like a professional badass. Alex recorded the whole thing. I can make the best shrimp fried rice, and—"

"What are you doing?" I asked.

"Telling you about myself."

"Yeah. But…why?"

He brushed his hand against the back of his neck and slightly shrugged. "So I'll no longer be a stranger and you can talk to me."

Oh, Jackson...

First, he's sour, then shockingly sweet.

The gentle monster.

His gesture surprised me, but perhaps he was learning to zoom in like I was learning to see him. Maybe, for the first time, the two of us were truly seeing one another.

"I don't know how to talk about it," I confessed. I didn't have a clue what to say.

"What's the hardest part?" he asked me. "What hurts the most?"

"Oh, that's easy." I lowered my head and wrapped my arms around me. "The betrayal of the situation, and the next hardest part is being alone. I don't know how to be alone. When Finn and I got married, I believed it was set in stone. You build your whole life around another person, and you think you'll never be alone again, but then you are. It's the hardest feeling to deal with. Loneliness hurts. It burns in a way that feels worse than fire."

"The burning never stops," he told me. "You just kind of become numb to it."

"How long have you been lonely?"

He gave me a broken smile, which told me his deepest truths.

"Oh, Jackson," I whispered, my hand gently brushing against his cheek. "You're way too young to be this sad."

He closed his eyes, and I felt his warm breaths falling from his slightly parted lips. "You're doing that thing that you do, princess."

"Doing what?"

"Putting others' hurts before your own."

I smiled and slightly shrugged. "It's my gift, my curse."

"It's not a selfish thing, you know." He opened his eyes, and the intensity I felt as he stared my way sent chills down my spine. He leaned in close, whispering against my ear as if he was revealing the biggest secret in the world. "You're allowed to choose yourself first."

What a wonderful thought, though the world I grew up in taught me the complete opposite. Where I came from, it was always give yourself to others first and whatever was left was what one used on themselves.

It just turned out that most of the time, nothing ever remained, and my tank for self-love was left on empty.

When it came time for me to leave, he offered to walk me home, and I once again declined. "But thank you for this…for helping me."

He gave me a halfway smile, or at least I pretended he did. "Are you all right?"

"No."

"That's fine," he declared. "You don't have to be."

Why did that make me feel a little bit better?

"Jackson?"

"Yes?"

"You're nothing like your father."

He frowned and cleared his throat as he looked down at the ground and crossed his arms. "I am when he's sober."

CHAPTER SIXTEEN

Grace

As I walked back to Judy's house, I smiled as I saw a friendly face sitting on my front porch. "Hi, friend," I said, walking up to Josie who had two extra-large cups from KitKat's 1950s Diner.

"Hi, friend," she replied, standing up.

"How long have you been waiting?"

"Long enough to finish two of these drinks and go back to KitKat's to grab two new ones." She frowned, studying my face. "What happened?" she asked, nodding toward the bandage.

I touched my cheek. "Just some emotional release."

"Are you all right?"

"If what's in that cup of yours is what I think it is, I'll be better soon enough."

She smirked, handing a cup my way. "If I remember correctly, you were a Diet Coke girl with a few shots of whiskey." When we were younger, we always used the extra-large cups from KitKat's

Diner when we wanted to get wasted in town but didn't want anyone to know that the perfect Harris girl even knew what alcohol was. It was, of course, Josie's idea. She was pretty great at secretly letting me break free for a small bit of time.

I grabbed the cup and laughed. "Yes." I took a sip and made a face. "Geez, Josie!"

"I might have been a bit heavy-handed with that whiskey," she told me.

"This is straight-up whiskey with a splash of Diet Coke, I think."

"Confession—there's no Diet Coke in that." She placed her hand on my shoulder and lightly squeezed. "If anyone deserves straight whiskey, it's you right now. How are you holding up?"

"I could be better."

"Want to go egg Autumn's house? I have a dozen eggs around the corner," she joked. Well, I thought she was joking until I saw the seriousness in her eyes.

"No, Josie, we aren't egging her house."

"But can we toilet paper it? I got two-ply tissue. Only the best quality, too. It's quilted. Soft as a down comforter. If anything, it'll be like we're wrapping the jerk's place in a soft blanket." She bit her bottom lip. "And then we'll throw egg yolks at the tissue."

I laughed, which felt so odd. Josie had that ability, though, to make the saddest person find a second of laughter. "I think we'll hold off on the revenge."

"Okay, but when it's time, just say the word."

"I promise I will."

"Want to go to our old stomping grounds where we would people watch and get drunk without them knowing?" Josie asked, wiggling her eyebrows in hopes that I'd agree.

"Sounds like a plan."

We walked through town to Kap Park and sat down on the bench that faced downtown Chester. When we were younger, we'd see so many insane things from that park bench. The drama that unfolded as we sipped our "Diet Cokes" and laughed was always entertaining.

But that day, everything felt different. The small town that used to make me laugh felt like a foreign country to me.

"You're okay, buddy," Josie said as we stared out at the events of the night. "I mean, you're not, but you will be."

Part of me believed her, while another part thought it to be nothing but a lie.

"Josephine and Gracelyn Mae, I haven't seen you ladies sitting on this bench together in what seems like forever," Charlotte stated, walking over to us in her high heels. Her pink painted lips curved into a wide smile on her face, and my stomach turned. The last thing I wanted to do that afternoon was deal with Charlotte's nosy self.

She made herself at home and sat down right beside me. "How are you doing, Grace? You know, I've been hearing rumors. And I actually just saw you a bit earlier running through town with Jackson Emery's hand in yours. What was that about? Is everything okay?" She said the words as if she was concerned about my well-being, but I knew better now.

She was just being Charlotte—a gossip queen.

If I wasn't careful, I'd read about my life in her newspaper column come Sunday afternoon.

"What makes you think you have the right to ask her anything like that, Charlotte?" Josie barked, backing me up because she knew I wasn't going to stand up for myself.

I didn't know how.

"I'm sorry, did I say something wrong?" Charlotte questioned, pressing her hand to her chest.

"You said everything wrong. Now, if you don't mind, Grace and I were having a private conversation, and we'd like to get back to it without having busybodies like you interrupting," Josie told her.

"Well, the attitude isn't needed," Charlotte huffed, standing from the bench.

"Yeah, well, neither were your invasive questions. Have a blessed day," Josie remarked, smiling brightly toward Charlotte, who was walking off in annoyance.

I couldn't help but laugh. "If I would've ever said that, my mama would've shamed me for life."

"Yeah, well, I'm not you, and my mama can't stand that girl as much. Plus, Charlotte is, after all, my own cousin. If anyone should've told her to shut her trap, it should've been family."

"Thank you, Josie. For being you."

"It's all I know how to be," she remarked, nudging me in my shoulder. "Now if you just want to sit here in silence, we can do that. Or if you want to talk, we can do that too, okay? Whatever you need, we can do."

"I just hate her…" I confessed. "I know I shouldn't because I was taught that hate doesn't do anyone any good, but I do. I hate her so much."

"You're not alone in your hate for her. Autumn has always been a hard one for me. She always seemed so…fake."

"Everyone always said she and I were just alike."

"Well, everyone's an idiot. You're genuine. You always have been even when people didn't deserve your kindness. But her? She's just…ugh. I mean, I really hate her. And her parents, too. They always rubbed me the wrong way. Who names their kid Autumn when they were born in February? Seriously! Who does that?! You could've named her anything. I have lists of names I would've given her. Like Karla."

"Or Mia."

"Or Rebecca, Becca for short," she offered.

"Or Evette. Maybe Harper."

"Oh, I love Harper." Josie nodded, placing the lip of the mug to her mouth and gently blowing the tea to cool it off. "Or Alexandria."

"Lexie for short."

"Or Andie for short."

"Or Alex."

"I love those names. That could be used for either a guy or girl. Like Jamie or Chris or Dylan," she explained.

"Morgan, Reese, or Taylor."

"Jordan. Sawyer."

"Emerson," I whispered, the words dancing from my tongue and stinging my heart. I took a deep breath and shut my eyes. "I would've named my daughter Emerson."

When I opened my eyes, I saw the hurt in Josie's stare. I gave her a tight smile and shook my head. "Sorry." I always tried my best to keep my infertility struggles to myself. I always tried to keep a smile on my face in front of others, but sometimes, I slipped.

Especially when my best friend was pregnant by my husband.

No apologies, Josie signed my way. "Don't be sorry. You're allowed to hurt." She gave me a broken smile, and I knew what it meant. "A while back, your mom mentioned to me that you and Finn were trying to start a family and how hard that had been for you," she said, her voice as gentle as ever. She must've seen the hurt in my eyes by her comment because she quickly added more words to the conversation. "I'm sorry, I don't mean to pry. I just…" She took a deep breath and rolled up her left sleeve. On her forearm sat three small heart tattoos, each one with angel wings attached to them. "I just want you to know you're not alone in those feelings."

I released a breath I didn't even know I was holding. "I see people with children in town, and I wonder if they know how lucky they are," I whispered, my voice shaky.

"Yes, and you're happy for them, you are, but you're also really pissed off too, right?"

I slowly nodded, feeling guilt for my resentment. I've resented myself for so long. I felt anger with my body, with my inability to do the one thing I was supposed to be able to do: create a family.

Josie's voice was so soft as she continued to speak. "I don't want to make you uncomfortable, but I wanted to let you know you aren't alone in this. If you ever need someone to talk to…or someone to just be mad with, I'm here."

"Thank you, Josie. That means a lot to me."

"Anytime. I know how lonely this road we walk can get, and with everything else going on with you…" Her words faded, and she grinned. "I just want you to know if you need a friend, you got one in me."

I took in her words and held them tight. I needed a friend more than anything lately.

Home is healing.

"I'm so sorry," I stated, nodding in the direction of her tattoo. "For your three hearts."

"Thank you. That means a lot to me. How many for you?"

I took my next breath slowly. "Seven."

"Oh, honey…" Her hands landed against her heart because she knew. Any woman who'd ever lost a child knew of the hollowness that remained within the soul. "I'm so sorry."

"It's okay. I'm fine."

She frowned. "You're tired."

"Yes," I whispered, taking my next breath even slower. "I'm tired."

She pulled me into a hug. A tight one that I couldn't break away from even if I wanted to let her go. I fell into the comfort she brought me, and I held her back for her three hearts as she honored my seven.

The simple feeling of not being alone washed over me as I held Josie tightly.

As she embraced me, she softly spoke. "Ellis." She pulled away from me and wiped her own tears as she smiled and signed my way, *"I would've named the last one Ellis."*

"And they would've been beautiful."

"God. I bet they would've had Harry's eyes," she said, laughing slightly as she shook her head, thinking of her husband.

"And your smile," I signed.

She grinned, and that made me happy.

"It's just hard, that's all. Autumn was able to give Finn the one thing he always wanted, the one thing I couldn't, without even trying," I explained. "It's like they are living my fairy tale. They are getting my happily ever after."

"Yeah well, there's one major issue with their storyline."

"And what's that?"

"She's not you. She'll never be you, and they cannot steal your happily ever after. It's yours, after all. Just because it didn't come to you the way you thought it would doesn't mean that it's not on its way."

I heard her words, but believing that I'd find a happy ending when I was trapped inside my own horror story was almost impossible to do.

We sat on that bench until the sun and whiskey had faded away.

When she offered to walk me home, I declined, knowing it was out of her way. As I walked through town, I noticed Jackson leaving The Silent Bookshop, and his eyes locked with mine. He was giving me that same frown from earlier with his hands stuffed deep into his pockets.

I gave him a smile, and he shook his head. *Deep breaths.* I gave him a tiny frown, and he slowly nodded. *Yes, yes, that feels right.*

He didn't want my fake expression, but the true one. The one that I never allowed myself to express in public.

He took a step in my direction, and I shook my head slowly, making him stop.

I couldn't have him near me because he made it seem like it was all right for me to be broken regardless of who was watching. If he came near me, I'd fall apart, and he'd catch me. Then I'd cry. Even though a big part of me wanted that, to feel unleashed, I knew I couldn't have his comfort. I knew I couldn't be sad on the streets of Chester with Jackson Emery's arms wrapped around me.

Too many people would wonder.

Too many people would care.

He lowered his head and turned away from me. He walked off into the direction of his cabin, straight into the shadows of the night.

A chill raced over me, and I knew it was due to him.

Even though we didn't truly know one another, his heaviness felt so familiar.

Out of everyone in town, I knew my heart most closely resembled the monster who I'd been told was nothing but darkness.

That was what I craved.

I wanted to sit in the dark and be okay with my feelings.

I wanted to bathe in the darkness and let go of the light.

I wanted to be free to feel whatever I wanted to feel without the fear of others' judgments being placed upon me.

I wanted to be free.

If only for one night…

CHAPTER SEVENTEEN

Grace

Mama set me up.

When she called me to say she wanted to apologize for everything that happened at the church service, I should've known something was up. She wasn't one to apologize—she was more one to request apologies.

When I arrived at her house a few days after finding out about Autumn's pregnancy, and I saw the bright smile on Mama's face, I knew something was off. I should've just stayed at The Silent Bookshop and avoided humans at all costs.

Especially Mama because her loyalty seemed to lay elsewhere.

My eyes locked with the man standing in front of me. "Finley."

He was dressed in that yellow polo that I hated, and he'd recently shaved.

I hated that I noticed.

"Why are you here?" I asked him.

Mama walked over to me and gave me a small smile. "I think it's about time you talk with your husband."

I huffed. "Are you kidding me?"

"Grace, I've been calling you," Finn stated.

"Have you? I couldn't tell because I blocked your number."

"Listen, I—"

Slap.

I slapped him hard against the cheek, and Mama gasped.

"Gracelyn Mae! What in the world has come over you?!" she barked, horrified.

I tilted my head in her direction. "Why in the world would you invite him here?"

"You wouldn't speak to him any other way," she told me.

"Can you blame me? After what happened?"

She looked baffled by my words, and I turned back to Finn. "You didn't tell her, did you? I shouldn't be shocked, seeing how you didn't even have the guts to tell me yourself. It's crazy I had to hear it from Autumn."

"Wait...she told you?" Finn's shoulders drooped, and he looked so pathetic. "Grace, I—"

"What's going on?" Mama asked, but I didn't have the patience to explain it to her.

I turned her way and shook my head in disbelief. "Would it kill you to choose me, Mama?" Would that honestly be the end of the world for you to put your daughter first?" I barked her way before storming out of the house.

"Grace, wait!" Finn said, chasing after me. I tossed off the high heels and hurried into the town square, which was packed with people and live music. Finn stayed right beside me, and as he caught up, he grabbed my arm and yanked me back, making me stumble.

"We have to talk," he told me.

"I have nothing to say to you," I snapped.

He grumbled and shook his head. "We need to discuss everything. Grace, I know it's probably hard to believe but, I still love you. I'm so confused and—"

"Finley, I swear if you do not take your hands off me, I will murder you," I shouted, making a few people turn our way. My heart rate kept climbing with each second. He was making me physically ill. The way he could stand there with his hands on my body and confess his love for me made me want to vomit.

It was so ridiculous—the whole concept of it.

He was just wasting his time speaking words of love, because I no longer believed in love.

"You're acting outrageous, Grace. Stop yelling in public," someone said behind me. "Keep your voice down." I looked up and saw Mama speaking my way, and her word choices stunned me.

"Mama, for the love of God, just butt out of my life!"

"Do not use the Lord's name in vain, Gracelyn Mae," Mama ordered me, but I rolled my eyes.

"What does it matter, Mama? He's not even real."

"What is getting in your head? Or should I say who?" she asked.

"What's that supposed to mean?"

"You've been seen around a lot with Jackson Emery, Grace," Finn stated. "Your mom called me because she's been worried about you."

I huffed. "She's worried about me being seen around with Jackson, but she wasn't worried about my husband being a cheater."

"Are you sleeping with him?" Mama asked.

"Excuse me?" My jaw dropped at her question.

"She wouldn't," Finn said, defending me, which irritated me more than ever. "She's too…well, she's Grace."

"What's that supposed to mean?" I asked him, my chest burning.

"What I mean is you're *you*. You would never do anything that would be…wrong. You'd never cheat on me."

"Said the cheater."

"I'm just saying, you're not…I don't know… You're just you. You're not a rebel or anything. You just don't have it in you to do such a thing. You never act out. You were always the safe choice."

I hated him. I hated him because it was clear he was calling me tame, boring, basic. I hated him because he was right, too.

I was loyal to others, and I always had been. I never acted out, no matter how tempted I was, because I feared how it would affect others' lives. I worried how people would label me. I was afraid of how others would view me if I did certain things they deemed ungraceful.

I lived my whole life quietly, staying in line in order to live the life Mama taught me I was supposed to live.

I did it all right, too.

I was faithful, honest, kind, and well-behaved.

Yet at the end of the day, when all was said and done, none of it mattered. He still chose her even though I was everything I thought he'd ever wanted. He still fell into her bed even though I was the "safe choice."

"I'm never going to speak to you again. Do you understand that, Finley James? Never," I told him repeatedly.

"Please, Grace. Stop talking," Mama scolded me. "Now, let's go inside to discuss this in a private setting. You're acting immature."

Immature?

She hadn't even seen immature, but I was tired that afternoon. I was tired of being told what to do, how to act, what to be. I couldn't even think of the last time I made a choice that was mine and mine alone.

Yet she had the nerve to call me immature.

So, that's exactly what I became.

"Excuse me, excuse me," I said, hurrying to the stage where a band was playing. I cut right in. "Sorry, Josh, I'll get the microphone back to you in just a second," I said, using my deep Southern belle charm voice as I grabbed the microphone from the stand. "It's just that I wanted to clear up some of the rumors circulating around town lately about Finley's and my relationship."

"Gracelyn Mae, get off that stage right now!" Mama barked from the wing of the stage.

I gestured toward her. "If y'all didn't notice, the Queen of Chester showed up tonight. Let's give my mama, Loretta Harris, a big round of applause. Isn't she a beauty?" Everyone started clapping for Mama, and she gave her big Southern fake smile and waved.

Then she hissed toward me, and said, "Give me the microphone."

"Sorry, Queen," I stated, slightly bowing toward her. "You can have the microphone in a second, but first Princess Grace is going to say a few words if that's okay." I turned back to the group of individuals staring my way, and I took a deep breath. "First and foremost, it feels good to be back in Chester. This place is the best home I've ever had and—"

Before I could finish speaking, the microphone went out, and I turned to see Mama holding the unplugged cord in her hand. She looked pleased that she cut me off, and that only made me angrier.

I dropped the mic. "It seems we are having some technical difficulties, so I'm just going to need y'all to stay really quiet for a second as I give you all the great news! It turns out that we're expecting a child!" I exclaimed, and I listened to the gasps in the area, and my eyes zoomed in on Finn. "But by 'we' I don't mean Finley and me. That's not the 'we' he has anymore. His 'we' is now him and Autumn Langston, my best friend. You all know her. Bible study teaching Autumn, the woman who's been screwing my husband for the past few months." When I spotted Autumn in the crowd, she was frozen. "They are expecting their first child, so if we could all just give them a big round of applause." The space stayed quiet, and I began slow clapping. I was the only one clapping at all. I then stared straight into Finn's eyes and took a deep breath. "Congratulations on the pregnancy, Finley James." I blinked once and fought the tears that were trying to come. "I know it's what you always wanted."

With that, I stormed off the stage, and Mama had a horrified look in her eyes. "Grace…I didn't know…" she told me, but I didn't care.

"Don't you have a son you should be consoling during this hard time?" I asked her. "I'm sure Finn could truly use your support."

I brushed past her, and past everyone who was now whispering about me and the nightmare that was my life. I just kept walking faster and faster until I found myself standing in front of Jackson's cabin door, banging on it repeatedly. I had finally done something outside of my good girl nature. I hadn't done the right thing, Lord knows I was wrong, but still, somehow it felt oh-so-good.

CHAPTER EIGHTEEN

Jackson

Grace was out of breath as I opened my front door. She'd been pounding on the wood like a madwoman, and when caught sight of her, she even looked the part.

"Hi," she said, her breaths heaving in and out.

"Hi," I replied.

"Can I come in?"

I stepped to the side, allowing her access.

She began to pace the living room, and I could almost feel how crazed her mind had to be. Her steps were quick and erratic, her mind spinning fast.

"What is it?" I asked her.

"I need you to sleep with me," she blurted out.

"What?"

"I said I need you to—"

"No, I heard you."

"Then why did you say what?"

"Because even though I heard you, it just seemed so damn ridiculous." I raised an eyebrow. "Are you drunk?"

"Nope, and I'm thinking straight for the first time in a while."

"And thinking straight means wanting to sleep with me?"

"Yes."

I kept my eyebrow raised. "Are you drunk?" I repeated, and she began to blush.

"No, Jackson. Come on, I'm serious."

I leaned against the wall and crossed my arms. "Who pissed you off?"

She kept pacing. "It doesn't matter. All I need to know is if you'll have sex with me or not."

"Princess—"

"*I'm not a princess!*" she snapped, pausing her steps. She looked my way, and her stare was heavy as she released a weighted sigh. "I'm tired of this. I'm tired of being the princess, the good girl, the girl next door. I've been that all my life, and it's gotten me nowhere. It's gotten me nothing."

"So the next step, obviously, is sleeping with me," I joked. She walked over and stood in front of me.

"Yes."

"Why's that?"

"Because you're the exact opposite of good."

"I'll take that as a compliment."

A smirked lifted the corner of her mouth. "I knew you would."

"Grace, you don't want to do this…" I warned as she moved closer.

"Yes, I do."

"People in town say I'm dangerous, and they aren't wrong. I'm unstable sometimes, lashing out without warning."

"That doesn't scare me. Besides…" Her steps moved her closer until we were standing inches apart. My back was still resting against the wall, and her breaths were coming faster and faster with each second. "Maybe I need a little danger in my life."

Her hand brushed against my neck, and I closed my eyes as the feel of her fingertips danced across my skin.

"You'll regret it," I promised her.

She lightly snickered in disbelief. "Do you ever regret sex?"

I opened my eyes and burned my stare into her blues.

She heard my reply without me speaking a word. Hesitation hit her for a moment as confusion swarm in her stare.

"I use it to forget," I confessed.

"To forget what?"

"Everything."

She nodded slowly. "I want to forget, too."

"Forget what?"

"Everything."

Two people who wanted to forget everything together…there were only a million ways that could go wrong.

"This is a bad idea," I warned.

"Yes," she agreed. "But still, I want it."

I grimaced. "You're sad."

"Yes." She nodded. "You're sadder."

Yes.

Her hands landed on my chest, and she looked up into my eyes. "You don't scare me, Jackson Emery."

"I should."

"Why's that?"

"Because sometimes I scare myself."

She still stayed so close. Her body pressed against mine, and dammit if I didn't pull her closer—how could I not? Gracelyn Mae invoked that odd sense of familiarity I hadn't ever felt before.

Even when you didn't want her near you, you somehow found yourself moving closer.

My hands against her lower back as her hips made contact with mine. What was it about her that forced my body to go against my mind?

"I've read about boys like you in books, ya know," she whispered, her fingers slowly spinning spirals on my chest.

"Oh, yeah? What did those books teach you about boys like me?"

"Well…" She bit her bottom lip, and with a small inhalation, she whispered, "They taught me to stay away."

"Then why are you so close?"

She tilted her head up, looking me straight in the eyes. "Because in those stories, the heroine never ever listens."

"And then there's trouble?" I asked.

"Yes, and then there's trouble."

From the way she said those words, I knew trouble was exactly what she was in search of. We were the classic cliché. She was the good girl next door, I the monster from around the block. We were perfect opposites for the perfect storm, and she was asking me to be her next flaw, her greatest mistake.

And, well, who was I not to live up to her request?

"I could destroy you," I warned.

"Or save me."

"Is it worth the risk?"

"Isn't it always worth the risk?"

The more she touched me, the more I wanted to touch her back. I wrapped my hands around her wrists flipping us around so she was now against the wall with her hands above her head. "I have rules." I leaned in closer, lightly brushing my lips against her neck. God, she smelled good, like peaches and my next sin. "You can't break these rules, either." My tongue rolled from my mouth and circled against her neck before I gently sucked her skin.

She shivered at my touch. "What are they?"

"Rule one," I whispered, my mouth moving across her collarbone. "You never stay the night."

"Check."

"Rule number two," I said, dropping her left arm to the side. Taking my hand to the bottom of her blouse, I slowly raised it up and massaged her skin. "You never develop feelings."

"That's easy enough," she replied, her breaths uneven as I teased at the top button on her jeans. "I don't believe in feelings anymore."

I didn't know why, but that made me sad for her. I, too, didn't believe in falling for people, but that was my norm. Grace seemed the type to believe in something bigger than love, so the fact that her belief was completely gone was a bit surprising.

Maybe we had more in common than I thought.

"Rule number three…we don't talk about my life."

"Like ever?"

"Never."

"Okay."

"And lastly, rule number four…" My mouth brushed against hers, and I slid my tongue slowly across her bottom lip. "If your favorite pair of panties get ripped, don't expect me to replace them."

Her cheeks reddened. She blushed so easily, and my new mission was to make her blush throughout the whole evening.

Our lips stayed lightly pressed against one another, and I breathed her in as she rested her left hand against my chest. "I have a rule, too," she told me.

I cocked an eyebrow. "And it is?"

"You don't sleep with anyone else while we're sleeping together." She looked up and locked eyes with me. "I just need to be the only one for the time being. I can't do this if you're doing it with someone else."

"You want my loyalty?"

"Yes."

It wasn't just a want, but a need. The betrayal in Grace's life recently was so overwhelming that her heart needed something that was hers, even if only for a few moments in time. She needed me to only place my lips to hers, to only slide between her thighs, to only make her moan.

"Here's the thing," I started, staring down at the band on my arm. "I use sex to forget. I use it to keep me from using…other things. So, if it came down to me needing you at a moment's notice…"

"I'll be here," she promised. "I won't leave you alone."

My finger trailed down her neck, and I couldn't take my eyes off her. She was beautiful, that was a given, but she was also broken, just like me. My broken pieces stayed shattered, and hers intermixed with them.

We were just two broken people, uninterested in being fixed.

"Do something for me?" I said softly against her neck, kissing her lightly, slowly, breathing her in.

"What's that?"

"Go into my room and take off your pants."

She swallowed hard, biting her bottom lip. "Right now?" she asked, a bit unsure.

"Yes." I nodded. "Right now."

She walked past me and began to unbutton her blouse on the way to my bedroom. I couldn't help but smile at her, too, at her uncertainty, at her shyness, at her nerves.

It was always amusing when a good girl tried to be bad.

"And Gracelyn Mae?"

"Yes?"

"You might want to toss a prayer up to that god of yours and ask for his forgiveness."

She turned on her heels and gave me those wide doe eyes. "Why's that?"

My eyes locked on her pink bra, cupping her perfect breasts, more than enough to keep my hands full. I pulled my shirt over my head, walked in her direction and said, "Because you're about to sin tonight."

CHAPTER NINETEEN

Grace

My nerves were strung tight, and even though I wanted to do this—I wanted Jackson's body pressed against mine—everything I'd ever been taught was racing through my mind, telling me of the flaws in the activities I was about to partake in.

You're still legally married.
He's dangerous.
You are not this girl.
You're a good girl.

I silenced the voices in my head as best I could, because this good girl was tired of being tame. For once in my life, I wanted to roam in the wild and see what it felt like to be uncensored.

"You okay?" he asked.

I nodded slowly. "I'm okay."

"Good." He proceeded to walk toward me, slowly, with no missteps. "Now sit down on the edge of my bed." I did as he said, and he kneeled in front of me. "You're beautiful," he told me, and it made my skin tingle. "Do you know that, Grace? Do you know that you're beautiful?"

I couldn't reply. I couldn't remember the last time I'd been called such a thing, and even though I wanted to believe it, it was almost impossible to do so.

After enduring a betrayal as I have, you couldn't help but doubt every bit of your worth, but it seemed that night, Jackson was prepared to remind me with every single touch.

He placed his hands on my bare legs and gently kissed my inner thigh before looking up at my face. "You're nervous."

"Yes."

"You want me to stop?" he asked.

"No."

His fingers rolled against my panties, and he began circling his thumb against my clit, making me shut my eyes. I lay back, falling against the mattress, and my fingers clenched the bedsheets. My heart began to race faster than I'd known possible as he slowly pulled my underwear down, allowing his warm breaths to hit me. I arched my hips toward him, but he teased me slowly.

"Patience, princess," he whispered, kissing my inner thigh. His hands wrapped around my ankles and spread them apart. "We have all night."

Then, with no haste, with such perfected timing, he slid his lips against my core, tasting me, sucking me, sliding his tongue slowly inside, pulling his mouth away only to bring it back seconds later.

I didn't know it could feel like…

I didn't know it could be so…

Ohmygosh.

"Ja…" I exhaled, grinding my hips against his mouth as he began to destroy me in the best possible way. The more I moaned, the faster his tongue slid inside. *Deeper…deeper…* "Yes…" My breaths were uneven as his hands wrapped tightly around my thighs and his mouth explored me even more, my hands tangling in his hair and gently pushing his head farther down.

I'd never felt anything like that…had never known fingers and tongues could create such—

"*Jesus!*" I gasped as he slammed his tongue deep inside, faster and faster, pumping it in and out as I began to lose my grip on reality.

"No." He smirked. "Quite the opposite, actually."

The way he controlled every shake of my body with only his tongue…the way he pinned me down as my legs twisted and turned…the way I lost myself, and he tasted each drop—it was almost too much.

He moaned against me as if he was enjoying the act as much as I was. The more I wiggled, the more he explored, deeper and deeper, making me fall apart against his tongue.

As he pulled away, my legs trembled, and my chest rose and fell rapidly as I tried to gather myself.

"That was…that was…yeah." I heavily breathed out. "That was…holy crap."

He smirked as my body dripped in sweat. As he rose up from the floor, he began to unzip his jeans then slid out of them, removing his boxers next.

My eyes fell to his hardness as he licked his fingers clean, tasting me.

I knew it was foolish, but I couldn't stop staring. I felt my cheeks heating from my desires, from my nerves, from my wants and needs, which, at the moment, seemed to be the same thing. I wanted and needed him so much.

I'd only been with one man in my lifetime, and it was no secret that Finley wasn't working with the same type of equipment Jackson had.

He wrapped his hands around my ankles and locked his stare with mine. "That was only the appetizer." He effortlessly flipped me over to my stomach, and I moaned gently as I felt him climb on top of me. His hardness brushed against my ass cheeks, and his lips trailed up my back before he moved in closer to my ear and whispered, "Are you ready for the main course?"

Even though I eagerly said yes, I wasn't ready at all.

When Jackson Emery slid into me, thrusting against me,

pounding deeper and deeper, I knew I was making the choices no one thought a good girl like me would've ever made.

I was being the opposite of what the world expected me to be, and being bad? Oh, being bad felt so good.

He slapped my ass, and I asked him for more. I wanted it harder, and he fulfilled all my requests.

He didn't stop there…

He flipped me over again, he placed me against the wall, and he took me from every angle possible. I moaned, I cried, I begged for more and more.

He was untamed and uncensored as he fucked me hard and whispered dirty words into my ear. As he placed me on top of him, my nerves began to rise once more as my mind began to worry about his viewpoint of my body.

Yet with one small touch to my back, he lowered my face down on his and rolled his lips against mine. "You're beautiful," he told me once again. "Now fuck me harder than you've ever fucked."

And I did.

I rode him like he was mine and mine to keep even though that was so far from the truth. Our false reality was worth it, though. Those few moments together helped my mind slow down to a speed my heartbeats could keep up with.

He wasn't mine, and I wasn't his, but that night, we were something. There wasn't a name for it, only feelings.

It felt scary yet safe.

Fast yet slow.

Wrong yet still so unbelievably right.

He was able to get me off that night more times than I ever had at once in the past fifteen years of my marriage.

I now understood why bad boys were worth exploring. I understood why good girls found their way to Jackson's front porch. Never had I known what true trembling legs felt like up until that night.

When the time came for me to leave, I got dressed, and he walked me to his front door.

"I'll walk you home," he offered.

"It's okay," I replied. I bit my bottom lip and looked up at him. "Tonight was…"

"Yeah." He nodded and leaned against his doorframe as if he'd read my mind. "It was."

"Is it okay if this stays between us? Our arrangement? Not because I'm ashamed or anything, but this feels like the first thing that's just…mine."

"Princess, come on…" He smirked, and I felt it. It was the first time I'd seen him do it, and when that small dimple appeared in his left cheek, my broken heart pieces began to skip a few beats. "Who would I even tell?"

CHAPTER TWENTY

Grace

Our secret was Jackson's and mine alone. The only time we ever make contact was when we were in his cabin. Each time he touched me, he showed me a new world. He kissed me deep and hard sometimes and other times, so timid and slow.

I loved the way he made me feel, and how he almost cared for me in a way. He explored my body as if it was the only thing he'd ever craved, and then I'd leave his place with only the memories of his kisses until the next time I fell into his bed.

Nobody knew, and that made it more fun for me. I was creating this new world that was just for me. No one could scold me for any of my actions, and each choice I made was from my own mind, not filtered through others' thoughts and opinions.

That was my favorite part of it all, well, besides when Jackson's mouth explored every inch of me.

That was truly my favorite part.

When we crossed paths in town, we didn't even glance at one

another. Yet I knew he was there, and I was certain he was aware of my presence, too.

It was fun having our own secrets the world couldn't taint.

Each time I left his place, a different part of me ached in a beautiful new way.

I hadn't known that hands could fall against a body in such a way where it was gentle and wild all at once. He made me feel the safest I'd ever felt while bending my body in ways I didn't know it could move.

Jackson Emery kissed me in a way I'd never been kissed.

He kissed me in places my husband had never explored.

I loved every single second of it.

He went full beast mode when he undressed me, but he did it in such a thoughtful way.

A gentle monster…

I was in his control, yet somehow, he made it seem as if I was steering the ship. Every moan I made, caused him to work even harder. Every time I came, he made it his mission to make me come even harder the next time.

Every time I left, I was already thinking about the next time he'd let the monster come out to play.

"Did you twist your ankle?" Josie asked the next morning as I walked into The Silent Bookshop with a slight limp. The truth was, every single muscle in my body was sore from the night before at Jackson's. It had taken me about ten minutes to even get out of bed without crying, seeing as how every inch of me ached.

I smiled at Josie as she set a cup of coffee in front of me. "I had a crazy workout yesterday," I told her.

"That's good. Working your energy out is a good thing."

She had no clue.

She picked up her mug of tea and sipped at it as the bell dinged above the front door, and we both turned to see Jackson walking in. On all the previous days when he walked in, didn't look at a single soul, going straight through those magical doors to his darkened corner.

That morning, though, he did something different. As he walked into the shop, he looked up in my direction and gave me a half grin. I gave him the other half. Then he looked away and headed back to the reading area.

It was a quick moment—our brief interaction. For only mere seconds, our eyes locked and our lips turned, but it was enough to make Josie raise an eyebrow.

"What was that?" she asked, confusion covering her face.

"What was what?"

"Did…" She paused, doubting her own thoughts. "Did Jackson just…smile at you?"

"That was hardly a smile," I remarked.

"But he looked your way."

"It's not a big deal," I told her, feeling my cheeks heat. "It was just a glance."

She narrowed her eyes. "Why are you blushing then?"

"I'm not."

"You look like Ronald McDonald's nose—red as red can get," she told me, making my face heat even more.

"Stop it, Josie."

Her jaw dropped. "Oh my gosh." She gasped, leaned forward, and slammed her hands on the countertop. "What kind of exercise were you doing yesterday, Gracelyn Mae?"

I swallowed hard and placed my hands on top of hers. "You cannot say a word about it, Josie."

The level of excitement that filled my friend's eyes was legendary. She began quietly celebrating with a small dance. "Oh my gosh, you and Jackson Emery? You and Jackson?! How? What? But, what?!" she whisper-shouted.

"I know, it's crazy."

"It's brilliant," she corrected. "Gosh, if anyone deserves to get laid by the town bad boy, it's you." She raised an eyebrow. "Not that it's any of my business, but are the rumors true? About the size of his…*member*?"

I blushed more, pressing my hands against my cheeks.

"Sweet home Alabama, heck yeah!" she shouted, jumping up and down. "I mean, don't get me wrong, I love my husband more than life, but I've seen that Jackson Emery guy shirtless, and I just imagined that a man who was that built upstairs couldn't be that built down below."

"The rumors are more than true," I told her, leaning in. "Times a million."

"I see why you're walking with a limp," she joked.

"It's weird. It's just…my life is a mess," I confessed. "Every single aspect of it is hard and confusing except for my time with Jackson. It's not…complicated. It just is. And, when I go back to Atlanta after the summer, it will be over and done with."

"A summer of love," she expressed.

"A summer of *lust*," I corrected. "Lust and nothing more."

"Well, regardless, I'm glad you've found an escape from the madness. Every person deserves a haven, Grace, a place they can go to breathe fresh air, because sometimes life can be toxic."

"Yeah, I'm just worried, I guess. If people found out, it would be a mess for both of us, for my family—my mom would flip out."

"Well, that's easy," she told me. "Just don't let people find out. You'll both need to stop looking at each other like that, though."

"Like what?"

"Like you have a secret between your legs."

"It's so stupid, but it's fun, you know? Almost like a game. It feels dangerous in a way."

"You deserve a bit of living on the edge. Have fun. You've lived your life being everything to everyone else, and now it's your turn to live a little. Now, tell me everything—like how good was it?"

I bit my bottom lip and leaned in again. "Have you ever heard of a move called the spider?"

"Oh, yeah." She nodded. "I'm guessing you've recently been tied up. Have you tried the wango tango?" she asked me.

I raised an eyebrow. "I've never heard of that."

"Here, give me your phone." I handed it over, and she quickly moved her fingers around. "Okay, I just downloaded the karma sutra book Harry and I rushed through in no time. You'll love it. Plus, you don't even have to go to the gym anymore. I didn't sculpt this butt of mine doing squats in the gym, that's for sure."

"All of this is so new to me. All Finn ever did was missionary."

Josie cringed. "Not even with you on top?"

"He said he didn't like seeing my body in that position."

"Ohh, I get it," she remarked, nodding slowly. "He's gay."

"What?"

"Honey, no straight guy would ever care about the shape of a woman on top of him. All he would see is boobs in his face, and he would be a happy camper. So either he's gay or just a straight-up asshole, and no matter what, you're better off without him."

I smiled.

I was so glad I'd reconnected with Josie. I needed her humor more than I knew.

"Next time you see Jackson, do the firecracker move," she told me. She shimmied her shoulders a bit and gave me a wicked grin. "It's explosive."

CHAPTER TWENTY-ONE

Grace

"Gracelyn! Gracelyn Mae! It's me, Grace! It's Charlotte!"

My body tensed as I walked through the streets of Chester and heard Charlotte's voice shouting my way. I only had two choices. I could break out into a sprint—*no thanks, running is gross*—or just stop, engage for a few minutes, and then go off on my own to hide away from the world.

I paused my steps, took a deep breath, and then put on the biggest fake Southern smile I could muster. "Oh hey, Charlotte. How are ya doing this wonderful Friday morning?"

"Oh, look at you, all chipper," she remarked, patting my arm. "I'm glad to see you're in high spirits after that weird speech you gave at the music festival last weekend." She pursed her lips and crossed her arms with that big ole smile. "It's a shame, ain't it? You think you know someone, and then, BOOM, they just turn out to be somethin' else, though I'm sure there were warning signs you ignored, right?"

I parted my lips to speak, but she cut me off.

"But what is your papa always saying? God works in mysterious ways, and ain't that the truth. I hope you're still praying each night."

Only to Jackson's body...

"Well, thanks for the chat, Charlotte, but I really need to get a move on. We'll talk later."

"Yes! Tonight at the get-together," she told me.

"Oh, sorry, I can't make it today. I'm busy tonight."

"But your mama said you'd be there, so I'll see you later! I put you down for an apple cobbler! Okay, I gotta run! Bye!" she said, hurrying away before I could answer.

I was on my way to Judy's house, but I did a quick one-eighty because it was time for me to have a heart-to-heart with Mama.

I couldn't take any more of her trying to control my airwaves.

"You're going to Charlotte's for chitchat night, Gracelyn Mae," Mama ordered as she shifted through binders of the workshops held at the church throughout the summer. I paced the living room, beyond annoyed with her antics.

"No, I'm not. You can't just do this, Mama. You can't tell people I'm going to do things that I'm not."

"But you are," she commanded, closing the binder. "Especially after that outburst you had in town last weekend. Look, I get it—you're going through some kind of midlife crisis right now, and you feel lost, but you cannot keep running from the people trying to help you."

I huffed, blowing out hot air. "Charlotte Lawrence is not trying to help me. None of the girls who go to that type of gathering are trying to help. They're just digging for gossip."

"Well, maybe if you didn't show up, tossing around comments about a cheating husband, people wouldn't have anything to gossip about."

And just like that, I was to blame once again.

"I'm not doing any of this, Mama. I don't want to do any of this at all."

"That's fine," she agreed, nodding slowly as she stood. "Keep thinking of yourself."

"Someone has to think about me, seeing as how you aren't."

"What do you want me to do, Gracelyn Mae? You want me to have an outburst in town toward Finley? You want me to publicly humiliate Autumn? You want me to blacklist their families and make such a scene in public that Charlotte has enough gossip for months to come? We are not those people. We do not grab microphones and air our dirty laundry. I raised you better than that."

"I had a moment," I said quietly, feeling a knot form in my gut.

"We don't get moments!" she barked, standing tall. "We aren't allowed to stumble. How do you think your little antics affected everyone around you? How do you think it fell upon me? And okay, if you don't care about me, at least care about your father—how do you think this makes him and the church look? People are asking how he can run a church if he cannot even control his own daughter."

I didn't have a word to say to her because I hadn't thought about any of that.

"Your actions have consequences, and your choices affect others. So, you can keep throwing a fit and acting out like a five-year-old, or you can remember all you have been given, all that was handed to you by your father and me, and you can fall back into line, Gracelyn Mae."

"Leaving so soon?" Jackson asked as he walked back into the bedroom after grabbing us two glasses of water.

"Yeah, I'm sorry. I just…I have this stupid meeting at Charlotte Lawrence's house."

"Charlotte Lawrence? That gossip nut?"

"That's the one." I sighed.

He placed the glasses on his nightstand and crawled up on the bed, wrapping his arms around me from behind. "She's batshit crazy."

"I know, but after my outburst, my mom's convinced I have to do damage control, which includes attending Charlotte's events."

"Bullshit," he huffed, turning me around to face him. "You didn't do anything wrong."

"I'm a Harris, and we don't act out in public—that's the rule."

"Fuck the rules. Your husband was an asshole, and your best friend was a bitch. They deserved to be called out."

"Maybe, but not by me. I don't have that right."

"Wow…" He whistled low. "Your queen really did a good job of brainwashing you into believing you have no power of your own."

"You don't understand," I told him.

"You're right, I don't." He dropped his hold on me and pulled back a bit. "You allow these people to control every aspect of who you are. It's like you don't even care," he said, his voice sterner than I thought it should be.

"It's fine."

"It's not."

"It's just one meeting."

"You can't be that naïve, Grace. Come on, you're their fucking sheep, and you are walking into a lion's den."

"Why do you even care? I thought we were just sleeping together," I asked him, narrowing my eyes in his direction.

"I don't care," he barked, his face red as he shifted his glance away. "Go ahead and be exactly what they want you to be. That seems to be working out great for you. You married the guy your mom wanted you to—perfect. You had the best friend your father probably pushed you toward—awesome. Everything anyone has ever done for you has worked out swimmingly. It would be a shame if you made a choice for yourself, wouldn't it? But you must be too weak to do such a thing."

"Fuck you," I snapped, my eyes watering over.

"You already did, princess," he snapped right back.

I leaped up from his bed, feeling like a fool as I collected my things. "Maybe you're right. Maybe I am controlled by other people but look at this—the one time I do make my own decision, I end up with a monster like you," I shouted, my chest rising and falling quickly.

"Yeah, that was a shitty decision. You should've rethought it." He was becoming cold again; being with Jackson oftentimes felt like whiplash—first sour, then shockingly sweet, then vice versa.

He sat there snapping the bracelet on his arm, and then I looked up at his face.

"I came to you because you felt familiar," I confessed. "I came to you because out of everyone in this town, you were the only one who made any kind of sense to me because you were no one's puppet, but then you act like this. You snap for no reason, and I just don't get it. You're not a monster, Jackson, and I don't understand why so often you find the need to act like one. I'm done trying to understand," I told him before turning to leave. I reached his front porch, but when I heard his hard voice calling after me, I paused.

As I turned to face him, his face was red, and his breaths sawed in and out. His hazel eyes locked with mine, and I saw the debate in his mind as he leaned against his doorframe.

"I'm not good with words," he confessed. "I have all these thoughts in my head, and I don't know how to express them, so instead, I snap. I come off as hard and aggressive when I can't express myself in the right way."

"And what were you trying to express just now by shouting at me?"

"I…" He took a deep breath and closed his eyes, snapping the bracelet on his arm. "It pisses me off." His eyes reappeared, and when I stared into them, I didn't see his anger, just the gentleness that sometimes slipped out of his soul. "It pisses me off the way these assholes treat you. It pisses me off watching you not stand up for yourself. It pisses me off that you act like you don't have a voice. It pisses me off that I don't know how to talk to you…"

My heart was racing as he stuffed his hands into his pockets, and looked down at the ground. "I know it makes no sense, Grace, but I just think you deserve more, and the people in this town aren't going to give it to you. They are tearing you apart, not stitching you back together, and it pisses me off that I can't express that in a clear way."

I swallowed hard. "I think you just did." He looked up, and I wiped the tears falling from my eyes. "I don't know who I am," I confessed.

"What do you mean?"

"I mean exactly that. I don't know who I am. Someone else has always handled everything I've ever done. I went out with Finn on a blind date. I became a teacher because my mama told me it would be a good choice. I followed Finn around like a sad puppy dog. I never made a choice that was of my own doing. The only thing I've ever done for myself is get that pink car years ago." I waved my hands back and forth and began pacing, my heart rate climbing higher. "Who am I? Who is Gracelyn Mae? Do I even exist or am I just a robotic creation of the environment I was brought up in? You know what I mean?" I asked.

"Grace…"

"I don't know how I like my eggs."

He narrowed his eyes, confused as ever. "What?"

"My eggs—I don't know how I like my eggs. Whenever I go out, for as long as I can remember, I've never ordered for myself. I always say, 'I'll have what he's having or what she's having.' Not once have I ever chosen my own food. Finn always ordered scrambled eggs, so guess what I always had?"

"Scrambled?" he said, playing along with my crazed mind.

"Exactly! But that's not all," I exclaimed. "I just realized I don't know anything about myself. I don't know what kind of movies I like. I don't know what clothes look good on me. If I could go on a solo trip anywhere in the world, where would I go? I know where my sister would go. I know where Finn would go. Heck, I even know where Mama would end up—but me? I have no dang clue because I don't know what I like or what I would want to experience. I think that's the hardest part of being alone right now.

"I don't know how to do it. I don't know how to be alone with myself because I don't know who I am. I've always been the pastor's daughter, then I went straight into becoming a wife, then I was a teacher to my students, and if the universe hadn't fought me, I would've gone straight from being a wife to becoming a mom. There has never been a moment when I've been able to just fully be Grace. Now I'm in a place where I have that opportunity, but I have no idea how to go about finding myself."

Jackson studied me for a moment with his eyes narrowed and his arms crossed. The way he tilted his head to the left and then to the right intrigued me. What was going on in that mind of his? What was he thinking?

"Okay," he finally said, dropping his hands and rolling his shoulders back. "We're gonna start with the basics."

"What do you mean?"

He took my hands into his and walked me back into his cabin. He moved me over to his kitchen table where he pulled out a chair and had me sit. He then went into the refrigerator, grabbed a carton of eggs, and set them right in front of me. "We're going to find out how you like your eggs."

I smiled and felt a fresh wave of tears coming my way. "Sounds good."

I sat patiently waiting as Jackson began cooking. "First, we're going to do scrambled—both hard scrambled and soft scrambled."

"I didn't know there was more than one way to scramble eggs," I told him.

"By the end of the night, you'll be shocked by my egg-making skills. I eat eggs every day before I work out."

"Oh? You work out?" I mocked him. "I couldn't tell at all. You're kind of skinny for a guy who works out," I joked. Jackson had more muscles than I knew a human could have. To put it frankly, he looked like a Greek god.

"Shut up," he huffed but in such a light way. I swore it almost looked like he was blushing.

"Do you get embarrassed by how handsome you are?" I asked.

"Don't call me handsome."

"Aww, it makes you nervous, doesn't it, *handsome*?"

He gave me a hard look, but those eyes still looked playful. "Don't make me spit in your eggs."

"Touché."

He brought me the first round of self-discovery: hard scrambled and soft scrambled.

I picked up a fork and ate them.

Meh.

Not a fan.

"I don't like how they feel in my mouth," I told him.

"Rumor has it most girls like it to be hard in their mouths to make it easier to swallow," he stated matter-of-factly.

"Yeah but…" I started, but then I paused. I replayed what he'd said in my head as my cheeks heated, and I began to blush. "Oh my gosh, Jackson! You're so inappropriate."

"Of course I am—I'm a guy." He finished eating the eggs for me. "Okay. Next up is an omelet," he declared, going back to the stovetop.

The omelet did nothing for me. He ate that, too. He also finished off the poached egg, the hard and soft boiled eggs, and when he set the over-easy egg in front of me, and I cracked it open, I literally gagged.

"You forgot to cook this one!" I shuddered.

He laughed, and I swooned at the sound. I hadn't known he knew how to do that—laugh.

"It's supposed to be—runny," he told me.

"It legit looks like an alien's brain landed on my plate, and then all of his insides oozed all over. That's disgusting."

He walked over to his counter, took out a piece of bread, and returned to the table. He proceeded to scoop up the nasty, runny guts and eat every last drop. Then he pulled out a chair and sat down. "Well, that's a wrap. All out of eggs."

I nodded slowly. "You know what? I don't think I like eggs."

He smiled, and I felt it. "So, first discovery of Gracelyn Mae: she's a woman who hates eggs."

"You have a dimple when you smile," I mentioned. "In your left cheek."

He dropped the grin, and I was sad that I'd even brought it up. "My mom had the same one in her right cheek."

"I'm sorry," I told him, growing somber. "About your mother."

He shifted around and shrugged. "It's fine. People die."

"Just because people die, doesn't make it fine, Jackson."

His brows wrinkled and he shook his head. "Yeah, well, I'm not the case study tonight. You are. So, let's get back to focusing on you. What's the next self-discovery task you have?"

"I don't know." I shrugged. "But I'm interested to find out who I actually am. Can I tell you a secret, though? One of the hardest things for me?"

"What's that?"

"I have a ridiculous fear of letting people down."

Jackson grimaced and shrugged. "You're gonna have to let some people down in order to find yourself."

"Is it even worth it, though?"

"Yes," he replied adamantly. "It's always worth it, and those who care will stay. Those who don't should've faded a long time ago."

"Have you found yourself, Jackson?" I asked him, curiosity filling me up inside.

"Nah." He gently shook his head and fiddled with the band on his wrist. I zoomed in on it and read what it said: *Powerful Moments*. "I don't know if there's anything left to find."

I was certain he was wrong, but by the way his body tensed up, I knew he was done with the conversation.

"I should probably get going," I said, clearing my throat. He nodded and stood from the chair. "Thank you for tonight, though. Truly."

"Of course, and I am sorry for my sometimes harsh personality."

I smiled, and as we walked to the front door, I thanked him once more. His arm brushed against mine, and chills raced up and down my body.

"Good night, Gracelyn."

"Good night, Jackson."

As I walked away, somehow still felt his touch.

"Grace?" a high-pitched voice said behind me, and as I turned, I mentally sighed as my eyes landed on the speaker.

"Hey, Charlotte. Hey, girls," I said to the gossip queen and her group of followers. "What's up?"

"Oh nothing, just coming from girls' night. We're off to get some ice cream. We were low on desserts, seeing how you didn't bring that apple cobbler." She pursed her lips and narrowed her eyes. "I don't mean to pry"—*Oh gosh, here we go*—"but did I just see you with Jackson Emery?"

I blinked my eyes, uncertain how to reply because she had obviously seen us, otherwise, she wouldn't have asked.

"Yeah, we just crossed paths."

"Oh, I see." She gave me a wicked grin and bit her bottom lip while the other ladies giggled, whispering things to one another. "Well, you know what they say about that man—he's all rock, even down below, if you know what I mean…and I'm sure you do." She giggled.

I gave her my fakest smile. "No, I don't know what you mean, Charlotte." Sweat was dripping from parts of my body I didn't even know could sweat even though I tried my best to play it cool.

"I'm just saying, I get it. Sometimes a girl just needs a break, and I can't even shame you for breaking with him. He's an awful human, but you can't deny how hard it is to breathe when he takes off his shirt to work down at his shop."

"His abs have abs," one of the girls noted.

"You don't know what you're talking about," I stated, trying not to lose my composure.

"No, sweetie, it's fine. Your secret is safe with us." She winked as she and her gaggle of women walked off in their high heels and fake personalities.

A knot formed in my stomach, and I tried my best to swallow it down.

Rumors of me and Jackson Paul Emery were beginning to float around, and I knew those rumors could lead nowhere good, especially with them starting from Charlotte's lips.

DISGRACE

I could already hear Mama's voice, ringing in my ear, saying, *I told you so.*

"I told you so," Mama hissed beside me as we sat in the church pew Sunday morning. The whispering voices were still speaking about me, but now their narrative included Jackson's name.

I felt like vomiting, but I didn't. I sat tall with no slump in my shoulders. *Fake it till you make it, Grace.* I wasn't fully confident in the realm of being myself, but I knew those people who sat behind me whispering would've judged me whether I was hooking up with Jackson or not, because that was what small-minded individuals do: talk about others.

"Are you happy?" Mama asked me. "Are you proud of yourself for what these people are saying?"

I took a deep breath. "I don't care."

"Excuse me?" she barked, somewhat stunned.

I stared forward at Dad preaching and shrugged. "I said I just don't care. I don't care what people think of me."

"Then you are a fool," she whisper-shouted.

"Quiet, Mama, you might miss an important message Dad's preaching your way."

She sat up straight, the veins in her neck popping out, but she didn't say another word.

For the first time in forever, I had stood up to Mama, and I'd have been lying if I said it didn't feel good and terrifying all at once.

My foot tapped against the floor rapidly as I tried to keep my conflicting emotions in check. Just in time, Judy placed a comforting hand upon my knee.

"You okay?" she asked, leaning in slightly.

"No." I placed my hand on top of hers and squeezed. "But I'm working on it."

Sometimes to find yourself, you have to let others down—parents included.

CHAPTER TWENTY-TWO

Jackson

"You need to stay away from my daughter!" Loretta Harris hissed, storming into the auto shop late one Tuesday afternoon. "She is not one of those women you use for your sick sex-capades!"

I looked up at her as a heavy sigh rolled across my lips, then went back to working on the car in front of me.

Did she just say sex-capades?

I had a new favorite word.

"Unless you got a car with you, I reckon you should leave," I muttered, grabbing a wrench from my toolbox.

She click-clacked over in her high heels and placed her hands on her hips. "I mean it, you-you-you *animal*. Keep your hands off Grace or else!"

"Or else?" I cocked an eyebrow. "I don't take well to threats," I warned her.

"Well, I don't take well to people coming for my family," she countered.

"No one's coming for your family, your highness," I mocked. "So, if you would please leave…"

"What's your deal with her anyway, huh? Are you just trying to get back at me for something?"

I pressed my hands against the car, rising to meet her stare. Her eyes matched her daughter's, yet hers were filled with hate. "What in the hell would I have to get back at you for?"

"When you came to me as a kid, asking for my help."

I snapped my band. *Deep breaths.* "I ain't got time for this." I rubbed my palms against my jeans and turned to walk away. "Let yourself out."

"You need to stay away from my daughter, or you'll regret it," she ordered once more, making me tense up.

"Once again," I growled, snapping my band, "I don't do well with threats."

"It's not a threat; it's a promise. If you keep crossing paths with Grace, I'll make you suffer."

I cocked an eyebrow. "How is that any different than what you and yours have done to me for so many years?"

"Listen—"

"No, you listen," I howled, moving in closer to her. "You don't come into my shop barking demands at me. You don't tell me what to do or how to do it, all right? This is my life, and you don't get to control it. I know you're used to having your minions do everything you want them to do, but I'm not your show pony, all right, woman? When you tell me to jump, I don't say how high, so how about you take your empty threats and get the hell out of my sight?"

"I wished you would've stayed gone all those years ago when you went to rehab," she told me.

"You should've prayed harder to that god of yours."

Her bottom lip trembled, which was the biggest sign of weakness Loretta Harris ever let herself show. Then she reached into her purse and pulled out a checkbook. "How much?"

"What?"

"How much do you want? I'll pay you any amount to stay away from Gracelyn Mae."

"Is that how you always get your way? With a check?" I huffed. "I don't want your money."

"How much?" she badgered, pulling out an ink pen. "I'll pay you for all of your land, too, if it means keeping you and your lowlife of your father out of my town."

"The last thing you want to do is talk about my father," I hissed. Even though I hated him, a Harris had no right to spit on his name. "Get out."

"Jackson—"

"Out."

"But you have to stay away from her!" she cried, her body starting to shake. I'd never seen her like that. She seemed terrified.

"What are you so afraid of?" I questioned, narrowing my eyes. "Are you afraid you won't be able to control her like you used to?"

"You don't know what you're talking about but just stay away. I swear to you, Jackson, if you don't, I will ruin your life."

"What life?" I asked her. Nothing about my existence resembled any kind of life. "Now, this is the last time I'm gonna say it. Get the hell outta my shop."

She began to walk away, and I called after her once more. "It must be killing you, huh? Being unable to control her." She raised an eyebrow, and I continued. "But maybe instead of attacking me, you should go after the asshole who broke her heart and got her best friend pregnant. Your loyalties are facing the wrong direction."

With simply perfect timing, Dad walked into the shop to see Loretta standing there. He held a bottle of whiskey in his grasp, and I cringed as he spoke. "What the hell are you doing on my property?" he barked.

"Just leaving," she snapped back. "I cannot wait until the day you leave this town. You and your son are nothing but trouble."

"Fuck off," Dad shouted as he threw the bottle in our direction. It shattered dramatically against the wall.

"*Jesus*, Dad!" I barked. "Are you fucking crazy?"

"Are *you*? Letting this woman into our shop," he grumbled, stumbling left and right.

"It seems the apple doesn't fall far from the tree," Loretta remarked. "When you're ready to sell this place, give me a call. In the meantime, stay away from my daughter." She stormed off, leaving me to deal with the mess that was my life.

"Bitch," Dad muttered, before looking my way. "I need you to get groceries," he ordered before turning to walk back to his place. "And more whiskey."

I hated the grocery store because there were always people inside strolling around like they had no damn better place to be. As I turned down the aisle to go grab some peanut butter, I paused when I saw Grace and felt my chest tighten.

I should've looked away, but I didn't...I couldn't.

She walked around nervously as people stopped her to speak at almost every turn. It was almost as if they didn't see her discomfort, or they saw it and just didn't care about her feelings.

She spoke with complete poise, hugging each person tightly and giving them the biggest smiles known to mankind, but those weren't the traits I noticed. I took note of her body language and the way her movements told her truths. Her shoulders rounded forward, her fingers tapped rapidly against her shopping cart, and her big smile was more forced than I'd ever known a smile could be.

When she'd hug one person goodbye, another set of nosy townspeople would stop her. The questions they asked her were so insulting and invasive, but Grace handled them very well—better than I would've.

She lived up to her name and the royal role she played.

After she left their side, I'd hear the individuals' nasty remarks, judgments, and lies.

It took everything inside me not to attack each person in that store. Maybe my father and I deserved the rude remarks. Maybe we made ourselves so dark and mean that the ugliness from the town was earned, but Grace?

She hadn't done a thing wrong.

I wanted to say something, but I didn't know what. I didn't know how to start conversations, especially with her, but still, I wanted to try.

"I'm shocked to see you're not buying any eggs," I said, walking up behind her in the frozen food aisle. Then I realized what a cheesy and corny comment that was for me to make. *Just do better, Jackson.*

She nearly jumped out of her skin as she turned to face me with a tub of ice cream in her hands. "Jesus, Jackson, you scared me."

"Sorry, didn't mean to."

She smiled, and I was pleased it wasn't her forced smile.

Why was I pleased?

I shouldn't have cared.

But still…she smiled, and I took note of it.

"No, not your fault. It's good to see you. I was actually thinking about you today. I saw you reading *This Savage Song* by Victoria Schwab a few weeks back so I picked up a copy. It was so, so amazing."

"Wait until you read the second book in the series, *The Dark Duet*. It's one of my favorites."

"It kind of shocks me that you love young adult so much," she confessed. "I just didn't picture that as your type of read."

"What did you picture?"

"I don't know." She shrugged her shoulders. "Horror."

She smiled, I smirked, and then we stood awkwardly in silence.

"Oh!" She cleared her throat and rocked back and forth on her heels a little. "I forgot to tell you—I learned how I like my eggs."

"Oh? And how is that?"

"In cake form."

I laughed.

"Gah, I like when you do things like that," she told me.

"Do what?"

"Laugh, smile, smirk—anything but frown."

I didn't reply, but I liked how she made me laugh, smile, and smirk.

"Your mom stopped by the shop to have a little chat with me," I told her, and she instantly cringed.

"Oh gosh, I have no clue what she said to you, but since I know my mother, I'm guessing I owe you an apology."

"It's fine. She's just a bit protective of you."

She raised an eyebrow. "Did she threaten you?"

"Only four or five times."

"Wow, sounds like she took it easy on you," she joked.

"Maybe with old age, she's becoming a softy," I replied.

Just then, a person walked by and made a crude remark about the two of us being seen together. I watched as Grace tensed up a bit.

"I've heard people talking about you, about your relationship with your husband," I remarked.

She nodded. "Outing my cheating husband didn't bring me the best attention. My mama ripped me a new one, claiming I acted in such a disgraceful manner. Now the nosy people are just loud and looking for more dirt. I didn't really think it through, I guess. I was just…I don't know, living in the moment."

"Sometimes you have to do that."

"Yeah, but it didn't help that I was recently caught leaving your place, and now they think you and I are…" Her words faded away and her cheeks reddened. "Doing what we're doing."

"Does it bother you? Them knowing?" I asked.

"Not because it's about us. It just bothers me that people have no tact at all. Now they have made up the idea in their minds that Finn and I were both unfaithful to one another, and they love to talk about it. They act like I can't hear their nasty comments when I walk away, but I can."

"Yeah, you always do."

"You know what's worse, though? When they have the nerve to say it straight to my face. Just earlier today, a woman said to me, 'You know, honey, maybe God would bless you with a child if you went back to your husband and stopped sleeping with bad seeds.' Can you believe that? Right to my face, even after I made it clear that Finn got Autumn pregnant! But all she heard was that I was sleeping with you, and she ran with that."

"I hate people," I blurted out, feeling anger building inside me for her.

How could someone say that to her?

How could people be so cruel?

Then I thought of all the nasty things I'd said to her when she first came into town. I was no better than the rest of them.

"It's fine, really. I'll get over it. I mean, it could be worse—I could be them, after all." She smiled, and it was beautiful. "They call you the fixer, you know."

"The what?"

"The fixer, and it's not just because you fix cars."

I cocked an eyebrow. That particular nickname hadn't made its way back to me. "Please, tell me more."

"The rumor is that after women sleep with you, they fix the issues in their lives, be it relationships, or job issues, or self-esteem. It's like your sexual prowess has the ability to fix any and every problem known to mankind."

"Not all superheroes wear capes." I smirked. "I'm just out here trying to make Chester the best town it can be, one vagina at a time."

"Well, I'll tell you this, if we keep up the wango tango, my life should be fixed in a few weeks at the latest." She grinned, biting her bottom lip.

God, she was breathtaking, and she didn't even know it.

"I'll wango your tango for the next week straight to help you out."

"Don't make promises you can't keep," she warned.

"Trust me, princess," I whispered, leaning in close, "I always keep my promises."

I loved the way her body reacted when I moved in closer. Then I remembered where we were, and I knew that touching her, even if ever so lightly, was a no-go.

She bit her bottom lip and looked up toward a few people

staring our way. It was as if we were everyone's favorite reality show. "I bet you they're having a field day with us just talking right now."

"I can go," I said quickly, not wanting to add to her torture.

"No, no. I mean, we're already sleeping together, right? Plus, I'm tired of always changing my life to try to fit into others' expectations."

"Another Grace discovery?" I asked.

"Turns out it's kind of fun learning who you are. If they want to gossip, they can, but I'm not going to stop talking to you or be ashamed when I know we're just two grown-ups doing grown-up things. Might as well give the people more of a story to make up."

"Careful," I warned, "once you start hanging out with the black sheep of the town, your wool starts shifting to a darker shade."

"My wool has already been changing. I'll take my chances talking to you. Is this what it's been like for you, though? Do you always get their harsh looks?"

"Yeah, but you get used to it. It only truly bothers me a few times."

"When's that?"

"When they talk about my father, or even worse, my mother."

She gave me those gentle eyes, and I had to fight to keep from losing myself in them.

"I think I owe you an apology," she said, looking right at me. "Before we even met, I had these ideas of the person you were. I was afraid of you because of the rumors people around town spread. I heard these horror stories about you and your father, and I just feel awful that I believed them."

"It's not a big deal," I told her. "No apologies needed. I'm sure some of the stuff you've heard is true. Plus, I'm sure you remember our first few meetings—I can be an asshole."

"Yes, but a nice asshole," she remarked.

"That's not a thing."

"It's definitely a thing."

"I judged you, too. I had this awful idea of who you were before I knew you."

"Why did you hate me so much?" she asked.

That was easy enough to answer. "Because I was taught to do exactly that."

"Well, do you still hate me?"

"No," I said. "Are you still afraid of me?"

"No," she replied.

"Well, that's unfortunate. I was really hoping to keep up my monster persona around these parts."

"Don't worry," she said, gesturing to the left where a group of girls were whispering. "I'm sure there are plenty who still think you're the spawn of Satan."

"Good. I can't lose my street cred," I remarked, and she laughed.

I liked it most when she laughed.

"Well, if you want to maintain your street cred, you should stop doing that."

"Doing what?"

"Smiling."

I turned my lips down into a dramatic frown. Before I could say anything else, out of the corner of my eye, I saw a grown man recording my interaction with Grace on his cell phone, and I listened to him call her a "church girl whore".

She heard it, too, and must've seen me tense up. "Let it go, Jackson," she whispered.

Apparently she'd forgotten our roles in this town.

She was the town's good girl.

Me?

I was the monster.

Without second thought, I walked over to him, snatched the phone out of his hands, and snapped it in half. Then I dropped the pieces into his cart and stared him dead in the eyes. "Do something," I threatened, crossing my arms. "I dare you."

His eyes widened with fear, and he swiftly pushed his cart away.

I walked back over to Grace, and she stood there stunned. "I didn't know phones could snap in half."

"Yeah, me either," I replied honestly.

"I know I should scold you for what you just did, but truthfully, that made me feel really good inside."

It made me feel good inside, too.

"It's a strange thing, though," she told me.

"What is?"

"When my Prince Charming is the rest of the world's Beast."

CHAPTER TWENTY-THREE

Grace

Each day that passed felt like a dream intermixed with nightmares. I saw both Autumn and Finn almost every time I left the house, and when I didn't see them, they still crossed my mind. My thoughts were trying their best to destroy me, but novels and Jackson both served as great distractions.

Even when the world was dark, words in books existed. Therefore, I knew there would always be light around me even on the darkest of days. I often wondered if that was why Jackson read, too—for a few moments of light.

When I arrived at The Silent Bookshop, Jackson was sitting in his corner, and when he looked up, he smiled right away, revealing that left dimple. I hoped that was a new regular thing—him smiling my way.

I smiled back and walked to my corner. When I got there, I saw a book sitting on my table with a Post-it note on it. The novel was *The Hate U Give* by Angie Thomas, and the note read:

I think you might like this, Princess.
-Oscar

My fingers ran over the cover, and I sat down and read for what felt like hours. The way the words pulled me in and didn't want to let me go made my heart beat faster and faster. You knew a book was amazing when you missed the transition from the sun shining to the sky fading to black. I sat back there until the store was about to close, and then I walked to the front counter where Josie's mom, Betty, was working.

She looked just like her daughter with those same loving eyes, and she signed my way as she said, "You've been here for quite a while—I'm guessing it's a good read."

"Better than good," I told her, holding the book to my heart as my eyes watered over. "It's one of those stories that just makes you want to yell and scream all at once." It was the kind of book that made your chest ache, and even though you want to put it down to take a breath, you'd rather flip the page to know more than worry about such a small thing like breathing.

Jackson was right; I did love the story.

"I saw Jackson leave it back there on the table for you," she mentioned as she rang me up. "Are you two friends?"

"No," I answered quickly. "But we aren't enemies either."

She signed, *"He's a good man."*

She was the first person I'd ever heard say such a thing about Jackson Emery.

"He's broken," she continued, "but good."

The idea that broken things could still be good was a thought that would stay with me for a while.

"I'm starting to see that in him—the goodness," I told her.

"His mother was in the same car accident with my husband the night of that huge thunderstorm. Did you know that?"

"Oh my gosh, no…I had no clue."

"Yeah. He was just a boy when he lost his mother. He adored her, and she adored him. After she passed away, I think a big part of him died, too, which is sad. I watched him go from this quiet boy in town to this bad seed. He loved her more than anything and losing someone that close to you is enough to make a person's mind go dark. So him coming here to this bookshop means a lot for me. Even though he doesn't speak my way or let me close, it's almost as if I can watch over him. I'm sure that's what his mother would've wanted. It's what I would've wanted for Josie if I ever passed away. Someone to look after my loved one."

"You're a good woman, Betty."

She smiled. "And he's a good man."

"Is it okay if I leave a book in his corner for him to find tomorrow?" I asked her.

"Of course, honey. I won't move it."

Walking back into the bookshop, I went in search of a novel to leave for Jackson. I thought back to books I'd read, and which ones made my heart race, wondering which one might do the same for Jackson.

My fingers landed on *Long Way Down* by Jason Reynold.

It had been a stay-up-all-night novel for me.

I grabbed it and a Post-it note and wrote:

It's written in verse,
and you'll feel each word within it.
-Princess

We kept it up, too, exchanging notes with different books. It was good to escape my current reality into the world of novels. Plus, Jackson had great taste in books, which made it easier to fall into every single word. Each time I found a Post-it note, I felt as if I was walking into a new adventure. Even though the words we exchanged were only on small pieces of paper, I felt as if I was learning more about the hard man who didn't let people in.

I was finally zooming in on the town's black sheep, and he was zooming right back in on me.

This one will hurt you.
Let it.
-Oscar

This one will heal you.
Let it.
-Princess

This heroine reminds me of you.
She cries on every page.
-Oscar

This hero's a total jerk.
Are you related to him?
-Princess

The last book you gave me was
fucking sad. Is the town's good girl
really that dark inside?
I loved it. Now, read this one, which is even darker.
-Oscar

You always give me books that make me cry.
-Princess

I've learned it's not too hard to bring you to tears.
-Oscar

Wow. Wow. Wow.
Five-star read.
More like this, please?
-Princess

Saw you at the bakery today. Your eyes looked sad.
Here's a book you can't help but laugh at.
-Oscar

He'd noticed me in town when I hadn't even seen him. It made me think of all the times I saw him walking around town with Tucker in his arms, or just exploring when he didn't know I'd seen him.

How many times had we stealthily noticed one another?

I started reading the novel he'd left me, and he was right—I couldn't stop giggling. I was shushed a few times by others in the bookshop for my laughter being too loud, but I couldn't help it. Sometimes, the best thing for a sad heart is a book that makes you laugh.

I knew I wouldn't be able to get through the next few chapters without breaking into a giggling fest, so I stood to go back to Judy's to read in my bedroom where I wouldn't bother anyone.

As I walked through the space, I thought about the characters in the novel and kept giggling to myself. Then I passed Jackson's corner, and he looked up at me.

I gave him half of a grin and held the book to my chest. "*Thank you,*" I mouthed.

He gave me the other half of my smile and nodded once before looking back down at his book. A half smile from Jackson Emery felt like so much more than the average person's full-blown grin.

CHAPTER TWENTY-FOUR

Jackson

Grace went against everything I'd been taught to believe about her. She was kind, gentle, and funny, the complete opposite of the snobby, rude, inconsiderate woman I had believed her to be.

That was hard for me to accept.

When you are taught to hate a stranger your whole life, it's humbling to realize you wasted energy hating something that wasn't even real.

Gracelyn Mae Harris was on a path of discovering who she was while I was on a path of erasing my judgmental thoughts about who I thought she was.

As she was learning about herself, I was learning about her, too.

She was weird, and spunky, and broken, yet somehow whole. I'd never come across a person who was so broken yet still whole.

The truth of the matter was that I liked her.

That was weird, too—for me to like a person. I didn't know

what that meant, mainly because I didn't understand my messed-up feelings.

On the following days, I tried my best to shake off my thoughts of her. If I'd learned anything about feelings, it was that they made no sense whatsoever. So I kept busy in the shop. When my head was inside a car engine and music was blasting through my headphones, I was able to tune out the world around me.

I was able to get her eyes out of my mind for a small moment in time.

When I heard the bell above the front door ding, I took out my headphones and looked up at the front of the shop. A man in a suit stood there with his hands stuffed in his pockets. Tucker walked toward him, wagging his tail as he always did, to greet the stranger.

The guy pushed Tucker to the side with his leg and told him to go away.

My body tensed.

The dude was already on my bad side.

I walked over to him and cocked an eyebrow. "We're closed."

"What? Your sign says open," he commented.

"Yeah. Then you shoved my dog. So, we're closed. You can fuck off and take your car elsewhere."

"I'm not here for my car. I'm here to talk about Grace," he told me. "I'm her husband, Finn."

"I don't care," I replied dryly.

"What?"

"I don't care who you are. You pushed my dog, so you can still piss off."

"Dude, that dog is hanging on by a thread. I probably did it a favor."

"Are you trying to die today, or are you just fucking stupid? Leave."

He didn't.

"I need you to stay away from Grace," he ordered me.

"I'm tired of people coming into my shop and telling me what to do."

Finn looked like the type of asshole Grace would've married. He stood as if he came from money, wearing a suit that probably cost more than my whole wardrobe. If that princess were to ever fall for a man, it would be that knight in shining armor. He and I were different in almost every single way.

I couldn't help but wonder how she found her way to me.

"Listen," he started, "she and I are on the course of figuring things out between us."

"You fucked her best friend. I think that case is closed."

He narrowed his eyes. "Don't act like you understand the whole story when you only know a few chapters."

"I don't care about the story, and I don't care about you."

"You're messing with her head, man. Her family is worried about her—I'm worried about her. She's not acting like herself."

"Maybe that's a good thing."

"*It's not*," he snapped. Obviously, my comment got under his skin. "She's not herself. She would never fall for a guy like you."

"A guy like me?"

"You know…" His words faded away, and he shrugged. "You're just not her type."

"She must be more into cheating assholes."

"Don't act like you know me or my wife. We've been through more than you know. So, do me a favor and stay away from her."

"No."

He cocked an eyebrow. "Excuse me?"

"She's a grown woman. She can make her own choices. Now, get out of my shop before you're unable to leave on your own."

He let out a low whistle. "Quite a temper you've got there. Okay, I'm going. But if you're smart, you'll keep your distance from Grace."

"I've never been known to be a smart man," I sneered.

He nodded and turned to walk away. Before leaving, he glanced over at Tucker. "You should seriously think about putting that thing down. It's a bit inhumane to keep him alive like that."

He flung the door open and left, but not before his words hit me hard in my soul.

I walked over to Tucker, who was back in his dog bed, and I pet his head. "You're a good boy, Tuck," I told him, rubbing right behind his ear. My voice cracked, and I studied his tired self.

You're a good boy.

After I finished up at the shop, I headed over to Dad's house to check in on him. He'd been pretty quiet over the past few days, which normally meant he was drunk, or…well, drunk. When I walked into his house, he was sitting on the couch, eating a TV dinner with a beer can in his grip. The only thing he ever watched was the news because he liked to remind himself exactly how much the world sucked.

He heard my footsteps, but he didn't turn to greet me. He never did, really. We didn't have the type of father-son relationship where we truly talked. We mostly just grumbled in each other's general direction and complained about the other being a pain in the ass.

"That shit is still in my shop," he sneered, stuffing a forkful of food into his mouth before chasing it down with the beer. "It's been weeks now, and that bitch's car is still in my shop."

I cringed. "Don't call her a bitch."

He glanced over at me and gave me his narrowed stare. His thick gray eyebrows lowered, and he let out a sound like a growl. "Who the hell are you to tell me what to do? Don't forget whose house this is, boy."

He loved to use that line about the house—and about the shop, and about the cabin next to the shop. He loved feeling as if he was the power behind everything we had. What he never seemed to notice was who paid the bills, who showed up to work, who cleaned the house. He hardly did anything with his time except drink and watch the news.

My father wasn't a person. He was the walking dead.

"I'm not gonna tell you again—get that car out of the shop," he ordered, but his words meant nothing to me. He didn't have the focus or the work ethic to actually have the car removed himself. Therefore, it would be fine.

He was all bark, no bite, just a bitter old man with a heart that no longer beat.

I had my mom to thank for that one.

"Don't you know what those people have done to this family, Jackson?" he asked me. "How they never once helped us? They put us through hell."

"Yeah, I know." But did he? Did he know how Grace had pulled him halfway across town to get him out of harm's way? Did he know how she'd showered him, cleaned his place, and sat with him just to make sure he didn't choke on his vomit?

Did he see her blue eyes when she cried, her shaking when she was afraid?

Did he not see how she was more than just a Harris? How she, too, had had things done to her? That she, too, had been through her own hell?

I blinked my eyes shut.

There she was again, filling my mind.

Why couldn't I stop thinking of her?

Shake it off, Jackson.

I walked over to his refrigerator and opened it, seeing all the food I'd bought was already gone. "You're supposed to tell me when the food's low," I told him.

"I ain't gotta tell you shit," he replied, flipping me off. I flipped him off right back.

Like father, like son.

"Is it true?" he asked.

"Is what true?"

"The rumors about you fucking that girl?"

Every inch of my body tensed. "What did you just say?"

"Is it true that you're fucking a Harris?"

I didn't reply because he didn't deserve a reply. It was none of his business what or who I was doing.

He stood and slowly approached me. "You stay away from that family."

"Don't tell me what to do," I growled, my anger building.

"No, I absolutely will tell you want to do! You are my son, and you live on my property. You will do as I say. You stay away from that girl," he barked, shoving my chest.

I allowed it the first time.

"Dad, keep your hands off me," I warned.

He shoved me again. "What are you gonna do? Huh? You gonna hit your old man? You gonna fight back?!" he snapped, slamming into me again. I took a deep breath as my hands formed fists. "Fight me, Jackson!" he hollered. "Fight!"

Still, I wouldn't lay a hand on him. Not once had I ever laid a hand on my father; no matter how many times he had put his on me. If I did, I would be just as bad as him.

"You're drunk," I told him.

"You like that girl, don't you?" he asked, narrowing his eyes at me.

"What?"

"Well, shit," he huffed, stunned. "You fell for a Harris? I shouldn't be surprised because you're weak. You're a piece of shit, and you're fucking weak," he hissed. "I shouldn't even be shocked that you're screwing a Harris," he barked. "You're a no-good lowlife."

"Shut up," I warned.

"You're a dumbass for thinking she'd ever truly want you."

"Stop talking," I told him, but he wouldn't. He couldn't.

"She's never going to choose you, Jackson. People who live in the heavens never fall for the ones in the slums. You think she'd actually fall for a monster?"

"Go away."

"No. You think she'd ever want something like you? A lowlife? Scum? A monster?"

"I'm not a monster."

"You are," he said, nodding. "I guess you get that from your old man."

"I'm nothing like you."

"No—you're even worse." He took a deep breath. "I treat people like shit 'cause I'm a fucking drunk. What's your excuse?"

He began to stalk off toward his bedroom, and I closed my eyes, taking deep breaths.

"Stay away from that Harris girl. I mean it."

I inhaled deeply and snapped the band on my wrist. My mind was spinning as I tried to wash my thoughts away. He was the worst one for me, the only person who was truly able to get under my skin and make me doubt every choice I'd ever made.

I want to use…

My heart was racing fast, and my vision began to blur as I paced back and forth.

I want to use…

I snapped my bracelet.

Powerful moments, Jackson. Stay strong.

My father was my worst nightmare, and I hated that when I stared into his eyes, I saw my own reflection staring back at me.

I want to use…

"Fuck!" I barked, raking my hands through my hair as I sat down on my father's couch. My foot tapped rapidly against the hardwood floor, and I pulled out my cell phone. I began scrolling through my old contacts, the people who were so good at supplying me with everything I needed to keep me high and fucked up.

That was all he thought I could be. Maybe that was all I ever would be…

I want to use…

I dialed the number. I listened to it ring, and when the voice answered, I swallowed hard.

"Hello?"

I sighed. "Hey," I whispered, feeling a knot in my stomach. "I need you."

CHAPTER TWENTY-FIVE

Grace

Jackson's voice sounded so broken over the phone, and it only took seconds for me to slide on my shoes.

When I made it to his house, he didn't say a word. He pressed his lips hard against mine, kissing me deep, kissing me long, kissing me as though he hadn't yet kissed me before.

He pulled my shirt over my head, and with one snap of his fingers, he had my bra unhooked. Our bodies tangled together, and as he moved on top of me and slid in, I almost cried out from the way he took over my body. Each thrust felt like a broken part of his soul intermixing with mine. He was low that afternoon, yet I welcomed the feeling. The truth was, it wasn't a good day for me either. I needed him to roll inside me, needed it hard, fast, rough, painful…

His hands wrapped around my wrists, and he pinned my arms over my head as he thrust deeper inside me, making me moan out his name as ecstasy overtook my body. We dripped in sweat and misguided emotions as he lowered himself on top of me and whispered into my ear. "I want you." He sucked my earlobe. "I need you." He slid in deeper and pulled out slowly. "I want you." he repeated as he slammed into me, making me gasp for air. "I need you."

My hips arched up, begging for more, and more, knowing it would never be enough.

The way we used one another was more than just sex, more than just wants or needs...

It was shockingly healing.

Without our bodies against one another, there was a real possibility that both of us would just drown into nothingness.

Our mutual sadness was the only thing keeping us afloat.

It was odd, how two sad people could make one another breathe.

"Are you okay?" I asked, getting dressed as he sat with his hands wrapped around the edge of the mattress.

"I'm always okay," he replied coldly.

I crawled over to him, kissing his shoulder blade. "You can talk to me, you know."

He grimaced and shut his eyes. "I don't talk."

I sighed, sensing the weight of the world on Jackson's shoulders. All I wanted to do was help him with his load, but he was completely against that. He lived in a world where he felt as if he had to carry all his baggage alone.

As I opened my lips to speak once more, Tucker walked past the doorway of the bedroom, moving slowly in the direction of the living room.

"He's been limping," Jackson whispered.

"Is he okay?"

He shrugged. "He's old, blind in one eye, and can hardly get around without my help."

"Is that why you carry him throughout town?"

"He loves the park. Even with all his issues, he loves the park."

"I saw you swinging with him one day," I told him. "With Tucker in your lap."

He nodded his head and looked down at his hands, which were clasped together. "He's a good boy. I'm just debating how selfish I'm being by keeping him around. He's just…" He took a deep breath and turned to me. I gave him a half frown as he kept talking. "He's all I've got, really."

"Tell me more about him." I climbed into his lap and wrapped my legs around his waist.

His lips parted, and he cringed as he placed his forehead against mine. "I don't know how to open up to people."

"Well, you don't have to open up to people, just me."

Before he could answer, his cell phone began to ring, and he released a heavy sigh as he moved me from his lap. As he answered the call, I tried my best to give him his space.

"Hey, Alex, what's up?" he said, then paused. "Are you shitting me? No, it's fine. I'll be right there. No, really, it's fine. All right, bye."

He hung up, and the weight of the world was solidly back on his shoulders. "I gotta get going," he said, gathering his clothes, and tossing them on.

"Is everything okay?" I questioned, standing quickly and wrapping my arms around my body.

"Yeah—well, no. My dad's just a fucking drunk, and is causing a scene down at the shop. I just gotta go handle him."

"Oh, well, do you want me to come with you?"

He shook his head. "No. If he saw you, he'd lose it even more. I'll talk to you later," he told me. "Just close the door on your way out."

CHAPTER TWENTY-SIX

Jackson

He'd lost his damn mind.

I made my way to the shop, where Alex was trying his best to contain Dad's drunkenness. I glanced around and saw broken glass everywhere. When my eyes made it to Grace's car, I cringed. All the windows were shattered, and the hood had marks on it that had probably come from the bat Alex was trying to pry out of Dad's hand.

"For fuck's sake," I muttered, rushing over to them. "Dad, what the hell are you doing?!" I barked.

"I told you to get that shi-shit outta my shop!" he shouted, slurring heavily.

I wrapped my hands around the bat and yanked it from his grip then tossed it to aside. I didn't even try to talk to him because I saw his level of gone in his eyes. He was seconds away from blacking out. In the morning, he wouldn't recall a thing.

There were many problems with what he'd done to Grace's

vehicle, but the main issue was that he took his drunkenness out on more than just her car. He'd messed up all kinds of things in the shop. Each breath I took only pissed me off more as I wrapped my arms around my father and forced him to walk away. I took him to his house and tossed him into his bedroom.

He kept grumbling about the Harrises family and how much he hated them. He went on about me, how much of a pain in the ass I was in his life, and then he passed the hell out.

Finally.

I went back to the shop and sighed as I looked around, resting my hands on top of my head. Alex already had a broom in hand and was sweeping up some of the shattered glass.

"Sorry I had to call you, man. It's just…he snapped. I was working on Grace's car when he walked in and blew up out of nowhere," he told me.

"Yeah, well, sounds just like good ole pops to me," I sarcastically remarked. "You don't gotta clean it up, Alex. I got this."

"Nah, it's no big deal."

"But it is," I groaned, looking around. "This is gonna cost us a lot of money in repairs. Of course, he'll never even know the damage he caused."

"He needs help, man—like real help, or one day he's gonna end up…" Alex's voice faded away, but I knew what he was hinting at—dead.

My greatest fear was getting that call, someone delivering the news that my father was dead, and with every day that passed, the fear seemed more valid.

I helped Alex straighten up the shop the best I could, but then I told him to call it a day and we'd get back to it tomorrow. He headed out, and I went over to Dad's front porch. I sat on the top step, listening closely to make sure he wasn't making too much of a fuss inside. I stayed there for minutes, hours, and the only time I moved was to go check on him in the bedroom to make sure he was still breathing.

Then I'd return to my spot on the porch where I'd probably end up spending the night. I couldn't go back to my cabin out of fear of what I'd wake up to come morning.

"Jackson?" a small voice said, making me look up from my hands, which I'd been staring at for the past few minutes. Grace was standing there, giving me a soft grin.

"What are you doing here?" I asked.

"I wanted to check in…I know you said not to, but I waited a while and wanted to make sure you were okay."

I took a deep breath. "I'm fine. I'm always fine."

She grimaced. "Can I sit with you?"

"If you want to."

She walked up the stairs and sat directly beside me. She didn't say anything at first. Maybe she didn't know what to say, or maybe she felt as if I just needed silence for a while. Having her sit there felt weird, like a comfort I hadn't even known I wanted.

"I hate apples unless they're cut into slices," she finally said, making me tilt my head in her direction. "I know magic isn't real, but whenever I see a good magic trick, I feel totally shocked. I suck at playing Uno, but I'll destroy you at Monopoly."

"Random facts?" I asked her.

She nodded. "To make you more comfortable."

Each moment, I liked her more. I took a breath. "I love hip-hop and country music in equal amounts. I sing in the shower. I eat Mexican food at least three times a week, and sometimes when I have a bad day, I sing 'Tubthumping' by Chumbawamba."

She inhaled. "I can't whistle."

"I can't snap."

"I cried during every Marvel movie," she whispered.

"I still tear up at *The Lion King*."

She smiled the kind of smile that could make even the saddest person feel better. "I think you're a good person."

"I think you're a better one," I replied. I swallowed hard and looked down at my hands. "And I think my life is easier when you're around."

"Oh." She said softly, tilting her head toward me. "So I guess that's a mutual thing. More facts?"

"Real ones or stupid ones?"

"Real is good," she replied. "I like real. I just didn't know if you liked to share that kind of stuff."

"I don't."

"Okay, then share whatever you want."

I took a deep breath and felt her arm lightly brush against mine, but I didn't say a word. There was an extended moment of silence before I built up the nerve to speak again. It was as if my brain was debating how real I wanted to get with her. We'd pretty much skated the surface of truths without ever really digging into them.

"Tucker was the last gift my mother ever gave me," I confessed. "She gave him to me a few weeks before she decided to leave my father and start her life with another man. I remember it like it was yesterday. My parents didn't let me have pets when I was little, said I was too young, but when I turned ten, they said I could get a dog. I think it was because I was bullied so badly and had no friends. They felt bad for how lonely I was as a kid. Then a few weeks later, she was packing her bags to leave."

"How did you find out she was going?"

"I saw my parents fighting in the living room. They fought for what felt like forever until Dad was just exhausted. I remember the defeat in his eyes. I think that was the exact moment he realized she was never going to be his again. She had chosen someone else, and he had a hard time with that. She was his everything—our everything—but, well, just because someone's your everything doesn't mean you're theirs. I'd begged her to stay. I literally threw myself at my mother and sobbed, pleading for her not to run away. My father had left the room because it was just too much for him. He'd checked out, I think. He'd already given up, and his heart was already so bruised, but I was just a kid. All I knew was that I wanted my mom to stay with me. I sobbed against her, pulling on her clothes, clawing at her, and she kept promising me it wasn't forever, that she would never leave me and we'd find a new normal. You know the last thing she said to me?"

"What?"

"She kissed my forehead, looked me in the eyes, and said, 'Take care of your father.'"

"Wow..."

"Shortly after, we learned about the car accident with Josie's father. My mom died instantly. We hadn't even had time to hate her for leaving before we were forced to mourn."

"Jackson, I'm so, so sorry," Grace said as she breathed out. "I cannot even imagine what that would do to a person's soul."

I felt my chest tightening, and as I spoke, I remembered why it was a subject I never opened up about. It was hard—too hard to relive those memories. It was too hard to face that guilt all over again. Whenever I thought of the night of Mom's death, I swore it felt like I was right back there, drowning all over again.

"Maybe if I had begged for a few seconds longer, then she wouldn't have been on that road at that exact moment. Maybe if I'd held her tighter..." I whispered.

Grace shook her head. "It's not your fault, Jackson. There's no way it was anyone's fault."

"I could've fought harder to make her stay."

"No. That's been a hard lesson for me to learn. It turns out it doesn't matter how much you beg someone to stay. If they want to go, they are going to leave regardless. All we can do—all anyone can do is learn the art of letting go, and no matter what, it's clear she loved you."

"She was my world, and after I lost her, Tucker became my best friend. I felt as if somehow, he was a part of her." I lowered my head and closed my eyes. "Say something to change the subject," I begged. "Say anything to make my mind stop spinning."

Grace cleared her throat for a second, and then she began to sing "Tubthumping" by Chumbawamba.

Almost instantly, I laughed. I needed that. I needed her there with me to ease me away from the darkness. "Great timing," I told her, releasing a breath. I allowed my shoulders to roll back and relax.

"I am really sorry, though, about your mother."

"It's all right. It's just the main reason I don't believe in love."

"You don't believe in love? Like at all?"

"Nah. I've just seen what love can be when it's found, and what it can become when it's lost. My father is who he is because of a broken heart, because he lost the love of his life. For months, he wouldn't get out of bed. He turned to the bottle to try to feel better. He tried to drink my mother out of his memory, and when that didn't work, he kept drinking and now he's just…broken."

"What was your father like? Before he changed?"

"Happy," I said. "That's the only word I can think of. He had the deepest laugh, you know, the kind that would rocket through your system and make you laugh yourself, and he was so in tune with cars. He could fix pretty much any and everything. I remember being young and watching him in awe."

"And now he's the way he is because she broke his heart."

"Exactly. I hate who he is right now, hate seeing him in this light because he pisses me off daily. I don't know who that man in that house is anymore, but I can't really blame him. The love of his life died in a pretty awful way right after telling him she didn't love him anymore. If I were him, I'd be crazy, too."

"Do you think someday he'll be okay?"

"I don't know. I hope so, but I really don't know. I've tried to get him into rehab clinics, but he doesn't want to hear it. I think he feels like what's the point? No matter what, she'll still be gone, sober or not. Plus, he'd still be sad sober—probably even sadder."

"Do you think broken hearts can be fixed?"

"Yes," I said matter-of-factly. "They just beat a little differently."

"So maybe someday your dad's heart can be fixed."

I shook my head. "For a broken heart to be fixed, the person has to want to repair it. It's kind of like a car engine—you can fix it if you take the time to work through the broken parts, but I think my dad's gotten used to how it feels—the hurt. I think that's where he's most comfortable now."

"What about your heart?" she asked. "Is your heart okay?"

"My heart left me the day she passed away."

"Oh, Jackson…" Her voice lowered, and my chest ached. "It hurts me that you're so sad."

We didn't say another word, but she didn't leave my side for a good while.

Grace didn't know it, but at that moment, I was so happy she stayed.

I was in desperate need of someone staying with me.

CHAPTER TWENTY-SEVEN

Grace

One Monday afternoon, I ran into Finn in town, and he kept calling my name.

I tried my best to ignore him, but he wouldn't let up. "Gracelyn! Grace!"

I gave up and turned to face him. "What is it, Finn?" I whisper-shouted, not wanting to draw any attention to us.

"I…" He raced his hand over his buzzed haircut. "I think we need to talk about things. I know you're angry, but we're still married, Grace. You can't just avoid dealing with me."

"You mean how you avoided dealing with me for the past eight months?"

"I know I didn't handle that well, and I want to apologize for that. Things have been a bit complicated."

"Autumn's pregnant with your kid. Plus, she told me you told her that *I* left *you*. Really, Finley? Is that how you get women to bang you? By making me out to be the monster?"

He lowered his head and cringed a bit. "I've made a lot of mistakes, but I'm trying my best to learn and own up to them. I owe you more apologies than I can even express, and I just want to have an open dialogue so we can talk. I think maybe marriage therapy… Or maybe we could start praying together again? Remember when we used to pray together?"

"Yes, and then each night you told me you were too tired to kneel beside me."

"I've been so lost, Grace. I just…I need you back. I don't do well without you in my life."

What?

I was baffled.

Completely baffled by his words.

"You disgust me," I told him, turning around and walking away.

There was nothing therapy, prayer, or apologies could fix between us.

He shattered our relationship all on his own, and the pieces would never fit back together.

"Why are you sleeping with him?" Finn asked, his voice not low at all, forcing me to turn back around.

"Excuse me?"

"Is it to get back at me? Because I hurt you?"

"I cannot believe you right now."

"He's dangerous, Grace, and like, what? Half your age?"

"He's twenty-four, Finley. That's nowhere near half my age."

"Yeah, but he's pretty much a kid compared to you. Plus, he sleeps with everyone in town."

"It seems that you two have something in common," I remarked, rolling my eyes.

"Do you really want to be just another number to him? You're not being smart, Grace, or safe. He could have caught something from those other women. He could be passing it on to you."

He didn't see it, did he? How ironic it was that he—my cheating husband—was telling me how I was being unsafe when he had the nerve to crawl into bed with me many nights after his countless affairs.

"We're not talking about this," I told him.

"Okay, well, it's clear that you won't talk to me or your mom, but you need to talk to someone. Maybe Judy? She's always been levelheaded. You need an outlet that isn't Jackson Emery."

"You don't get to have any input on my life anymore. You are no longer involved in what I do during my free time. The same way I'm no longer involved in yours."

I walked off to Judy's house, trying my best to shake off Finn and his words.

He was like a nasty tick that wouldn't leave me alone. Worst of all, he seemed delusional. Almost as if he expected me to simply let his infidelity slide because my love should be strong enough to forgive any wrongdoing he bestowed on me.

As I returned to Judy's place, I paused on her front porch as I glanced through the window. My sister stood behind a podium with a wooden spoon in her hand as if it were a microphone, and she projected her voice as if speaking to a packed auditorium. The more I listened, the more I understood what she was doing: she was giving a sermon.

My heart jumped a little because she was doing amazing, too. I'd never seen that side of Judy. I didn't even know she was interested in preaching.

When she turned to look out the window and saw me, she quickly dropped the spoon. Rushing in my direction, she flung the door open. "What are you doing, Grace?" she asked, red in the face.

"Judy"—I stared at her with my eyes wide—"you're preaching."

"I'm not," she snapped, smoothing out her dress. "I'm not a preacher. I was bored and just messing around."

I shook my head. "Well, you looked and sounded like a preacher for a second there."

Her eyes glassed over, and a flash of hope filled her gaze. "Really?"

"Really, really."

She puffed out a breath of air. "It's just silly," she told me. "I just play around a bit, that's all."

I walked into the foyer and gave her a small grin. "But if you did want to do it as more than playing around, I could talk to Dad…"

"Please don't," she said quickly. "It's not worth it. I'm happy teaching Bible study and running events around town."

"You deserve more than that, though," I told her. "Before Dad found out I was going to be a teacher, he talked to me about taking over the church after him. Lord knows that's something I would never want, but you'd be great at it! I mean, if you just—"

"Grace, come on, just drop it, okay?" she begged, clearly uncomfortable with the idea. I saw how she flinched, so I did as she asked and dropped it. "Are you excited for the Peach Festival coming up?" she asked me.

Each year, the town held a big festival to celebrate the sweetest peaches in all of Georgia. It was a huge event with carnival rides, barbecue, and fireworks that had been going on for years, but it was the first year Judy was fully in charge of every aspect of it.

"I am! Anything you need, let me know."

She bit her bottom lip. "Do you mean that? Anything?"

I cocked an eyebrow. "What are you getting at?"

"Well, the day of the event Mama needs some help with some baking…"

I groaned. It was no secret that Mama and I weren't on the best terms. Then again, I knew how much the festival going well meant to Judy, so I'd do my best to put up with Mama's annoyance for her.

"I can do that for you."

She squeaked. "Thank you, thank you. You have no clue how much stress that takes off me."

"Always and always," I told her. "I was actually just coming to change real quick before going out."

"Oh? Where are you going?" she asked, raising an eyebrow.

My cheeks heated up in response to the way she asked her question. As if she already knew where I was heading.

"There's been a lot of talk about you and Jackson Emery," she told me. "Mama is pretty livid about it."

"When isn't Mama livid about something I'm doing lately?" I joked, feeling my nerves build in my stomach. I'd have been lying if

I'd said it didn't bother me that my relationship with my mother seemed so damaged lately. All my life, I'd done my best to make her proud, and now it seemed as if all I did was disappoint her.

Judy gave me a small frown. "I just want to make sure you're okay. I know what happened with Finn and Autumn is a lot, and I cannot even imagine what's going on in your head, you know? I just don't want you to get hurt even more by the likes of someone like Jackson Emery. He's a terrible person."

"He's better than Finn," I told her, my voice shaky.

"Just because he's better doesn't mean he's good."

"Judy—"

"I don't want to parent you, Grace. Lord knows the last thing you need is another Mama coming down on you, but I just want you to be careful. I know your heart is broken, and I don't want anyone else adding bruises to it."

"You worry about me too much, little sister," I joked.

"It's not too much worry. It's the perfect amount. I just love you, is all."

"I love you too," I told her. "Always and always."

If Mama had approached me the same way Judy did with her worries for me, it would've been different. Where Mama was harsh, Judy was gentle. They both wanted the best for me, it seemed, but Mama had a hard time expressing it in a kind way. Perhaps she and Jackson had more in common than they thought. They struggled with expressing themselves.

I understood why everyone worried about Jackson being in my life lately. They were still looking at the out-of-focus version of him the people of small-town Chester had crafted.

Me, on the other hand—I was fully zoomed in.

When I arrived at Jackson's place as we had planned, I was a bit thrown off. I sent him a text message and waited for a while, before giving up and heading home. It was the first time in all our time together that he hadn't answered my messages or returned my calls. Plus, whenever I planned to head over, he was always waiting.

I did my best not to overthink it. Jackson had his own life, and I had mine. It was just nice when they crashed together.

A few days passed, and I still hadn't heard from Jackson at all. I knew we didn't have the kind of relationship where I had any right to worry, but I did. It was hard not to, knowing that there were so many storm clouds in that head of his.

I left novels in his corner at the bookshop, but each day when I returned, the Post-it notes were untouched, which only made my nerves build more.

After not hearing from him for five days, I tossed on some clothes and headed over to Jackson's place to check in on him. When he didn't answer the door, I walked toward the auto shop, but he was nowhere to be found. Then, I walked around the building and saw him with that sledgehammer in his grip, hammering away at a new broken-down car. His white shirt was tucked into the side of his jeans as he swung the hammer into the glass windows.

His arms were muscular and tan as if he'd spent the past few days standing directly in the sun. I cleared my throat loudly, and watched his body react to the sound. He knew I was there, but he didn't look my way.

After opening and closing my mouth a few times, I finally built up the nerve to ask him a question. "Is everything okay? I haven't seen you around the bookshop lately, and when I called you, I didn't get a reply."

He swung the hammer up and then dented the hood of the car. "Been busy."

He still hadn't turned to look at me.

"Oh, well…okay…I just wanted to make sure you were okay."

He didn't reply.

I wished I could crawl into Jackson's head and see what he was thinking about. I knew his issues went much deeper than he let on. I should've let him be and allowed him to have his alone time, but something in my heart told me not to leave. Something in my heart was asking me to stay.

"Jackson, what's wrong?"

"Nothing."

"Jackson, come on. You can talk to—"

"Can we not fucking do this?!" he barked. The sledgehammer dropped to his side, and he finally looked up at me. "Can you just leave?" he snapped, sending chills down my back. He was acting like the monster I'd first met when I came into town, and I didn't have a clue why.

A tear fell from my eye. His coldness stung me a lot harder than I'd thought it would. The last time I'd seen him, it had felt like we were finally getting somewhere, like he was finally knocking down the wall he'd built up over the years.

Plus, lately, he seemed like the only thing that brought me comfort, and I was convinced everyone in town was wrong about him. Now, though, he was acting exactly how the townspeople viewed him—like a nasty beast.

I sniffled a bit before wiping the tear away and then nodding. "I'm sorry."

I turned to walk away and heard him mutter, "*Shit,*" before he called my name. When I turned around, he was facing me, sweat dripping down every inch of his body as if the sun was only beaming its rays on him. Every inch of him was soaked, every inch of him wet. I felt my cheeks heat as my stomach began to flip back and forth.

"I'm in a shitty mood," he said, wiping his forehead with the back of his hand. I pretended the nerves forming in my gut weren't real as I nodded his way. He crossed his arms, and kept talking. "And my mind is really messed up right now."

He dug his palms into his eyes before he moved those same hands to his mouth and tapped repeatedly while his spoke. "Like *really* fucked up, but instead of trying to decipher my thoughts, or go find some shit to make me forget, I've decided to be in a really shitty mood and fuck up this car in my backyard. I understand where you're coming from, and I appreciate the hand you're reaching out to me, but if I talk to you right now, I'll probably be an asshole, and I don't want to be an asshole to you because you're *good*. You're a good thing, but I will break if you keep pushing me, and I can be a real asshole, Grace. Then you'll hate me, and I'll feel bad about it, so…I just need my alone time to feel like shit for a while."

I nodded once more. Beating up on that car was his outlet to his anger, to his hurt. It was the safety belt keeping him from falling down the rabbit hole, and I'd interrupted that.

Walking back home, I felt foolish for crossing the line with Jackson.

How naïve was I to think he'd let me in?

CHAPTER TWENTY-EIGHT

Grace

It had been a few days since Jackson asked me to leave him alone, and I hadn't heard a word from him until he walked over to my corner of the bookshop on a Wednesday evening.

"Hi," he whispered, standing tall with his hands stuffed deep into the pockets of his black jeans.

"Hi," I replied just as quietly.

"I owe you an apology—" he started, but I cut him off.

"No, I owe you an apology. You made it clear that you needed time, but I didn't listen, and I'm sorry for that. You asked for your space, and I didn't give it to you."

A person shushed me, but then when they saw Jackson give them an intense look, they said, "Never mind," as they stood and walked away.

I'd never seen a stare so powerful.

He brushed his hand against the back of his neck and sighed. "I don't know how to handle people wanting to know if I'm okay. I reacted poorly, and I just wanted to apologize for the way I treated you. You deserved better."

"It's truly okay, I promise. Are you okay, though?"

"No," he replied. "But that's normal."

I wished he understood that there was nothing normal about not being okay.

"You can talk to me, you know. I know it's against the rules and all, but you can, Jackson. I'm a safe place."

I watched his Adam's apple move as he swallowed hard, and his body began to tremble. He parted his lips to speak, but his eyes glazed over before any words could escape his mouth. He fought hard to keep the tears at bay, but by the way his body shook, I knew he was close to losing the battle.

I stood from my seat and moved closer to him. "What is it? What's wrong?"

He cleared his throat, and his bottom lip twitched. "Tucker's gone."

"What?" I gasped, placing my hand on his arm. "What do you mean gone? What happened?"

"He, um, he passed away five days ago. I woke up, and he couldn't even walk. I took him to the vet and was told he was in organ failure. They said he probably wouldn't have made it through the week, so I had to make the decision to put him down."

"Oh my gosh…Jackson…" I moved to hug him, and I watched his body tense up. "I'm so sorry."

"It's fine."

"It's not."

"Yeah, but—"

"Jackson, this isn't the part where you argue with me."

"Then what part is this?" he asked.

"This is the part where you let me hold you."

He separated his lips to speak but surrendered as his shoulders slumped forward. He nodded his head a little, and within seconds, I'd wrapped my arms tightly around him. I held on as I felt his tense body slowly relax against mine.

When he asked me to let go, I held on tighter because I knew he needed me close in that moment. After a while, he stepped back and pressed the palms of his hands against his eyes, shaking his head.

"Will you do something with me?"

"Anything," I promised. "Whatever you need, I'm there."

We walked through the wooded area of Jackson's property. He held a box in his hands, and as we walked farther through the trees, we reached a clearing. There was open land, and the setting sun touched every corner of the space. In the middle of the field sat an easel with a canvas resting on it. There were paint supplies surrounding the stand, and a small cross made with paintbrushes.

"That's where we buried my mother's ashes," he told me. "This is where we were supposed to build her art studio. I just thought it would be nice to have Tucker buried beside her."

"I think that's a beautiful idea, Jackson."

He set the box on the ground then pulled out Tucker's stuffed elephant toy and his water and food dishes. Then he pulled out the small urn of ashes and set it down. He cleared his throat, and as he stood, he grimaced. I took his hand into mine and squeezed it lightly.

"He saved my life," he told me with a somber look. "A few years ago when I overdosed, Tucker found me and led Alex from the auto shop to me." He swallowed hard, and his voice cracked. "He's the reason I'm alive today."

My heart kept breaking for Jackson's pain. I held his hand a little tighter but didn't offer any words. There were no words for a story like that. Just thankfulness that Jackson was still alive and well.

"I don't know how to say goodbye," he softly spoke, staring at the empty bowls.

"Then don't. Just say good night until tomorrow."

Jackson closed his eyes and took a deep breath before he moved over to Tucker's final resting place and kneeled. I stepped back a bit, wanting to give him as much space and time as he needed. I didn't move too far back, though, because I needed him to feel my presence. I needed him to know he wasn't alone even though he had his space.

"Hey, buddy," he said, his voice smooth like whiskey. "I don't know how to do this. I don't know how to let you go." He sniffled, wiping his nose with his hand. "You were a good boy, the definition of unconditional love. When everyone left me, you stayed near. You loved me on the days I didn't deserve it. You stood by my side on the good days and the bad. You put up with my moods and loved me regardless of my shortcomings." He sniffled and lowered himself to the ground, laying his hand upon the grass. "You were there when I had nothing. You're the best friend I've ever had, and I'm not gonna lie; this hurts.

"This hurts more than I knew it would, but you wouldn't want me to fall apart, so I won't. I don't believe in heaven, but today I will for you. I hope you're running through the biggest park filled with bones and chew toys. You were the best dog I could've ever wished for, and I can never thank you enough. I love you, Tuck. I always will. Always and always. Good night until tomorrow."

My ears perked up as the words 'always and always' fell from Jackson's tongue. He didn't even know what he'd said, but my family's words had just fallen from his lips. I felt the chills as they caused goose bumps all along my arms.

As he stood, he wiped the tears from his cheeks and turned my way with the saddest gaze I'd ever seen. Without a word, I wrapped my arms around him.

He rested his forehead against mine and inhaled slowly. "Gracelyn Mae?"

"Yes?"

His lips brushed against mine as his eyes slowly shut. "I'm really glad you exist."

CHAPTER TWENTY-NINE

Jackson
Ten Years Old

"Really?" I gleamed, staring at my parents. "I can really get one?!" My face hurt because I was smiling so hard. We were standing in the pet store staring at the cages with all different types of puppies.

"Yes. You've been doing so great with your grades. Plus, we think you're old enough to have a bit more responsibility now. So"—Dad gestured toward the dogs—"let's find you a new friend."

I wanted to cry because that was what I wanted.

I'd always wanted a friend, and now I was going to get one.

My parents walked through the shop with me, pointing out which dogs they liked. They didn't agree on anything, and then they'd say something mean to one another. Even though they tried their best to hide it, they fought underneath their breaths. I didn't get why they were so annoyed with one another lately.

All they had to do was say I love you to fix things.

I didn't let their fighting get to me that afternoon, though.

I was on a mission to find the right dog to be my new partner in crime. That way, when my parents were fighting, I'd have someone to keep me company.

"What about him?" I asked, nodding toward a black puppy who was wagging his tail so fast as he looked at me. It looked like he was excited about finding a new friend, too.

The employee got the dog for us. He then took us into a room to interact with the puppy to see if it was a match. The second they placed the dog down, he leaped in my direction, jumping in my lap. He began licking my face and hugging me as I hugged him tight.

Ma smiled. "I think we found the perfect guy for you."

I laughed as he kept kissing my face.

"Now all we need is a name," Dad remarked.

Whenever I would pull him back a little, he'd dig himself deeper into my lap. "How about Tucker?" I laughed. "Because he keeps tucking himself against me."

"Tucker." Ma nodded, still smiling. "I love it."

"Me too," Dad replied.

They agreed.

It must've been right.

"Hi, Tucker," I whispered, holding him close to me. It felt like he was hugging me back, and I liked that the most. I never, ever wanted to let him go. "I'm going to love you forever."

CHAPTER THIRTY

Grace

"Gracelyn Mae! Get down here, will you?" Mama hollered the morning of the peach festival. I'd been helping at her house by baking cupcakes all morning. The whole town was in a rush to get it set up, and I'd just finished putting on the red sundress Mama had picked out for me.

We hadn't truly spoken about anything, and the truth was, I was glad. I was certain if we did talk, it would just result in another disagreement, and I was tired of having those conversations with her.

Soon enough, I'd be back in Atlanta teaching. Therefore, I didn't see a point in arguing with her.

As I walked downstairs, Mama tilted her head toward me. "Oh," she muttered. "Is that how it looks on?"

"Mama, don't start," I warned, feeling all my insecurities bubbling up.

"No, no, it's fine. You look fine."

Then Judy walked into the room, and Mama gasped, her hands flying over her mouth. "Oh my gosh, darling, you look stunning!" she remarked about Judy's white sundress.

The sundress was identical to mine, just a different color.

Judy beamed so brightly and twirled. "Isn't it fun? Oh my gosh, I'm so excited for today and for the fireworks display tonight. I think we are going to raise so much money for charity."

"With that beautiful smile of yours, you'll get everyone to hand over their money for the cause. Did you choose which one you wanted to donate to?"

Every peach festival, the church held a big barbecue and carnival, and all the money raised went to a charity. Seeing how Judy was in charge of organizing the event, she got to choose where the money from the event would go.

"Yes," she replied, looking in my direction. "I want to donate to the MISS Foundation," she said.

My heart skipped a beat. "Judy," I whispered, and she gave me the most gentle smile.

"I just think it's important, you know? The work they do; their values and support—it save lives."

I tried to blink away my tears, and I nodded. I knew from personal experience how much they could save a life.

The MISS Foundation helped families who'd suffered from the unbearable loss of a child. When I had my first miscarriage, they were who I turned to. When I had my seventh, they were who kept me from drowning.

I'd once mentioned the foundation to Judy years ago; I hadn't had a clue she remembered.

But, of course, she did. She was, after all, the one who restored my faith in humanity each day.

I walked over to her and gave her the tightest squeeze. "Thank you," I whispered.

"Always," she replied, squeezing me even more. "The dress looks better on you, by the way."

Oh, sister, you and your lies.

The carnival began, and everyone in town was there—except

for the Emery men, of course. I had asked Jackson if he would attend, and he'd said he would rather eat five hundred cans of anchovies than be surrounded by all the folks of charming ole Chester.

I couldn't blame him. If it wasn't for me being Chester royalty, I would've avoided it, too.

It was probably a good thing he wasn't there because the number of times his name was upon someone's tongue was infuriating. Jackson never talked about anyone in town. Heck, I was almost certain he didn't even know most of their names, but they were true fanatics about tossing his around.

Every time someone said something ugly about him, the hair on my arms stood up. Every time someone called him a monster, I wanted to stand up to them. He wasn't a monster at all, not the real Jackson. He was so gentle and kind. He saved me when I felt so alone.

When Susie Harps remarked that the town would be perfect if we didn't let white trash stay, I was seconds away from leaping at her and pulling out her extensions. "I'm just saying, it would be best if his father just went ahead and drank himself to death. Then maybe Jackson would off himself next," she said in such a despicable tone.

How could those words ever leave someone's mouth?

How could someone be so shockingly evil? Wishing death on someone? Really?

My arm reached out and if not for a hand landing on my forearm, she would've been on the ground.

"Whoa there, slugger," Alex whispered. As I turned around, I saw his smiling face, and he shook his head. "It's not worth it."

"Did you hear what she just said?"

"Yes, but still, it's not worth it," he told me. "The more you react to their comments, the more power they have over you. Just walk away. Come on, let's get some cotton candy." He placed his arm around my shoulders, still smiling, but I felt sick to my stomach.

"They wished him dead," I barked.

"Yeah, well, that's their karma to deal with. If you pulled out that girl's hair, that would be your karma, but look! Now your karma is clean, *and* you get cotton candy. I call that a win-win." He bought me a cotton candy, and I shook my head at him in disbelief.

"How do you always stay so positive? With everything and everyone?"

"Oh, that's easy—I smoke a lot of marijuana." He smirked. "I've been meaning to talk to you about Jackson, actually. I just wanted to say thank you."

"For what?"

"Giving his darkness a chance. As you know, he's a good person once you peel back those layers, and it means the world to me that you took the time to do that."

"It's not just a one-way thing, Alex. He's done the same thing for me. Whenever I feel like falling apart, he's there to catch me."

"That's the type of friend Jackson is—loyal and always there for you."

My heart skipped a beat. "You think I'm his friend?"

Alex snickered and cocked an eyebrow. "You think you're not? Rumor has it he sends you texts."

"Yeah…"

"Not to sound dramatic or anything," he said, leaning in, "but the asshole doesn't even text me back. You might be his new favorite person. If it was anyone else, I'd probably be pissed, but since it's you"—he shrugged—"I'll allow it."

"So what does he do for the festival days? Does he hang out with his dad?"

"Nah. Normally he sits on top of the shop and drinks while watching the fireworks."

"Alone?"

"Yeah. I've tried to join him, but he won't have it. Alone is something he's used to, I think, and he has a hard time breaking that pattern."

Well, maybe it was time to have someone try to break it for him.

"What are you doing here?" Jackson asked as I made my way onto the roof of the auto shop, holding a bag in my hand.

"What does it look like? I'm bringing you barbecue." I handed him the food, and he gave me a somber look.

"Thank you. You can leave it and go."

"*Orrr…*" I smiled brightly, sitting beside him. "I could stay."

"*Orrr*," he responded, frowning sharply, "you can go."

"Even though I brought you food? That just seems rude. I won't talk, I swear. I just want a nice place to watch the fireworks."

"Did Alex tell you I was here?"

"He might have mentioned it."

He rolled his eyes. "Of course, he did. How was the carnival?" he asked.

I smirked. "Do you really care about the ins and outs of Chester events?"

"Not at all, but it seems like a big deal to you, so I thought I'd ask."

Swoon.

Wait, did I just swoon?

When was the last time I swooned?

"It was good. They raised a lot of money for a great cause." I told him about the MISS Foundation and what it meant to me, how they'd helped me through my miscarriages.

"Seven?" he questioned.

I nodded slowly. "Seven. I spoke with Josie about it a few weeks back. She's lost a few of her own, too, and she has little hearts on her wrist with angel wings in memory of their lives. I thought about doing that, too, but my family's a bit against tattoos. It's not classy, as my mama would say."

"Your body, your choice," Jackson said, making me smile a little. "I think it's a good idea to have a reminder of them."

"Yeah…maybe. I'm just a bit tired of disappointing my mom."

"Sometimes, you have to disappoint people to better yourself," he told me.

"Maybe," I said, still uncertain.

"You'll get there," he told me. "To the point where you don't care what other people think."

"That sounds like a great place to be."

"Trust me, it is." He turned toward me, locking those beautiful hazel eyes with mine. "You would make a great mother."

Oh, Jackson…

"Ah, come on, princess. I thought we were past the crying thing," he joked, brushing his thumb beneath my eyes.

"Sorry, I…that was a really nice thing to say, Jackson. Thank you."

"Just the truth."

We sat in silence, and it wasn't long before the big show began. If there was one thing Chester was extremely good at—other than gossip—it was putting on a fireworks display.

"This peach festival was the last chunk of time I spent with my mom," Jackson told me, staring out at the sky as it lit up. "We sat up here eating Bomb Pops and Cheetos Puffs, watching the display. We were quiet, and I just remember feeling whole, like for the first time in a long time, everything would be all right. I mean, sure she passed away shortly after that, but at that moment, the world was still. At that moment, I was happy."

"Those are the things you have to hold—the moments."

He gave me a half smile. "This is a good moment," he said, his voice low as he turned back out toward the fireworks.

Yes, it was.

"So, Jackson, are we like…friends?"

He groaned, rolling his eyes in the most dramatic way. "Come on. Don't do that, Grace."

"Do what?"

"Be corny."

"How is that corny?"

"Because you don't ask people if they are your friend. They just…are."

"Oh." I nodded slowly, staring out into the night. "So, we just…are?"

"Yeah." He nudged my shoulder with his. "We just are."

I wouldn't tell him how good it felt—just being with him.

As he looked out, his voice dropped low. "Listen, I know I'm not easy all the time. I'm a bit cold and hard to read, so thank you."

"What are you thanking me for?"

"Being my friend. I never knew I needed you, but I did—I *do*." He tilted his head my way and gave me a small smile, the kind that always made my heart skip. Jackson Emery didn't smile a lot, so whenever he did, it felt like a secret gift he was only giving to me. "The only friend I've ever had was Tucker, you know? Then came you."

"You want to know a secret?" I asked him.

"Yes."

"I think you're the most graceful person in this town."

He laughed. "Bullshit."

"No, I mean it—not the you they make you out to be, but the real you, the one who gives his all to care for his father, the one who holds a girl who's having a panic attack, the one who doesn't fight back when the world is fighting you. You have the most grace I've ever seen."

"Princess?"

"Yes, Oscar?"

"You make it really hard."

"For what?"

"For me to hate the whole world."

CHAPTER THIRTY-ONE

Grace

Jackson and I began seeing one another most days. It was as if I was his escape from reality, and he was mine—or more so, we were each other's escape from the façade of superficiality in Chester. The town had been my home all my life, but lately, it felt as if I didn't fit there anymore. The only time I felt like anything made sense was when I was with Jackson.

In his darkness, I found my light.

We began doing all types of activities together as a way of learning more about each other and ourselves. His life was spent caring for his father, and mine was spent being perfect for my mother, so for the first time ever, we took the time to learn who we were as individuals—together.

We went to movies we would've never seen before and loved them. We went hiking, which I hated. We tried to build furniture just to say we could do it. (He could. I couldn't.)

Some of my favorite times, though, were sitting in the back of The Silent Bookshop beside one another, flipping through different novels together. It was so easy to be quiet with him. The silence felt a little like home.

My other favorite moments were spent on his couch doing nothing but talking about anything and everything. Those were the times when I felt as if I learned the most about the man across from me. Those were the small moments I adored.

"I didn't learn to swim until I was seventeen years old. I've only ever had one pet, and it was a cat named Mouse. My two front teeth got knocked out when I fell face first during the Founder's Day parade one year. I can understand Spanish but can't speak a word of it, and I think cardinals are my favorite bird," I told him, giving him random facts.

He melted into the couch cushion a bit. "I was named after Jackson Pollock. My middle name is Paul because that was Jackson's real first name. I almost fell in love once when I was nineteen with a girl passing through town. I think I chose her because I knew she wouldn't stay. I hate peas but think they work fine in beef stroganoff. I'm obsessed with *Game of Thrones*, and I secretly judge anyone who isn't."

"Confession: I've never seen *Game of Thrones*."

His eyes darted over to me before quickly looking away. "Oh, well, that's okay."

I laughed. "Stop it."

"Stop what?"

"Secretly judging me."

He arched an eyebrow. "I'm not."

"You totally are! I see it in your eyes."

"No, I mean, I get it—it's not your fault you're shockingly uncool."

I snickered and shoved him. "Screw you."

"Nah, I don't screw people who don't fuck with Jon Snow."

My cheeks heated at his comment, and I hoped he couldn't see the redness of my face in the partially darkened room.

"I bet you're the type of person who's never seen *Breaking Bad* or

The Walking Dead either."

"Guilty as charged."

"*Sons of Anarchy?*"

"Um, never heard of it."

His eyes bugged out. "Geez, Grace! What exactly do you do with your time?"

I smiled and shrugged. "I don't know, live life?"

He grimaced. "I bet you crochet for fun."

I blushed.

He narrowed his eyes. "You do crochet, don't you?"

I bit my thumb.

I freaking loved to crochet.

"Oh my gosh, you're an old woman," he groaned, slapping his hand against his face. "Well, hell, if we are going to keep crossing paths, you'll have to sit through a few episodes of *Game of Thrones*. I'm going to un-old you."

I kept laughing. "Well, if we're watching *Game of Thrones*, I'm crocheting as I do it."

"You can't crochet while watching. You need to be one-hundred-percent focused on the show, otherwise it's just a waste of time. You won't know what's…Grace?"

"Yes?"

He glanced down, and I saw that somehow, at some point, my hand had found its way to his. I'd laced my fingers with his fingers. I'd moved in close enough to touch him, and I hadn't even noticed.

I quickly pulled my hand away and took a deep breath.

"Sorry," I whispered.

"Don't be," he replied. His hand slowly inched closer to me, and his pinky finger brushed against mine. "You miss this, yeah? The small moments?"

I closed my eyes at the touch. "Yes."

His hand slowly slid on top of mine, our fingers intertwining. "And this?" he asked, his voice deep and smooth. "Holding hands?"

Take a small breath…

"Yes."

He moved his body closer to me then took his other hand and

placed it on the nape of my neck. His fingers slowly began to massage my skin, making me tilt my head to the side. "And you miss this?"

Yes…

Oh, yes, I missed that.

Our thighs brushed, our breaths sawing in and out in sync.

Yes…yes…yes…

"I miss this," I confessed, placing my hands on his chest. "I miss being touched…miss being held without the hooking up and all."

"Let me do this," he said softly, placing his forehead against mine. His gentle breaths caressed my lips as I kept my eyes closed. "Let me hold you."

He lifted me into his arms and placed me on his lap. My legs wrapped around him, and he held me close. I was so close that my head fell against his chest. We were so close that each time I took an inhale, I could listen to his heartbeats.

One breath, one beat.

Two breaths, two beats…

"Jackson," I whispered as his fingers played with my hair. "Can I ask you to do something crazy?"

"Say the words."

"Can you carry me to your bedroom and lie down with me and just…hold me for a little while?"

Without another word, he placed his hands beneath my legs and lifted me into the air. We moved to his bedroom and he gently lay me down then climbed right beside me. As he pulled me closer, I curved into his body. His warmth covered me whole, and I took in his scents. He felt like my favorite blanket, and I wanted to stay wrapped in him as long as I could.

There were no sounds around us, only his inhalations and my exhalations. He nuzzled his lips against my neck, and for the first time in a long time, I felt as if I were exactly where I was meant to be.

"Jackson?" I whispered, moving my body even closer to him. We were from two different puzzles, yet still, we seemed to fit perfectly together.

"Yes?"

I took a deep breath and exhaled it slowly. "I like the way your heart beats."

CHAPTER THIRTY-TWO

Jackson

"Hey," Grace said, standing on my front porch on Tuesday afternoon, beaming ear to ear with a sly look. "Want to do something crazy today?"

"Okay, wait, wait, wait!" Grace cringed in Alex's tattoo parlor as he was seconds from putting the needle against her left shoulder blade.

"We've been waiting for the past thirty minutes." I laughed. "It's now or never."

"Will you hold my hand?" she asked.

I took hers in mine. "Always and always."

She stared at me for a moment as if she'd seen a ghost, her lips parting as if she was going to speak, but she didn't say a word. She tilted her head Alex's way and nodded once. "Okay. I'm ready."

That was a lie.

The moment the needle touched her skin, she screamed bloody murder and nearly hopped up as she squeezed my hand ridiculously tight.

"Think happy thoughts, princess," I told her.

She inhaled sharply and nodded. "Eggs in cake, puppies, dresses, tacos."

"Pizza, waffles, parks…"

"Bookshops, Christmas, Hallow—holy fudgeknuckles!" she barked, squeezing my hand tighter.

"You okay?" Alex asked. "Are you sure you want seven of these hearts with wings? We can do fewer of them."

"No," she said sternly. "I can do this. I just…" She took a breath, and I took her other hand into mine. "I can do this."

"Okay, and while we're doing this, can we discuss the fact that instead of cussing, you just said holy fudgeknuckles?" I asked.

She laughed. "I've been staying with my sister too long. I'm starting to express things like her."

"Are you two close?"

"She's one of the only things that gives me faith in humanity. Judy is a saint, a truly good person."

"I'm glad you have her."

"Yeah, me too. Ouch!" She jumped slightly.

"Focus on me, princess," I told her. "Talk to me. Ask me questions—anything to keep your mind off the needle."

"I can ask you questions?"

"Anything."

She bit her bottom lip then nodded toward my wrist and the band around it. "What does that mean? Powerful moments?"

I grimaced a bit. "Just diving right in, aren't you?"

"You don't have to tell me. I just always notice you snapping it against your wrist."

I moved around a bit in my chair. Alex gave me a look and nodded once, almost as if telling me it was okay to open up a little. To let someone else see my scars.

"I got it from rehab. Whenever I felt like using, the doctor had me snap the band against my wrist as a reminder that this life is real, and the pain I felt from the snap was to remind me that the next step I took would be real. It was my chance to be powerful in dark moments."

"Powerful moments," she whispered, nodding slowly. "I like that a lot."

"Yeah. It works for the most part."

"Do you ever almost fall off track?" she asked.

"Only every single day." I smiled. "But I think it's a fight worth fighting."

"It is," she agreed. "Can I ask you another question?"

"Will it stop you from thinking about the tattoo?"

"Yes."

"Then yes."

"Why did you start using drugs in the first place?"

My brows knitted, and I shrugged. "Because I was tired of hurting, and I thought that was an easy fix."

"Was it?" she asked.

"Yeah, it was…until I came back down from the high. Then I ended up hurting even more. The higher the high, the greater the fall."

"I'm really proud of how far you've come," she told me. "I can't even begin to imagine what you've been through, but you're here and strong now. That's amazing."

That meant more to me than she'd ever know. "Thanks."

As Alex hit a sensitive spot on Grace's back, she squeezed my hands even harder, and I let her. "You've got this. Powerful moments, okay?"

She nodded. "I can do this."

And she did. It took some time, and a few tears slipped from her eyes, but the final product was perfect. As she stood in front of the mirror, glancing over her shoulder to see the artwork, a small smile crossed her lips. "Do you like it?" she asked.

"I love it." I placed my hands on her waist and kissed her cheek. "It's perfect."

"It is, isn't it?" she agreed as she turned to face me. "There's one more thing we have to do," she stated.

"What is it?"

She pulled out a small card. "I hope this is okay, and if you hate the idea, we don't have to do it, but I saw that the veterinarian sent you a card for Tucker with his paw prints inside. I thought maybe you could get his paw print tattooed somewhere in his memory."

I pinched the bridge of my nose and cleared my throat. "Are you always like this?"

"Like what?"

"Perfect."

I got Tucker's paw prints on my shoulder blade, and beneath it, I added the words *powerful moments*. Grace added the same words beneath her angel wings.

She didn't have a clue how much comfort she'd brought me that afternoon. She didn't have a clue how much comfort she'd brought me over the past few weeks.

"Okay. Now what?" I asked, kissing her forehead after we finished everything up.

She smiled ear to ear, and her grin made me find my own. "Ice cream, but first I'm going to run to the bathroom."

"Sounds good. I'll meet you up front."

As she left, Alex smiled my way and shook his head back and forth. "What?" I asked.

"Nothing. It just looks good on you, that's all."

"What looks good on me?"

"Happiness."

CHAPTER THIRTY-THREE

Grace

"You have to choose, Grace," Jackson told me sternly. "I know this is really hard for you, but you have to do it. In the next thirty seconds, you have to make a choice."

"But..." I bit my lip as I stood in line at the ice cream shop, staring at the menu. "I don't know. What are you getting?"

"There's no way I'm telling you what I'm getting because then you'll just get the same thing."

"That's not true!"

He cocked his eyebrow.

Okay, that was true. Even though I'd discovered how I liked my eggs, I was still learning other things I enjoyed on my own without the influence of the people around me.

"Fine, fine. Okay, I can do this." I took a deep breath, and when we made it to the counter, I told Jackson to order first, but he wasn't falling into my trap. I looked at Mary Sue, the cashier, and gave her a big smile. "Hey, Mary, I'll have the peanut butter swirl sundae, please."

"For sure, and what can I get for you?" she asked Jackson, and I saw it in her eyes—the way she drooled while looking at his face.

While the men were saying rude things about Jackson Emery, many women secretly yearned for him.

"I'll have the same," he told her.

"What?! You just got what I was getting!" I hollered.

"That's what he gets every time," Mary Sue said, smiling at Jackson with her flirty eyes. *Gross.* "Are these together or separate?" she asked.

"Separate," I said quickly.

"Together," Jackson replied, handing her his credit card.

"You don't have to do that."

"I know." He gave me a small smile before taking his card back. "I'm gonna run to the bathroom. I'll be back."

I moved to go grab a table, but Mary Sue called out to me. "Grace! Grace."

"Yes?"

She bit her bottom lip and placed her hands on her hips. "Not to pry, but are you and Jackson on a date right now?"

"What? No. We aren't—we don't—we're not…we don't date. We're just…" My words faded away. "We're not seeing each other."

"Oh good!" she exclaimed, clapping her hands together. "Well, I know this might be too forward of me to ask, but as I'm sure you know, Peter and I recently broke up, and Lord knows I'm heartbroken over it. So, I was just hoping maybe you could put in a good word for me? I just feel like if I got a chance with the fixer, I might be able to get Peter back into my life."

What a screwy little town we lived in.

"Oh, uh, well, I don't know, Mary Sue. I think maybe that's something you should do for yourself."

"Oh, please, Grace! You know how shy I get. I just couldn't face him and ask him to hang out with me for a little while."

"Well, okay. I'll see what I can do."

Not a chance in hell will I help her.

"Thank you! You're such a sweet little peach! It truly means a lot to me. Also, do you think maybe we could keep this between us girls? I don't want to be a part of any rumors."

"Trust me, Mary Sue, your secret is safe with me."

She thanked me again then handed me the two sundaes. I walked over to an available table and sat down.

It might've been the most uncomfortable conversation I'd ever had in all my time in Chester, Georgia. Mary Sue was asking me to be her wing-woman to help her snag the man I was sleeping with.

"Why the weird expression?" Jackson asked, walking over to me.

"Mary Sue wants to sleep with you," I told him flatly.

"Who the hell is Mary Sue?"

I gestured toward the cashier, who was staring our way, smiling brightly. She gave Jackson a nervous wave before blushing and turning away.

"Why does she want to sleep with me?"

"To fix her relationship."

"Oh," he said, sitting down. He began to eat his ice cream. "Not interested."

Those two words brought me more comfort than I'd thought they would. "But why not? She's pretty, and well, I'll be heading back to Atlanta soon enough."

"So?"

"So, you're free to do whatever you want when I'm gone." Just saying that made me want to vomit. The truth was, lately, I'd been coming up with hypothetical situations where Jackson and I somehow found a way to make something real work between us.

But that was just my silly mind messing around with my heart.

There were a million reasons Jackson and I couldn't work…but my heart kept telling me I only needed one good one to give it a try.

He grimaced. "You want me to sleep with Mary Sue?"

"What? No. I'm just saying, there's a line of women waiting for you once I leave."

His brows knitted. "I don't want to do that anymore. I don't want to just hook up with random women."

I narrowed my eyes. "Why not? Isn't that what we've been doing?"

He lowered his spoon. "Come on, princess..." He gave me a look. "You don't really believe that's all we've been doing, do you?"

"I know we just had it yesterday, but it's a craving," a voice said as someone walked into the ice cream parlor. As I looked up, I saw Autumn walking in as Finn held the door open for her. The moment they saw me, their faces went pale, almost as if they'd walked straight into a ghost.

"Grace," Autumn muttered, her voice shaky.

My eyes fell to her stomach where a small bump was forming, and nausea overtook me.

Finn was quick to drop his hand from her lower back, which he had been massaging as they entered. His eyes darted back and forth between Jackson and me then he cleared his throat, but he didn't say a word.

Autumn's eyes watered over, but I groaned. "Don't do it."

"Don't do what?" she asked.

"Cry."

"I...I won't. It's just..." She began crying, and she was still beautiful.

That made me want to cry.

"I'm just going to run to the restroom," she said, hurrying away.

Finn kept standing there, and he awkwardly stuffed his hands in his pockets. "So, you two are like...buddies now?" he asked, his voice deeper than it had ever been, which was odd.

"Finley, don't do this," I warned. "Just go."

"It's just a question," he said, moving in closer. He tilted his head my way. "I've been calling you."

"I blocked your number, remember?"

"We should talk."

"I think you should go," I said sternly. The wave of comfort that washed over me as Jackson placed a hand on my knee and squeezed it under the table was shocking. I needed that. I needed him there.

"Yeah, but—" Finn started.

"You should do as she said," Jackson said harshly.

"Or maybe you should mind your own business," Finn shot back. He looked at me, then toward my ice cream. "Since when do you like peanut butter ice cream? You always get strawberry."

"I'm trying something new."

"Yeah?" he huffed, glancing at Jackson once more. "Is that what you're doing?"

"All right, on that note, we're leaving. Enjoy your date with Autumn," I said, standing up from the table.

"It's not a date. It's just…ice cream. She's been having cravings."

"I don't care."

"What's that on your back?" he inquired, seeing the plastic covering my new tattoo. "Jesus, did you get a tattoo? Your mom's going to flip out."

"Finn, can we stop this? We aren't having conversations anymore, okay? Come on, Jackson. Let's go."

As we began to walk away, Finn quickly grabbed me by the wrist and pulled me closer to him. "This isn't you, Grace. Whatever's going on between you and this guy…this isn't you."

"You have no clue who I am," I told him.

"Maybe not, but you have no clue who *he* is."

"Let me go, Finley."

"No. I can't let you go with this guy," he insisted as I tried to twist out of his grip.

Jackson stepped forward and lowered his voice as his gaze pierced Finn. "You have five seconds to let her go before I rip your arm from the socket."

For a moment, Finn debated, uncertain if he should believe the threat or not.

"You better listen to him," I warned. "Last time a guy stepped out of line, he snapped his cell phone in half."

Finn dropped his hold on me and took a step back. "It's only a matter of time before he hurts you, Grace. People like him always snap."

"And people like you always let people like me down."

"You're acting like a fool," he barked, but I didn't even give him a reply.

I was so tired of being in his presence.

I took Jackson's hand in mine and we walked out, my stomach in knots and my mind spinning. I hated how Finn still had that effect on me, how he could make me feel so small and naïve.

That was the biggest difference between the two men standing in front of me.

Finley always caged me.

Jackson allowed me to fly.

CHAPTER THIRTY-FOUR

Jackson

After the run-in with Finn and Autumn, we went back to my place where I had a night of watching *Game of Thrones* planned. I had everything ready—popcorn, cherry cola, and her favorite candy: Reese's peanut butter cups.

It amazed me that I knew her favorite candy.

I'd never let anyone close enough to learn their favorite things.

I hoped the distractions would help get Grace's mind off the interaction with the two people who'd hurt her the most.

After I set everything up on the coffee table, I went to grab the cola from the fridge, and I stopped when I saw Grace glancing at the tattoo in the mirror. There was a small smile that looked more like a frown upon her lips.

"Are you okay?" I asked.

"Yes, I'm fine. It's just..." She turned to me and lightly shrugged. "Today's my anniversary."

"Oh, I didn't know…" A knot formed in my gut at the thought. I'd been pretty stupid lately—letting my feelings for her grow. There was no real point, really. She was still a married woman, and she could go back to her husband at any moment when she got sick of doing whatever it was she and I were doing. Plus, it wouldn't be long before our summer fling came to an end, and she went back to her reality in Atlanta.

We'd made a deal, and it was perfectly clear that come the end of August, she'd go her way and I'd go mine.

She owed me nothing.

Still…I wanted all of her.

"Seeing Finn in town with Autumn must've been hard for you," I remarked.

"No, Jackson." She shook her head, placing her hand on my forearm. "Not that anniversary. It's the anniversary of my first miscarriage."

"Oh, God. I'm so sorry."

I felt like such a dumbass.

"No, it's fine. I mean, it's not, but it is, you know? That's why I wanted to get the tattoos today, to honor them. I'm not gonna lie, though—running into Autumn and seeing her pregnant today of all days really hit me hard."

"I cannot believe that happened," I whispered, combing her hair behind her ear. "I cannot understand how the two of them could've ever done that to you."

"She gave him the one thing I couldn't," she replied. "That's all I ever wanted to be for him, ya know? For me. All I ever wanted was to have a family, to be a mother, and for some reason, I couldn't do the thing women are supposed to be able to do. I couldn't…" She took a sharp inhale and closed her eyes. "All I wanted was to give him a family, and instead, he went out and created one for himself."

"I'm so sorry, Grace."

She gave me the saddest tight smile and shrugged. "Sometimes life is so unfair, but I guess that's the way it is. I guess I'm just an almost girl."

"An almost girl?"

"You know…" She released a hard exhale. "The girl who almost gets the dream. I almost had a forever love, I almost had a forever marriage, and I was almost a mother, but after seven losses, I finally realized it wasn't in the cards for me. The doctors said if we kept trying, my body wouldn't be able to take it, but truthfully, I was more worried about my mind. I felt like I was losing it with each day that passed. I hadn't even had a chance to come to terms with that fact before Finn walked out on me. My mind was too broken. My heart was too sore. I'm just tired of being an almost person, that's all."

"That's not a thing," I told her, taking her hand in mine. "Being an almost mother isn't a thing. You have seven children, whether they made it here or not doesn't take away from the fact they existed. They were yours, and they were loved fully if only for those small moments. You are a mother, Grace. I am so, so sorry you were never able to hold your babies, but you are, and always will be, a mother."

Her body began to tremble, and I pulled her in closer, trying my best to let it be known that she wasn't alone that night.

"I sometimes pretend I knew their genders, and I gave them all names," she confessed.

"What are their names?"

"Emerson, Jamie, Karla, Michael, Jaxon, Phillip, and Steven," she said, tears rolling down her cheeks.

"Those are beautiful names."

It came in waves, her pain. For a few moments, she was fine, but then it was like the truth overtook her once more, the truth of all the losses she'd faced over the years.

No words I could say to bring her comfort.

Nothing I did would make her pain go away, so, I did the only thing I could for the remainder of the night—I held her. I let her fall apart in my arms, and let her not be okay.

I held her so tight for so long and when it came time for her eyes to rest, she faded to sleep against my chest. It broke my heart that in her dreams, the tears still fell.

Even in her dreams, the place she was supposed to find peace, she was still falling apart.

She deserved more, more than this world had given her. She deserved happiness more than anyone else out there. I hated that life had been so hard for someone so good. I hated that bad things swallowed the heart of the most graceful woman.

I hated that I couldn't fix her cracks that night.

She just deserved so much more.

We stayed in bed longer than we should've, and I held her body against mine longer than I'd planned. She was still sleeping, her breaths weaving in and out as her chest rose and fell against me. I hadn't even noticed it until it happened, my lips falling against her forehead. She'd spent the previous night broken, telling me about her darkest days, and as she spoke, I knew she was reliving each moment.

Emerson, Jamie, Karla, Steven…

The children she never got to hold, the lives she craved so much, the souls who'd said goodbye before they ever had a hello.

I couldn't imagine her pain. I couldn't imagine her hurts.

All I could do was hold her and hope my touch was enough to help her through those memories. If ever there was a woman who deserved to be a mother, it was Grace.

The world was selfish, unjust. How could so many undeserving people be given the opportunity to raise children they didn't even want while so many worthy individuals didn't get the chance?

She shifted a bit and snuggled closer as a yawn left her lips.

"I slept over," she whispered.

"You did," I replied.

"I'm sorry. I know the rules." She sat up and stretched. "I'll get going."

"Or well…"

"What is it?" she asked, looking over her shoulder. Her hair was a mess, and I wasn't certain how she could get any more beautiful.

"Are you all right? After last night?"

She turned my way and gave me a tired smile. "I'm always all right."

"Yeah, I know…but if you're not, you can…" *Stay. You can stay with me.* "I mean, if you ever need someone to talk to, I'm here."

Her eyes softened before she broke her stare away from mine. "Careful, Jackson," she whispered, raking her fingers through her hair. "Summer's almost over, and you shouldn't make my heart skip like that. Now, come on," she said, sitting on the edge of the bed beside me. "Say something less sweet. Say something mean to me."

"I don't want to say anything mean."

"Yes, but if we are going to keep things going, we need to balance out the nice moments with some mean ones. Say anything. Think of something nice you'd like to tell me, and just say the opposite."

"All right. I think you're the ugliest person I've ever seen. Your face reminds me of a garbage can, and every time you leave, I'm happy you're gone."

She leaned in closer and rested her forehead against mine. "Oh," she said softly. "So the truth is the opposite of that?"

I nodded slightly. "The opposite is the truth."

"Jackson Emery?" She shut her eyes.

"Yes?" I shut mine.

"My heart's doing that skipping thing again."

"Well, maybe that's okay, you know? Maybe sometimes hearts have to skip in order to keep beating."

"Can I stay a few more minutes?" she asked, her voice shaky and unsure.

"Yes, and then you can stay a few more after that."

I wrapped her in my hold, and we lay back down on the bed. The way she melted into me made my mind fog up, but I didn't mind. I hadn't felt this way in so long—intimate, protective. I wanted to protect her from the world, from her hurts, from her pain, yet also, selfishly, I just wanted to keep her close to me. I wanted to feel her against my skin, against my lips, against my chest. I wanted to feel her in my heart…

My heart…
Damn my heart.
I didn't know it still knew how to beat.

CHAPTER THIRTY-FIVE

Grace

"You guys, this is stupid!" Judy complained as Hank and I sat across from her in their living room. "I just don't think this is a good idea, and the timing is all wrong. Mama and Daddy are already doing so much, and they are as busy as ever. I think this is just silly," she whined, pulling on the hem of her dress.

"Judith Rae, I swear to God if you try to back out of this now, I'm going to kick you so hard you'll land in California. Now, come on, do it again," I ordered, sitting on the couch beside Hank as my sister stood with a stack of paper her hands.

"But..." She frowned and bit her fingernails.

Hank stood, walked toward her, and took her hands in his. "Babe, look at me. You are the best woman I've ever known, and you are the best preacher I've ever had the pleasure of listening to, okay? You deserve this chance, and I can promise you there ain't no way we are going to let you pass it up, okay? Now focus. You got this. You can do this."

"How do you know?" she asked, her voice shaky. "How do you know I can do it?"

"Because you're you. You can do anything."

I loved them so much it was almost sickening.

"Now come on," Hank barked, slapping her butt. "Preach that sermon for Grace and me." He went back to the couch and sat down.

Judy took a deep breath and released it slowly. Then she began to deliver one of the most moving sermons I'd ever sat through. She felt the words, and I could hear in her voice how much she believed in what she was saying. It was a beautiful thing to watch, my little sister growing up into her own person.

She did this on her own; this was her gift, her talent, not anyone else's. She was born to be a preacher. She'd found her light, the thing that made her happy, and no one could take that from her.

I couldn't have been prouder.

When she finished, I wiped my eyes, ridding myself of the tears she'd brought to life.

"Was it okay?" she asked, still nervous.

I stood and pulled her into the tightest hug ever. "It was more than okay. It was so freaking good, Judy, beyond words good. Now just do that same thing at dinner tonight with Mama and Dad."

She took a breath and nodded. "Okay. Thank you, both of you, for believing in me. I wouldn't be doing this crazy thing if it wasn't for y'all."

"Always and always," I told her, squeezing her hands and smiling. "Now I better get to dyeing my hair before dinner."

"I'm sorry, come again?" Judy's mouth dropped open. "What do you mean dye your hair? Grace, Mama would have a fit! Does she even know that you have a tattoo yet?"

"No, but she'll be fine."

"Are we talking about the same Mama?" she joked.

Hank narrowed his eyes. "This seems like a sister conversation, so I'm going to go watch ESPN in the bedroom."

He snuck away, leaving Judy to stare at me with concern. "Grace..." she started. "Is this you? I mean, listen, if you always wanted to do these things like dye your hair and get tattoos, I'm all about it. Lord knows if anyone deserves to find themselves, it's you. I just want to make sure this is of your own doing and not Jackson's influence."

"Judy." I took her hands into mine. "This is all me."

"Promise?"

"Promise."

She nodded. "What color hair?"

"Burgundy."

Her eyes widened. "You want to kill her." She laughed. "You want to kill our mother."

"Think of it this way. If she doesn't die from this, she'll probably live forever."

"Okay, well, come on. Let's get this over with."

"What do you mean?"

"I'm not going to let you dye your hair alone. I'm going to help you color it. Two set of hands are better than one, I'm guessing."

I loved how my sister was always there for me, even if she didn't understand my choices.

She loved me enough to let me explore unmarked territory, and she never let me walk it alone.

We headed to dinner, and Judy's nerves were all over the place. Mama and Dad sat down at the table as their chef served us dinner. Hank and I couldn't stop smiling from the excitement of what was about to take place.

The meal was wrapping up, and Judy hadn't spoken up once. So, I decided to take charge. "I think Judy has something she wants to share with us all," I said, getting everyone's attention. Judy shot me a harsh look, but I just grinned.

"Oh?" Dad asked, looking over at my sister. "What is it, Judy?"

"I, uh, I…" she started, her voice trembling.

"Spit it out, Judith," Mama ordered.

"Well, I was just, I was thinking, maybe, I mean, maybe one day

I could do a sermon at a Sunday service. I even—" Before she could even reach for the printed copy of her sermon, Mama and Dad broke into laughter.

"You doing a sermon?" Dad remarked, tickled pink by the idea, which made me more upset than anything. He was supposed to be different. He was supposed to support Judy's dream, but then again, in my parents' minds, Judy was just a pretty little girl who didn't have big dreams.

"Oh, honey." Mama giggled. "That's a good one. Now what did you really want to say?"

My parents missed it—the way my sister's spirit wilted.

Hank started to open his mouth, to protest their laughter, but Judy placed a hand on his knee and gently shook her head.

"I was just gonna say I'm really looking forward to the Founder's Day parade," Judy choked out, holding back her tears as she sat up straight like a proper young lady.

"Yes, it's going to be fantastic, and you get to ride on the float, too! You're going to be the prettiest girl in town, Judy," Mama remarked.

"She's more than just a pretty girl, Mama," I barked, more than irritated.

"Grace," Judy said softly, giving me a look that begged me to drop it.

For her, I would, but still, I was pissed off.

"Oh, I forgot Hank and I have a meeting for the parade in about fifteen minutes, so we're going to head out." Judy pushed her chair back from the table and kept her smile on her face. "Come on, Hank," she said.

"But…"

She bit her bottom lip to hold back her tears. "Please, Hank, we can't be late."

He reluctantly stood and left with her, and then my parents went back to casual conversation as if nothing had even happened.

"Are you kidding me?" I snapped, making the two of them look in my direction.

"I beg your pardon?" Mama questioned.

"What is it, Grace?" Dad asked.

"How could you do that to her? How could you laugh in her face when she brought up preaching a sermon?"

"Oh, Gracelyn Mae"—Mama rolled her eyes—"that was just your sister being her silly self."

"No, it wasn't. She's been practicing for weeks, probably months, and when she finally built up the nerve to tell you two, you laughed in her face. How did you not see it? How did you not see how your laughter hurt her? She pretty much bolted out of the room."

"She couldn't be serious," Dad said, baffled. "Judy isn't a preacher."

"What's that supposed to mean?" I said with narrowed eyes, confusion swimming through my brain.

"Well, you know, your sister is into different things like shopping, throwing events around town, party planning—things like that. She's more like the town cheerleader. She's not one to run a church," he said. At that moment, for the first time ever, I saw my father in a different light.

"You think she's stupid?" I asked.

"I didn't say that."

"You didn't have to," I snapped. "I'll have you know she is a preacher. I've listened to her, and she is one of the strongest voices I've ever heard. She has so much heart and compassion for every person in the world. She is gifted beyond compare, and you had the nerve to laugh in her face when she came to tell you her dream!" I hollered, overly passionate about trying to get them to understand.

"Grace, lower your voice," Mama ordered.

"No. I won't be silent about this. She worked so hard for this, and you two were so disrespectful. If you ever had a dream and you took it to Judy, she would cheer you on for the rest of your life. She'd believe in you more than you'd believe in yourself, and you two didn't even give her a moment to breathe."

"I think it's time for you to leave the table," Mama said, her voice low and annoyed.

Dad didn't speak a word.

That hurt me more than anything else.

My eyes stayed on him, and I couldn't help the tears that filled my eyes. "I'd expect this from her, Dad, but you too? You're supposed to be the one who believes in us. You're supposed to be the one who listens to our dreams and tells us we can fly. The person you were tonight? The way you laughed at my sister? I don't even know who you are right now."

"That's comical, coming from the girl having an affair," Mama snapped.

"Excuse me?" I asked, perplexed.

"You know exactly what I'm talking about. Just go, Grace. Leave. Go run off to see that delinquent boy of yours."

I sarcastically laughed. "Wow. I've been waiting for you to throw that in my face, but I think your timing is off. That has nothing to do with the issue at hand."

"It has everything to do with the issue at hand. Your word and your character are void to me right now because you are running around town like a wild woman. I mean, seriously! Tattoos?! Burgundy hair?! What is going on with you? This isn't you. And you're skipping around with a filthy dog who doesn't even deserve a bone. Yet you're just giving him all of you like a disgusting whore."

My mouth dropped open. "What did you just call me?"

"Do you know the damage control I've had to do because of your rampage these past few weeks? Tattoos on your skin…leaving Jackson's place late at night—do you know how hard it has been for me?"

"How hard it's been?" I huffed. "For you?"

"Yes. Do you know what people have been saying to me? What they have been saying about our family?"

"No. Do you know what people have been saying about *me*? You know what, I can't do this. I cannot talk to you."

"You're a disgrace to this family's name! Sleeping around with that dirty monster when you're married."

My heart was breaking, and she didn't even notice. I swallowed hard and lowered my head. "Finley cheated on *me*, not the other way around, but what do you care? It seems you're determined to choose everyone but your daughters lately. I'm done with it all. I'm done with the church and their judgments, and I'm done with you and yours. By the way, over the past few weeks, Jackson has treated me with more respect than you ever have in all of my life, so if he's a monster, Mama, that must make you the Devil."

CHAPTER THIRTY-SIX

Grace

"I didn't know she was serious," Dad said, standing on Judy's front porch later that night. His hands were stuffed in his pockets, and his shoulders were rounded forward. Judy and Hank were still out when he showed up on their doorstep. The guilt that filled Dad's eyes was so heavy.

I rubbed my temples and sighed. "That's because you guys never take her seriously. She's good, Dad—great, actually. If you give her a chance, she'll prove to you that she's beyond right to take over the church someday. Just give her the chance. Give her the opportunity to be something more than the event planner."

He sat on the top step of the porch and rubbed his hands together. "I think today was a parenting fail overall."

"It doesn't have to be if you fix things with her. It's hard for me to watch how Judy gets treated sometimes. She's more than a pretty face, so much more than that, but it's as if this town has painted her into that frame of little miss beautiful, and they won't allow her to break free. She deserves more than that. She deserves a chance to have a shot—a *real* shot—at her dream."

"I'll make sure to talk to her."

"Thank you, and I am sorry about how dinner went. I get overwhelmed by Mama sometimes."

"I think you both get overwhelmed by each other. You're very much alike, you know," he told me.

I cringed. "We're nothing alike."

He smiled and shook his head. "That's what your mama said when I told her, too. Buttercup, are you okay? Now, you know I'm not one to follow along with any rumors, but the fact that you are running around with Jackson Emery is a little worrying for me."

"Why is everyone against him?" I asked. "He's not evil."

"No," he agreed. "But he is damaged, which can be dangerous. I don't want you to get hurt, especially when you're already hurting so much. Maybe putting a little distance between the two of you wouldn't be a bad thing, especially as you figure out what's going on with your marriage."

"What do you mean 'figure out what's going on'? Finn chose someone else, and for goodness' sake, she's having his child."

"Yes, but don't you think it's important to be more than what Finn has been to you? To have the elegance to completely resolve one situation before moving on to another? I know you're hurting, and your mind is jumbled, but that's why I'm being so protective of you right now. Jackson Emery has never been one to make people's lives easier. He makes messes, and I don't want him to do that to your heart, not after it's already been broken."

"He's not as bad as you think, Dad," I whispered, my voice shaky.

He pinched the bridge of his nose, then placed his glasses on the top of his head. "If he's really not that bad, then he'll be around after you figure out the details of your marriage."

"So…what? You want me to avoid him because the town thinks he's a bad influence?"

"No, not at all. I just want you to take a second to breathe. It seems as though your life has been spiraling, and I don't want you to go from one bad situation to another. Just take the time to heal before rushing into something else." He placed a hand on my knee and squeezed it. "You'll be all right, Grace. Just don't rush into something that probably won't last. Jackson Emery doesn't have a history of many friendships, and I'm sure there's a reason for that. I just don't want you to find out the hard way."

"I wish you could see what I see when I look at him," I whispered.

"And what is it that you see?"

I swallowed hard and shrugged my shoulders. "Hope."

Before he could reply, Hank and Judy walked up to the house. "Dad? What are you doing here?" she asked, looking perplexed.

Dad stood and stuffed his hands into his pockets. "I was hoping I could hear a sermon."

Judy's eyes glassed over, and as the tears fell, she was quick to wipe them away. "It's stupid, Dad. Don't even worry about it."

"It's not stupid," he replied, walking over to her. "I'm stupid. The way I responded was wrong and cold, and I apologize for hurting you. I'd love to go inside and hear your words, Judith Rae, if you'll let me."

She smiled and nodded.

The two walked inside, and Hank came to stand by me. "Thank you," he whispered.

"Always and always," I replied.

CHAPTER THIRTY-SEVEN

Jackson

"Are you okay?" I asked when Grace showed up at my place. She hadn't said much of anything, but I could see in her eyes that she wanted to use sex to forget that night.

"No," she told me as she began to unbutton her shirt. Her eyes swam with emotion as I placed my hand over hers, bringing her movement to a stop.

"What is it?"

"Nothing, really. Can we just…" Her words trailed off as she tried her best to blink her tears away, but Grace wasn't one to hide her emotions easily. She felt everything in the complete opposite way of me. Her emotions lived on the surface while mine swirled in the depths beneath.

She shut her eyes and took a deep breath. Her thoughts must've been flying through her mind quickly because as she parted her lips, no words came out.

I placed my hands on her lower back and pulled her into a hug.

"We don't have to talk," I told her. "But we don't have to have sex tonight. I can just hold you."

She shook her head back and forth as her body trembled against mine. "That goes against our arrangement."

"I think we're miles past our arrangement, princess."

With a sharp inhale, she spoke. "Everything's a mess. My father thinks I'm making a huge mistake being close to you. He didn't say those exact words, but I know he's disappointed in the way I'm dealing with everything, and my mother…" she muttered, her voice cracking. "She's so hard on me."

"Don't take it personally. She's hard on everyone because the world made her that way."

"Same as you?" she asked.

"Same as me," I replied. Even though I couldn't stand Loretta Harris, I saw how we shared some of the same traits.

She sniffled and laid her head against my chest. "Every day, it's hard to breathe. I do fine when I'm with you, but when I leave your side, it's hard again. I feel like I'm using you as a temporary Band-Aid for my pain."

"You can use me all you want," I told her. "In any way you wish."

I felt my heart skip a beat.

Lately, my heart had been skipping a lot of beats around her, and I wasn't sure what to make of it. I simply allowed it to happen, not wanting to read too much into it all.

"I'm broken," she warned me.

"Yeah, I know." I took her hand and kissed her palm. "I am too."

She placed her hands against my chest and felt my heart beat against her fingertips. "Fix me for a while?"

"I'll fix you all night long, and then I'll continue tomorrow."

CHAPTER THIRTY-EIGHT

Grace

He didn't fix me with his body but with his words. We stayed up talking about anything and everything in our lives, which made it a bit easier for me to breathe. Knowing more facts about Jackson made life seem less lonesome.

"When did you know you wanted to work on cars?" I asked him.

He grimaced a bit and shrugged. "I didn't. I wanted to go to art school. I took more so after my mom than my dad, but after everything that happened, I figured I should help out at the shop."

"You never wanted to be a mechanic?"

"Never."

That made me sad for him. He couldn't even find the time to chase his dreams after spending most of his life caring for his father. "You can always go back to school," I told him.

He shrugged. "I'm fine here."

"But are you happy here?"

"Happiness never really seemed like an option for someone like me."

"You deserve it more than most."

"But less than you." He somewhat grinned. "You deserve it the most."

We lived in a strange world, he and I. A world where we weren't exactly free to express how we really felt for one another, but in my mind, I told him over and over again.

I adore you. I adore you. I adore you...

His finger traced my wrist and then he pulled my arm closer to his and kissed it. "You're bruised from the last time I pinned you down."

"There are worse ways to get bruises." I smirked. He frowned a little, looking at my wrist. "It's okay, Jackson. I'm fine."

"I just don't want to hurt you."

"Lately, you're about the only thing *not* hurting me." I moved in and kissed his lips softly.

He closed his eyes for a second, and when he reopened them, his hazel stare sent chills down my spine. "When do you go back to Atlanta to teach?"

We hadn't really spoken about me leaving. Over the past few months, we'd simply fallen into one another's arms and hadn't exchanged many words outside of moans. When we did speak, it was always about our pasts, never about the future.

"In about three weeks," I told him.

He looked down, a hint of disappointment in his stare. "Oh, okay."

"What is it?" I asked.

"It's just...I'm going to miss you, that's all."

My heart skipped another beat.

"Jackson Paul Emery misses people?" I joked, trying to control the feelings raging in my chest.

"No, not people...just you."

I adore you. I adore you. I adore you...

My fingers fell to the side of his neck, and I began to massage his skin as he wrapped his arms around me. My stare stayed on his lips. That same mouth had been all over my body, but what touched me the most were the words that fell from between those lips of his.

"I'm going to miss you, too," I said softly. "Without you, I would've drowned this summer."

He kissed me, and something shifted that night. His kisses felt different, more real than the fictional story we'd been telling one another every single day for so many weeks. He hadn't said the words, and I hadn't either, but our kisses felt like we were begging for a little more time, a few more touches, a few more skipping heartbeats.

I stayed longer that night as our touches almost mimicked something that could've been confused with love. As the sun began to rise, I began to put on my clothes and started heading back to my place.

"I'll walk you home," he offered.

I smiled and yawned. "You know I'll decline."

"Text me when you make it back?"

"I can do that."

"Okay." He smiled, leaning against the doorframe.

"Okay," I replied.

"Gracelyn Mae?"

"Yes?"

He cleared his throat and placed his hands into his pockets. "Do you think I can take you out on a date sometime? Like a real date?"

Butterflies filled me up inside.

"I didn't know Jackson Emery dated people."

"Not people…only you."

More butterflies.

"Actually, I was going to ask you if you'd do something with me."

"What's that?" he questioned.

"Each year, for as long as I can remember, my parents host a summer gala at the town hall ballroom to raise money for charities. It's a big deal, and everyone in town dresses up like it's the Oscars or something. There's a big dinner and dance and literally everyone in town will be there."

"The Harris Gala. Yeah, I've heard of it."

"Be my date?" I asked him. He grimaced for a moment, and I felt my heart crack. Embarrassment hit my cheeks. "If you don't want to, you don't have to. I swear, I just thought—"

"I want to come," he told me, giving me some reassurance. "I just worry people will give you a hard time if you show up with me. I don't want to stress you out and add more drama to your life. People will talk."

"Let them," I told him, placing my hands against his chest. "We just won't listen."

He smiled. The kind of smile that made my heart skip a few beats. He leaned into me, placing his forehead against mine.

His lips grazed mine, and I knew I was ruined.

"So…" He whispered. "It's a date?"

"Yes." Chills raced throughout my body. "It's a date. Good night, Jackson Paul."

He kissed me gently on the lips, and I felt it in every fiber of my body as his hands fell behind my neck. He massaged my skin then softly spoke with his smoky voice. "Good morning, Gracelyn Mae."

CHAPTER THIRTY-NINE

Jackson

"Closing early today?" Alex remarked, a bit stunned. "You never shut the shop down early."

"Yeah, well, I got plans tonight."

He cocked an eyebrow. "Plans? With a woman named Grace?"

"Don't do that," I told him.

"Do what?"

"Smile."

"I always smile."

"Yeah, and it's annoying," I joked, tossing all the dirty towels into the back room.

"So, are you two, like…a thing?"

"What? No. We're just…friends."

"With benefits."

"Something like that."

"But it's more," he commented. "It's so much more."

"Alex, I'm going to need you to shut up right about now."

"All right, but I'm just saying, it's okay for you to like people, man. I know you think it's not, but it is. It's part of what makes humans…human."

I frowned and shrugged my shoulder as I began tossing my supplies back into the toolbox. "I can't like her, Alex. Even if I did, she's leaving town in a few weeks."

"So? Go with her."

I rolled my eyes. "Right."

"Dude, I'm serious. Get out of this hellhole and go live your life. Even if it's not with Grace, you're allowed to leave this place."

I huffed. "It's not like I can leave my dad. The only reason I was able to go off to rehab was because you stepped in, and I wouldn't ask you to ever do that for me again."

"Buddy, your father is not your burden."

"I'm not going leave him to die. I'm all he has."

"Okay, I'll drop it because I can tell you're getting upset. I just want you to know that the world will keep spinning even if you go off and live your own life. My main point is this: you are allowed to be happy—maybe more than most people, and I think Grace makes you happy. I think you make her happy, too."

I swallowed hard. "You think so?"

"She was about to rip out some woman's hair at the festival because they were talking about you. She's as protective of you as you are of her. I've never seen something that made no sense yet made complete sense until I laid eyes on the two of you together."

"She's just so…good."

He laughed, walked over to me, and patted me on the back. "So are you. I'm going to get out of here. Have a good time tonight, all right?"

"Okay. Have a good night."

He headed out of the shop, and I kept cleaning so I could finish up before going back to my place to jumped in the shower. I rented a suit for the event because there was no chance in hell anything in my closet was going to be good enough for the Harris Gala.

I wanted to look my best for Grace. I didn't want to let her down.

Her taking me to this event, her allowing my arm to be wrapped around hers was more than just a small gesture. She was making a statement to the whole town that she was free to live however she chose to live.

I loved that fact, and I loved that I was going to be the one holding her hand.

She showed up at my place around seven thirty p.m., and when I opened the door, I took a few steps back.

She was beautiful.

From her burgundy curls to her fitted silver gown, she looked like a goddess.

"Wow," I breathed out. She began to blush, and I loved it.

"Wow," she replied, eyeing me up and down. She held her hand out toward me. "Shall we?"

I took her hand into mine, and we walked down the streets of Chester together. People saw us, and we didn't care. People judged, and we didn't listen.

When we arrived at the town hall ballroom, everyone's eyes turned to us. I felt it hit my gut, and I could only imagine what they were thinking.

How I wasn't good enough to be holding Chester's royalty.

How I was simply a deadbeat.

Right as I was about to ask Grace to retreat, she squeezed my hand, giving me comfort. "Powerful moments," she whispered, pulling me closer to her. She then raced her lips against mine and kissed me as everyone watched. I kissed her back, because how could I not? All I ever wanted to do was kiss those lips lying against mine.

"Powerful moments," I replied as we slowly pulled away.

Somehow, at that exact moment, everyone's opinions were officially void because she chose me.

In front of the world, she held my hand.

CHAPTER FORTY

Grace

People gathered around me right away and started asking me questions about Jackson and me as he wandered off to get drinks. It all felt overwhelming, but I took it the best I could because he was worth the risk of people judging us.

And boy, did they judge.

"It's a bit soon, isn't it? To be dating again."

"You should be by yourself for a while."

"I think Finn and you can work things out."

"Finn obviously still cares for you."

So many opinions. So many nosy souls.

I just smiled through it all and did my best not to let it get to me. "If you'll excuse me, I have to go find…something," I said, grinning ear to ear.

The second I got away from the crowd, I ran into Marybeth Summers.

Marybeth was a quiet soul and always kept to herself. She looked my way and nodded once. "Hey, Grace."

"Hey, Marybeth."

"I think you two are beautiful together."

"Thanks." I smiled, still feeling a knot in my stomach. I was waiting for her next comment to be like everyone else's.

Yet instead, she just said, "You deserve to be happy."

She gave me a hug, and it felt so sincere. I held on a bit longer than I probably should've.

Maybe not everyone in town was filled with a gossiping heart.

Perhaps some did truly wish me well.

"Gracelyn Mae," Mama stated, walking my way. She seemed stunned to see me as she smoothed out her dress.

"Hi, Mama."

"What are you doing here?"

"I've never missed a gala. I didn't think I'd start now."

"Are you…" She shifted around in her high heels. "Are you here to just make a scene? To act out?"

"What?"

"I saw you walk in with that boy. I just don't want any drama. Did you bring him here to get back at me for our last conversation? For what I said?"

"Oh, Mama." I smiled her way and moved in close. "Not everything has to do with you."

I walked away and ran straight into Josie, who was grinning ear to ear as she looked my way. "Oh, my, my, my. Did I just witness you telling your mother off?" she asked me, sipping at her champagne.

"I think you did."

"I see you brought a certain guy as your date tonight," she remarked with a wolfish grin.

"I did."

"Good for you, Grace." She held her glass up in a celebratory fashion. "Good for you."

As the band struck up their instruments, Josie perked up. "Oh! The band is starting! I better go find my husband before some Chester girl tries to claim him for first dance. I'll check in later!"

The first dance of the Harris Gala was always a fun one to witness. The tradition stood that whoever was the first to ask for you for a dance, you had to agree. No ifs, ands, or buts.

That was how I was able to get Finn to dance with me all those years ago.

That was how I began to fall in love with him way back when.

My eyes darted around the room for Jackson, and I started in his direction as I saw him still standing near the bar, but my heart landed in my throat as I heard the words, "Gracelyn Mae, may I have this dance?"

I turned around to see Finn standing there in a suit and tie. He looked so handsome, and I hated him for it.

"No," I barked, turning away, but he kept talking.

"It's tradition, though. You can't say no."

I groaned.

"He's right, you know," an older woman stated, walking by us with a young man who looked underwhelmed. It was clear he didn't choose her. "It's tradition."

I rolled my eyes and looked at Finn. "One dance. That's it."

"That's all I want."

"That's all you're getting." We walked to the dance floor, and he tried to place his hand on my lower back, but I didn't allow him to do so. His hands sat on my shoulders, as if we were at a middle school dance.

"Thank you for this," he said, his breath dripping with whiskey scents.

"You're drunk," I remarked, staring into his glassy eyes.

"I had a few drinks, yeah. I was just trying to build up the nerve to talk to you, to ask you for this dance. I thought it would bring back some memories of us."

I didn't reply.

"Well?" he questioned. "Does it?"

"Finley, where's Autumn?"

"I don't know. I don't care about her. I care about you."

"Since when? Since I started talking to Jackson?"

He grimaced. "It drives me crazy to see you with him, you

know? It drives me batshit crazy." His eyes watered over, not from the alcohol, but from his emotions. "Grace. It kills me seeing you with another man."

"Now you know how I felt."

"I'm so sorry, Grace. I really am," he told me, tears rolling down his cheeks. I couldn't think of the last time he'd cried in front of me. "After the first miscarriage, I lost myself. It hit me hard, and I had to try to hide my pain because I knew you were hurting so much. I just needed space to think and clear my head."

"Using other women's bodies? How long did you expect me to wait for you? How long did you think I'd sit here praying for you to love me again?"

"You don't understand. After everything that happened, I couldn't breathe."

"I like how you're using the miscarriages as an excuse for your disloyalty when it should've been the complete opposite. I…" I blinked my eyes and took a sharp inhale. "When I needed you most, you weren't there for me. When I needed you to catch me, you watched as I began to fall, and right as I was seconds away from hitting the ground, you turned and walked away."

"Grace…"

"I'm done, Finn."

"This isn't you. This is that guy getting in your head. You love me," he told me. "You do, and I know you do. You can't just give up on us, Grace. You can't—"

"I want a divorce," I cut in. I was tired of him coming and going as he pleased. I was tired of him trying to tell me who I was and what I stood for. "I don't want to do this anymore. I don't want to beg you to love me. I don't want to sit up at night wondering if you're loving someone else. I don't want you to want me just because you believe someone else does. I want to be free from the chains, Finley. I want to let you go."

"What? No." He tensed, trying to keep his hold on me, but I pulled away.

"You're the only woman I've ever loved, Grace."

I didn't know why, but that stung me. "Then I don't think you know what love is."

I turned to walk away, and Finn's hand landed against mine. "Gracelyn, please." His grip was a bit tight, and his eyes were pleading. I stared into those crystal blue eyes for a moment. Those same eyes I'd thought I'd spend the rest of my life gazing into. Those same eyes that I'd thought would always bring me peace during my darkest storms…

"Finley James…" I whispered, looking past him to where Autumn had just entered the room. She looked beautiful in her golden dress that somewhat showed her curve. Each and every one of her curves. "Let me go."

He dropped his hold and looked over at her.

"Dammit," he muttered.

I walked away quickly, trying to shake off my nerves. As I was going to escape, Jackson walked over to me. He gave me a halfway smile, and I gave him the other half.

"What's wrong?" he asked me.

"Nothing."

He narrowed his eyes. "What's wrong?"

I shook my head. "Really, I just need a bit of air. That's all."

He stood tall and cleared his throat. "Is my being here bringing you more stress? Because if it is, I can go. I know this is a big deal for you and your family, and I don't want to cause any kind of harm."

Oh, Jackson… "You being here is the only thing keeping me from drowning."

"What happened? Did someone hurt you?"

"Yes, no, well…they just hurt my heart."

He moved in closer and combed a fallen curl behind my ear. "Those are the worst kinds of hurts."

A tear rolled down my cheek, and I didn't bother to dismiss it.

Jackson frowned. "What can I do for you?"

"I just need to step outside for a moment. Can you just…wait," I whispered, laying my hand against his chest. As I looked up into his hazel eyes, I saw such softness. I stared into those hazel eyes for a moment. Those same eyes that helped me take small breaths… Those same eyes that brought me peace during my darkest storms…

"Please, Jackson," I begged, "just wait for me."

"Princess…" His thumb moved to my cheek, and he wiped away my falling tears. He tilted his head to the left and gave me a smile. It was small…tiny, really. Most people would've missed the expression, but I'd been so zoomed in on Jackson that I noticed every move his lips ever made. The comfort that swept over me as he softly spoke words my way. "How could I not wait for you?"

CHAPTER FORTY-ONE

Jackson

Grace walked away for a minute to get some air, and I waited for her return. I stood in the room, feeling completely out of place. The suit was itchy. The people were rude, and the food was bite-sized.

I was officially in hell.

"Not your normal crowd, huh?" a woman remarked.

"Not in the least."

She held her hand out toward me. "I'm Judy. Grace's sister."

Of course—they had the same eyes. I shook her hand. "Nice to meet you. I've heard a lot about you."

"Same with you." She smiled and shifted around in her heels.

I arched an eyebrow. "Is this the part where you tell me to stay away from Grace?"

"No. Why would you think that?"

"That's what everyone seems to be telling me to do."

"I see. That's not why I'm here. I'm just here to ask you to be gentle with her, okay?"

"What do you mean?"

"Her heart...it's fragile. She's been through more than I think she even realizes, and I don't think she can take much more. If you are going to allow her to fall for you, please be ready to catch her because I'm not certain she'll be able to stand again after being dropped."

She loved her sister, and it was apparent through her words. She wasn't shouting at me to stay away from Grace, only requesting that I be easy with her heart and soul.

"I can do that," I told her.

"Promise?"

"Promise."

She smiled, rubbing her left hand up and down her right arm. "You like her."

"I do."

"She likes you."

I hope so...

"Have fun tonight, Jackson, and please ignore everyone at this party except for her. She's all who matters tonight, okay?"

Judy thanked me before she walked off to go entertain others. I could see so much of Grace's personality in her sister. It was nice to know other good people existed in the world besides Grace.

I wanted to go check on her since she'd been gone for a while, but I was working on being patient. She needed to breathe, and I'd be there when she came back to me.

"You must be real proud of yourself, huh?"

I turned to see Finn walking my way. He looked a bit wild in the eyes as he spoke to me.

He was drunk.

I'd seen the look in my father's eyes enough times to know.

"Finn, let's not get into it tonight," I told him.

"Stay away f-from my wife," he ordered, slurring his words a bit.

"Wife?" I huffed. "We're using that term a little loosely, aren't we?"

"Don't get slick," he warned, stumbling in my direction.

I groaned.

This is the last thing I want to deal with.

I took a breath and tried to calm my natural instinct of stepping up to him. Even though he was an asshole, he was still Grace's ex, and I didn't want to do anything stupid that might tick her off.

"Look, buddy, you're drunk and not in your right frame of mind. Go find yourself some water."

"Oh, fuck off," he hissed. He obviously wasn't going to make it easy for me. "You think you're so amazing for banging my wife, huh?"

"Again, that word," I remarked. "Using it rather loosely."

"She's been mine for fifteen years."

"And then you let her go."

He grimaced, running his hands over his face, and then he moved in closer and lightly shoved me in the chest. "I'm getting her back."

"I need you to not touch me," I warned, feeling my anger building with each second.

"I need you to not touch my girl," he countered, annoying me more and more. Nothing about Grace belonged to that guy. He had walked away from her, and it was clear he was only coming back around because he felt threatened.

"Fine, go ahead. She's all yours." I turned and headed for the front door because I didn't want to make a scene. I wasn't going to feed into the conversation because that was exactly what he wanted. He wanted me to act out. He wanted me to unleash the monster he was sure lurked inside me. He wanted to prove that I was no good for Grace.

Especially in front of the whole town.

So, I walked.

I released a weighted sigh as I listened to drunk Finn follow me.

"I just want to make it clear to you that if you go anywhere near her, I'll kick your ass!" he barked.

That actually made me laugh. Finn wasn't a built guy, and I was certain I could take him out with one hit. "Okay, buddy, that's fine. Now, just leave me alone."

"Come on," he said, racing over and shoving me from behind. "If you're such a badass, fight me."

I stopped my steps.

He's not worth it.

He shoved me again.

I took a deep breath and snapped my band against my arm.

He's not worth it.

The sooner he left me alone, the sooner Grace and I would be together, yet it was becoming more and more clear that he was really itching for a fight. He wanted to release the beast, and I didn't want it to come out.

"You aren't going to fight me back?" he asked, annoyance filling him up inside.

"No. I'm not."

"Why, because you think Grace will be disappointed? You think she'd be disgusted by the monster you really are? I mean, hell, what do you think would happen? You think she'd choose you or something?" I looked at him, and for a split second, I felt my heart skip a beat. He must've seen the look in my eyes because he laughed out loud. "Holy shit, you actually thought she'd pick you."

I kept quiet.

I snapped my band.

"You have nothing to offer her," he bellowed, his words filled with hatred. "You're the bottom of the barrel, and she's never going to pick you, you know. You might be a summer fling for her, but you'll never have her. She's broken, not stupid. You're nothing. You have nothing, you'll never be anything. After some time passes, she'll find her footing again without you, and you'll still be nothing."

"Okay. You're right, Finn. Congratulations."

He walked over to me and shoved me hard. "You're nothing but scum, and we'd be better off if you were dead like your bitch of a mother."

He spoke against my mother, and then I blacked out.

Next thing I knew, the two of us were rolling on the ballroom floor, fists flying. I slammed him into the floor, and he slugged me hard in the eye. As I rushed to get my bearings, Finn dived at me, sending me flying backward, straight into the table where the five-layer cake was sitting. It crashed to the ground, shooting frosting in all directions.

We kept hitting one another as a crowd formed and people tried to pull us apart.

He kept swinging, so I did the same, over and over again.

We were finally separated when Sheriff Camps arrived and yanked us off of each other.

Before I could even explain, he slammed us both behind bars.

Great.

That was exactly how the evening was not supposed to go.

Jackson
Ten Years Old

"Get out of here, freak!" Tim barked at me the first day I was back at school after Ma's funeral. He and his friends shoved me back and forth. "Nobody wants you here!"

He kept mocking me and making fun of me, but I didn't care.
I didn't care about anything.
Ma was gone, and life didn't matter anymore.
I let them push me.
I allowed them to shove.
I couldn't feel anything anymore, anyway.
"You're such a loser! You're never going to have friends, you freak," one of the guys said, tripping me as I tried to walk away.
My body slammed hard against the floor, and I groaned. As I tried to stand up, one of them kicked me down again.
I didn't say a word.
We went to class, and Tim kept kicking the back of my chair.
"Freak, freak, freak," he'd whispered.
I kept ignoring.

I tried to repeat what Ma would've told me.

I'm extraordinary. I'm extraordinary...

I didn't want to feed into Tim because I didn't care if he liked me anymore.

I didn't care if anyone liked me.

I just wanted my mom back...

"I'd wished you'd disappear and never come back," Tim hissed. "Like your stupid dead mom."

And then, without thought, I snapped.

CHAPTER FORTY-TWO

Grace

"Sheriff Camps, he doesn't deserve to be behind bars," I bellowed, blasting into the police station. The moment I heard about the fight breaking out and Jackson's arrest, I headed straight to the station.

Sheriff Camps was dressed in his suit and tie from the gala as he sat behind his desk. "Yeah, well, I don't deserve to be sitting here filling out this paperwork because it seems your two men cannot keep themselves from acting like damn monkeys in public," he grumbled.

"Yes, but it wasn't his fault! He did nothing wrong. And I think—"

"Time out. Which 'he' are we talking about?" he asked. "Which one are you here to save?"

"Jackson," I stated matter-of-factly. "I'm here for him."

"Good call. It seemed that Finn was the one who started the fight, which is a bit shocking."

That wasn't shocking to me at all. Not in the least.

"Can I go back to see them with you?"

He shook his head a bit. "I don't know, Grace. We don't really let people back there."

"Sheriff Camps…it's me. Lil' Miss Gracelyn Mae. I just want to talk to them both, that's all. I swear."

He sighed. "I guess it wouldn't hurt any. Come on back, but don't tell anybody I let you, all right? I don't need people thinking I'm going soft."

I agreed to the secret, and as he walked us to the back, I felt my heart racing. When my eyes fell upon Jackson, I gasped a bit. He was cut up and black and blue all across his face. His tie hung around his neck, and he looked so defeated.

Jesus, Finn. What were you thinking?

"Hey," he muttered.

"Hey," I replied.

"It seems you got yourself a get-out-of-jail-free card, buddy, thanks to this little ole lady. Be thankful, too—I would've kept you sit overnight." Sherriff Camps remarked as he fumbled with his keys before unlocking Jackson's cell.

The moment it opened, I wrapped my arms around him. "Are you okay?"

"I'm fine. I'm sorry."

"Sorry? For what? You didn't do anything wrong."

"Yeah, but still, I shouldn't have engaged with Finn." His voice was so low, almost a whisper. I could tell his mind was spinning, and I hoped he wasn't slipping too far away from me.

Stay here now, Jackson…

"I'll meet you up front in a second, okay?" I told him, rubbing his arm. He nodded and made his way up front. I walked over to Finn's cell. He looked up at me, his face just as beat up as Jackson's.

"I'm guessing you're not here to bail me out, too, huh?" he joked.

I could hardly look at him. He felt so much like a stranger to me. "You're still drunk."

"A little."

"You don't get drunk, Finn."

DISGRACE

"Well, maybe you aren't the only one who's changed a bit." He stood and walked over to me. His hands wrapped around the bars. "What are you doing, Grace? Running around with an addict?"

Wow, he was shooting low.

"He's clean," I told him. "He's been clean for years."

"For now. I mean, look what he did to my face. I told you he was dangerous."

"You did the same thing to him, too, Finn."

"Yeah but…" He sighed and turned away before looking back at me. "I love you."

"Stop saying that."

"No, I won't because I do. We have fifteen years of history together, and I cannot stand by and watch you run into the arms of that asshole. I love you too much for that."

"I prayed for you to say those words to me again," I whispered, shaking my head. "I prayed for you to want me back, to come back to me, but that's not what you wanted."

"Yes, it is. I'm telling you right now, you're who I want. I know things are messy but—"

"You only showed interest in me when another man did, Finn—that's not love, that's jealousy, and I don't want to play that game. I don't want to play any games. I just want you to let me go."

"I'm not going to quit," he warned. "I'm not going to give up on us, on this."

"There is no us, Finn."

"Because of that lowlife?"

"No." I shook my head. "Because of you."

"It's fine," Jackson grumbled as I pressed the warm cloth to his eye as he sat on his couch. "It's not the first time I've gotten a black eye for sleeping with another man's woman."

"I'm not his woman," I stated sharply, watching him wince as I pressed the cloth to his eye. "And he is not my man."

He tilted his head up. "If you're not his, then whose are you?"

"My own," I said breathlessly, feeling my heart began to beat faster. "Before I am anyone else's, I will always be my own."

"Geez," he whispered, shaking his head as he bit his bottom lip. "You have no clue how good it feels to hear you say that."

I smiled at him and went back to tending to his eye.

"You're doing it," he whispered, placing his hand against mine to stop me from patting his cheek.

"Doing what?"

"Finding yourself."

I grinned and wrung out the cloth. "I think you'll live to see another day."

"That's good to hear," he mumbled, looking down and fiddling with his fingers.

"What is it?" I asked. "What's wrong?"

"What do you see when you look at him? What do you see when you see Finn?" he asked, his voice filled with uncertainty.

I paused for a moment, lowering myself to the floor, and then I looked up at him. "I see my past. I see everything I was, and everything I was not."

"And what do you see when you look at me?"

I swore there was a small spark in his eyes that healed parts of me that I hadn't even known were broken. I ran my hand through my hair, bit my lip, and gave a slight shrug. "Possibilities."

CHAPTER FORTY-THREE

Jackson

I was shocked when Sunday morning rolled around, and Loretta Harris was knocking on my door. As I opened it, I noticed her in her Sunday best outfit with her big floppy hat and steamed dress. Standing there poised, she looked as southern as a woman could look.

I hated that her face matched her daughter's. It made it harder for me to despise her.

"Shouldn't you be on your way to praise that God of yours?" I asked her, leaning against my doorframe with my arms crossed.

She didn't arrive with the same spitfire that she'd brought my way the first time she barged into my shop. She wasn't barking demands or shouting at me. She was hauntingly calm and collected.

That brought about some unease.

"I haven't spoken to my daughter in days," she told me. "And the last time I saw her, I said things I regret."

"Yeah, well, perhaps you should've thought things through

before speaking. Now, if you'll excuse me, I have things to do." I began to close my door, and she blocked it with her arm. I cocked an eyebrow. She quickly dropped her arm.

"I'm sorry, it's just…" She sighed and shook her head. "I saw her in town, and she looked away. She has this crazy red hair and tattoos, and this just isn't who she is. She hasn't even been attending church."

"I wouldn't either if the people talked about me the way they do her."

"You think I enjoy it? Hearing what those people say about her?"

"No"—I shook my head—"I know you don't enjoy it, but I also don't think you try to stop it."

She parted her lips but paused. Reaching into her purse, she pulled out a check.

"I thought I told you I didn't want your money," I scolded her.

"Maybe you would if you looked at the price. It's enough to give you and your father a good life. You could start over anywhere in the world."

I took the check and ripped it in half. "I don't care about your money. You're not gonna run my father and me away from our own land. Besides, what does it matter? Grace is going back to work in a few weeks."

"Yes, but she'll be back for holidays, and you'll still be here. Then she'll make weekend trips to visit you. Then she'll find a job closer by. Don't you see? You're messing with her mind, making her think she could someday fall in love with you. You don't see it, do you? The way she looks at you?"

How?

How did she look at me?

"I don't want any trouble," I told her. "You should leave."

"Jackson, please, you must be realistic. Gracelyn has already been through enough, and on her path to finding her footing, she doesn't need distractions that might knock her off-kilter. I know you're trying to help her, but you're really hurting her, and yourself. I'll write a new check," she said, going to dig into her purse.

"Again, I don't want your money. Plus, Grace is a grown woman. I'll let her make the choice of shutting me out." I went to close the door, and she shouted my way, making me come to a full halt.

"It was my Samuel!" Loretta shot my way.

I cocked an eyebrow. "What?"

"It was Samuel." She cleared her throat, and a few tears fell from her eyes as I watched her body tremble. "It was my husband—the man who your mother loved. Samuel was the one she was leaving to be with that night."

My hands formed fists, and my mouth grew dry. "What the hell is wrong with you? Why would you lie about something like that?"

"I'm not lying. I found out the night of the storm. Samuel told me about how he'd fallen in love with a woman who he was leaving me for. Though, he didn't tell me her name." She narrowed her eyes and shook her head back and forth as she studied the wooden porch. "Before your mother, the women were just an escape. He never developed feelings for them, and he always came home to me. Because even when he faltered, I was still his end game. I was the one he crawled into bed with each night and whispered 'I love you' to. I was his forever, and he was mine.

"Then one day, a new family bought property in this here town, and a woman with eyes that matched yours walked into our church. She was beautiful, and Samuel noticed, as did I. I didn't take offense to it because, at the end of the day, he'd come home to me. We had that arrangement. Out of respect and loyalty, he'd come back to me. But then, he'd end up working later each night. Some nights, he'd come home so late, I swore I'd see the sun rising through the blinds. He'd stopped saying I love you, and I could smell her all over him. Honeysuckle and raspberries." She closed her eyes as more tears fell down her cheeks. "I had my suspicions about who the woman was, but it became very clear once the news came out that your mother was killed in a car accident. I'd never seen a man truly mourn until I watched my husband fall to the ground and cry out for your mother."

"You're lying," I choked out, stunned.

"I'm not, and I think you know it."

"Get off my property," I barked.

"Why do you think your father attacked the church all those years ago, Jackson? Why do you think he's so hell-bent on hating my family?"

"I said leave."

"Fine, I will. But tell me this… Can you really be with my daughter—the woman whose father is the reason your mother left all those years ago—and fully love her? Can you give yourself to Grace without resentment and anger? Can you stare into her eyes that match her father's and not attach her to that horrific event? I know I couldn't do it."

I didn't reply because I didn't have a clue how to gather any kind of words. I marched straight into my home and closed the door behind me as her words invaded every inch of my being.

"Is it true?" I barked, barging into Dad's house. He was sitting on the couch with his eyes half-open as he watched the morning news. The place was once again trashed even though I'd just cleaned it a few days back.

He looked like a zombie. Heavy bags under his eyes, greasy hair, filthy clothes. Nothing about my father resembled life.

"Well?" I badgered, tossing my hands up in annoyance. "Is it true?"

"What are you talking about? Is what true?"

"Was Samuel Harris the man Ma was having an affair with?"

The way his brows lowered and his lips slightly parted made it apparent to me that it was, indeed, the truth.

"Are you shitting me right now? Are you telling me this whole time you've known Samuel Harris was the man pretty much responsible for my mother's death, and you didn't find the need to tell me?"

"I told you to get that car out of my shop. I told you to stop fucking with that girl. What more did you want?"

"Oh, I don't know, maybe the fucking truth, Dad? Why didn't you tell me?"

"It was none of your damn business, boy," he told me, picking up his whiskey bottle and taking a swig. "You had no right to know."

I snatched it from his hand and threw it across the room. "I had every right to know."

"Piss off, Jackson. I don't have time for this."

"My mother's dead because of this situation, and your life is shit due to it all. You could've told me. I would've never let that family anywhere near our shop. I would've fought for you, for us. I would've—"

"That shit is over and done with. Get the hell out of my house."

"But Dad—"

"Look, your mother is dead, and she ain't ever coming back, all right? Let it go. Don't make me tell you again. Get out. I don't want to see your face."

He spoke to me in his drunken state as if it wasn't a big deal. As if my mother's death was nothing but a passing memory instead of a daily soul-burning sensation. He spoke as if he didn't relive the nightmare each day, the same way I did. He spoke as if she were nothing when, in fact, she was everything.

And the man responsible for her tragic ending lived right down the road.

The father to the woman who I had the nerve of almost falling for.

A few more days and I would've let her into my heart.

A few more days and I would've told her words that I'd never discovered before.

Yet that morning, the chains on my soul locked up tight once again, and there wasn't a chance I'd let Gracelyn Mae anywhere close to me.

CHAPTER FORTY-FOUR

Grace

"Okay, Jackson, two things. One, I only have about a week left in town to finish the last two seasons of *Game of Thrones* with you, so we better start doing two-a-day marathons. And two, I'm hungry, so I think we should order in Chinese food for the episodes tonight," I expressed, walking into the auto shop where Jackson's head was under the hood of a car.

He didn't respond right away, so when I walked over to him, I placed my hand on his shoulder, feeling him tense up.

Knots formed in my stomach. "Hey, is everything okay?"

"Yup," he replied shortly, not looking up.

Obviously, that was a lie. "Jackson, what's going on?"

"I'm working."

"Okay…but…you're also being super short with me."

He looked up in my direction, and I was taken aback by his cold stare. I hadn't seen those hard eyes in so long, and I was almost confused as to why he was shooting them in my direction.

"What is it?" I whispered as the palms of my hands grew moist. "What's going on?"

"I think it's best if we cut off this whole arrangement right now," he told me, going back to working on his car.

"What?"

"I just don't see the point. We aren't going anywhere, so we might as well end it now."

"What are you talking about? Where is all this coming from?"

"I just been thinking, and the truth is, I don't want anything to do with you."

"You're lying. What we have…what we are…" My voice was shaky because I was so thrown off by his change.

He locked his eyes with mine, his chilled stare piercing my soul, and he grimaced. "We aren't anything, princess, all right? Everything that happened this summer was a mistake—you were a mistake, and it's one I won't make again, all right?"

"Why are you acting like this?"

"Because this is who I am," he snapped. "This is who I'll always be."

"No. You're good, Jackson. You're kind, and gentle, and—"

"Drop it, Grace. I ain't got shit to say to you. Turn around and walk away because this conversation is over."

"Who's in your head right now?" I asked, gently placing my hands on his cheeks, staring into his eyes. I saw it, too. The small tremble in his bottom lip. "Who's feeding you these thoughts? Is it your father? Finn? My mother?"

He wrapped his hands around my wrists and lowered them from my face. "Walk away, princess, and don't look back. There's nothing here left for you."

My eyes watered over, and I took a few strides backward.

What changed so fast? How had it happened?

Just the other day, we saw possibilities. How did we go so quickly to the final chapter of our story when I was convinced we were only on chapter two?

"I know you," I swore to him. "This isn't you."

"You don't know me," he said, his voice sounded flat and somber. "You never did, and I never knew you. You were nothing more than another lay, and I'm done taking off your clothes, so you can go now."

I stumbled back a bit more by his words. I felt betrayed. Stung. Unbelievably hurt. "You don't mean that. You don't mean any of this. When we had no one, we had one another. I don't know what's going on in that head of yours, but whatever it is, we can figure it out together because that's what we do, Jackson. We help one another."

"Stop making it out like we're something we're not. I am not your friend. I am not your lover. I am nothing to you, and you are nothing to me." He turned away and went back to work, leaving me standing there stunned.

I wiped my tears away and turned to walk back toward the front door. I didn't see a point in continuing the conversation with Jackson. It was clear he had no goals of letting me back in.

"Grace?"

I turned to face Jackson as he stared my way.

"Yes?"

"Don't come back."

Those three words hurt the most because they meant that all our possibilities were officially gone.

"Grace, what are you doing here?" Finn asked as I stood in the hospital hallway. I'd been waiting for him to come past so I could speak to him. "What's wrong? Are you okay?" he asked me, sounding alarmed.

"Did you say something to him?" I asked, crossing my arms. "Did you tell Jackson something?"

"What?"

The blank stare in his eyes made me frown. His confusion was strong as if he hadn't a clue what I was talking about.

"I haven't seen him since the fight," he told me.

"Don't lie to me, Finn."

"I'm not. I swear. Why did…?" He cocked an eyebrow and shook his head. "He let you down."

"You don't know what you're talking about," I told him as I turned and walked away.

Finn called after me. "You can't really be surprised, Grace. That's what everyone's been trying to tell you. He's a ticking time bomb, and it was only a matter of time before he hurt you."

"He's not what you think he is," I swore. I knew Jackson. I knew the corners of his dusty soul that he never shared with anyone else. Something happened, and it had to be bad if it meant he'd pushed me away like he did. "He's kind."

"Look at my face, Grace. How kind could he be?" Finn argued.

"You started that fight."

"I was drunk. He did this sober. Besides, I know you. I know you better than you know yourself. He's not the right move for you, Grace. You're better than him."

I snickered. "That's funny."

"What's funny?"

"That you think you know me. The truth is, the girl you knew died the moment you betrayed her."

"He's a monster, Grace. He'll keep hurting you and letting you down." I walked away without responding as a tear rolled down my cheek. Yet Finn kept calling my way. "I'm not giving up on us, Grace! I'm not going to stop fighting for us."

It was insane to me how life worked.

As Finley was going on and on about "us," my mind was locked on Jackson and what scarred his heart.

"Gracelyn Mae," Autumn said, sitting at the reception table. She stood slowly, revealing her growing baby bump.

Every time I saw her, a part of me wanted to die.

She hurried around the desk in my direction. "What are you doing here? Is someone hurt?"

"Don't act like you care, Autumn," I softly spoke.

"But I do. I…" Her eyes watered over, and a chill raced over me.

The last thing she needed to do was cry. I didn't have time for her tears. "Were you talking to Finn?"

I raised an eyebrow but didn't reply.

She continued as her body began to shake. "I know it's not really my business, but, well, everything's a mess. My own family won't hardly talk to me, and now Finn is so distant. Are you two…is there something…?"

I crossed my arms. "Are you asking me if my soon-to-be ex-husband is cheating on you with me?"

Her tears fell.

I hated her beautiful tears.

"I just… I'm so lost. I don't even know how to deal with it. Finn made all of these promises to me about a future, and I just can't—"

"No," I cut her off. "You do understand why none of this is my concern, right? I'm not your person anymore, Autumn. You don't get to confide in me when you're the one who stole my life. You get that, right?"

She took a few steps back. "Yes, of course. I'm sorry."

As I started to walk away, I heard her break into a sob, and my stomach knotted up. Even though I hated her, a part of me that still felt sorry for her. Call it stupidity, or call it ignorance, but her loneliness was something I once lived. The place where you wonder about all your faults for Finn not coming home to you. The place where you doubt every heartbeat in your chest.

Autumn wasn't a good friend. She hurt me to my core in more ways than one, but those words that Dad taught me slowly danced through my head.

If you turn your back on one, then you turn your back on all.

"Do you love him?" I asked as I looked up at her.

With such unease, she nodded, ashamed to admit her love. "Yes."

"Do you love yourself?"

More tears fell as she shook her head. "No."

I sighed because, for the first time since the news came out about Finn and Autumn, I saw her. I truly studied her beyond her beauty, beyond her being everything I thought I was supposed to be. I saw the cracks in her soul and the scars on her heart.

She made a choice, just as Finn had. They decided to betray me, and their choices changed the course of all our lives. Now the two of them had to deal with those consequences, the same way I had. In her eyes, it almost seemed like she hadn't known who she was, or where her life was heading. On top of that, she had to somehow find a way to be strong for the child she'd be bringing into the world someday soon.

In those eyes, I saw her regret.

Her sorrow.

Her pain.

Autumn hadn't a clue what she was doing.

She was broken, shattered, and alone. Her family turned on her, and the father of her child was pining after another woman. Autumn had hit rock bottom, and she didn't have a clue who or what she was anymore.

I knew what that was like—to be in such darkness that you forget what the light feels like.

"You can't love him if you don't love yourself, Autumn. It's impossible," I swore to her.

"I know, I know. It's just…I'm so lost," she cried.

"I know," I said in understanding. Even though she wasn't my friend, and she hurt me, I understood the meaning of being lost. Maybe more than most. "But it's not my job to find you. It's not Finn's job to find you. The only one responsible for you is you. You have to find yourself. You have to have your own back. Otherwise, you'll spend your life trying to be everything for everyone else, and one hundred percent of the time, you'll still not be enough. So, you gotta choose yourself. From this point on, you have to be your first choice. Otherwise, you'll drown."

"Thank you, Grace."

I almost replied, always and always, but I wasn't in the position to tell Autumn a lie.

"Mama, did you say something to Jackson today?" I asked her, walking into her living room.

"It's good to see you too, Gracelyn Mae. I'm glad to see you still remember where your family lives. If only you could recall where the church is, then we'd be fine," she sarcastically remarked.

"Mama. Did you talk to Jackson?"

"Grace—"

"Tell me the truth." Her bottom lip quivered. My heart dropped. "Mama, how could you?"

"Look at you, Gracelyn Mae. You aren't yourself," she said, gesturing toward me.

"I wish people would stop saying that."

"It's true. You're not yourself, and you haven't been for a long time. I spoke to him because I love you. I'm all about you finding yourself, but Jackson Emery isn't the way you make that discovery."

"You don't get to make that choice for me. You don't get to run my life, but now, Jackson won't even talk to me. What did you say to him?"

"It doesn't matter."

"Mama. Tell me."

But she wouldn't. Her lips wouldn't part, but her truth wouldn't spill out from her tongue. I couldn't even imagine what she could've told him to make him that way, to make him so cold after a summer of melting beside me. "I'm done. I'm done with this town, with this lifestyle, and with you, Mama. All my life, all I've ever done was try to make you proud, and the one time I choose myself over you is when you turn your back on me. All while claiming you love me. That's not love, Mama. That's manipulation, and my mind is no longer yours to control."

"Gra—"

"I don't want to see you again."

"You don't mean that," she warned. "I am your mother."

"No. You're just the woman who gave birth to me. You are no mother of mine."

I turned and walked away, feeling more alone with every step I took. When I got to Judy's house, I began to pack my bags. There was nothing left for me in Chester, Georgia, anymore, and I'd rent a car and be out of there before I could blink my eyes shut.

"Grace?" Judy said, walking into my bedroom. "What's going on? I just got a frantic call from Mama. Are you okay?"

"I'm leaving."

"What? Why? What's going on?" Her voice was so alarmed as she walked to my side. "Talk to me."

"I can't. I just have to go. I'm going to rent a car and drive back to Atlanta and get a rental place for a week before I move into my place. I just can't…" I took a deep breath. "I can't breathe here."

"Okay." She nodded. "I'm coming with you. I'll drive."

"What? No. Judy, you don't have to do this. I can go on my own."

"I know you can, but you're not going to. I'm driving." She wouldn't let me argue with her, and before I knew it, my suitcases were packed into the back of her car.

We drove down the streets of Chester, and we paused at the stop sign right near Mike's Auto Shop. I could see Jackson hammering out on the broken-down car around the building, hitting it repeatedly. When he looked up, my heart skipped.

Judy turned my way. "Do you want to say goodbye?" she asked.

"No," I told her because even though my mom told him something, it was on Jackson that he chose to turn cold. He was allowed to make a choice, just like all humans were allowed to do. Our choices defined us. We could go left or right. We could say yes or no. We could hold on, or we could let go. Jackson chose to let go, and in response to that, I let him go, too.

He and I were a summer of lust. We were a summer of finding ourselves. Of losing ourselves. Of finding each other. Of losing each other.

Even though it was over, I had no regrets. If I could go back in time, I'd still fall into Jackson Emery because, to me, he represented possibilities. He stood for the idea that even on the dark days, one could still find light. During that summer, he became my faith, and I swore for a small moment, I was his.

In the dark, vacant trunk of Judy's Honda sat two pieces of

mismatched, tattered, and torn luggage. They each held a part of me within them. They each told a story of the woman I was and the woman I was becoming. And Jackson Emery, the man I crashed into, the man who made me remember how it felt to breathe again, watched them all drive away.

CHAPTER FORTY-FIVE

Jackson

She'd been gone for a few weeks, and I hadn't stopped thinking about her. I did my best to get Grace off my mind, but she made it her mission to stay wrapped in every thought that crossed me.

I didn't mind.

If I couldn't have her, I'd at least have the memories of what we shared.

On a cold evening in September, I received the call I'd been dreading for so many years. The call that rocked my world upside down and left me dazed and confused.

"Jackson, it's Alex. Your dad is in the ICU."

The second the words were spoken, I felt as if I'd died. I rushed to the hospital, and when I got to the reception desk, I panicked. "Hi, my dad was brought in. He's in the ICU, a-a-and—" I began to stutter as the receptionist stared my way.

Autumn.

"Mike Emery, yes. Let me look up which room he's in, Jackson," she said, typing in some information. "He's in room 234, on the second floor. Elevators are down the hall to the left."

I started moving before she even finished talking. I broke out into a run, and instead of taking the elevator, I shot up the stairs. My heart sat in my throat as I hurried to 234, and when I arrived, Alex was standing in the hallway talking to a doctor.

"What's going on?" I barked, barreling forward. "What's the deal?" The anger that raced through my chest when I looked up and saw Finn staring my way only pissed me off more. "You're his doctor?"

"Yes, and—"

"No. We want someone else."

"What? I'm sorry, I'm the only one on the floor tonight and—"

"I don't give a damn. Call someone else," I ordered. The last thing I wanted was that asshole to be dealing with my father's care.

"Jackson, look, I know we've had our issues, but please believe that my patients are always my top priority," Finn stated. "None of my personal issues are going to affect your father's treatment."

"Bullshit. Get a new doctor," I said through clenched teeth. My blood was racing, and I hadn't had a chance to slow it down since getting the call from Alex.

"Jackson," Alex cut in. "Just listen to him. He was updating me on Mike's condition."

I grimaced but didn't say another word. I crossed my arms, and my eyes were locked on Finn. I didn't trust the asshole, but at that moment, I didn't really have a choice.

"Your father suffered from acute alcohol poisoning. Your uncle found him passed out with vomit in his mouth, and he called an ambulance right away. Though he hasn't woken up yet, we are closely working to stabilize him. We are watching his airways and maintaining his circulation and breathing. Now, it's mainly a waiting game until he actually wakes up."

"That's it?" I growled. "All you have to offer me is waiting? Are you kidding me?"

Finn frowned, and I wanted to slam my fist right into his face. "I wish I had more information for you, but that's where we are right now."

I wanted to cuss him out, but I didn't. I walked into Dad's hospital room, saw him hooked up to all those machines, and I swore my heart died all over again. "Fuck," I said on an exhalation, pulling a chair up beside his bed. I lowered my head and sniffled.

He looked like shit. He was so skinny and weak, and it seemed like those machines and wires were the only thing keeping him alive.

"I can't believe you did this," I said, taking his hand into mine. "Listen, I don't really have time for this, so can you just wake up? All right?" I nudged him in the arm. "Just wake up, all right?"

"Jackson…" Alex's voice was low, but I ignored him.

"Wake up, you fucking asshole," I said to my father, the man who had once been my hero. My chest burned as I choked on my words and tears began to fall from my eyes. My head fell to our embraced hands, and I began to fall apart. "Please, Dad," I whispered. "Just wake up."

Seven hours had passed, and he was still not waking up. They used the term alcoholic coma and told me there was nothing they could really do except for wait.

I was so damn tired of waiting.

"Jackson," a voice said from the doorway. I'd been in the same chair in the same position since I'd arrived. I looked up to see Judy standing there. She gave me a small smile. "Hey, Jackson."

Seeing her eyes made me miss her sister.

"What are you doing here?" I asked.

"I heard about your dad. As you know, rumors get around this town fast. I figured you could use someone to sit with you." My stomach knotted up, but I didn't reply as she walked into the room. She sat down beside me and gave me a small smile. "Are you okay?"

"No."

"Okay. It's okay not to be okay. But just know that you're not alone."

I lowered my head, bewildered by Judy sitting beside me. She owed me nothing, not an ounce of her time or energy, yet there she was, sitting beside me, letting me know that I wasn't alone.

"Why are you here?" I asked her.

"Because I made a promise."

"To who?"

"My sister."

I turned to look at her, confused. "What do you mean?"

"I drove her to Atlanta a few weeks ago, and when I was getting ready to leave, she asked me to do only one thing."

"And what was that?"

"To look after you."

I grimaced and clasped my hands together. My feet tapped rapidly against the floor tiles. "I miss her," I confessed.

"I know," she replied. "And she misses you, too. Which makes it hard for me to understand why you aren't on speaking terms."

"It's complicated."

"No." She shook her head. "It's not. Falling for someone isn't hard. It's the easiest thing in the world. It's all the other things that surround the fall that make it hard. But those feelings that you both feel for one another? That's easy, and if you allow yourself to let it in, you'll be happy that you did. But you both are allowed to figure things out on your own time. For now, I'd just like to sit here with you if that's okay."

"Yes." I nodded. "That's okay."

We sat in silence, watching the lines dance around the machines as my father fought for his life.

"Can you not tell Grace about this?" I asked her. "Please. I don't want her to worry."

"If that's what you want, then I'll respect that. But it's okay for you to need her. It's okay to need people."

I didn't reply to her comment, but I simply thanked her for sitting beside me that afternoon. She gave me the warmest smile and lightly squeezed my knee. "Always and always."

If only she knew how much that meant to me.

DISGRACE

Days passed, and nothing changed. Judy stopped by each day and would sit beside me whenever Alex wasn't around. We didn't talk about anything at all; we merely sat in silence wishing and hoping for my father to open his eyes. When Friday evening came, I sat in the room, and when a voice was heard at the door, I looked up.

My chest burned.

"Gracelyn," I muttered, standing up.

"Hi."

"What are you doing here?"

Grace stood in the doorway. "Can I come in?"

I nodded, and she walked into the room slowly. The look of fear in her eyes when she saw my father hurt me.

He looked awful, and it was apparent.

Then she looked at me. The look of sadness that found her eyes when she saw me hurt me.

I looked awful, and it was apparent.

She didn't say another word, but she wrapped her arms around me and pulled me close.

God, I missed this.

I missed her. I missed us.

"I'm so sorry," she whispered.

"I'm so sorry," I replied.

I held her for a while, afraid to let go because I feared if I did, she'd just fade away like a mirage.

When I finally let go, I walked over to the window and took a deep breath.

"He's in a coma," I told her, my voice cracking. "He's been this way for days now, and if he doesn't wake up..." My words faded off, and I jerked my hand through my hair. "I hate him," I told her. "I've hated him for so long—for the person he became, for the person he turned me into—but if anything happens to him...if I lose him..." I shut my eyes. "He's my dad, Grace. He's all I have, and if I lose him, I lose my world."

I wiped a stubborn tear that fell from my eye.

"Jackson, come here," she said softly. I hated how her gentle voice brought a small dash of ease to my mind.

"No," I said. "I'm fine. How did you even know I was here? I asked Judy not to tell you."

"And she didn't, but you live in Chester, Georgia—word spreads quickly, even to Atlanta. Now, come here."

"I'm fine, really. You can go," I told her, looking at my father.

"Jackson," she said, this time placing her hand on my shoulder. She then held her other hand out toward me. "Please, come here."

I sighed and placed my hand in hers. She pulled me into another tight hug.

She wasn't a mirage.

She wasn't a dream.

She was real…she was there.

"I'm okay," I told her.

"You're lying," she replied.

"Gracelyn—"

"No." She shook her head as she laid it against my chest. "You don't get to argue your way out of this one, okay? You have to let me hold you for a while. So just be quiet and don't let go, okay?"

I took a deep breath and pulled her closer to me.

Comfort.

I wasn't used to comfort, but pain I knew a lot about. That afternoon, Grace gave me so much comfort, and even if I had wanted to let her go, my heart wouldn't have allowed me to do it.

"Thank you," I whispered, pulling her even closer and resting my forehead against hers. "Thank you for coming back."

"Always," she said softly, her exhalations falling against my lips. "And always."

CHAPTER FORTY-SIX

Grace

I hadn't left the hospital since I'd learned Jackson's father had been admitted. I wandered off to go find food and coffee for Jackson because I knew he wasn't going to leave that spot, and as I was heading back to the room, I felt chills race up my back.

"Grace, what are you doing here?"

I turned around to see Finn staring my way. "What do you mean what am I doing here? Jackson's father is here, and I'm staying by Jackson's side."

"He called you?" he said, sounding somewhat surprised.

"No, but I'm surprised you didn't. I know we are going through things, Finley, but for you not to let me know Jackson's father was here… You should've told me."

"I couldn't. Patient-doctor confidentiality."

"Oh, screw your confidentiality, Finn. You could've told me!"

"No, I couldn't have, and frankly, I don't know how it got back to you," he said.

"I told her," Autumn replied, walking up behind the two of us.

"You what?!" he barked at her. "Why would you do that?"

"I just figured…" She sighed. "I walked past Jackson's room and saw him sitting there alone. His uncle went to work, and Jackson had been alone all day. I just thought he could use someone."

"That wasn't your place," Finn growled, growing red in the face. "You crossed a line."

"I'm happy she crossed it," I told him. I couldn't look at Autumn because seeing her still seared the broken pieces of my heart.

"It wasn't her place, and Grace…Jackson Emery isn't the type of person you need to be around."

"You don't get to decide that for me."

"He's dangerous—*violent*."

"We aren't doing this again, Finn." It felt like we were running on the same hamster wheel getting nowhere every time we crossed paths. "You started that fight."

"He's the one who swung!"

"You gave him a black eye!"

"He deserved it!"

"You don't get to decide that. You went to him and started a fight! He did nothing wrong," I snapped back at him.

"He's a burden in your life. You shouldn't even be friends with him."

"You don't get to make those decisions for me."

"She's right, Finn," Autumn said, stepping into the conversation.

"Autumn, will you mind your own fucking business for a second?! I'm trying to have a conversation with my wife here!" he barked, and as the words rolled off his tongue, I felt how they must've stung Autumn.

His wife.

I finally looked her way and saw the heaviness in her stare.

Then came the embarrassment, the guilt, the shame.

"Sorry. By all means, have your talk with your wife," she said, before turning to walk away.

Finn sighed and pinched the bridge of his nose. "Jesus, that's not what I meant. I just..." His voice faded off, and Autumn kept walking. "*Shit!*" He stood there for a moment, staring at me, unsure what to say. "I'm not sure what to do," he confessed.

I inhaled deeply and shook my head once. "You have two choices: you can stay here with me, or you can go after her," I told him straightforwardly. "But trust me, staying here with me isn't going to get you anywhere whatsoever."

He sighed and nodded. Then he turned and walked in Autumn's direction.

"And Finley?"

He looked back toward me with those blue eyes I used to love so much. "Yes?"

"You don't have a wife anymore. It's time to let me go."

Not another word was spoken because he knew. He already knew we were over and done.

It was no secret that our story had reached its final chapter, and some stories didn't get the happily ever after.

Some stories simply ended.

Mike hadn't awoken for two days, and the worry that filled me was sickening. Jackson was falling apart, and I wasn't certain how to keep him together. We sat on the couch in the hospital room, and I lay against him as he closed his eyes and focused on his breathing. Sometimes I'd bring a novel with me and read out loud to him to try to keep his mind from spiraling.

"We should go to your place so you can shower," I told him, and he shook his head.

"I don't want to leave."

"It's been days, Jackson. The moment anything changes, they will let you know. We should just get you home for some rest, just for a few hours."

He nodded slowly and finally agreed.

We walked back in complete silence, and when I saw his body

began to fold, I placed my hand in his and gave it a light squeeze so he knew he wasn't walking the path alone.

Once we got to his place, I turned on his shower and grabbed him a change of clothes. I set the clothes on the bathroom counter then went to grab him from the living room.

He was standing in front of his mother's paintings, staring at them with such sadness in his eyes.

"Your shower's ready," I told him.

"Thank you."

He cleared his throat and walked into the bathroom. Then he peeked his head out. "Grace?"

"Yes?"

"Come in with me?"

Yes.

I went into the bathroom with him, and we took off one another's clothing so slowly. The only sound was from the water streaming from the showerhead. I climbed into the tub first, and he followed me. We stayed quiet, him rubbing soap against my back, and me lathering his hair with shampoo. We cleansed our skin, our hurts, our fears, and when the soap washed away from our bodies, we remained standing under the hot water.

Jackson pressed his forehead to mine and closed his eyes. I felt his breaths coating my skin as he inhaled deeply and exhaled slowly. "I can't lose him, Grace," he said softly, and I watched as his tears intermixed with the water falling against his skin. "I can't lose him."

I felt the heaviness of his words, and I wasn't certain how to fix this, how to fix his heartbreak, or how to heal his father, so for the first time in a while, I did the only thing I could think to do when life felt out of control.

I closed my eyes, took a deep breath, and began to pray.

Dear God, it's me, Gracelyn Mae…

CHAPTER FORTY-SEVEN

Jackson

He wasn't waking up, and each day that passed made it more unlikely that he would. On Sunday morning, I was tired of looking at his small figure in that hospital bed, but I wasn't certain what more I could do. I couldn't leave for long periods of time because I felt he'd pass away while I was gone, and I wouldn't be there when it happened.

I knew it sounded stupid, but when I lost my mother, she was alone. She'd died alone, by herself, and I couldn't imagine that happening with my father.

I'd never forgive myself if I wasn't there beside him when he either woke up or fell asleep forever.

"We'll have to start making big decisions soon," Finn told me, standing in the hospital room as Grace stood in the far corner. Whenever he came around, she made sure to drop hold of my hand, just to make it a little more comfortable for everyone.

Finn went on about options, and then even mentioned that my

dad might not ever come out of the coma so next steps needed to be addressed.

"You mean unplugging his machines?" I asked him.

He frowned. "I mean making the best choice for his life. I'll give you some time to think everything over."

I nodded, and before he left, he glanced at Grace one more time.

"He still loves you," I whispered, lowering my head and staring at my hands. I didn't know why that bothered me, but it did. I hadn't known Grace for long at all, and we had made it very clear where we stood with one another. Yet, still, seeing how he looked at her hurt me.

Part of my mind wondered if, over time, she'd ever look at him in the same way again.

"He loves the idea of me," she said matter-of-factly. "But truthfully, he doesn't even know me anymore. Plus, I think it's more of a 'I want what I can't have' type of thing. He only wants me because he thinks you have me."

I turned toward her a bit and gave her a broken smile. I wanted to speak my mind. I wanted to open up my heart and tell her what it'd been feeling, but I held my tongue.

Late that evening, she'd be on her way back to Atlanta to fall into her future, and I'd still be in Chester, stuck in my past.

But, if there was ever a way, I'd wish she could be mine because so many parts of me wished I was hers.

"I was thinking," she told me, walking back over to me on the couch. She sat down, and her hands fell into mine. "Every now and then, my family hosts a person in need, and we do prayer and a dinner to help those going through difficult times. I was thinking maybe you could be our guest tonight before I head back to Atlanta."

I raised an eyebrow. "I thought you said you didn't pray anymore."

She shrugged. "I didn't, but I recently started again."

"For me?" I asked.

She nodded. "For you."

I didn't pray, and I didn't believe in God, but for some reason, that meant the world to me, more than she'd ever know. "Your family hates me."

"Only my mother, and don't worry, she might hate me more than she hates you," she joked.

"No, she doesn't."

"How do you know?"

"Because no one can hate you, Grace. Trust me"—I rubbed the palm of her hands with my thumbs—"I've tried."

"I haven't really seen or talked to my mom since the blowout we had, so it might be a little weird to see her, but I think if she sees you —the *real* you—she'll understand where I'm coming from."

"Even if she doesn't, that's okay. You should make up with your mom regardless of any misunderstandings or drama," I told her, glancing toward my father. "Because in the end, those disagreements don't matter. What matters most is family, even if it's a bit messed up."

She swallowed hard. "Are you encouraging me to make up with my mother?"

"You'd never forgive yourself if you didn't."

"You're not wrong… So, will you come? It could be a nice break for a while. Just to get away for a bit." She was good at that, good at making me take breaths whenever I forgot how to breathe. "Say yes?" she begged.

So, I did.

I felt oddly nervous as I stood on the front porch of Grace's parents' house. If my dad knew I was standing in front of the Harrises' home to receive prayers for his life, he would've come back to full health just so he could murder me.

But Grace had a way of making me do things I wouldn't normally do.

"Are the flowers stupid?" I asked. I'd brought a dozen red roses for Loretta Harris—the sky was falling, and hell had frozen over.

"They're perfect," she told me. "You're fine." She squeezed my hand, giving me a burst of comfort, but it didn't last long once the front door opened and Loretta stood there.

"What in the world is he doing here?" She gasped, staring my way.

"I told you I was bringing the person in need today, Mama, remember?"

"Yes," she said, her voice low and cold. "But you failed to mention it was *him*." She spat out the last word as if I were diseased.

I couldn't blame her—I used to do the same with her family's name.

"Yes, but we welcome all into our home, right, Loretta?" her husband said, walking into the foyer. He looked my way and nodded once. I did nothing in reply. The longer I stood there, the more I began to regret my decision.

I cleared my throat. "I brought flowers."

Loretta eyed them up and down. "Yes," she muttered. "It seems you did."

"That's nice," Samuel remarked. "Thank you, Jackson."

Loretta turned toward her husband and grumbled as she moved past him. "This is a huge mistake," she whined before walking away.

Samuel looked at me and smiled. "We're glad to have you here, Jackson. I'm very sorry to hear about your father."

I still didn't reply, but when he held his hand out toward me, I shook it.

As we walked into the house, my eyes fell to a painting on the foyer wall, and my gut tightened.

I was almost certain that this home was the last place I was supposed to be.

The dinner was odd for me. When everyone sat at the table and they all began to pray, I wasn't certain what to do, so I studied the clock hanging on the wall. How long did it take one to pray? And if prayers were real, did you have to do it for a certain amount of time?

I felt unease throughout the whole meal, but the saving grace of it all was Judy, and her husband, Hank. They seemed so much like

Grace that it made it a bit easier to breathe. They seemed like genuinely good people.

"Mama, aren't you going to do the tour of the property with Jackson?" Grace asked. Then she turned to me. "She always shows the guests around the property. This place is her pride and joy."

She shot Grace a dirty look. "No. I'm going to do these dishes."

Judy laughed. "Since when do you do dishes, Mama?"

Loretta scolded her daughter as she stood and started clearing items away. "Since always, Judith Rae. Now come help me, will you?"

Judy rolled her eyes toward Grace and made a face, which made me smirk. At least I wasn't the only one Loretta drove insane.

"I'll show him around," Samuel said, standing up from his chair. "I was hoping to have a moment to talk to him a bit anyway."

Grace's face went pale. "Talk to him about what?" she asked, her nervousness evident in her expression.

"Just things between the two of us, that's all. How about you and Hank finish clearing off the table? Come on, Jackson, let's take a stroll."

I knew I didn't have a choice, not really, so I stood and followed him.

As we walked around the acres of land, Samuel began to tell me all about it. He went into the stories of the orchards, the berry bushes, and the swimming pool used for baptisms, but I cut into the conversation once we started talking about tennis courts.

"We don't have to do this," I told him.

"Do what?"

"The small talk."

He grimaced and stopped his steps, knowing exactly what I was getting at. He crossed his arms and looked my way. "We've never really spoken in all these years, have we?" he asked.

"I never had anything to say to you," I stated harshly, feeling my chest tighten. He didn't flinch at my words, probably because he knew he deserved them.

"Jackson…Loretta told me you know about your mother and me."

I tensed. "Yes."

"I can only imagine what finding that out could've done to you. I'm so sorry you had to find out like that. That you had to find out at all."

"The artwork in the foyer...does your wife know who painted it?"

He pinched the bridge of his nose and shifted his glasses up. Then he shook his head. "No."

"Does anyone know?"

"No."

I sighed and turned his way. "She told my father. She told him how much she loved you, how much you meant to her. She never told him it was actually you who she was in love with, but that there was another man. She said all the words that killed him inside, and you hang my mother's artwork in your home. Right in front of your wife's face. That doesn't seem very God-like."

"If things had ended differently..." He paused, took a breath. "I wouldn't have kept it a secret."

"Well, lucky for you, you can take it to the grave. Your legacy will be left unmarked."

"Jackson, it's complicated."

"It's not. It's just sad because my mother..." My palms began to sweat as I blinked my eyes shut. "My mother deserved to be loved out loud, and you mourned her in silence."

He lowered his head. "I loved her like I never loved before, and I blame myself for what happened every day."

"It wasn't your fault, not yours alone, at least. You knew my mom was married, and you knew you were married, too, but still, you betrayed both families by creating a story that should've never come to life. My father spent years trying to use alcohol to heal the heartbreak she left him with. Before he even had a chance to hate her, he had to mourn her death, and now he's fighting for his life against the demons you set free inside him."

"I'm truly sorry about your father. I've been praying—"

"We don't want your prayers," I said bluntly. "I didn't come here for this, for your guidance, for you or your god. Honestly, I don't believe in either one."

"Then why are you even here?"

"Because she asked me to come. Grace wanted me to come. I don't believe in you or your god, but I believe in her. No one has ever stood by my side in all my life except for her, so the least I can do is stand beside her in the same fashion. This family means more than words to her, so that's why I'm here. For her and her alone."

He lowered his brows and guilt washed over him. "If she found out about what happened…"

"She'd never forgive you, I know, which is why she hasn't heard a word about it from me. You're the apple of her eye, and just because you're my family's demon, that doesn't mean you can't be her angel. I won't ruin the image she has of you."

"Thank you," he said sincerely. He cleared his throat and crossed his arms. "Can I ask you something? Your father attacked the church because of what went on between your mother and me, correct?"

"Yes."

"How did he even find out about the two of us?"

"I have no clue," I told him. "He doesn't talk about it."

His brows lowered. "I cannot imagine what that did to him."

"You don't have to imagine. His current situation is living proof of his scars."

He frowned. "Thank you again, for not telling Grace."

"Yeah. It just makes me wonder… You don't want to tell her because you don't want her to see you in a different light, right? Because you want her to keep loving you for who she thinks you are?"

"Exactly."

"But do you really want that? Do you want someone's love by keeping secrets from them, or do you want their full love when they see all your flaws?"

He didn't reply as he removed his glasses and pinched the bridge of his nose again.

"You two look quite serious," was heard behind me, and I cringed as I turned to see Grace standing there. "What's going on?"

"Nothing," I said. "Just guy talk."

"You're lying. You smile too much when you're keeping something from me. Dad? What is it?"

"It's nothing really," I told her, taking her hand into mine. "But I'm going to get back to the hospital."

"I'll come with you," she told me, but I shook my head.

"No. Stay here with your family for a little while. Just stop by before you leave town tonight?"

She nodded and pulled me into a hug. "Okay, but if you need anything, let me know." As she held me, I held her tighter, and I felt it in every inch of my being.

I loved her.

I was in love with every single part of her soul.

CHAPTER FORTY-EIGHT

Grace

"That was good," Judy told me as we finished cleaning up the kitchen that evening. "I'm glad you brought him."

"You think it went okay? Mama didn't really say much." I frowned. It still amazed me, after everything we went through, that I still craved her approval. Maybe that would never truly go away. Maybe a person always craved their parents' love and understanding.

"Maybe her not talking was a good thing," Judy remarked. "Maybe that meant she was taking it all in."

"I hope so." I truly did.

"I've never seen that look before," Mama commented, walking into the kitchen and leaning against the doorframe. Her voice was so soft and low that I was almost confused if she was my mother after all. "The way that boy looked at you. The way you looked at him…" Her eyes watered over, and she wiped away a few falling tears. "I didn't understand."

"Mama..." I whispered, stunned to see emotion falling from her eyes. In all my life, I'd never once seen my mother cry. Not even during the darkest days.

"My stubbornness kept me from understanding. My pride got in my way, but Gracelyn Mae, the way the two of you look at one another floored me. It was as if you could truly see each other. I've never seen that in all my life."

"Except for you and Dad," Judy remarked.

Mama frowned.

Tears kept falling.

"What's going on?" I asked, completely confused by her emotions.

She couldn't talk. Judy and I hurried over to her and wrapped her into our arms. I didn't have a clue what was breaking her. I didn't have any idea why she was falling apart. All I knew was that she needed me there for her, and right there was where I'd be.

There was something so heartbreaking about seeing your parents fall apart.

It was as if you were watching Superwoman fall from the sky.

"Is everything okay?" Dad asked, walking into the room. His glasses sat on top of his head as always, and he stuffed his hands into his pockets as we released Mama.

"He loves her, Samuel," Mama confessed, gesturing toward me. "That boy loves her."

"What? No..." I whispered. Jackson didn't love me...

Jackson Emery didn't love at all.

"Yes," Dad agreed, "he does."

Mama wiped at her eyes. "Even after what I told him, he still stood by her side. For the past years, I'd been trying to delete that woman from our lives, and then her son has the nerve to fall in love with my daughter."

"That woman?" I questioned. "What's that supposed to mean?"

Mama sighed, wiping her eyes, and then she walked out of the room, leaving a confused Judy and I standing there.

I turned to my father. "Dad? What is she talking about?"

He swallowed hard, and I watched as the emotion that once lived in Mama swarmed his eyes. "We should have a talk."

"You're upset," Dad remarked, meeting me on the front porch where I'd been sitting for the past ten minutes after he told me about his past.

"I'm confused," I corrected.

He sat down beside me, guilt written all over his face as we both stared out into the night sky.

"Jackson's mother…did you love her?" I asked.

"Yes."

"If she were alive, you'd still be with her?"

He frowned. "Yes."

"Do you love Mama?"

"Your mother has been my rock for years now."

I gently laughed, shaking my head. "That wasn't my question."

"I know."

"Before Hannah Emery, were there other women? Or was she the only one?"

"Grace…you must understand…" he started, but I rolled my eyes.

"No. I get it. You were unfaithful to a woman who stood by you no matter what. It all makes sense to me now. Mama being so pushy about me going back to Finn. She truly believes that no matter what, you're supposed to stand by your man. That's all she's ever done, too. She's always stood by you, and you kept betraying her."

He sniffled, glancing up at the stars in the sky. "I've made plenty of mistakes."

"You're not wrong, and you used her loyalty to abuse her heart. No wonder she's so cold. She doesn't know what love is anymore."

"You hate me," he remarked.

"Yes." I paused. "No."

It was complicated, my feelings for my father. I felt as if I'd been hit by a freight train, and I was left trying to gather all the pieces of my soul.

"You told me when I came here this summer that we were created to feel, and sometimes our feelings came out of order. You said in one second, your heart can beat for love, and in the next, hate could show up. That's how I'm feeling right now. Just confused."

"I'm sorry."

"Yeah. It's just funny. I always wondered where I went wrong with Finn. How I stumbled into a relationship where the foundation of loyalty didn't exist." I took a deep breath and looked up at the same stars he studied that night. "It just turns out that I married a man who was exactly like my father."

"I've let you down."

"Yes, but I'll heal. I'm stronger than I ever thought I could be. It turns out that we all are. But just do me one favor, will you?"

"Anything."

Mama swirled in my thoughts. I couldn't imagine how lost she felt. How hurt her soul must've been. I lay my head on his shoulder and softly spoke my one request. "Love her fully, or let her go."

CHAPTER FORTY-NINE

Jackson

My father woke up that evening.

Doctors and nurses were in the room with him, and I was waiting outside for them to allow me to come back. I didn't know how to handle it. My heartbeats wouldn't slow down.

He was awake, and the first person I messaged about it was Grace.

Whenever something good or bad happened, she was the first one I wanted to tell. Whenever I fell asleep, she was who I'd wish was beside me. I wasn't a praying man, but if praying meant I'd receive Gracelyn Mae, I'd fall to my knees each night.

"He's awake?" Grace asked, coming my way. Before I could reply, she wrapped her arms around me.

"Yeah. I'm just waiting until they let me back in."

"Jackson, this is amazing." She smiled, bright. "So amazing."

"Maybe your family's prayers worked," I joked.

"My family…" Her eyes darted away from my stare, and she stepped back. Her smile faded, and her lips turned down. "I have to tell you something."

"Okay."

She swallowed hard. "It was my father. He was the one your mother was having an affair with."

I stuffed my hands into my pockets. "Yeah, I know."

"What?"

"That's what your mom told me all those weeks ago. It's what pushed me away, and I hate myself for it. For allowing our parents' scars to make me want to run. I owe you an apology for that—for how I walked away. It was selfish and childish. I just…it felt as if I was losing my mom all over again. Only this time, I knew why."

"No. I feel like I owe you the apology. My father is pretty much the reason your mother's gone. If he hadn't…" Her eyes watered over.

"That's not true. Whatever you are about to say isn't true. None of this was anyone's fault. The truth of the matter was two people fell in love, and then life got in the way of it."

She kept frowning. "Why didn't you tell me? Once you found out?"

"Your dad is your world. I'd never take that away from you."

A doctor came out of the room and told me that I could go in to see him. I grimaced and nodded, looking toward Grace. "Do you want to come with me?"

"No," she replied, shaking her head. "He just got out of a coma. The last thing he needs is to see a Harris smiling in his face." She gently snickered. "Besides, you two need that time together and I should get back on the road, seeing as how I work in the morning."

I pulled her close to me and kissed her forehead. "Thank you for coming down here to see me."

"I'll be back next weekend."

"You don't have to," I warned.

"I'll be back next weekend," she replied matter-of-factly. "Keep me updated on your father, will you?"

"I will." I placed my lips against her forehead. "And princess, can you do one thing for me?"

"Of course, anything."

I combed her hair behind her ears and looked straight into those beautiful blue eyes as I spoke her way. "If you ever fall in love again, please let it be with me."

CHAPTER FIFTY

Grace

Mike had been out of the hospital for a few days now, and he was lucky enough not to have suffered any brain damage. Ever since Mike had returned home, Jackson kept a close eye on him. He was terrified of his father relapsing, which wouldn't have been uncommon.

The amount of alcohol that Mike Emery consumed on the regular was terrifying. I couldn't even imagine the amount of worry that existed in Jackson's soul.

When I got back to town Saturday morning, I headed straight for the auto shop to check on Jackson, where he said he'd be.

As I waited, I watched as the back door of the shop opened and Mike walked in with a coffee mug. He headed straight for the coffee machine and poured himself a mug of black coffee.

Then he topped it off with a small bottle of whiskey that he pulled from his pocket.

"Are you kidding me right now?" I asked, completely baffled.

After everything he'd been through, after Jackson almost lost him, he had gone right back to the bottle.

That broke my heart more than words could express, and I knew if Jackson found out, he'd lose it.

"What the hell are you doing here?" he barked.

"Waiting for your son. Are you really drinking? After everything you just went through?"

"Don't come in here judging my choices like you know me."

"You're right, I don't know you, but I know your son, and what you're doing is destroying him."

"You don't know anything about that boy. You spend a few weeks with him, and now you know the ins and outs of how his brain works? You don't know anything. That kid is messed up."

"I wonder what made him that way."

He grimaced, turning to walk out.

"You're stealing his life away," I told him.

He paused. "Pick your next words wisely."

"You are. Do you know he doesn't even like working on cars? He wanted to go to college to study art, like his mother. He wanted to see the world."

"Now I know you know nothing about Jackson. He loves cars."

"No, he learned so he could help out around here. He wanted to help take care of you."

"Nobody asked for his help."

"Yes." I nodded. "They did."

He raised an eyebrow and grumbled, "What are you talking about?"

"The last thing your wife said to him was, 'Take care of your father.'"

"You got some nerve walking into my shop and talking about my dead wife. You know nothing about her."

"No, but I do know my father loved her, and I know she loved him, too. I know that when she told you she was in love with another man, it cracked your heart. I know you know what betrayal feels like. Trust me, I know it, too." He didn't say a word, so I continued speaking. "Jackson knows how much you've been through. Even on your darkest days, he still loves you. He loves his mother too, which is why he'll never leave your side. That was the last request she ever made of him, for him to take care of you, but while he's picking you up, he's missing out on living himself. On the day he lost his mother, he lost his father too, and every morning he wakes up scared he's going to be burying you any day now."

"So what, are you here to just tell me what a fuck-up I am? How I ruined his life?"

"No, I'm here to say you always have the opportunity to make things right. Right now, you have a choice: whiskey or Jackson."

He looked down at the alcohol in his cup and let out a low sigh. "You should leave."

"Okay, but for once in your life, how about you be the parent to your son instead of it being the other way around?"

"She's right, you know, Mike," a voice said behind me, and I turned to see Mama standing there. "You've been a child to your own son for years, and I'm not judging you, because I have been the same thing to my girls. All those years ago, both of us were betrayed. We were both hurt by the two people who meant the most to us. We took that heartbreak out on our own children. Even with all the darkness we sent their way, they still managed to have goodness in them." She walked over to Mike and frowned, placing a hand on his forearm. "Aren't you tired of being angry?" she asked him.

His upper lip twitched as he lowered his mug down to the table. "He wanted to study art?"

"Yes," I told him.

"He hasn't spoken about art since Hannah..." His words faded off, and I felt my gut tighten. He was so unbelievably sad. It was painful to watch.

"When was the last time you two have actually spoken to one another? Had a real conversation?"

The pain in his expression only intensified as he turned to leave the shop.

I stepped toward him to try to express my thoughts more to him, but Mama placed a hand on my shoulder. "Let him go, Gracelyn Mae."

"I just want to break through to him."

"Trust me." She shook her head. "He heard every single word you said."

"How can you be sure?"

"Because his eyes showed me exactly how my heart feels."

It made me sad to know Mama was hurting so much. Had she been hurting as long as Mike had? Why hadn't I ever taken the time to zoom in on my own mother? Perhaps it was because children oftentimes forgot that their parents were human, too. Perhaps it was because we assumed they had everything figured out, due to the fake smiles they delivered our way.

"What were you doing here, anyway?" I asked her.

"Looking for you. I heard you were seen walking into the shop."

"I just got here," I mentioned. "How could you hear that already?"

"It's Chester, darling. News travels fast. Which is why I wanted to be the first to tell you. Your father and I decided to separate. Well, he decided. I was forced to agree."

"Mama," I started, but she shook her head, giving me a sad smile.

"It's okay. I'm okay. I owe you an apology, though. For the past summer, for the past forever years. I put too much pressure on you and your sister to be perfect, to be loyal to people who didn't deserve your loyalty."

"Is that how you feel about Dad?"

She shut her eyes and took a deep breath. "I love that man. More than anything, I love him, and I tried to be everything I could for him. I wanted to be perfect so he could love me back. The truth is, he'd never be able to love me the way I love him, and that breaks my heart."

"Oh, Mama…"

"I guess this is what I get for treating you the way I did. I guess this is my humble pie."

"I'm so sorry you're hurting."

"For so long, I thought I was unworthy of love. I prayed on it each night, asking God to heal my broken pieces. To make my husband love me, but he couldn't. And now, Samuel says he doesn't want to be with me. That I deserve more. What does that even mean? More than what? All I know, all I've ever known was how to be his. To be the pastor's wife. And now, he's leaving me, and I'm…" She took a breath and closed her eyes. "I don't know how to be alone."

"You're not alone, Mama. I got you."

Her eyes stayed close, and her body began to shake. "I've been so hard on you."

"Yeah, but I get the feeling you've been harder on yourself."

When her eyes opened, I felt as if I saw myself staring back at me. "How did you do it?" she asked me. "How did you begin again after years of being someone else's?"

"You take small breaths. Whenever you feel overwhelmed or heartbroken, just remember to take small breaths."

"Small breaths…I can do that."

"Yes, you can."

"I just don't know who I am anymore. Without Samuel, do I even exist?" she asked me.

How odd was that? Hearing my mother repeat all the same questions I'd asked myself. "You probably exist more in this moment than you ever have in all your life. You'll be surprised by all the things you learn about your heart and how it beats. And if you need to get away, you can come stay with me for as long as necessary. I have a spare room."

"You'd do that for me?" she questioned, her voice cracking as if my offer stunned her.

"Oh, Mama." I pulled her into a hug and held on tight. "I'd do anything for you."

She inhaled deeply and exhaled slow. "Small breaths," she whispered.

"Yes," I replied. "Just take small breaths."

CHAPTER FIFTY-ONE

Jackson

As far as I knew, Dad had been able to stay away from the bottle. I was thankful for that, too. I never wanted to see him in that shape ever again. I'd never been so terrified in my life.

On Thursday afternoon, I walked over to the auto shop, and I felt a knot in my stomach as I looked up at Dad on a ladder as he hammered away at the Mike's Auto Shop sign in front of the building.

"Dad, what the hell are you doing?" I asked walking over to him.

"Closing shop," he replied.

"What? What do you mean closing shop?"

"That's exactly what I mean." The sign dropped to the ground with one more hit, and then Dad started climbing down the ladder. "I sold the place," he grumbled, walking into the shop, leaving me flabbergasted.

"Are you drunk? You can't just give all this away," I argued, following right behind him.

"Actually"—he shrugged—"it turns out I can. I sold the shop and the cabin along with all the land. Got a pretty penny for it, too."

"Are you kidding me? That's my home."

"Yeah, well, now it's not."

"Who did you sell it to? I'll get it back. It's obvious you're not in the right state of mind. You've been through a lot these past few weeks, and your mind just isn't making sense."

"Nah. For the first time ever, I'm thinking straight."

"But—"

"What type of art?" he asked me, throwing me off completely.

"What?"

"What art style would you study? Where would you travel to see different techniques?"

"You need a nap."

"I've been sleeping long enough. Now here." He nodded me over to him, and I hesitated. "Come on, boy, I ain't got all day. Get over here."

He handed me a check with a huge amount written on it. "What is this?" I asked him.

"Your cut from the sale. Of course, you won't see any real payoff until the paperwork goes through and all that bullshit, but that's enough for you to live off of for a year or so."

"What?"

"You're free, Jackson," he said, giving me a half smile. "Go find yourself."

"Dad, you're being ridiculous. I know exactly who is behind this, and I'll get everything figured out. Don't worry."

Before he could reply, I was already on my way to Loretta Harris's home. It was clear that she was the one behind the sale of the property. She was the only one ever pushing for land for that church of theirs. This situation had her name written all over it.

As I stood on her front porch, I took a deep breath as she answered the door.

"Jackson? What are you doing here?" she asked, confused.

"You really couldn't help yourself, could you?" I barked, feeling my chest rise and fall.

"I don't know what you're talking about."

"Let's not play stupid. The property, my dad's shop," I told her. She raised an eyebrow. "Him selling everything to you and the church."

"What?" she said, flabbergasted. "I'm sorry, I have no clue what you're talking about…"

"Stop with the games and pretending."

"She's not pretending," Samuel stated, walking onto the porch from their household. "She had nothing to do with the deal. It was between Mike and me."

"What?"

"He came to the church the other night and asked me if the offer that Loretta had given him still stood," he explained.

"Why would he do that? Why would you allow him to do that?"

Samuel's brows lowered, and he crossed his arms. "He came to me and told him he was tired of hating. He was sick of being angry, and as long as he stayed on that property, the hate would stay inside him. So he wanted it to be gone for good. Yet he wanted enough money to make sure you'd be okay without it. I understood, too. Wanting to let go of the past hurts. There was only one thing I requested of him if we made the deal."

"And what was that?"

"Rehab."

My chest tightened. "Rehab?"

"Yes. He's going to spend some time at one of the best rehab clinics in America. He'll receive the best treatment from the best doctors over the next few months. It's going to be tough for him, but he agreed to it. Your uncle said he'd drive him to the clinic this Thursday."

Rehab?

I pinched the bridge of my nose. "He's really going to go?"

"Yes."

Without another word, I wrapped my arms around Samuel and held on tight.

All I'd ever wanted was for my father to get help. All I'd ever wanted was for him to find his way out of the darkness.

"Thank you," I whispered, feeling overwhelmed. "Thank you."

When Thursday came around, I stood outside the auto shop while Alex loaded Dad's suitcases into the back of his car.

"Are you sure you don't want me to go with you, Dad?" I asked, uncertain about them heading off to the clinic without me.

"Yeah, I'm sure." He gave me a frown and scratched his beard. "Look, can we not make a big fuss about this? I ain't no good at goodbyes."

"Well, let's not say goodbye," I told him, pulling him into a hug. "Just good night until tomorrow."

He pulled back and placed a hand on my shoulder. "My boy."

"My dad."

"I'll see you on the other side," he told me, going to climb into the car.

"Wait, Dad! Here," I said, hurrying over to him. I took off the band on my wrist and handed it to him.

"Powerful moments?" he asked me.

"To help you get through the hard days."

He thanked me. "That Harris girl? You really care about her?"

"I do."

"Then take my advice…give yourself time to find yourself and give her time to find herself. If it's meant to be, you'll find your way back."

"And if it's not meant to be?" I asked.

He lowered his brows and chuckled with a slight shrug to his shoulders. "Just don't drink the whiskey." He smiled—something I hadn't seen him do in such a long time. "When the time comes, you let her in, all right?"

"Will do."

We said our last good nights before tomorrow, and I watched as my father drove away to find his own self.

It turned out self-discovery was a process that everyone continued to explore. One never stopped growing therefore, they never truly stopped discovering.

"So he's safe and sound?" Grace asked over the phone as I lay in bed Thursday night.

"Yeah. Alex sent me a message to let me know they arrived."

"How do you feel?" she asked me.

I took a deep inhale. "Free."

"I was thinking I could come down this weekend to see you, or you could come up here. Either way, I'd love to see you if I can."

I cleared my throat and closed my eyes. "I'm falling in love with you, Gracelyn Mae," I confessed, feeling my chest tighten from saying the words. "I'm falling in love with every part of you, but before I can give you all of me, I think I need to learn more about myself. About my wants, my needs, before I can be what you deserve."

"What do you mean?"

"My dad gave me a check, and it's enough for me to explore the country for a little bit of time. I can stop places and find out who I am, and what I believe in. I can start healing the broken parts of me."

She went quiet for a moment, and I was terrified she'd be against the idea. That she wouldn't want to wait for me to explore the world. That perhaps, our time was up.

"Okay," she said.

I sat up a bit. "Okay?"

"I mean, I haven't really been alone, not really. I think it could be good for the both of us to take a few months and truly discover the ins and outs of our hearts and minds. Then, once we truly come together, it will be because we are two whole individuals, not two broken ones leaning against one another to keep from falling."

"Exactly. We'll learn to walk alone, and then we'll walk together."

"Can you let me know where you are every now and then? Can you check in with me to let me know you're safe?"

"Always and always," I told her.

She released a small sigh. "Those words…who do you think created them first? Your mother or my father?"

"I don't know. I guess it's one of those things, though. The origin of the saying doesn't matter. All that matters is the meaning behind it."

"I miss you already," she confessed.

I fell in love with her some more.

"I miss you already," I replied.

"Jackson?"

"Yes?"

"When you find you, come back to me."

On the day I was leaving town, there was a knock on my front door. When I opened it, I saw a cage sitting on my porch with a ribbon on top of it along with a note.

Dear Jackson,

I know today marks the first day of your new adventures, and I wanted to send my love. Plus, how could one go on a road trip without a nice companion? This is Watson—Wats for short. He's a three-year-old golden retriever who loves playing catch and riding in cars. He's always wagging his tail, and he loves cuddles almost as much as I do.

I thought that even though you're finding yourself, you shouldn't ride in a car alone all the time. I don't want you to think of this as a replacement to Tucker. Tucker was a good boy, and his love can never be replaced, but I think Watson can add a little more love your way. That's the thing about love—there's always room for more.

Here's to new friendships and new beginnings.

-Gracelyn Mae

P.S. I'm falling in love with you, too.

I smiled at the note and read the words over and over again. I bent down and looked at the dog in the cage. He wagged his tail back and forth and stuck out his tongue.

"Hey, buddy," I said, grinning. He was so handsome. When I opened the door on the cage, he leaped my way and began licking away at my face. "Whoa, slow down there, slugger."

He kept licking, and I kept laughing. "Will you stop, stupid dog?" I joked, but he didn't reply. That tail of his kept flying back and forth, and I finally surrendered to his love.

Good boy, Wats, I thought to myself, holding him closer. *Good boy.*

CHAPTER FIFTY-TWO

Grace

We gave each other space because we didn't want to use one another as a crutch any longer. If we were going to be together, we'd first have to be whole on our own. I fell back into teaching, and when I wasn't teaching, I was out and about trying new things.

For a while I thought I was the yoga type of girl until I got stuck in killer praying mantis for a good bit of time. I couldn't paint or sketch at all. When late autumn came, Mama and I took a pole dance class. I wasn't sure what was more disturbing—the fact that Mama loved it so much that she continued with the classes on her own, or the fact that she was ten times better than me.

Dad didn't know what he was missing out on.

She laughed more, too.

I almost forgot how much I loved the sound of Mama's laughter.

One late November night, I received a package in the mail with a novel and a Post-it note attached to it. My heart skipped as my fingers raced over the book cover, and then I read Jackson's words.

I'm currently in Cave Creek, Arizona, watching the sunset with Watson.
The night before, I read this novel, and all I could do was think about you and
what you'd think
of the words within the pages.
It's a hard read, but worth it.
-Oscar
P.S. I learned I hate sushi.

I liked the ending but struggled with the middle. I cried, which isn't surprising.
I still cry so easily.
Try this book.
It will break your heart.
-Princess
P.S. I hate sushi, too.

Alex sent me this read for Christmas.
If you read this book backward, it's better.
-Oscar

I don't know why I'm even sending this book, just skip to chapter five.
Chapter five is so good it makes up for all the other pages.
-Princess

Today I missed your heartbeats.

-Oscar

Today I missed your touch.
-Princess

It's March 23rd.
Today I sat in California watching the sunrise, and I painted the sky.
You would love this place, Princess.
Or maybe I'd just love if you were here.
Tell me something I should know.
-Oscar

Something you should know?
That's easy.
Today is April 4th, and I still love you.
-Princess

It's May 3rd, and I still love you, too.
-Oscar

When late May came around, I was getting ready to finish yet another year of teaching. It was chilling how much had changed in the past year, how much I have grown, and how much I've learned about my heart and how it beat.

On Sunday morning, Mama always headed off to church. That was something she realized about herself—no matter if she was still with Dad or not, she held on to her faith. Sometimes I went with her, and other times, I stayed and prayed on my own.

Over the past year, I learned that faith wasn't a building, yet it was a place in one's heart.

I could go to a church and be surrounded by others and join them in prayer, or I could close my eyes in my own solitude and find peace. Both ways were worthy. Both ways were right.

There wasn't one correct way to believe—there were a million possibilities out there.

That was one of my favorite discoveries. I didn't have to be a perfect Christian in order to exist in the world.

When Mother's Day came around, I went to church with Mama and sat in the pew holding her hand tight in mine. Throughout my life, there were a few hard days. Days where even when I tried to be happy, my heart still cracked, and Mother's Day was one of those. For others, it stood as a celebration. For me, it spoke of loss and failure.

I'd somewhat come to terms with the fact I wouldn't be one who had children. It wasn't in my cards, and I'd learned to accept that.

But still, some days were harder than others.

Mother's Day was one of them.

"That was a beautiful service," Mama told me as we walked home from the church with our arms linked.

"It was."

She smiled my way and tilted her head. "Are you okay?"

"Yeah, just tired. Judy is driving in tonight for dinner, so I think I'll just grab a nap before she gets here."

"Sounds like a perfect plan." She took my hand in hers and squeezed it. "Today's a tough one for you?"

"Yes, it is."

She squeezed my hand again and didn't say another word. Though her comfort was enough.

That was all I ever wanted from Mama—her comfort.

As we walked up the steps to my apartment, and I unlocked the door, my eyes watered over, and I gasped as I looked around.

Scattered throughout the living room and dining room were bouquets of red roses.

Seven to be exact.

"Mama…" I started.

She shook her head. "They aren't from me."

I walked over to the roses sitting on the coffee table and grabbed the note attached to them.

Instant tears fell from my eyes.

Because there is no such thing as an "almost" mother.
Seven bouquets from your seven angels.
Happy Mother's Day, Princess.

My heart skipped as I read how the card was signed.

- Emerson, Jamie, Karla, Michael, Jaxon, Phillip, Steven, and Oscar.

There was one bouquet from each child I'd lost.

All of my babies.

All of my loves.

Mama moved over to me and read the words on the letter. "Oh, honey," she breathed out, just as stunned as I had been. "He's the one."

He was so much more than the one. Even though we were apart, he still controlled my heartbeats.

Just then, there was a knock on the front door, and when I opened it, everything inside me began to heal completely.

"Hi," Jackson whispered, holding a bouquet of roses in his hands. Watson sat right beside him, wagging his tail back and forth.

"Hi," I replied, feeling my body tremble.

"I, uh…" He brushed his hand against the back of his neck. "I've seen so many places over the past few months. I've witnessed a million sunrises, and I've seen the sun set. There were thousands of roads I've driven, and no matter which one I took, no matter if I went left or right, north or south, it seemed that they all led me right back to you."

"Jackson…" I started, but the tears and love in my soul made my words fade away.

"You're my world, Gracelyn Mae," he told me, moving in closer. Mama removed the roses from his hold, and Jackson took my hands into his. "You're my faith. You're my hope. You're my true religion. I'm a better man because you exist. I'm me because of you. And if you'd allow it, I'd love to spend the rest of my life worshipping your heartbeats."

I held his hands in mine and moved in close. My head tilted up, and I released a small breath as my eyes locked with his. A small, tiny, breath.

My mouth grazed across his, and I whispered against his lips. "Worship me, and I'll worship you."

Then he kissed me.

He kissed me slowly, gently, and filled with love.

He didn't even have to say it, but I felt our love. I felt it shoot through my body as his lips pressed against mine. Our souls intermixed, and our flames were infinite.

It was simple, the way we loved. We loved the scars of our past, and we loved the unknown of our future. We loved the mistakes. We loved the celebrations. We loved our darkness, and we loved the light.

Our connection wasn't something built around hurt anymore.

We existed only on hope.

I didn't expect Jackson Emery.

Out of all the prayers I'd prayed, I never thought I'd receive a man like him. We didn't believe in the same God, but still, that was okay. We didn't always love the same things, but still, that was okay. We didn't always agree, but still…*that was okay.*

Because love—real love—didn't mean always holding the same

beliefs. It didn't mean we had to see eye to eye on every subject. Yet what it did mean, what real love stood for was a mutual understanding. A respect for one another's dreams and hopes and wishes and fears.

Jackson respected my choice to pray to God while I respected his not to do the same.

We took the time to learn how each of our hearts beat, and in that journey, we learned that oftentimes, in the most important moments of the night, that our hearts? Our hearts beat in sync.

From that point on, we were inseparable. We were committed to our future and learning to let go of our past. I was thankful for all my blessings I didn't even expect to kiss my life. The blessings I was too blind to even realize were coming my way. That was a lesson I had to learn over time. The lesson that sometimes for the blessings to arrive, one had to get out of their own way.

Everything happened exactly as it had to unfold. Even the hard days led me to where I needed to be. All the dots connected, I just couldn't see it while I was walking down my path. Without Finn betraying me, I would've never crashed into Chester, Georgia, all those months before. Without all the heartbreak, I would've never known what love was truly supposed to feel like.

For that, I was thankful. For the ups and downs, for the wrongs and rights, for the heart breaking and healing. I was thankful for it all, and each night as I lay down to sleep, I'd closed my eyes and softly speak my prayers.

Dear God, it's me, Gracelyn Mae...

CHAPTER FIFTY-THREE

Jackson

"My dad's retiring," Grace stated over dinner one night in late June. "Judy is taking over, and she's preaching for the first time in front of the church this Sunday. Will you come down with me?"

"Of course."

That was a given. When something was important to Grace, it was important to me. We hadn't been back to Chester in months, and I'd be lying if I said returning wasn't hard for me. That town stood for a lot of demons to me but showing up with Grace's hand in mine made it a bit easier to swallow down.

Loretta came with us because even though she wasn't looking forward to seeing Samuel, she loved her daughter enough to get past her discomfort.

We arrived at the church Sunday morning, and I could see Loretta's nerves as we walked up the steps. I placed a hand on her shoulder and squeezed lightly. "You good?"

She nodded. "Just taking small breaths."

Samuel was standing at the door greeting people, and when we walked up, I watched his eyes dance across Loretta's figure.

"Hi," he spoke.

Loretta stood tall. "Hello, Samuel."

"You look...stunning." He was a bit shocked and overtaken by Loretta's beauty—which seemed odd to me—all the Harris women were beautiful.

She gave him a small smile and shrugged her left shoulder. "Of course, I do." Then, she walked inside.

"Hi, Dad," Grace said, moving over to her father and kissing him on the cheek.

"Hey, Buttercup. You doing okay?" he asked her.

She wrapped her arm around mine and grinned ear to ear. "Better than okay."

We walked into the church and sat in a pew. I couldn't think of the last time I'd been inside a church, let alone watching a person preach, but it was a big moment for Judy. I didn't believe in church, but I did believe in family.

So, I sat, and I listened.

Judy preached about the power of forgiveness. She spoke on how life sometimes came with its twists and turns, yet at the end of the day, you were always promised a reset button come morning.

She stood there confident, as if all she was ever meant to do was preach sermons. She found her passion, and it was powerful to watch her live it out loud.

After the service, she came over to Grace and me, and I swore I never saw a person look happier. "How was I?" she asked.

Grace pulled her sister into a tight hug. "It was perfect. Every second was absolutely perfect."

"She's right. You were made for this," I commented. Judy smiled and thanked me.

"Oh! Have you been by your old place yet? I'd love to know your thoughts," Judy commented. I raised an eyebrow, and she turned to Grace. "You didn't tell him?"

"I thought it would be best to show him," Grace replied.

"Show me what?"

The two girls grinned ear to ear and gave me those doe eyes. "You'll see," they said in unison.

We headed over toward the place I once called home, and I was stunned when I saw Dad's house, the shop, and the cabin were completely gone. Instead, there were trails going through the land. There were beautiful flowers throughout the space, and a small playground where children were playing, making a ton of noise.

"You turned it into a park?" I asked, somewhat stunned.

"Yeah, and we named it after someone close to you," Grace commented, pointing at a sign. I looked in the direction. *Tucker's Park*. "I figured there are enough dogs running through the area that they could use a place to come play. So we made a few paths to the open land in the way back. Come on, let us show you."

We walked down one of the paths to the open land where both Tucker and my mother were buried. Their burials were guarded with a gate, and there was a sign that read, *In Loving Memory*.

Owners were walking their dogs and playing fetch with them, and I could feel the happiness running through the area. It was beyond amazing.

My heart soared as I looked past the memorial to a building in the background. It was new to me, but I knew exactly what it was when I saw it.

"You built my mother's art studio?" I asked, my voice cracking as I read the sign over the door. It was created with Dad's auto shop sign, but it now read, *Hannah's Paint Shop*.

Grace's hand landed on my arm. "Is it okay?" she asked concerned. "I just thought…"

I cut her off as my lips fell to hers.

In a way, it was as if my mother was alive that day.

"We teach art classes there," Judy remarked. "The kids love it. Sometimes we sit outside and paint the sunsets at night."

"That's amazing," I stated, still stunned. "That's beyond amazing."

"If you're ever in town and want to teach a class, we'd love to have you." Judy smiled and nudged her sister in the arm. "Grace, how about you go show him the studio? It's closed right now, so you two can look around in peace."

"Of course, come on." She took my hand in hers, and we headed to the art studio, and we walked inside.

It was beautiful. Against the walls were some of Ma's artwork that I hadn't even seen. "Where did you get this stuff?" I asked.

"We found it in your father's basement, and he told us we could use it. I thought it would be a nice touch. I also studied some of her earlier work and figured charcoal drawings might be great for the younger kids. And in the back room, we have an open canvas each Saturday night where people can toss paint around like crazy. They call it the Jackson Pollock room, but I prefer calling it Jackson Emery, obviously." She went on and on about the space, and the way it excited me made my heart soar. As she was speaking fast, she caught herself and then slowed down her words. She frowned a bit. "Is this all okay? I just thought—"

I cut her off again with a kiss.

"Marry me," I whispered as my lips lay against hers.

She gently laughed, thinking I was joking at first, then she pulled back a little and looked me in the eyes. She slightly tilted her head. "Marry you?"

"Yes. Marry me, Gracelyn Mae."

Her fingers landed against my chest. She bit her bottom lip and nodded slowly. "Okay," she whispered, grazing her lips over mine. "I'll marry you."

CHAPTER FIFTY-FOUR

Jackson
One Year Later

"You look good, man," Alex remarked, straightening out my tie. "But I'm gonna need you to stop sweating through your suit."

I couldn't help it. I was a case of nerves as I prepared to walk down the aisle toward the woman of my dreams. I didn't know days like today could exist. I didn't know I could be so happy.

"This is all I've ever wanted for you, Jackson," Alex stated, patting me on the shoulder. "You to be happy."

"Me too," a voice said from the doorway. I looked up to see Dad standing there in his own suit and tie. He looked healthy—something I thought I'd never be able to say again. Ever since rehab, he'd found his footing. Not without a few slip-ups, but with every fall, he got back up. And when he stumbled, I'd help him walk.

Because that was what family did—showed up even on the dark days.

Luckily, that afternoon was a day filled with only light.

"Can I have a word with my son, Alex?" Dad asked. Alex nodded and left us alone for a minute. Dad stuffed his hands into his pockets and gave me a small grin. "You look great."

"You don't look half bad yourself."

"Look, Jackson…I know I've let you down over the years and I'm not good with words, but I want you to know that you are my world. I haven't been a good man. I've made mistake after mistake, but the greatest thing that has ever happened to me, is you. I'm thankful each day that you became a better man than I could've ever been. I'm thankful that you hold within you the best parts of your mother and me. You are more than we could've ever wished for. I love you, son."

Those words…

Those damn words…

"Don't be a punk and cry," he joked, wiping at his own eyes.

"Sorry. My bad." I pulled him into a hug. "I love you too, Dad."

As we separated, he wiped his eyes again and sniffled a bit. "Oh, one more thing. Your mother had this thing that she did the week you were born. She wrote you letters for special occasions. She wrote you a letter that she, um, wanted to give to you on your wedding day. I mean, she wrote you other letters, too. For your sixteenth birthday, for your graduation, and crap, but I messed up and missed those occasions." He frowned, his guilt taking over. Being sober for him was hard at times. It meant facing all the missteps he'd taken in his past.

"It's fine, Dad."

"It's not; it's not at all. But I'll give you those other letters on another day. Today, you get this one." He reached into his pocket and pulled it out. Then he reached into his other pocket and pulled out a small box. "Plus, rumor has it that you're supposed to give your bride a gift. So, if you don't have one already, I figured this might work."

He opened the box.

My eyes watered over more. "Mom's ring?"

"Yeah. I figured Grace might appreciate it."

"She will. More than words, she will. Thank you, Dad."

"Yeah, of course. I'll let you read the note, and I guess I'll see you at the ceremony." He hugged me once more, and then started toward the door before pausing. "You know what? That Grace girl ain't so bad." He smirked a bit and shrugged his shoulders. "Even though she's a Harris."

"Yeah." I laughed. "She's growing on me, too."

"Treat her well." He nodded once. "For as long as you both live, you treat her well."

He left the room, and I took a deep breath as I opened the letter that Ma left for me.

My Sweet Jackson,

Today you swear your life to a woman that I hope is everything and more to you. You will say, "I do" to her as she says the same to you. You will make promises of forever. So, I thought I'd tell you a few things about how to love a woman to make it easier for you.

Be easy with one another's hearts. Some days she'll wake up angry with no warning. Hold her tight on those days. Other times, she'll wake crying. Hold her tighter on those ones. Remember to laugh out loud, the kind of laughter when it becomes hard to breathe. Hold her hand, even when she doesn't want you to. Tell her she's beautiful when she's sick.

Dance together.

Miss her when she's gone.

Tell her you love her every day.

Every. Single. Day.

Love her, but let her be free to soar, too.

Support her dreams as she supports yours.

Watch the sunrise and love the sunsets.

Always know that I'm here for you whenever you need your mother. I was the first woman to have the honor of loving you, and even when I'm gone, when the sun fades and the stars sparkle bright overhead, remember my love for you.

This life is beautiful because you are here, son.

Enjoy this moment. Enjoy this day. This is your happily ever after.
I love you, Jackson.
Always and always.
-Mom

"Can I interrupt for a minute?"

I turned to see Samuel standing there in his suit and tie. I nodded him into the room, and he walked in my direction.

"Are you nervous?" he asked.

"Yes, but ready."

"Good." He grimaced for a second, sliding his hands into his pockets. "Listen, Jackson… I've been trying to figure out what to say to you today, or how to approach you, but words are slipping from me. So I'm just going to say congratulations. Thank you for treating my daughter the way that you do."

"She's my best friend," I told him.

"And you are hers." His eyes glassed over, and he nodded once. "Don't let that fade."

"I won't."

He turned to leave the room and paused. "Your mother would've been so proud of the person you became."

That meant the world to me.

"Samuel?"

"Yes?"

I inhaled slowly and exhaled even slower. "I get it, you know… you falling for my mother. I loved her, too." I gave him a smile, and I hope he felt the forgiveness in it. "I mean, how could one not?"

He moved over to me and gave me a hug. I saw it in him, the hurt from losing the love of his life. I understood how that would haunt him forever; therefore, there was no reason for him to feel as if I'd hate him for the rest of his life.

He was already heartbroken.

No one would be as hard on him as he was on himself.

So, I let him free.

"Thank you for that, Jackson," he said to me, his voice low. "Always and always."

CHAPTER FIFTY-FIVE

Grace

"Am I supposed to be panicking like this? I don't know if I'm supposed to be panicking like this." I swarmed in my dress. "I look fat, don't I?" I asked Judy. Then, I turned to Mama. "Do I look fat?"

"You look beautiful," a person remarked.

I turned to the door and saw Mike standing there, leaning on the doorframe. "Sorry I didn't mean to interrupt, but I'm just doing my rounds. I know you're on a tight timeline, but I was wondering if I could steal you for a minute to give you something?" he asked me.

I smoothed out my dress, the nerves still strong in my stomach. "Yes, of course."

He held his hand out to me, and I took his hold.

"So, I know the saying is something old, something new, something borrowed and something blue," Mike remarked as we walked down the hallway, stepping through a set of doors that led us outside. "But I figured pink would work just fine."

In front of us was a car.

Not just any car, but my car. My pink Rosie with a big bow on top of it. "Mike," I breathed out. "What…"

"It took a lot of time," he told me, shrugging his shoulders. "And a lot of the parts are new, but I figured after all I put you through, I could at least fix your car."

I walked over to it and ran my fingers across the hood. "It's beautiful. I cannot even thank you enough for this."

"You don't have to," he told me. "You saved my son, and in saving him, you saved me. You are the most graceful woman on this planet, and we are so lucky to know you."

I pulled him into a hug and held on tight. "I'm glad you're here today, Mike."

The words hit him hard because he knew the meaning. There were so many roads that could've led to Mike not being around to celebrate his son's wedding day, yet he was standing beside me. We all made it through the storm.

We all felt the sun.

"Want to know a secret?" he asked.

"What's that?"

He smiled a smile just like his son's and sniffled a bit as he stared my way. "I always wanted a daughter."

We headed back into the building and crossed paths with my father, who seemed to be on a search to find me. "Grace, there you are. It's time to get this ball rolling." He looked up to Mike, and for a split second, there was tension.

The two men who loved the same woman stood face to face.

The silence at that moment was so loud, but then magic happened.

At that moment, they chose me over their own struggles.

Mike held his hand out to Dad. "Congratulations today," he expressed.

"You too," Dad replied shaking his hand.

And my heart exploded with love.

Dad looped his arm with mine, and I looped mine with his. "Are you ready, Buttercup?"

"Ready as I'll ever be."

We walked down the aisle, and I smiled as I saw Jackson standing there waiting for me. He smiled my way, and I smiled back. He cried, and I cried back. He was everything I never knew I always wanted.

"Hi," he whispered.

"Hi," I replied.

"You look beautiful." He grinned, wiping at his eyes as he took my hands into his. "You are so beautiful."

We didn't drop hands as the ceremony took place, and when it came time for our vows, I smiled as Jackson began to deliver his to me.

"I lost my first tooth when I was six years old. I can't pat my head and rub my stomach at the same time. I hate pickles unless they are on burgers." Oh, my heart. *Jackson Paul and his random facts.* He squeezed my hands as his words grew more serious. "The first time I saw you, I thought you were beautiful. The first time I held you, I didn't want to let go. The first time you kissed me, I knew I was yours. You are the definition of everything pure in this world. You taught me what love is. What it looks, feels, and tastes like. You taught me how to be my best self. You taught me that my struggles aren't flaws; they are just part of what makes me whole. So, today, I give you the random facts of our future. I promise I will show up each day, even when it's hard. I will breathe life into you whenever you need me. I will be your best friend, your person. I will love you in every way, shape, and form. I will give my all to you because you are my world." He took a deep breath. "You are my whole world, and I will never stop loving you. That's what I promise you, Gracelyn Mae. I promise you, *me*."

I inhaled deep and exhaled slow. "And I promise you, me."

That night, we sat in the middle of the field in front of Hannah's Art Studio—me still in my gown and Jackson still in his suit. We missed the sunset, but we were lucky enough to witness the stars that danced over us.

Our lives were whole.

Maybe we wouldn't have children. Maybe we wouldn't travel the world. Maybe we'd never be rich. Perhaps we'd live in a small house on the outskirts of an unknown town, and our lives would still be whole because our love was enough.

No matter what life shot our way, we were the winners of our story because we held onto one another through every storm.

With him, I was complete.

With him, I found forever.

"This is too good," he warned me. His voice was low and timid as I sat in his lap with my legs wrapped around his waist. "How do we keep this? How do we keep this feeling from fading?"

"We keep choosing this," I told him, placing my forehead against his. "You and me. We keep showing up for one another. Choose me today, and I'll choose you tomorrow."

"Always and always?" he whispered, brushing his lips against mine as I felt chills race over me.

I nodded slowly, so sure, so certain as I spoke so gently our greatest truth.

"And always."

The End.

ACKNOWLEDGMENTS

This book is for the mothers who had to say goodbye too soon. I see you, I hear you, and I honor your hearts with wings. You are the strongest individuals alive, and I'm blown away by your strength, your ability to love, and your ability to not quit on life.

This book is for my family. The people who hold me up when I feel like falling apart. My always and always. My heart and soul. I am the luckiest woman to be a part of the best tribe around.

This book is for my friends who understand me disappearing from time to time into the writing cave. Thank you for loving me and allowing me to go writer mode every now and then.

This book is for Staci Hart, who created a beautiful cover once again.

This book is for the betas who didn't give up on me. Talon, Christy, and Tammy…you saved this story. Thank you for reading a million drafts and not killing me.

This book is for the editors and proofreaders who moved and shifted when I had to change my deadlines. Who showed up when I felt as if I were a failure. Who stood by my side regardless of anything. Caitlin, Ellie, Jenny, and Virginia: you have no clue how much you mean to me. Thank you for being a part of my team.

This book is for my agent, Flavia: You changed my life. I adore you.

This book is for the man who held me during my panic attacks and told me it would be all right. The man who makes me laugh when I feel like crying. The man who lets me 'win' at games, even though I really almost always lose. The one who taught me that not all guys are the same. The one who makes me smile the kind of smiles where my cheeks hurt while my heart skips a few beats. The one who always gives me butterflies. The one who made me believe in love stories once again.

This book is for any and every person who has ever felt lost in their lives. It's for anyone whose world has been flipped upside down. For anyone who has been broken down, but didn't give up. You deserve to find your way once more. You deserve to re-introduce your heart to your soul. You're not broken because of a few missteps. You are not a failure because of some mistakes. You are human. You are growing, learning, evolving, and that is extraordinary.

You. Are. Extraordinary.

Thank you for reading.

Thank you for zooming in on me.

Thank you for seeing my flaws, and somehow calling them beautiful.

I love each and every one of you.

Always and always.

Printed in Great Britain
by Amazon